THE LOST DAUGHTERS

COMPLETE TRILOGY

VIOLA TEMPEST

The Lost Daughters
Complete Trilogy

© Copyright 2024 Viola Tempest
Website: www.violatempest.com

Any references to historical events, real people, or real places are used fictitiously. Names, characters, and places are products of the author's imagination.

Cover Design by Ann Fleur Art

The Lost Daughters

COMPLETE TRILOGY

VIOLA TEMPEST

KINGDOM OF PEACE
BAOSHU KINGDOM
HEPING
SHENHUA KINGDOM

ORPHANAGE
JINU KINGDOM
ISJAEN ISLAND
N
W E
S

CONTENTS

THE FORGOTTEN DAUGHTER

THE LOST DAUGHTERS TRILOGY
BOOK ONE

The Forgotten Daughter

THE LOST DAUGHTERS TRILOGY BOOK ONE

VIOLA TEMPEST

CHAPTER

ONE

HE FELL INTO SYNC WITH THE SKY, HER EYES FOLLOWING THE speeding birds, her nostrils inhaling the moist air with every breath. It was another ordinary day in the leaden winters of the kingdom of Heping, China, also known as the "Kingdom of Peace."

With her gaze shifted from the sky to the cluttered town, Xiuying looked over the small town of the colossal kingdom—its tiny homes, the busy streets, and wandering people—from the tall castle towers, thinking to herself, "Where did it all go wrong?"

Standing on the grand terrace, witnessing a spectacular sunset, and seized by an acute sense of loneliness, she held

5

a letter in her hand from her parents, remembering all the torturous memories of her past.

"After twenty years?" she asked herself with confusion. "Why now?"

Heping, China was divided into different kingdoms, ruled by the most powerful and wealthiest tribal families. Xiuying was born in the magical kingdom of Jinu, a kingdom unlike any other. It was surrounded by mountains, lakes, and trees, a scenic masterpiece, and people from all around the world would visit to see the eye-catching views for themselves.

The rulers of Jinu were the royal family, who had magical powers that controlled the sun and the moon, the ability to turn light into dark and dark into light. Because of this, they were respected by some and feared by many.

The king, Qianfan, was known for his bravery and brutal honesty. He was a tall, strong, and muscular man with sharp hazel-shaped eyes and short dark black hair. He was unforgiving, and he believed in punishing those who stepped out of bounds. Still, he was respected by his people, and for the most part, everyone obeyed his laws.

Qianfan was a strong ruler, and he made several beneficial decisions for his kingdom that led to prosperity. But as vigorous as he was, he had a soft spot for one person, one woman... his wife. Daiyu, with hair that fell down to her knees, rosy cheeks, and large eyes on a petite face. She was the most beautiful of all the queens in all the kingdoms and adored by all the kings.

In fact, Qianfan was often infatuated by her that he'd let her run his kingdom, though, the people of Jinu never minded. Daiyu had the kindest soul and a big heart.

Less than a year after they tied the knot, they decided to have a child and start a family.

However, during this time, the one child rule was still in place. This rule had been established during the last decade to prevent the increasing population. However, the rule was rejected by several kingdoms, but it led to the creation of norms that were going to leave a scar on many souls. Because of the rule, the families who still abided by it preferred to have sons over daughters so they could carry on their legacy, and having a daughter instead meant great shame for the family.

Qianfan wanted a son more than anything else. In fact, even *he* believed that Daiyu was carrying a boy because he knew he was too powerful and great of a man to breed something that would dishonor his name and kingdom. And whenever he spoke with Daiyu about the child, he'd always address the child as a *him* or a *he*, the security in his tone scaring Daiyu and making her anxious.

"What if it's a girl?" she'd ask cautiously.

"That won't happen, my love," Qianfan replied. "It *has* to be a boy; it just has to."

He'd then smile, kiss her on the forehead, and leave the room, not even waiting for her to reply. He didn't want to hear anything else she had to say about the matter; Qianfan wanted what he wanted.

The celebrations in the kingdom started months before the child was born, the castle receiving ample gifts and goods for the child. And this was all beginning to worry Daiyu. Everyone expected her to have a boy, and she started to worry about what would happen if that wasn't the case.

"What if I have a daughter?" Daiyu whispered quietly to Mei, her trusted maid and soon-to-be nanny of the child.

Mei was an incredible listener and Daiyu's only friend in the entire kingdom. She'd listen to the queen's concerns, her problems, and would give her advice whenever Daiyu needed it. Mei was in her early thirties, petite, with fair skin and shoulder-length hair. The queen always adored her and her presence.

"What do you mean, Daiyu?" Mei asked hesitantly. "Qianfan seems certain that the child is a boy."

"But what if it's not? I fear his reaction, and I fear what he will do to me and the child if he finds out."

"Oh, Daiyu. You're being silly. You know how much Qianfan loves you, and he's going to love the child as well, no matter what the gender might be. Sure, he's excited about having a boy, but he'll love a girl just the same. Trust me." She then walked over to Daiyu. "My dear, don't worry. Everything will be okay," Mei told Daiyu with a smile.

Daiyu sighed, hoping that Mei was right, but these words only brought her temporary comfort.

"I guess you're right," Daiyu said instead of what she was really thinking, that Mei didn't know what she was talking about, and Qianfan would kill her if a daughter popped out instead of a son. "Thank you."

As the months flew by, Daiyu continued to worry about the outcomes of giving birth to a daughter. What was coming ahead was uncertain, but something she would never have imagined would happen to her.

Eight and a half months in, Daiyu started experiencing labor pains. Mei rushed to call her doctor, and Qianfan joined her side as soon as he could, prepared for the premature birth of his firstborn son. And after six long hours of labor, Daiyu's screams awakening the entire kingdom and splitting Qianfan's ears, they finally heard a cry, the cry of a perfectly healthy little... girl.

Daiyu smiled when the doctor handed the child to her, her grin quickly fading away when she saw the baby's face. She looked over at Qianfan, who looked like he was ready to faint, or explode, whichever came first.

"This is *not* possible. My firstborn *cannot* be a daughter!" he yelled at the top of his lungs as his eyes grew red with anger.

He slammed the door shut as he left Daiyu's room, and ordered Mei and the doctor *not* to share the news of the child's birth to *anyone*. He then left the castle, Daiyu passing out on her pillow from the pain. But even in her dream, she couldn't help but wonder what the consequences would be for her... what the consequences would be for her daughter.

Hours later, Daiyu woke up. She was delighted to see the little girl by her side, and she held her in her arms.

"Where is Qianfan?" Daiyu asked Mei with a smile.

Mei shrugged, and as soon as Daiyu saw her face turn numb, she immediately knew that Qianfan was still upset.

"It's okay. I can go talk to him. He'll be able to accept our daughter because she's just like me," Daiyu tried to assure her friend.

However, while Daiyu was asleep, Qianfan did the unthinkable, and he told the people of his kingdom that the child had not survived the birth, that Daiyu had a miscarriage.

"This is a dark, dark day for us and for our kingdom. We are deeply saddened and would appreciate it if we were given some time to mourn. The funeral will be held tomorrow," Qianfan stated.

When he returned inside, he found Daiyu waiting for him. He still loved his wife, but he couldn't stand to look at the child. He refused to believe that *it* was his.

"But she's your daughter, Qianfan. She's just like me," Daiyu pleaded with teary eyes.

"No, she's not, and nobody can ever know of her. She is to remain unidentified and confined within the walls of this castle. This *disgrace* is not my daughter, and I do not accept her as my firstborn." Qianfan fumed with rage. "We are going to hold a funeral tomorrow to honor the miscarriage that I've told everyone you had."

Daiyu couldn't believe what she had just heard; it was almost as if the news of his daughter's birth fell on deaf ears. Qianfan ordered Mei to keep the child in her custody, and she agreed, taking the child away from Daiyu on the first day of her being a mother. Mei hated that she had to be the one to hurt the queen, her friend, like this, but she had no other choice.

Daiyu was distressed, but at ease with the fact that the child was with someone she trusted. The horrible night slowly passed away, and soon, the sun rose over the horizon. Daiyu couldn't sleep all night, though Qianfan slept like a baby, knowing that he had protected his reputation and honor.

He woke up and hugged his wife. "Forget about it, Daiyu. This never happened."

But she was stunned to see how cold-hearted Qianfan was about his own child. "What do you mean? How can you —how can *we*—forget an entire existence?"

"She's not welcomed or accepted, and it's better for you, for us, that you forget about her," Qianfan answered in a calm tone as she pushed him away.

"No! She's our daughter; we have to mark her with the stone, Qianfan. She's one of us, please!" Daiyu sobbed and fell to the floor.

The magical stone was kept safe and a secret in the kingdom, a stone used to engrave the symbol of their tribe onto the child's hand, giving them their magical power. It allowed them to control the light and the dark. They could use the light to grow plants and trees, or turn day into night whenever they wanted.

Each family member had a symbol engraved on their hand since birth. It was that symbol that gave them these abilities.

Qianfan begrudgingly picked up the child and said, "Alright, Daiyu, I'm going to mark her with the stone, but after that, you have to promise me that you are going to make yourself forget about this *abomination*."

Daiyu looked up at him with teary eyes, and then nodded her head in agreement. She knew he was never going to come around; he was *never* going to accept her. But at least their daughter would have her power.

Before the funeral, Qianfan and Daiyu went to go see their daughter. Daiyu took the girl in her arms and cried as she carried her toward the room where the stone was kept.

Qianfan recited the enchanting words, "From blood to blood and the bond it creates, mark what differentiates us from the rest of the mates," and placed the stone on his daughter's wrist.

The stone glowed and made its mark.

"Oh, my daughter. We're going to call you *Xiuying*. And no matter what anyone else says, you represent the kingdom of Jinu, and you are a precious gem," Daiyu whispered in her tiny ear.

Then, with a heavy heart, she handed Xiuying over to Mei, and Qianfan pulled his wife out of the room.

"I hope you keep your word, Daiyu, just like I kept

mine," he told her, to which she nodded with a crestfallen face.

As she stood beside Qianfan at the funeral, Daiyu realized that her family was forever going to be a jigsaw puzzle that never seemed to fit together.

"How does it feel having a funeral for someone who's still alive?" Daiyu whispered to Qianfan in the saddest tone he had ever heard.

"I don't feel anything because there's nothing to be upset about," he replied with a smirk.

"Maybe the funeral is for us, then. For our dead hearts, Qianfan," Daiyu remarked sarcastically.

Qianfan stayed silent. Her words stung, but he still loved her, more than he loved anything else. Although his patience was quickly fading, he tried not to talk back as he feared hurting her even more.

The castle was full of townspeople coming in to comfort the king and queen. They brought white flowers and dried fruits to offer their condolences. Qianfan could see that Daiyu was exhausted, and he told her to go get some rest. She nodded and walked toward her room.

She tried and tried, but she couldn't sleep, the daughter whom she had to forget eating her alive.

"She will always feel incomplete and abandoned," she heard herself say. Her thoughts continued to cloud her mind as she heard a knock on the door. "Come i-in," she stuttered, and the door opened.

It was Mei. Daiyu couldn't contain her emotions and started to cry.

"Mei, I gave birth to a daughter, and people are acting like I'd lost a child. Is it really that awful to let them know that I have a healthy baby girl?"

"Oh, Daiyu, it's not. Your daughter is a beautiful little girl, and she's right here inside the castle, under my care. I promise you that she's going to be well-loved and cared for. Stop letting your thoughts take control of you. It's not your fault. You fought for her, and that's what a mother does. Don't be so hard on yourself. I'm sorry that you were the one who had to suffer, Daiyu, but the rules of society were put in place to protect the honor of the kingdom." Mei tried to comfort her as Daiyu sat on the white marble floor and cried her heart out.

"From now on, no more tears, my queen," Mei said politely, and Daiyu nodded.

When the funeral ended, Qianfan entered the room and found Daiyu sitting on the floor. She was asleep, and for a moment, Qianfan felt regret. Because of his decision, Daiyu had fallen into great depression.

"Daiyu, wake up."

Daiyu opened her eyes, but she was too weak to get up, so Qianfan carried her to their bed. He started to talk about how the kings from other kingdoms had written to him, expressing their condolences, but she refrained from indulging in the conversation and remained quiet.

After a few moments of silence, Qianfan whispered, "I will always love you, Daiyu."

"But not more than your honor," she retorted.

Qianfan felt another sting to his heart, but walked away instead of saying anything back.

The day soon turned to night, and Qianfan started to question himself. He understood that Daiyu was *never* going to see him in the same light again. He knew that their relationship would change drastically. And he could only blame Xiuying for it.

"I wish you'd died, Xiuying," he whispered to himself. "You're the reason why Daiyu hates me, and I'll *never* forgive you for that."

BABY XIUYING WAS COMPLETELY OBLIVIOUS TO WHAT WAS GOING on, or how her life was going to end up. She was unaware of the fact that her mother never wanted to give her away; she was unaware that her father hated her. She was unaware that the woman who was looking after her was only her nanny, and not her mother.

Xiuying was an adorable child with a chubby face and bright smile. All the nannies inside the castle adored her, and they loved making her giggle. Mei stayed with her the most, but because of her other responsibilities inside the castle, she had to appoint different nannies for Xiuying.

And even though Qianfan didn't accept her as his first-born, and despite the hatred he had for her, he instructed that the staff take great care of her as so to keep Daiyu satisfied. The best cuisines, fruits, and clothes were given to her, and her innocence to her surroundings kept her happy.

However, Daiyu could see and hear everything that was happening around her. Her heart died every day, seeing her daughter being carried by one nanny after another. The burden of abandoning her child was too heavy on her. And the distance between Qianfan and Daiyu began increasing with every second, despite the attempts of Qianfan to make amends. What he did could not be fixed, and they both knew it. One blamed the other while the other blamed the child.

Days and nights passed, the seasons changing from winter to spring, from summer to autumn, and soon enough, six years had gone by. And though the marriage that had been hanging by a thread had become a little more robust over the years, things were never the same as they were before Xiuying was born.

Qianfan was still in love with Daiyu, and Daiyu was still trying to accept what had happened, but still numb.

Qianfan's mother, Qiang, had also come to stay with them. She was a petite and elderly woman, had a thin, wrinkled face, graying hair, and a terrible temper. Like her son, she, too, hated Xiuying because she felt like all the happiness had been stolen from the castle the day Xiuying was born.

And Xiuying, now six years old, was beginning to look more and more like her mother. She was taught at the castle by one of her nannies, intelligent and a quick learner. She'd even learned how to read and write proficiently by the age of four. However, she had no friends her own age, and she only ever interacted with Mei and the other nannies.

Mei and Xiuying were close; it almost felt like they were mother and daughter. Xiuying would come to her if she needed help with anything, and Mei would always comfort her, console her, just like she did with Daiyu. But still, Xiuying knew from a very young age who her true parents were. Daiyu begged her friend to let her daughter know, but to also tell Xiuying to never contact them, reach out to them, or even speak about them. Her parents lived on the other side of the castle, and Xiuying never saw them face-to-face. It was hard for her, knowing that her parents didn't want to be near her, but she still felt safe with Mei by her side.

Luckily, she was still too young to understand what this all meant, why this was happening. What she *did* know was that, whatever the reason was, it involved a lot of hate. She could sense the rage that her father had for her, and would often find herself questioning whether she had ever been loved, loneliness and sadness shivering in her soul.

She didn't hate her parents; she didn't know them enough to do so, but she still had questions that needed answers. Xiuying was much brighter than the other children her age. She could understand things that even adults could not comprehend, but she was awkward around new people and got anxious often.

Daiyu kept an eye on her daughter during the first few years of her life, asking Mei to bring her out into the yard to play so Daiyu could see her from through her window. She'd pretend that she was talking to Xiuying, tears flowing from her eyes when she realized that she wasn't, though Xiuying had been too young to remember. But eventually, she stopped, choosing her husband over the little girl.

Xiuying knew that she canopied under the mantle of secrecy and silence in the castle, and made peace with it at a very young age. Ever since Qiang came to stay, she was determined to ruin Xiuying's peace. Qiang moved closer to Xiuying's room in order to keep an eye on her, and she took every chance she could to insult her.

"She's an abomination! Ruining both my son and his kingdom. What would the people think if they were to ever find out?" Xiuying would often hear Qiang say from down the hall.

And she continued every chance she got, making sure the girl knew that she wasn't wanted.

"You're bad luck for our family. That's why your parents left you," Qiang told Xiuying once.

It shattered her, her reflection a constant reminder that she was a flaw and a burden to her own family. Qiang made Xiuying believe that she was unloved, and Xiuying believed it as the truth. She knew that her mother was never going to change her mind and suddenly love her again, and this made her hyperaware of all her flaws, feeling foreign in her own body, and like she didn't even belong in her own skin. Growing up, Xiuying had put Daiyu high up on a pedestal, something she was beginning to regret.

"I don't understand why she doesn't want me. Why they just abandoned me, forgot about me," she'd say to Mei while pacing back and forth.

Mei could see that her anxious thoughts had started to take over her, all these questions with no answers.

"Xiuying, I want you to do something for me, okay?" Mei said one day.

"What is it, Mei?" Xiuying asked politely.

"Every time you feel like your heart is heavy, or you feel anxious, I want you to close your eyes and think about a place where you feel calm, comfortable, and happy. It may be the beach, a forest, your bedroom, somewhere else. Imagine what this place looks like, sounds like, and imagine how good you feel when you're there. Try it; take a deep breath."

Xiuying closed her eyes, and she soon found herself out in the yard. She could hear the sound of the wind, feel the cold breeze, and smell the fragrance of the jasmine flowers planted nearby. Most importantly, she felt like her mother was watching her. She believed that she was seen, and that, was her happy place.

As soon as she opened her eyes, she realized that she felt much calmer. She saw Mei smiling in front of her and gave her a hug.

"Thank you, Mei," Xiuying whispered.

"Promise me that you'll do this every time you feel down, my child."

"I promise," she replied.

"I know, Xiuying, that this must be very hard for you to understand, but you need to know that you cannot control what other people say, and you cannot let their words get to you. Other people are other people, and you are you. The only words that should matter must be your own, and yours alone. You will be punishing yourself if you keep letting these harsh words get to you; you have to learn to let them go," Mei calmly said, and Xiuying nodded.

After this heartfelt conversation, Mei and Xiuying went into the kitchen and enjoyed their favorite dessert, red bean cake, like they always did. Daiyu hardly ever checked up on Xiuying, and Mei was surprised to see how Daiyu had moved on with her life, leaving Xiuying behind. Daiyu started getting caught up in her own life, going to social gatherings and taking up social welfare projects to keep herself occupied. It was obvious that she was running away from her feelings, but she was leaving a lot behind, and Mei feared that it'd be too late when she'd finally realize.

Mei hardly ever saw Daiyu anymore, and their friendship drifted apart with time.

However, while Mei had all these feelings, Daiyu was jealous, jealous that Xiuying was close to her and was getting closer to her day by day. She would often think that Mei took her place, took her daughter from her. She tried to remain modest; she tried to be understanding, but she envied the motherly bond that Mei had with Xiuying.

"At least Xiuying has a motherly figure in her life," she said to herself and decided to maintain distance.

She started to avoid Mei for the sake of her daughter, never wanting her jealousy to get in the way of the beautiful relationship that Mei and Xiuying had formed. But what Daiyu didn't realize was that, even though Xiuying had Mei by her side, she still craved for her mother's love, her mother's presence.

After all, her happy place was in front of her mother's eyes.

Qianfan's hate for Xiuying did not lessen over time. He tolerated her but could not accept her. He didn't care that he was missing his daughter's early years, or that his decision was affecting more than just himself. It was almost as if Xiuying didn't exist for him. Like he had forgotten about her.

It was another monotonous day at the castle, where Xiuying remained a trapped princess. She had a young soul and was determined to find silver linings in her life. She made herself believe that every day was a new day to learn from, to fix mistakes, and move forward.

She sat in her room, learning how to paint. Mei had given her some paints and several canvases. Xiuying always had a habit of painting the secret garden of the castle; it was her happy place, and nobody else visited it. The only thing she hated about it was that she had to walk past Qiang's room to get to the garden, and Qiang *always* had eyes on her.

Most of the time, Xiuying would only go into the garden when Qiang was away, but whenever Qiang noticed where she was going, she'd follow her, make sure she wasn't up to anything. There was a dark room at the end of the hallway, where they stored armors and old statues. Xiuying was not fond of that room. It always gave her chills, shivers throughout her body, whenever she looked inside it, her imagination making her think that the room had ghostly spirits inside it.

It was late afternoon, dark black clouds over the castle, and winds blowing hard against the trees, dark yet beautiful, and Xiuying decided that she wanted to paint out in the garden.

"It seems like a good day to paint, right?" Xiuying asked Mei.

"I think not. It's about to rain," she answered.

"I'll be back before it rains, Mei. I promise!" Xiuying answered and ran off with her paints, brushes, and a tiny canvas.

On her way to the garden, she passed by Qiang's bedroom door and felt relieved when she found her sleeping. She tiptoed her way through the hallway and reached the dark room. She always peeked through the windows but never stepped foot inside. But this time, something inside her told her to go in.

"Why not? Life is about trying new things, right?" she asked herself, opened the door, and entered.

There was dust everywhere. The armors were covered

with a white cloth that almost looked like they were possessed. She looked around and found a statue of her mother and father with a baby in her mother's hands. Xiuying walked closer and brushed the layers of dust off of them. It was dark, and the windows were slamming shut because of the wind, when suddenly, she heard a shrieking voice with the anger of a thousand dragons.

"It was *never* supposed to be you!"

Xiuying looked back in fear and realized that Qiang was standing at the door. Xiuying couldn't see her face, but she could see a black shadowy figure. As soon as Xiuying realized what was happening, Qiang closed the room's doors and locked her inside. Xiuying ran toward the doors and shouted at the top of her lungs.

"Grandmother! Qiang! Please, let me out; let me out! I'm scared of the dark, please!"

She continued to bang against the door, but Qiang ignored her pleas and cries. With an evil grin, she walked toward her own room and closed her bedroom door.

Meanwhile, little Xiuying was all alone. All she could see were white sheets covering armors, and a statue that she could not understand. It was dark, and getting darker as each minute passed. Xiuying couldn't help but cry, her body starting to shiver, and tears rolling down her cheeks.

"Mother, please, come save me! I need you," she screamed out loud.

The silence in the room forced her words to invade her mind. As a six-year-old, it was difficult for her to snap out of her own thoughts.

You are bad luck; you're not supposed to be here. The words echoed and whispered to her again and again. The voices were overlapping, and it almost felt like she was inside a well, and the harsh words were surrounding her.

Xiuying closed her eyes and tried to imagine her happy place, but she couldn't do it.

"My happy place cannot be someone who abandoned me." Her eyes were red and swollen as she stood up and walked toward the statue of her parents. "You are *nothing* to me anymore. You abandoned me, and I hate you and will *never* forgive you."

She shrugged as shivers traveled her spine. Before this, she had never hated her parents. She'd always hope that maybe the decision made by her parents had a valid reason and that maybe, only maybe, one day, they would take her back with love and open arms. However, the darkness inside the room had taken away the last tiny ray of sunshine that Xiuying had left in her heart.

Many hours passed, the thunder roared, and the room that Xiuying was trapped inside started to grow colder. When Mei realized that Xiuying was nowhere to be found, she checked everywhere, in her room, in the other nannies' rooms, out in the yard, in the kitchen. Nothing. There was no sign of her, and panic started to take over Mei's heart.

Soon, word spread like wildfire across the staff, and everyone started to look for Xiuying. Qiang stayed silent, watching everyone freak out and worry as if it were her own comedy show. The guards were looking for her, the maids were looking for her, the nannies were looking for her, and Mei was going crazy, running from one end of the castle to the other. The dullness of the night had taken over as the clock struck midnight, and there was *still* no sign of Xiuying.

Xiuying had fallen asleep for several hours before she awoken again, wondering if anyone had even noticed that she was missing. The questions that were popping up in her own mind made her cry, yet once again, but this time, with all her will and rage, she started to bang against the doors. Lucky for her, Mei was close by, and she ran to the direction where the faint noise was coming from… and found herself in Qiang's hallway.

The room that Xiuying was trapped in was in the corner of a dark alley. Mei rushed toward the doors and swung them open, and Xiuying quickly rushed outside.

"Oh, sweetheart, we have been looking for you for hours! I was worried sick. Don't ever scare me like that again." Mei pulled Xiuying into a warm hug. Xiuying's body was cold, and she was shivering with fear. "It's okay, Xiuying. I'm here," Mei told her, but Xiuying remained quiet.

Mei had showed up for her; that's what mothers do. And her own mother was clueless that her own child had gone missing this entire time. Xiuying started to realize that it was time to say goodbye to all the hopes she had for her parents.

She used to make excuses for them, but no more. It was time to move on.

As she broke free from Mei's grasp, Xiuying said, "Thank you, Mei."

"No matter where you are, where you go, I will *always* come find you, Xiuying. I will *always* look out for you," Mei replied.

LATER THAT NIGHT, MEI STAYED BY XIUYING'S SIDE AFTER SHE HAD tucked her into bed, and started to suspect that Qiang had been the cause of the little girl getting trapped inside that room.

"I'm sorry, my child. You don't deserve all this pain that you're experiencing. I wish I could do something, but there's not much in my control," she whispered to Xiuying as the child fell asleep.

Mei decided that she was going to go talk to Daiyu because the actions of Qiang were getting out of hand, and they were affecting Xiuying's well-being.

The next day, Mei went to the queen's room. Daiyu had changed a lot of things. Her room had a different color scheme, changing from pastels to darker shades. The paintings of natural sceneries were removed and replaced by faux animal heads. The room was lit up with candles, and the drapes were down even though it was the middle of the day.

It almost feels like all the joy has left her life, Mei thought as she knocked on the door.

"Come in, come in, whoever it is," Daiyu said in a cheerful tone, and after hearing her voice, Mei started to second guess herself. Daiyu *did* sound happy, or was it all fake?

"Oh! It's you. It's been so long. So happy to see you again!" Daiyu exclaimed with a grin.

"I'm glad to see you, too. There's actually something that I need to talk to you about," Mei replied.

"What is it?" Daiyu asked in a curious and slightly irritated manner.

"It's Xiuying, your daughter," Mei answered and told her what had happened last night.

However, Daiyu didn't respond like Mei had thought she would. "So, what? Are you accusing the king's mother of something so wicked?"

Mei stood silent.

"You do *not* question royalty, Mei. You are nothing but a mere maid, a servant. You do *not* question what's above and beyond your entire existence. I will suggest that you take these nonsensical thoughts of yours somewhere else. The girl is *your* responsibility. You must protect her. If that is something you cannot do, stop making excuses for it," Daiyu said as her tone grew harsher.

Mei felt devastated over the response that she had gotten from the queen, from her friend. "Yes, my queen. I shall obey," she responded and left the room with a heavy heart.

What had happened to Daiyu was beyond Mei's understanding, but after the conversation, Mei promised herself that she'd never go to Daiyu for anything ever again.

On the other hand, Daiyu was regretful for what her daughter was going through, for how she had spoken to Mei. She felt confused, about herself and about everything around her. After their conversation, she sat down in front of the window, feeling something that she couldn't explain with words, and wrote in her journal what was beyond her understanding.

We all have someone we don't speak about, someone who is everything to us, but the world keeps us apart. Xiuying's presence, her name churns my stomach, and the remembrance of her scent from when I held her for the first time is still fresh. Xiuying is someone I can never stop loving, even if I cannot have her in my life. Forgetting about her is an impossible task.

Her marriage with Qianfan was finally getting back on track after the chaos that had ensued when her daughter was born. It was his orders to forget about her daughter, and at this point, she only knew one thing.

"You do not question the king, especially when it is someone like Qianfan," she whispered to herself.

Days passed since the incident had happened, and Xiuying found herself struggling trying to return to normal. She started to grow afraid of the dark even more, sleeping with the room lit bright. Most of the time, in the middle of the night, she would wake up with fear and scream. She also found herself beginning to speak with a stutter, and she complained of hallucinations that Qiang was always around her, always near her, whispering words of hatred into her ears.

Mei, and everyone in the castle who interacted with Xiuying, noticed how differently she was behaving after the incident, and they all worried for her.

One evening during supper, Mei and Xiuying had one of their heartfelt conversations.

"Xiuying, you have to move on, my dear. I know it's hard, but you need to love yourself. I understand that, at this point, the most difficult form of love for you is self-love. You have always given more than you have received, and that is exhausting, I'm sure. You're worth every fight; you're worth this life. Laugh a little, get back to things that bring joy to you. Get rid of the loose ends that make you feel unseen."

Xiuying heard her, shook her head, and stated, "But how do I do that?"

"Xiuying, maybe you should write a letter about your feelings. I know it's hard for you to speak up to me or to anyone, and that is fine, but keeping your feelings to yourself will only haunt you. You have to let them out, or else they are going to affect you in ways you would not understand," Mei suggested.

Xiuying smiled, took a sip of her tea, and replied, "You always have such insightful suggestions, Mei. Maybe I will write a letter, but who do I write the letter to?"

"You can address it to anyone you want. Just write whatever you feel, whatever you are experiencing, and hide it somewhere. Nobody has to read it if you don't want them to," Mei answered politely.

That evening soon ended, and the darkness of the night started to take control while Xiuying was getting ready for bed. Mei tucked the girl into bed, kissed her goodnight, and left the room. Xiuying tried to close her eyes but could not get herself to fall asleep. All of her thoughts and memories were rushing into her mind, when finally, she decided that she was going to write them all down. She hopped out of bed, went over to her desk, and looked for a quill and ink.

"Where is it? Where is it?" she kept mumbling to herself. "Ah, finally."

She grabbed the items and a sheet of paper. This was the first time she had felt excited about doing something after the unfortunate event. She sat down on her desk and began to write.

Dear Friend,

I have been holding onto something that I need to let go of. It's something that no longer exists, but I still think about it all the time. I have been holding onto family that were not mine from the very beginning. I kept them safe in my heart because I was scared to give up on them and the hopes of being together one day. But a recent event made me realize that it's time to move on, that I don't need them anymore. That all I need is myself.

So, I am writing to let go.

I am writing to move on.

Yours truly,

X

She didn't sign her name because she didn't want to,

but she felt much better after writing the letter. She folded the sheet of paper and placed it inside a scroll.

"Mei was right; this does help," she told herself and smiled. "Mei is always right."

THE NEXT DAY, XIUYING WOKE UP AND WENT OUT TO THE CHERRY blossom tree that she could see from her window, and she tied the scroll onto a branch, hiding the letter in the tree. However, when she woke up the day after, she noticed that her scroll was gone, and there was another one in its place. Confused, she ran out toward the tree. She was right. There *was* another scroll. Someone had replied to her letter! She took the scroll down and rushed toward her room. Unable to maintain her excitement, she sat at her desk and opened it.

To the little girl with the strongest soul,

Sometimes we have to go through these tough times and learn what is and isn't right for us. And that is the most valuable thing we can learn in life because that is how we get to know about the people and things that are meant to be with us. So, always remember that letting go is a part of your journey, even if you have to go back and go down a different road. Letting go will take you to places you never knew you wanted to go.

Keep your head up high.

Yours faithfully,

A Well-Wisher

Xiuying was in awe while reading the letter. She couldn't believe that someone had *actually* answered her! And with such wisdom, too. The words touched her heart, and she believed in them, a pinch of hope for her future in this bewildering castle. But then she paused.

"What if it's Mei?" she asked herself and started to march toward Mei's room, where she was nowhere to be found. "Hm, where could she be?"

She then walked into the kitchen and found Mei making her favorite dessert, red bean cake with strawberries. The fragrance of the sweet sugar wafted throughout the room and almost distracted Xiuying from what she'd wanted to say.

"Hi, there, my dear. What a surprise seeing you down here!" Mei exclaimed, noticing that Xiuying's mood had suddenly shifted from crestfallen to joyful.

"So, remember how you told me to write a letter about my feelings?" Xiuying started, and Mei nodded. "Well, I wrote one and hid it somewhere, but apparently, someone found it and replied to it."

"What do you mean?" Mei asked, confused.

"I got another letter in the place where I had hidden mine. I thought it was you!" Xiuying said in suspicion.

"I certainly did not," Mei replied with a firm face, and then laughed. "You really think it was me? That's funny!"

"Mei, are you sure it wasn't you?" Xiuying asked again.

Mei knelt down, tucked a strand of the child's hair behind her ear, and whispered, "Yes, my dear. I am positive that it wasn't me. Trust me."

Xiuying still had her doubts, but she believed Mei. Now, the new mystery was this new person with such beautiful insights. Xiuying was now more determined than ever to find out who it was, because the person who wrote the letter clearly knew much about her. She needed to find out more, so she decided to write another one.

Dear Friend,

I'm surprised that you replied to a letter that no one was supposed to read, but I am genuinely grateful for the heartfelt response that you had written. You made me feel happy again, and it was something I had thought I lost. Since you know who I am, judging by your last letter, it would be fair for me to know your identity as well. After all, we are friends, right?

Yours truly,

X

Xiuying signed the letter with another X, tied it to the same spot on the tree, and waited eagerly for a response.

She woke up the next day, and there it was!

To the little girl filled with curiosity,

I will not reveal who I am because I wish to remain a secret. I cannot help but notice what you wrote about happiness. You must understand that happiness comes when we are listening to the words of another, or are noticing the beauty of the world around us. You've read and heard my words; hence, you felt the true joy of happiness. But remember, do not associate your happiness with someone else's presence because happiness comes from within.

Yours faithfully,

A Well-Wisher

Xiuying felt overwhelmed by the amount of extraordinary wisdom this person had. She was surprised that she understood what was written, but what bothered her was the wish to stay a secret.

"Why would this person not want me to know about them?" she asked Mei one night while heading to bed.

"Maybe it is for your own good, Xiuying. Don't think about this too much. Whoever this is, is a kindred spirit."

THREE

While Xiuying was struggling to figure out who this mysterious person was, Daiyu and Qianfan received exciting news. They were expecting another child! After six years, the queen was pregnant again, something the people in their kingdom began to spread around very quickly. Soon, presents from all around the kingdom started to come into the castle, congratulating the king and queen.

Daiyu was caught by surprise because she had not planned for this, and it was already three months into her pregnancy. The thought of having another child scared her, especially since she already had Xiuying.

The presents, the praise, the celebration, it all made her feel like the past was coming back to haunt her, from which she had tried to run from for a very long time. Qianfan, over time, had become even more of a pessimist, yet still proud because of all his achievements in the betterment of the kingdom. His entitlement had grown and overshadowed every meaningful relationship he had in his life.

Times had changed, but Qianfan had not. He was still expecting a son and calling the child a firstborn in front of other people. Daiyu felt lost, and the only person she wanted to talk to was Mei, whom she had pushed away. Ever since Daiyu heard the news of her new child, she had grown quieter. Qianfan noticed, and he tried his best to bring her everything she liked in an attempt to cheer her up, to provide her with the best of the best.

He'd work less to spend more time with her, but that wasn't what she needed. What she needed was the surety that she would *actually* get a chance at motherhood this time, no matter what the gender turned out to be. But Qianfan was so certain that it would be a son, just like last time. He addressed the child as a *he*, even in front of his wife, and he wanted what he wanted. He wasn't going to compromise at any cost, but this situation felt like a living nightmare to Daiyu.

History was repeating itself, and she had gotten no closure from what'd happened before. There were questions, and only questions, lingering in her mind.

Why me? I have given up so much, compromised so much for our marriage, that all I have left is emptiness. I've loved, lost, and Qianfan just doesn't seem to care. I wonder about the past; I look for closure, but there's none. The truth is, I'm still holding onto these unknown answers, so much that I've started to obsess over what could've been. She wrote to herself as she felt emotionally exhausted.

Celebration was in the air as months passed by, and the child was about to come into this world. Every day at the castle, new gifts were coming for the child, and it was happening right in front of Xiuying's eyes. The more she tried to ignore the festivities, the more they were prominently in front of her.

Mei was given the responsibility of hosting a dinner for some of the royal families who were coming to congratulate the king and queen. This kept Mei occupied, and she hardly ever got a chance to see Xiuying. Xiuying wondered if things were just as fast-paced and celebrated right before *her* birth.

"My birth was not celebrated, but was the news of my existence celebrated?" she asked herself.

She soon felt overwhelmed by all her emotions. This child was going to be her sibling! She often wondered how that would feel, but then she'd distract herself from such thoughts because she knew that she would never be given the chance to meet him or her. She would just be isolated from her baby brother or sister, just like she was isolated from her parents.

This month was also her birth month, and she was about to turn seven. She felt old, even though she was still only a child, like she had lived a lifetime. Every year, Mei would plan a mini surprise birthday party for her, where she'd bake Xiuying's favorite red bean cake, buy her presents, and decorate her room.

Xiuying's birth, birthday, and mini parties were always kept a secret. At the same time, the rest of the castle mourned the death of Qianfan and Daiyu's firstborn.

Xiuying looked forward to her birthday this year because Mei would always go out of her way to celebrate it.

It was only three days away, and Xiuying was eagerly waiting. She felt like a directionless balloon in the wind with no destination in sight. She sat in her room, looking through the window, and she decided to write another letter. She'd failed to find out who the mystery writer was and hadn't written a letter in a while, so she sat down at her desk and pulled out a sheet of paper.

Dear Friend,

I know that I have not written to you in a long time, and I'm sorry for that. I haven't felt like myself lately because of all that's going on inside the castle. A life is celebrated, but not mine. Every time I try to let it go and move forward, something comes up, and all the memories start coming back. I end up wondering about many things. I wonder what birds do when they get stuck in one place. Because I feel the same way, caged. The world is lonely and sad, especially if your family chooses to abandon you; it makes you question your entire existence. I don't know why I'm here or why they chose to forget me, and that not knowing, not having answers, is what's killing me.

Tell me, is coming back to the start and beginning again the same as having never left?

Yours truly,

X

The child wrote as tears fell onto the sheet of paper. Her hands shivered as she rolled the letter and placed it inside the scroll. She threw a cloak over her body, walked toward the same cherry blossom tree, whose leaves were now beginning to fall off, and placed the scroll in the same spot.

But three days later, the day of her birthday, she didn't get a response, not like she had before. Everyone inside the castle dressed in black as they mourned for someone who was still alive while Xiuying stayed trapped inside her room, unable to let them know otherwise. And she didn't know that they were all mourning for her, that they were all mourning for her death. To protect her from the truth, Mei had told her that a noble fighter of the kingdom died on her birthday.

The entire day passed, and it was almost dark. Xiuying was eager to see what Mei had planned for her, and as the thought crossed her mind, she heard a knock on her door.

"Oh, I wonder who that could be," she said to herself and chuckled.

She opened the door, and Mei was standing there with the biggest red bean cake in her hands, along with a few bags filled with presents and decorations. Mei came in singing, placed the items on her bed, and gave the child a hug.

"Happy Birthday!" she exclaimed.

"Thank you, Mei. I love you!" Xiuying cheered, unable to contain her excitement.

They started to decorate her room with candles, balloons, streamers, and a handmade birthday banner. They lit the candles and placed the cake on her desk.

"This looks so pretty! I wish my room could look like this every day of the year!" Xiuying yelled happily.

Mei chuckled. "But that would steal the charm from it, wouldn't it?"

They both laughed, and then suddenly, the door slammed open; it was Qiang!

"Well, well, what do we have here?" Qiang remarked. "A celebration for the unwanted spawn? I see. Do you ever wonder why you have to do everything in secrecy?" She glared at Xiuying as she stepped inside.

The life from Xiuying's face vanished. Mei was furious, but she had to stay quiet for the sake of Xiuying.

"Haven't you heard? A new child is coming. A boy. And your father is just *thrilled* about his birth, unlike when you were born." Qiang blew out the candles, one after another.

"What do you mean?" Xiuying muttered.

"Oh, you naïve child. Don't you realize that you've stolen the happiness from your father? Why do you think the castle mourns on your birthday?" Qiang asked with a smile on her face. Clearly, she enjoyed every second of torturing a seven-year-old.

"Please, stop; she's just a child!" Mei hesitantly interfered, but Qiang raised her hand and indicated for her to stop.

Qiang was royalty, and Mei was just a nanny. She had no power over her.

Qiang continued, "We mourn because your father declared his first child *dead*. You are *dead* to him, yet a living weight on the shoulders of your parents. He wanted a son, but you were born instead. You brought him disappointment, and your parents drifted apart because of *you*. They both hate you, and they never want to see your face ever again. You are alive, yet everyone thinks you're dead. It would have been better if you *had* died."

Xiuying's heart sank. Her room turned dark as Qiang blew out the candles, but she finally had answers. Still, they were too heavy for her to carry. She felt scattered in the sand like strands of dried seaweed.

The silence in the room soon broke with Qiang singing, "Oh, and Happy Birthday!"

"The *audacity* of this woman knows no limits!" Mei hissed to herself as Xiuying sat feeling helpless. But she knew that Qiang was right. She couldn't help Xiuying or protect her from the truths of her life.

Xiuying was shattered, broken to such an extreme that there was nothing Mei could say to remedy that.

"Mei, can you please leave? I need some time alone," Xiuying asked her.

Mei didn't know what to say, how she could possibly console her after all that.

"Okay, I'll be in the next room if you need me," she said in such a low voice that even Xiuying could understand that Mei was feeling hopeless.

Xiuying nodded, and Mei left. The child closed the door behind her and sat down on the floor.

"What if I weren't alive anymore? Would that fix everything? Make the wrongs right?" she asked herself, the question itself so intimidating for such a young child.

She thought about what Mei would always say to her. "Your inner monologue is something that can either make or break you as a person."

But Mei wasn't here anymore, and her inner monologue was becoming more and more demeaning, pushing her to make a decision that no one thought a seven-year-old could even make.

Xiuying went outside her room and started to walk down the dark hallway. It was almost time for supper, and everyone gathered in the grand dining room, so no one saw her. She walked over to the storage room and grabbed a tiny bottle of poison that was used to kill the rats in the castle and hurried back into her room.

"What a royal way to die," she whispered to herself as she held the tiny bottle in her hands.

All of a sudden, she felt like she had grown too fast and finally understood her destiny. It was to go away for good.

She wanted to write something before she left, so she sat at her desk for the last time, held her quill, and started to write.

Dear Friend,

I feel shattered. It feels like the sad days are winning, or maybe they've already declared victory. I've had times of despair and uncertainty many times before. Still, not quite like this. There is this feeling of sadness, mixed with a pinch of fear, that is creeping around inside of me. I am giving up. I have decided to go away because that is what my father wanted and my grand-mother suggested. That is what I need to do to make things right.

I will always be grateful for the amount of love that Mei has shown me. She is the closest person I have to a mother, and I cherish every moment with her. She does not deserve this, but I don't deserve this, either. I hope Mei lives a happy life after I'm gone. Well-Wisher, you've brought light into my life, and I will never forget your wise words wherever I go next.

Yours truly,

X

She finished the letter and left it on her desk. Without another thought, she drank from the tiny bottle. At first, she felt fine, though a bit dizzy, so she climbed into bed. Soon, her vision started to fade away, and her eyes closed.

In the other room, Mei was worried for Xiuying. She was an adult, and even *she* couldn't stand what Qiang had said. She couldn't even begin to imagine how Xiuying had taken it. Mei couldn't fall asleep, so she decided to go and check up on the child. She knocked on the door three times, but no one answered. That was very unlikely of Xiuying, so Mei opened the door and found the little girl tucked in bed. At first, she assumed that the girl had fallen peacefully asleep, but when she stepped a little closer, she saw white liquid coming out of her mouth, and she realized that it was poison and started to scream for help!

"Someone call the doctor. Xiuying needs help!" Mei's scream was so loud that it frightened everyone inside the castle. The doctor arrived instantly and checked Xiuying's pulse. It was still there, and that meant there was hope. "Please don't leave me; please don't leave me," Mei kept repeating and prayed for a miracle while the doctor treated her.

Everyone who loved Xiuying grew devastated by the news, and they all felt sympathy for the child. While the doctor treated the girl, Mei went outside with her soul wrecked and heart stabbed. She started to reflect on everything that she could not tell Xiuying. How much she loved her, how much she wanted to be there for her, and how much she believed in her.

The news soon spread quickly, and one of the nannies rushed to inform the king and queen.

"Your daughter, Xiuying, tried to end her life," the nanny said in a panic, and Daiyu stood up, her heart dropping down to her stomach. Qianfan hated the thought of seeing his beloved wife in such distress, especially over that child again, and he felt a seething rage for his daughter.

"We have to go see her, Qianfan. I have to go see her, please!" she pleaded. "I just need to look at her once. Make sure she's okay!" And Qianfan, for once, agreed, but only because she was carrying his unborn son, and he didn't dare risk doing anything that would compromise that.

The castle halls were lit with tallow candles, and guards were standing at every corner as Qianfan and Daiyu headed toward Xiuying's room.

Mei was still in disbelief, and all she could think about was all the pain that Xiuying must have experienced to make such a crucial decision, how heartbroken she must have been, how hopeless she must have felt as these thoughts were running through her mind. Then she heard footsteps approaching down the hallway, pulling her away from her thoughts. It sounded like an army was marching toward her, and Mei looked up. Her eyes made out two shadowy figures. Tears in her eyes blurred her vision, and when she focused harder, she couldn't believe her eyes.

It was Qianfan and Daiyu! Mei felt like her heart had sunk and emerged back with vengeful rage, and before she could think to say anything else, she screamed in tears, "Now you decide to show up?! After dragging her to the depths of despair? After leaving her on her own? Look what you have done to her! This is all your fault; you have *no right* to see her, and *no right* to be with her right now. You left her and let her be, leaving her to feel abandoned her entire life just because you two are selfish!"

All eyes were on her as she fell onto her knees and started to sob. The silence in the hallway broke as Qianfan spoke in a calm, yet firm, tone. "Have you forgotten your place, Mei? Have you forgotten who you are talking to?" His tone grew stronger. "Besides, do you really think we're oblivious to what you're planning? Taking care of a child with magic and rights to our wealth, keeping her by your side, putting up a pretense to show that you actually care just so you can claim our wealth one day? You are only motivated to take care of Xiuying because of *your* personal interests." He paused, and then continued, "You crossed the line before when you questioned my mother's intentions, but this ends here. Your time ends here."

"No!" Mei shouted. "I-I will never leave her like you did. Xiuying has yearned for love ever since she was born, and I have given that to her. I played the role that you and your wife should've played. I don't want anything from you. You two are monsters, and I feel sorry for you."

She spat, her breathing heavy from the rage welling inside of her. Qianfan ordered the guards to take her away, and they did. Two guards held her from her arms and chained her hands. Her cries and screams were growing louder with every second, but no one seemed to care.

"Please! Please, I beg you! She needs me; she needs to see me when she wakes up. Don't do this to her. Don't hurt your daughter more than you already have!" Mei pleaded, and her voice fainted as her body was dragged to the castle's prison.

The hallway went silent again, but the faint cries of Mei remained within the walls of the castle.

Daiyu witnessed everything, but she chose to stay quiet. Maybe it was her sorrow and shock that took over her body and made her numb, or maybe the pinch of jealousy sealed her lips. She knew every word that Mei had said was true, but she also knew that the truth was more brutal to accept and easier to overlook.

The doctor finally came out and told them the surprisingly positive news. Xiuying was going to live! Daiyu was relieved, and she rushed inside the room, holding her daughter's hand.

"Oh, Xiuying! Mommy is here now!"

Xiuying slowly opened her eyes and looked around. "Where's Mei? Why are you here?" she asked.

"Mei is gone. I'm here now, your mother," Daiyu replied, and she held onto her hand tightly.

But Xiuying moved her hand away and guardedly said, "You are *not* my mother. You have never been, and you will never be."

The words that Daiyu heard from her daughter left her

in a state of agony. She felt like someone took the meaning of her existence away, and she started to step back slowly in disbelief from what she had just heard.

You're not my mother. You're not my mother. Quiet whispers were on repeat in her mind, and before she realized, Daiyu fainted and fell.

Qianfan witnessed the scene, and the moment he saw Daiyu fall onto the floor, he decided that it was time for Xiuying to leave, and this time, forever. Everyone rushed to Daiyu's aid. Qianfan carried her in his arms and took her into their bedroom.

Daiyu remained unconscious for hours, but when she woke up, she was petrified, shaking like a crumbling leaf.

"I-I, s-she said I am n-not her mother!" Daiyu cried, and Qianfan could only comfort her. "I never want to see her again, Qianfan. She doesn't need me," she stuttered, sobbing as she rested her shoulder on Qianfan's arm.

He held her tight because he knew that nothing he'd say could make her feel better, but she said what he wanted to hear, and now, he was going to make sure that Xiuying's existence vanished from their lives. Forever.

"That child will no longer hurt my wife," he said as he summoned the chief royal guard. "You must take Xiuying away, somewhere miles and a full sea away from this kingdom, and you must leave her there. Give her some supplies, but nothing more," Qianfan ordered.

"But what if she dies there?" the chief asked.

"Are you questioning my orders?"

"Apologies, and yes, my king," the chief guard replied.

"Take her away at dawn," Qianfan continued, and the guard obeyed.

A small island that had been abandoned for decades, off in the Pacific Ocean. That was where they'd send her. It was surrounded by nothing but water, and the atmosphere was damp. There was nothing on the island but dead trees and sand, with a few large boulders scattered here and there.

It would take three days by sea just to get there. So, the preparations for departure began, baskets of food were prepared, barrels of drinking water were loaded onto the ship, and a group of five maids, ten guards, and five soldiers were going to escort Xiuying, almost as if they were preparing for another funeral. Because their plan was to leave her there to die.

And all while everyone was getting ready, Xiuying was oblivious to what was happening. Her mind was clouded with questions. It had been two days, and Mei was nowhere to be seen. And no one was allowed to tell her what had happened, keeping her locked in her room as they prepared to ship her away.

"Open the door! Open the door!" she screamed and banged against it, but there was no one around to hear her plea. "Please, I need to see Mei. You can't keep me locked away forever!" she shouted again, and suddenly, the door creaked opened. It was Qianfan.

"Calm down, you stupid child," he said with a smirk. "Don't worry, you won't be staying here for long." He paused and entered the room, his eyes looking around the pale walls and her desk.

Xiuying was stunned; she couldn't move or utter a single word. This was the first time her father had said anything to her, and even if she hated him, her heart started to beat faster and faster when she saw him. The castle's maids all piled into Xiuying's room and started to pack up her things into wooden crates.

"What? What's happening?" Xiuying asked.

"You are going away. I cannot allow you to hurt my

family anymore. Besides, you told Daiyu that she is no longer your mother, and because of that, you no longer have a place in this kingdom," Qianfan replied, the calmness in his voice sending shivers down Xiuying's spine.

"But, Father..." She couldn't even bring herself to complete her sentence, unsure of what to say.

"I am *not* your father. I never was, and I am *never* going to be," Qianfan replied as he stared into her eyes, eyes that were watery with tears.

Qianfan strolled over to the window, admiring the view while the maids packed her things, and Xiuying begged for them to stop.

"Please leave my things. Don't do this, please! Mei!" She sobbed and cried out, "Mei, where are you?!"

Qianfan turned toward her with a sneer. "Oh, haven't you heard? Mei is no longer here. You are *never* going to see her again. You made the mistake of hurting my wife, and you will pay for it for the rest of your life. Take her away!" And he waved them off.

Xiuying resisted and pushed the maids away, but no matter how hard she tried, she was much too weak. And after a few minutes of struggling, she fell unconscious.

The weather was rowdy, the winds racing, the trees rushing back and forth, the birds struggling to find their way, and the dark clouds above getting ready to shower over the kingdom of secrets. This time, the dawn was bringing darkness, and nobody knew what was ahead.

Xiuying was carried by two maids while she was still unconscious and placed in a carriage that would take her to the shipping port. The carriage started to move, and the child woke up, but was too weak and emotionally exhausted to move or make a sound. Her eyes opened a bit, but all she could see was the castle shrinking in the background as the carriage moved forward.

And just as Xiuying saw the castle shrinking, Mei saw a carriage leaving the castle and traveling down a road toward the seaside from her small window in the prison cell, but she didn't know who it was.

It was all a blur to the small child. One second, her eyes would open slightly, and the next, they would turn dark. She could faintly see the blue of the sea, the dark-colored waves, a giant wooden boat, and tons of wooden crates. She felt numb and lost consciousness again as she was carried onto the ship.

AT THE SAME TIME, DAIYU WASN'T DOING MUCH BETTER. SHE woke up with contractions, cramps, and went into premature labor once again, but this time, she didn't have Mei by her side. And yet again, Qianfan was there with the hopes of having a baby boy, curiously waiting outside the room after shipping their first child to the depths of despair. History was repeating itself, and Daiyu feared what it would bring. She prayed that another girl would not come out for the sake of both her and the child's life. She knew Qianfan loved her, but he could *never* love a daughter.

Daiyu was struggling during the procedure. It almost felt like she didn't want to bring this child into existence. She was aching with sharp pains, and it intensified as the clock continued to tick.

The silence in the hallway broke as cries of a baby were heard after seven hours of immense labor pains, and as a result, Daiyu was left in comatose, not knowing the gender of her child. Qianfan bolted into the room, and to his surprise, it was… another girl. His second-born was *also* a daughter, and he knew he couldn't get away with pronouncing her dead, not again. All eyes were on this royal birth, and the kingdom was eager to welcome a new child.

Qianfan slowly walked out of the room. He couldn't even look at his daughter or Daiyu. He made his way toward the main terrace and stood there as the thunder roared above him, and sprinkles of rain started to fall.

"How is this possible?" he asked himself in disbelief. "What have I done to deserve this? Is this karma? I send Xiuying away, and now she is reborn? What can I do to get a son? I deserve a son! Xiuying has brought nothing but terrible luck to my honor. She has ruined my life!" He shouted, looking toward the ocean, "It's all because of you!" And he grabbed the vase beside him and slammed it against the wall.

FOUR

Xɪᴜʏɪɴɢ ᴡᴏᴋᴇ ᴜᴘ ᴛᴏ ꜰɪɴᴅ ʜᴇʀꜱᴇʟꜰ ʟʏɪɴɢ ɪɴ ᴀ ꜱᴍᴀʟʟ ʀᴜꜱᴛʏ ʀᴏᴏᴍ. It had an uneven wooden floor, a single mattress with off-white sheets, a warm blanket, and two small round windows on the wall in front of her that only had a view of the aggressive ocean waves. The light in the room was a dull sunset orange, and it smelled like burning candles and drenched wood.

The floor creaked as she stood up and walked toward one of the windows. Everything seemed so uncertain, and she had no idea what was ahead, what was going to happen to her. She had cried, screamed, and yelled so much that now, she couldn't feel anything. All she had left were untangled thoughts, and she questioned herself.

"How am I always the problem, no matter where I go? I tried to end my life, and that too, became a problem. Is my gender my only flaw? Such an injustice to my parents? Maybe if I had welcomed my mother with open arms while she was beside me, I wouldn't be here right now; maybe she would've taken me under her wing instead. And Mei, she just disappeared on me. I trusted her, and she just left me. I don't even know who to trust anymore."

Her thoughts were interrupted as she fell onto the wooden floor. The ship was struggling to fight the strong waves caused by the storm. Things around her started to slide from one end of the room to the other, and the candle lights were flickering. Her heart sank and feared that the ship would, too.

Daiyu regained consciousness to receive the disheartening news that she had given birth to another daughter.

"This world is a treacherous and lonely place, especially if you're born a daughter in this castle," she whispered to her baby. "I'm afraid I cannot fight for you. Qianfan is too powerful; he will never allow it." She had given up hope that Qianfan would accept the little girl as his after what he'd done to Xiuying, and she prepared herself for what's to come next.

It was dusk, and Qianfan finally decided to see Daiyu. He entered their room. His gaze wandered around until he saw Daiyu resting on their bed with silks sheets, pillows around her, and their daughter in her arms. Qianfan walked closer and sat on the bed's corner.

"So? What have you decided?" Daiyu asked in a low voice.

"Nothing; my thoughts are conflicted. She's not what I wanted or expected. Disappointment is all I can feel right now," Qianfan stated with his eyes glued to the floor and with a voice that had lost its firmness.

"Perhaps, in disappointment, we are perfectly matched. I was a fool to think that you'd welcome our child with open arms," Daiyu replied.

"You know, I never want to hurt you or break your heart, Daiyu."

"Tell me, my dear, does a heart still break if it has stopped beating?" Daiyu asked while looking down at her newborn.

Qianfan stayed quiet. Although it felt like history was repeating itself, and Daiyu was prepared for another compromise, Qianfan felt different. He felt conflicted, and under the impression that he was only cursed with a daughter because he'd mistreated Xiuying. He'd sent her away, and Daiyu wasn't even aware of it yet.

The silence in their room grew as the hours ticked into the night, and Qianfan's thoughts grew louder. He assumed karma was coming back for revenge, and in order to receive a son next time, he'd have to change his ways.

"Maybe if I treat my daughter right this time, I'll be gifted with the blessing of a son," he told himself and tried to fall asleep.

But for Xiuying, the night got perturbed. She didn't know if the ship would make it to their destination without meeting an unfortunate event. The sky lit with thunder, the windows flashing, and all she could hear were waves crashing into each other. She was horrified, scared out of her wits, and even though she had wanted to die, the thought of dying alone, afraid, with no one to find her, terrified her.

It was also in this moment that she realized that, although she was being sent away and abandoned, this change was the next chapter in her life. It was going to be a new and different experience for her. It was time for her to move on and leave what had already left her. This was still a chance for her to start over, to build for herself the life that she'd always wanted. And lucky enough, the storm soon passed, the clouds bidding farewell, and her heart settled.

"Tomorrow's going to be a fresh start for me; it's time to leave everything behind," she told herself, wrapped herself in the blanket, and closed her eyes to fall asleep.

The next morning, the sky had turned a bright blue. Xiuying opened her eyes to see rays of sunshine entering her room through the round windows. The aura in her room felt different. It felt happier, as if the storm really *did* brush all the sorrow away.

She rolled out of bed and got dressed. She'd been locked away in this room for the past two days, and something in her made her feel like she was going to get out of here today. Over the past two days, she barely ate a thing, even though all the dishes that the maid dropped off for her were her favorites.

Today, the breakfast that she received was congee with green onions. This reminded her of Mei, but she tried to push away her thoughts, tried not to think of her. She still couldn't understand why Mei had disappeared, but she suspected that it had something to do with her father.

"I hope you are well, wherever you are. Even if there *is* a possibility that you left on your own. I will cherish your memory forever as the guardian who looked over me," she addressed Mei and said out loud.

As she dug into the bowl of congee, the warmth bringing life back into her, someone knocked on her door and slid a folded piece of paper toward her. She was surprised to see it there and couldn't understand who on this ship would write her a note. She leaned down and picked up the sheet.

THE NEW DAWN BROUGHT A BRIGHT LIGHT INTO THE CASTLE, TOO. The angry storm had left, flowers were in full blossom, and the grass looked greener. Daiyu opened her eyes and couldn't believe what she was seeing. Qianfan was holding their newborn daughter in his arms and smiled as he swaddled her. Daiyu rushed out of bed and stood there in shock.

"Qianfan?" she called over to him.

"Good morning, my sunshine. You are finally up! She was crying, so I picked her up. She looks just like you."

Daiyu was confused. She didn't know if she should be happy that he finally understood, or sad that his arrogance and dignity cost her their first child.

"So, what does this mean, Qianfan?" Daiyu found herself asking.

Qianfan walked toward her and handed their daughter to Daiyu. "I couldn't sleep last night because of something I did, and it made me realize that karma is haunting us. We need to fix things and do things the right way with our second daughter, so that we get a son next time. I promise you that we're going to give her everything she needs, love, admiration, time, us. She is going to be celebrated, and I promise that we will keep her close." Qianfan smiled.

Daiyu was still stunned, but disappointed at the same time because Qianfan thought a daughter meant bad karma. But still, he was willing to do everything for her and their new child, so she kept her worries to herself.

"That's great, Qianfan, and that makes me really happy. Finally, I get to be a mother, and we get to be a family," she said, and Qianfan nodded. "So, what made you realize this?"

"It's because I sent Xiuying away, far away from the castle. She hurt you, and us, and we needed her gone. But don't worry. She's safe. We'll just never see her again."

Daiyu fell silent. She wanted to scream, to blame her husband for all the pain in Xiuying's life, for sending away her child, but she couldn't. She'd become numb to anything related to her first daughter. Besides, she had another child now, and it was time to move on.

The next day, Qianfan and Daiyu got dressed in their finest garments and announced the birth of their daughter. They didn't give her the title of *princess*, but they called for a celebration and welcomed her in front of the entire kingdom. Visitors started to pour in, and the castle was filled with flowers, bouquets, and presents for the newborn.

Daiyu was over the moon. She felt important, she felt loved, and she felt like a mother. Qianfan has announced a grand ball, a celebration for their daughter, and had invited everyone to come. The castle was decorated with fresh white lilies and baby pink roses. There were ten main courses prepared and six different types of dessert on the menu, and it felt like serenity was in the air, and happiness had taken over the castle.

But there was one person who could not understand the sudden change in Qianfan's mindset. Qiang was suspicious of him and eager to get to the root of the reason that led Qianfan to open his heart to his second daughter.

THE PARTY WAS IN FULL SWING AT THE CASTLE, BUT MILES AWAY, trapped in a ship, curiosity had taken over Xiuying. She sat down on her bed, unfolded the note, and started to read.

To the little girl who is entering a new chapter in her life,

This new journey that you are entering is going to test you in every way possible. It is going to test your hope, patience, strength, and beliefs. You have always been a little girl who tries to overcome every obstacle that life puts in your way. In the end, you always win. You are always able to pick yourself up, and that's the most special thing about you. You are moving to a new place. Make this place your home. If you welcome it with an open heart, I promise you, it will give you the love, admiration, respect, and the sense of belongingness that you have always wanted.

I know that life has been tough for you, but do not let that change you as a person. Always be the person who cares, the one who makes the effort, loves without any hesitation. Be the person who bears it all for those who cannot. Be the one who never shies away from her feelings. Be the one who sees the good in everyone. If you do, you will only receive goodness in return. There is nothing stronger than a person who stays soft to a world that has never been kind to them.

You kept going, even when the world was against you, even when no one was on your side. You never gave up hope. I hope you never stop doing that, and I hope you know that I am proud of you.

Writing about your feelings always helps, so don't stop writing, especially when you are not able to understand how you feel. Even if you don't get a reply to your written notes, write them for yourself, and don't keep your feelings locked in your heart.

Your new life awaits you!

Farewell,

Your Well-Wisher

Tears welled up in her eyes, but this time, they were tears of happiness. She felt like someone was looking after her, and it made her feel less alone. She received the note from inside the ship, which meant that whoever her Well-Wisher was, was on board, and she was eager to see their face. She wanted to cherish this letter forever, so she folded it into a small square and kept it safe in a box that she knew she would take with her. Suddenly, the door of her room started to unlock, and someone opened it.

THE KINGDOM WAS EXCITEDLY WAITING TO SEE THE NEWBORN'S face. The ball had started, and after a few minutes, Qianfan appeared with Daiyu and their newborn child in her arms. They were showered with flowers as they walked toward their throne. When they sat down, a guard came in with the magic stone. The child was going to be marked with the stone to give her the magical power, just like they had done with Xiuying.

As the guard approached the throne, Qianfan held the magic stone in front of everyone and began to say those same words. "From blood to blood and the bond it creates, mark what differentiates us from the rest of the mates." As he recited, the stone glowed when he placed it on his daughter's arm and left a mark.

Everyone cheered and applauded while the room lit up

with the stone's glow, and Qianfan spoke, "Here, in front of the entire kingdom, we name our daughter, Xiaofan."

As the kingdom celebrated the birth of a sibling that Xiuying would never come to know, the door opened, and Xiuying saw a lanky, tall man, who appeared in his sixties, standing in front of her. He had a fair complexion, brown eyes, and black hair. He was dressed in a military uniform that was worn by the majors in the army.

"Can I speak to you for a second, Xiuying?" he asked.

"Who are you?" Xiuying asked.

The man came inside and answered, "I am the major your father appointed to escort you to the island. My name is Huizhong, and you might know me as your Well-Wisher."

Xiuying's mouth dropped open, and her eyes glowed with joy as soon as she heard him.

"Xiuying, I am sorry for what you have been through, and I regret that I had to be the one to take you away from the castle."

"It's okay, Huizhong. It wasn't your fault," Xiuying replied, paused, and then asked, "I wrote to you back at the castle. Why didn't you respond?"

"Your father was growing suspicious as to what I was doing, and I had to stop. If he knew that I was in contact with you, he would have done worse to me than what he had done to Mei. I empathize with you, my child, but I could not put you or myself at risk."

He sighed and moved toward the window.

"Mei? What happened to her?" Xiuying stammered while she stood behind Huizhong.

"You don't know? She fought for you. She went against all odds and said what needed to be said to the king and queen, but that only landed her in jeopardy," he mumbled as he turned to face Xiuying.

"Jeopardy?" Xiuying questioned.

"There is a lot that you do not know, Little One. But Mei loves you, and she did everything she could for you. Qianfan has sentenced her to life in prison because she talked back and questioned the intentions of the royal family. There's nothing anyone could do to help her."

Xiuying regretted having ever doubted the intentions of Mei. She felt overwhelmed with guilt and sorrow, for blaming her for getting her shipped away. It wasn't Mei's fault at all.

"This would never have happened if I hadn't attempted to end my life," she lamented.

"Oh, no, Little One, it is *not* your fault. It was all written and meant to be; it would have happened with or without what you did. Do not take yourself as a prisoner for the unfortunate event. Mei will always love you; she always has. All she wants for you is happiness. I visited her in the prison before we left, and the first question she asked was about you, how you were doing. She would want you to have a regret-free life."

Xiuying could no longer control her emotions, and she started to cry.

"My dear, you have to live your life for her. Wipe your tears away, Little One. Keep your head up, and I promise you that what's ahead is better than what you've left," he continued.

She wiped her tears and asked, "Where are you taking me?"

"I am taking you to where your father ordered me to take

you. You are being sent to an island, completely stranded and surrounded by the ocean. Your father wanted you gone. He wanted you to suffer and make survival a challenge for you, hence, choosing an abandoned island. But what he doesn't know is that this place has some wonderful secrets and presence of people who are going to make your life flourish. Good things are ahead of you," he concluded with a smile on his face.

Xiuying was furious about everything her father had done, but she was looking forward to her new home and the countless possibilities it would bring.

"I have told you all of this because I want you to know that taking your past with you will only affect your future. You have to accept the truth and move on, my child," Huizhong continued as he sat beside her. "And I am *always* going to be here for you. I will come visit you whenever I have to travel. I will *always* be your Well-Wisher, Little One." And he hugged her.

Xiuying looked up at him and smiled. "I'm glad," she whispered.

"We will be arriving at the island today," he told her and left the room, leaving the door open.

Xiuying had a lot of things to understand and overcome, but she was grateful that even though the universe never treated her right, it kept on sending people who looked over her.

"This is a sign to move on and start a new life," she told herself as she began to pack up her things.

IT SEEMED LIKE TIMES WERE CHANGING, AND FOR THE BETTER. Daiyu looked out the window and let the warmth of the sun touch her face as she held Xiaofan in her arms. The happiness that Xiaofan brought her made her forget all about Xiuying, not thinking about her even once ever since Qianfan accepted Xiaofan. Qianfan then came into the room with flowers and Daiyu's favorite dessert.

"I come bearing presents, my queen!" He laughed.

Daiyu turned around and saw Qianfan in a rather pleasant mood.

"Thank you, my king!" she exclaimed, her cheeks turning rosy.

Qianfan leaned forward and held Xiaofan in his arms. "Seems like everyone loves her already. The kingdom is celebrating her birth more than we are. I am already getting marriage proposals for her for when she grows up." He sighed with delight, and after a few seconds, his voice suddenly changed as he said, "Things would have been different, happier, if she were a boy."

Daiyu smiled and ignored his words, concentrating on the dessert that she was stuffing into her mouth and not the sentence that Qianfan had just uttered.

There were two knocks on the door before Qiang walked in. She'd been confused ever since Qianfan accepted his second daughter. She didn't understand why her son had changed his mind about wanting a son, and she needed to understand what he was thinking. So, she requested to meet with him in person... without Daiyu.

Qianfan kissed his wife and child on the forehead before walking out into the garden with his mother. The sun was about the set, allowing the dusk to take over the sky.

"Are you happy? How did your demeanor just change overnight? You abandoned your firstborn and sent her miles away, and now you welcome the second daughter with open arms?" Qiang interrogated.

"Oh, Mother, I do not expect you to understand, but Daiyu is happy, and her happiness matters to me," he replied.

"How come her happiness didn't matter to you before? When she begged you to accept your own child? Enough with the act! You might be able to fool everyone else, but it's *not* going to work on your own mother!" she declared.

Qianfan wasn't fond of his mother asking him questions. He hated it when Qiang tried to parent him.

He sighed. "Mother, I need a son, and in order to do that, I have to treat this daughter of mine right, whether I like it or not. I have to. Or else karma is going to keep providing me with daughters. I am not fooling anyone. I'm just trying to keep Daiyu happy so I don't lose my mind. I don't expect you to understand." Then he continued, "And I certainly don't want you to treat my daughter in any way that hurts her. Do not resent her, and I mean it!" he declared and walked off without listening to what Qiang had to say.

Qiang was left in a state of disbelief. Qianfan was standing up for his daughter, even if it was for all the wrong reasons. She also didn't appreciate the tone that he'd used with her, especially in front of all the guards.

"How dare he disrespect me like that?" she snapped and promised herself to teach him a lesson when she got the chance.

ALTHOUGH THE DOOR TO XIUYING'S ROOM WAS UNLOCKED, SHE couldn't bring herself to go out and explore the ship that she had been on for the past three days. The tiny room she had been confined in became her comfort zone. She had experienced her darkest days inside it, yet also her brightest. The place that gave her goosebumps now brought her comfort, and she couldn't stop thinking about Mei. She wanted to make things right with her, but she knew that could never happen.

The level of hatred she had for her parents had reached an extreme. Her eyes twitched around her room, and she saw her writing quill that she kept on top of a box.

"Maybe I can write one last note to her. Mei always told me to say or write what I felt, and maybe she needs this more than I do."

She got up from her bed and opened the lid of the wooden box, took out her scrolls and ink, then grabbed the quill and sat down at the rusty table beside her and began to write.

My beloved Mei,

Your prayers and blessings have saved me once again. I am well and in good hands. You do not have to worry about my well-being anymore, Mei. You have worried and compromised enough. I know what you did for me, and I cannot believe that someone would give their life up for me, but maybe that's what mothers do. You are my mother, and no one can change that, even if we are miles apart.

You have helped me become the best version of myself. You have helped me turn my weaknesses into strengths. And you have taught me to believe in myself. You told me that you were always going to be there for me, and you have proven that. Thank you for everything that you have done for me, for every compromise that you have made, and for putting me before everyone else, even yourself.

I wish I could've seen you before I was sent away, but

maybe saying goodbye would have been much harder. So, this is for the best, I guess. I finally found out who my Well-Wisher is. He is here with me, and his presence, his words, remind me of you. He's like a male version of you, Mei. You'll know who it is when you get this letter. He's looking out for me and has promised me that the place I am going to will become my new home. I am not scared. I am looking forward to this new chapter in my life. Leaving the castle and you was not my choice, but whatever happens from this point on, is. I will make sure to make every second of my life worth living for, for you and for myself.

I will keep writing to you, Mei. I know that you won't get my letters after this one, but writing to you will always make me feel like I am connected to you. So, I promise that whenever happiness or sorrow reaches my soul, I will always write them down. I will always tell you, even if I don't get a response. I will always keep our memories in my heart, Mother, and I hope you do, too. I'll always remember you. Hopefully, one day, we can meet again. I promise I will never forget you until then.

Love you forever,

Xiuying

She experienced a sudden wave of relief after writing down what she'd felt, almost like she was bidding Mei a farewell, and this was the end of something beautiful. Xiuying folded the note, placed it inside the scroll, and sealed it by dripping candle wax onto the lid. She decided to then go and find Huizhong.

She opened the door and heard a faint creak. She then found a winding stairway that led toward the deck, and she started to walk until she found herself standing on the deck of the ship, the small island only a short distance away. Her eyes wandered around, and she found Huizhong standing to her right, admiring the sun. She could feel the other maids and guards staring at her as she made her way over to him.

"Hi," she gasped softly.

"Hey, you made it outside. Delighted to see you, Little One!" he replied. "Look at the sunset, the sun leaving without any hesitation, welcoming the dark because it knows that time will bring it back... and that's exactly what our lives are like, a pattern of light and dark. We have to let them take over us sometimes because we have to experience different emotions. How else will we experience joy unless we know what sorrow feels like?"

Xiuying smiled and replied, "That's very insightful. I have never looked at it like that."

She moved her hand forward and handed over the scroll.

"What's this?" he asked with great curiosity.

"I wrote something for Mei. Can you please help me give it to her?" she asked.

"Of course, I will hand this over to her myself, and I'm sure she'll be delighted to hear from you."

Xiuying stayed quiet and let the moment sink in. She gazed at the changing colors of the sky as the cold breeze slowly touched her hair, chasing the ship's rumble.

"I want to remember this moment forever," she whispered to herself.

"Xiuying, I know that you've been through a lot, and at a very young age at that, but don't let that define you. Don't let the bad experiences speak for who you are. You are more than that, kind, affectionate, and talented. Let the good things take over, and let people see you for who you actually are, not for the bad things that have happened to you."

Xiuying agreed. She knew that people only sympathized with her, felt sorry for her, and she never liked that.

She had a chance now to change how people saw her, and she decided never to bring up anything from her past to anyone she'd meet.

"Yes, you're right. Happy people are the best kind of people, aren't they?" she asked.

"Hm, maybe not the *best* kind, but they *are* more preferable," Huizhong said, and they both chuckled. "We're about to reach the island. You should go and pack up your things."

When Xiuying got back to her room, she sat down on her bed. Her life was about to change, and hopefully, for the better. Although she was optimistic, excited, and looked forward to what was ahead, she was also scared. She was going to be on her own for the first time in her life. Mei wasn't going to be there, and her Well-Wisher would not be by her side. She knew she had to be brave, but how?

On the bright side, Qianfan and Daiyu weren't going to be there either, and that was a blessing in and of itself. As much as she tried to put herself in a healthy mindset, deep down, she knew that the memories of her past would come back from time to time, and they would affect her.

The ship spontaneously stopped and caused her to stumble onto her butt. She got up, dusted off the clothes that she was wearing, stood up, and realized that they had reached the island. She was wearing a dark pink dress with off-white embroidered sleeves and flowery cufflinks, and she tied her hair back with a white ribbon. She looked like royalty, the royalty that she now hated.

Huizhong knocked on the door, letting her know that it was time to leave. She opened the door and welcomed him in.

"Saying goodbye to the room?" he asked.

She laughed. "Yeah, I think I'll actually miss this place."

Huizhong looked at her. "Well, that's surprising."

"This journey has been insightful for me. There's a lot I have learned and overcome. As much as I want to hate the experience, I will *always* be grateful for it."

Huizhong stepped closer to her and sighed. "There is something that you need to know before you leave."

"And... that is?"

"Every child in your family is given a magical power, and that includes you. You were marked with the stone when you were born, and now you are old enough to understand how to use it," he said, and Xiuying listened. "Here, give me your hand."

Xiuying hesitated, but she reached over.

"Look at this mark on your wrist. It's a tiny flower engraved onto your skin. I cannot say for sure what your power is, but it has something to do with the Earth and its four elements. Earth, water, air, and fire. This power has been given to you. It exists inside of you. You just have to recognize it, feel the connection with it, and accept the power that the stone has bestowed upon you."

Xiuying looked down at her wrist and stood there, shocked. "I always thought this was a birthmark, and it meant nothing."

"It means everything, Xiuying. Generations upon generations of your family have been gifted with magical powers. Your father has control over the sun and moon, and your mother can communicate with animals. Your ancestors have made legacies for controlling the elements. Every newborn brings a new and different gift." Huizhong recalled and continued, "And it is rumored that the firstborn gets the most powerful gift. You are the firstborn, and you are *always* going to be more powerful than any of your siblings, no matter who or what they are."

Xiuying stayed silent for a moment before saying, "Maybe that's why father wanted his firstborn to be a boy."

"Maybe," Huizhong replied. "Remember to believe in yourself and your power," he added, and then it was time to leave. "Let's go, Xiuying. It's time."

He smiled at her and left the room.

Xiuying took a deep breath and looked around the tiny room, the round windows, the small rusty bed, and the tiny table on which she wrote the farewell note for Mei. This was a life-changing event for her. And now it was time to leave everything behind and start over.

The maids started to come into her room to transfer the wooden crates to the deck. After all the crates had been moved, Xiuying gave the room one last look and slowly closed the door. She walked upstairs and saw all the hustle. The deck was crowded with maids and guards, moving things back and forth, and the sun had almost disappeared.

The island looked beautiful but rugged. There were mountains surrounding. They were so tall that they made her feel even smaller than she already was. But there wasn't anything green on the island, nothing but sand and dead branches.

"How can I survive here?" she asked herself, but then realized that she had no other choice.

Huizhong tapped on her shoulder and asked her if he could escort her off the ship and onto the island. Xiuying agreed, and they both got off the ship. He strictly told all the other guards and maids to stay on the ship. No one was permitted to step another foot onto the island.

It was getting dark, and Xiuying felt scared.

"Are you going to leave me here alone? There's no one else here. I-I'll die out here!" she stuttered.

"Have patience, Xiuying. This place is not what it

seems; there is more than what meets the eye. Follow me," he replied.

She followed him quietly with worries that she could not dispel. She could see the mountains all around them. There were dead plants and shabby bushes, the land was infertile, and she could feel, with every step, dry branches being crushed beneath her feet. The ambience, the cold breeze, the night taking over, brought shivers down her spine; she grew pale, and her heart was racing.

She followed Huizhong, and suddenly, he stopped in front of a cave that had a dim light at the end of it.

"Remember what we talked about, okay?" he asked and entered the cave.

Xiuying hesitated at first, but she had no other choice but to follow him. The cave was dark, and she noticed tiny red eyes when she looked above her, before realizing that they were bats. She hissed but stayed quiet.

"Am I going to live in a cave for the rest of my life? So much for a new life," she said to herself sarcastically.

FIVE

AFTER WALKING FOR SEVERAL MINUTES, THEY REACHED THE OTHER side of the cave. Xiuying was looking down at her feet to avoid staring at the bats, and as soon as she looked up again, her eyes lit up.

She smiled with a sigh of relief; there was an entire civilization right in front of her, a small cottage town hidden and protected by the mountains.

The mountains were only surrounding the village, and they acted almost as a decoy. The streets were lit up by fire lanterns. They were bright, warm, and most importantly, welcoming. There were small cottages around every corner, with a small porch, oversized windows, wooden doors, and they were painted a dusty brown pastel color.

The streets felt alive with small children running around, and there were colorful decorations everywhere. Dark blue flags with flowers on them hung at every corner, the sky was a shade of dark blue and purple, and the view of the village was heartwarming. It was a small town where everyone knew each other and showed up for one another during times of need.

"Welcome to Naje." Huizhong smiled and squeezed Xiuying's hand. "I told you this place was more than what meets the eye, Little One." He chuckled with joy.

"Ha, you were right." Xiuying giggled beside him as they walked down the cobblestone pathway.

She couldn't get enough of the village. It left her in awe, the children playing marbles, the smell of freshly-baked bread, the aroma of love in the air; she loved every bit of it.

"Huizhong!" an elderly voice called out with admiration. "You are finally here; we have been waiting for you."

Xiuying turned around and saw a woman nearing her late eighties. She had braided white hair and tiny yellow flowers in them. She had wrinkles on her face, a fair complexion, and a lovely smile. She reached out and gave Huizhong a hug.

"It's so good to see you, Huizhong. You look well, my son!" she gushed.

"Oh, Hua, it's so good to see you as well. This is Xiuying, the girl I told you about."

"Yes, yes. Xiuying, my dear, you are so beautiful, and we are glad that you are here. It's about time I have some company. With Huizhong gone, it gets pretty lonely." She laughed while hugging Xiuying tightly.

Xiuying beamed and said, "Thank you for having me."

"Oh, no need to be polite, my dear. You are too kind," Hua replied with an upbeat tone and added, "Let's get you settled in. Come on. Let me show you your new home."

Xiuying and Huizhong followed her as she made her way through the lively streets of the village. After a short walk, they reached her cottage. It was the same as all the other ones, with a large wooden door, a front porch, and gigantic windows.

But there was one thing that stood out about her cottage. There was a tree with tiny yellow flowers all over it. It was the only one like it, from what Xiuying had seen in the village. Hua opened the cottage door and led them inside. It was beautiful on the inside. The place had an aroma of cherry blossom trees and fresh cookies, floral murals hung on the walls, and wooden furniture covered with soft, colorful cushions sat around the open rooms. There were three bedrooms in the cottage, a living room, and an open kitchen.

Of the three rooms, one belonged to Hua, and one was a library. The third room was given to Xiuying, already decorated with peach-colored paintings of flowers all over the center wall, and the lightest shade of pastel pink paint was used on the other three walls. Her room had a large window with off-white curtains on it, and she could see the street and other homes at the base of the mountains. There was also a desk in her room with some books on it and a light lantern, along with a small bed that was covered with a quilt and had a fluffy pillow on it.

"Do you like it?" Hua asked in hesitation.

"Like? I love it! Thank you, Hua." Xiuying sighed with joyful tears in her eyes.

"Alright, my dear. I'm glad you do. The villagers will bring your things here first thing in the morning, okay?" Hua said.

"Okay." Xiuying blushed.

"Now, let me make you both something to eat!" Hua turned to Huizhong and raised a brow at him. But he shook his head.

"No, I can't. I have to leave. I only came here to escort Xiuying, and now it's time for me to go."

Xiuying looked at Huizhong like she didn't want him to leave, but she knew she had to say goodbye to him. He, too, had to leave, as everyone else did. Huizhong thanked Hua as she showered him with her blessings and said her farewell.

Xiuying took a deep breath and walked toward Huizhong.

"Can we talk outside for a bit?" she asked him, and he nodded his head in agreement. "Thank you for doing this, for bringing me here and not leaving me stranded as my father told you to," Xiuying murmured when they got outside.

Huizhong laughed and asked, "Did you really think I was going to leave you stranded? I came here with a plan, Little One. I have known Hua for ages, and I promise you, you are in good hands. I am your Well-Wisher, after all. I have to live up to the title, right?"

Xiuying sniffed and replied, "Ha, right. So, how do you know Hua?"

"Six years ago, I was on a voyage and encountered a problem with my ship. I had to anchor it here, on this very island. While the rest of my crew stayed on to try and repair it, I got out to explore the island. That's how I found Hua, injured. Sharp rocks had wounded her foot, and blood flowed from her wound. I tried to help her as best as I could. I wrapped up the wound with my shirt and helped her to her cottage. After that, she always welcomed me with open arms, and I've always seen her as a motherly figure. But she made me promise to never mention the village to anyone else. No one else knows that they live here. They chose to disconnect from the rest of the world, happy with their own kind without any invaders. I try to visit Hua every now and then, once every six months or so."

"And what about her family? Does she have children?" Xiuying asked.

"Her husband died five years ago. He was a wonderful man who kept her happy. And after his death, her only son left the village because he wanted to explore life beyond these mountains. He left without realizing the worth of this place or his own mother, and Hua has been alone ever since." Then he added, "I wrote a letter to her, telling her about you, before we started our journey. She's excited to have you live here with her. She needs you as much as you need her."

"I already love her." Xiuying smiled. "And I love this village."

"I'm not sure when I will come back, Xiuying. But I will come back one day; this is my promise to you. Focus on yourself from now on. You have everything you need, and you will get everything you want here. It's time for me to leave now before the crew gets suspicious; everyone thinks I am leaving you in the wilderness," he told Xiuying.

She nodded. "I'll miss you. Take care of yourself, and don't forget to give my scroll to Mei, please."

"I will miss you, too, Little One. Stay happy, and I won't forget. I will deliver it to Mei myself." He hugged her.

"Alright, goodbye. Have a safe journey," she said, and Huizhong smiled before he left.

Xiuying watched as he walked away, a tear or two trickling down her cheek. He turned halfway back, saw her standing, and waved goodbye. But then he disappeared, and just like that, Xiuying's Well-Wisher was gone, and her new life was about to start. She walked back to her cottage and opened the door. During the time when she was gone, Hua had prepared all sorts of goodies for her, from cookies to baked bread to her favorite red bean cake.

"Oh! You're home," Hua exclaimed with excitement when Xiuying entered.

"Yes, I am home." She humbly smiled.

Xiuying woke up the next morning, slowly opened her eyes, and caught a glimpse of the warm sunlight coming through her bedroom window. She smiled, thinking to herself that her life would only change for the better from now on. She sat up and moved her eyes around her room. The painted flowers on the walls, the aroma of freshly-baked waffles—all made her fall in love with the place once again.

"Oh, my child. You're up! Just in time for breakfast. I made you waffles with chocolate syrup. Come on, rise and shine!" Hua sang.

"Thanks, Hua. I'll be right there," Xiuying replied with a humble smile on her face.

She got out of bed and tidied her room. She liked everything neat and organized, always. She found her way to the dining table, and it had the most delicious-looking waffles placed on it, decorated with a vase at the center that featured yellow flowers.

Xiuying took her seat, and it felt like she had been born all over again, but this time, the experience was going to be a pleasant one.

"I will take you to meet everyone today. You are staying

here, so it'll be good for you to meet the rest of the villagers and make some friends, my dear," Hua said as she pulled up a chair and sat beside Xiuying.

"Yes, of course," she replied. "Although, I've never made friends my age. I'm not sure if I'll be able to or if they'll like me."

Hua grinned. "This is something you should not worry about. Just be yourself, and everyone is going to adore you. I promise."

"I hope so. Hua, I've noticed that there isn't much greenery around here. There's only one tree outside your home. Why is that?"

Hua took a deep breath and explained, "This island has had its own history, and not a pleasant one. A long time ago, a noble warrior was left on this island to die, the scorching heat and lack of fresh water and food making it nearly impossible for him to survive for long. He was being punished for something he didn't do, framed by his very own confidant to a royal king. His family eventually came looking for him, but found nothing but rotting bones that had dissolved into the sand. Most others would've left, but this family didn't. They didn't want to leave their son behind, and that's how our tiny village came to be. The family settled here in secrecy, and their loved ones, along with the community who believed in the soldier, joined them. However, the island is mostly barren. The mountains and sand make it very hard for us to harvest food. It's almost as if the island is still mourning the warrior's death, even after centuries. The tree outside my home is known as the Golden Tree of Hope. It is the only one here because it's the only one that'll remain alive. I take care of it, and it takes care of us by giving us hope. Maybe one day, our village will become Lùhuà."

"Lǜhuà?" Xiuying repeated.

"Yes, it means *greenery*."

Xiuying was moved by the story she had just heard, and it brought goosebumps to her body. Her heart was beating fast, and she felt a tingling sensation in her fingers. The village with such pure souls living in it had such a dark past.

"Hua, do you believe the island will get its greenery back one day?" Xiuying asked.

"Yes, I put my trust in Mother Nature, my dear. Something, or someone, is going to help our island one day," Hua replied as she placed a tiny yellow flower from her tree in Xiuying's hair.

"This says you belong here, Xiuying. This yellow flower welcomes you into our family and our home. I just want you to know that I'm happy to have you here."

Xiuying hugged her with teary eyes, and Hua hugged back. Xiuying really *did* feel like she was home, finally. Hua reminded her of Mei, the same motherly warmth, and she realized how, even when things go wrong, she'll always have someone who will look after her without any hidden motives.

"Okay, then, get dressed. You have many people to meet, and I'm sure you'll love Meili!" Hua exclaimed.

Hua was the kind of person whom everyone knew and adored in the village, Xiuying quickly found out; she was known for her excellent baking skills, kindness, and helpful advice. Everyone in the village felt at home around her. It was who she was, and she loved it. She knew the impact she had on people, and she used it to her advantage. She had many connections, and people would listen to her like she was some sort of prophet.

And now that Xiuying was with Hua, she too, had a

special place in everyone's eyes. She barely knew anyone, but everyone already knew her. Hua packed some baked cookies for her closest friend's family and left the house to meet them. Xiuying, of course, followed her. She wore a light pink, knee-length dress with puffy sleeves that had tiny white flowers printed all over the fabric. This particular dress always made her feel comfortable, confident, and it made her feel like the best version of herself, which she needed to be today. She wore matching pastel sandals, let her hair down, and placed the tiny yellow flower on the side of her head.

She stepped out and whispered, "Here we go," took a deep breath, and started to walk alongside Hua.

The sky was light blue with hints of white clouds that had faded. The sun was shining bright, but still warm, in a comforting way. As they walked down the street, Xiuying noticed that everyone stopped to greet Hua. Hua introduced Xiuying as her adopted daughter to the other villagers, and they welcomed her with open arms. Xiuying was overwhelmed by the amount of love that she was already getting. They had only gone down two streets, and she had already gotten invites for both a tea party and brunch.

Hua and Xiuying finally reached Lifen's home. Lifen was Hua's childhood friend, and their families had moved to the island together several years back. Their friendship was solid; nothing could tear them apart. They laughed and cried together, and they shared with each other all their secrets. Hua even watched Lifen's daughter and granddaughter grow old right alongside her friend. They weren't just friends. They were like family to each other.

"Hua! You're here," Lifen screamed with delight and leaned in for a hug.

"And you brought your famous cookies!" her daughter, Yilin, added as Hua extended the basket to them.

"And you must be Xiuying. You might not be aware, but you are the talk of the town these days." Yilin chuckled as she welcomed Xiuying inside.

"I'm not a fan of attention, to be honest," Xiuying replied.

The interior of Lifen's home was the same as Hua's, almost identical. The walls had flowers painted on them, the furniture was wooden, and the color combination involved dark hues of white and blue. Yilin went into the kitchen to brew some tea, and Lifen accompanied Hua and Xiuying into the living room, as they sat by the window with a clear view of the mountains and the scattered blue sky.

"So, Xiuying, how do you like our little village so far? And how is our Hua treating you?" Lifen asked.

"Oh, Lifen. It's amazing. I was so lucky to end up here with Hua. She has been like a mother to me already. I am grateful for everything she's doing for me," Xiuying replied with a smile.

"There's no need to be such a kindred spirit, my dear. It's our duty now to look after you. Remember, we want you here. You're one of us now, and if anything ever happens to you, come straight to me, okay?" Hua reminded the child.

"Meili is going to adore you! I have a feeling you two are going to become the best of friends," Lifen chimed in.

The thought of having a best friend her age excited Xiuying. She never had one before, and often wondered what it felt like to have a friend whom she could share moments of happiness and despair with.

"Where is Meili, anyway?" Hua asked.

"She's at school, learning to read and write. She's going

to be back any minute now," Yilin replied as she placed the tiny teacups on the center table, served with the cookies that Hua brought.

"Why don't you get Xiuying enrolled?" Lifen suggested.

"What do you think, Xiuying?" Hua looked at her and asked.

"I would love to."

Although Xiuying could already read and write as any normal adult could, she still said yes because she didn't want to give up on the chance to experience what school was like. She wanted to experience what being a normal child was like.

"Alright, that's settled. I will get our Xiuying enrolled tomorrow, first thing in the morning," Yilin declared.

Meili suddenly rushed through the front door and stomped her feet on the floor.

"I am *never* going back to that place!" she screamed and plopped herself onto the couch right beside Xiuying with her arms crossed in protest. "They *never* treat me right. Mr. Zen doesn't understand that I'm trying my best, and he keeps pointing out my mistakes." She started to stuff her mouth with cookies. "Ah, I love these, Hua!" she added with her mouth full.

Yilin spoke up, "You know, Meili, that's what teachers are supposed to do. They help you fix your mistakes so that you can learn."

"Ugh, but it annoys me!"

Hua and Lifen laughed while Xiuying smiled.

"I'm so sorry! Where are my manners?" Meili chuckled and went in to hug Xiuying. "It's so great to meet you, finally. I can already tell that we're going to be best friends, just like Hua and my grandmother."

"Me, too," Xiuying whispered, and they started to talk over tea and cookies.

Meili told Xiuying how she loved writing and wanted to be a writer when she grows up. She had all these imaginations and stories that she couldn't wait to put into words. Xiuying told her how she loved to paint, and she liked to capture moments into pictures so that she could cherish them forever. They clicked instantly, and their friendship began, even though they were different from each other in so many ways. Xiuying was calm and collected while Meili was the definition of *chaotic mess*. Xiuying stayed quiet and kept her feelings to herself while Meili blurted out the first thing that popped into her mind. But together, they were part of one equation, and *that* was the foundation of a strong friendship.

"So, where are your parents, if you don't mind me asking?" Meili asked as they looked toward the fleeting rays of the sun disappearing behind the dreaded mountains.

"They died when I was very young," Xiuying replied.

Xiuying couldn't believe that she had just said that, but she wanted to take Huizhong's advice and start a new chapter in her life. She wasn't going to let her past traumatic experiences define her and speak for her, for who she was. She wanted to do things her way, and she was writing her own story.

"I'm sorry to hear that," Meili replied.

"It's fine. It doesn't really matter anymore. What about your father? Is he around?" Xiuying mumbled.

"He's not around much. You see, our island needs food, wheat that we cannot grow on this soil. He's one of the merchants who arranges all the basic necessities for the village. So, he's traveling almost all the time. He comes home for two days at best after ten days gone." Meili sighed.

"It must be hard; you must miss him."

"Yeah, I do, but at least he's here. The house lights up when he's around. He's caring and compassionate, and he makes up for the times when he's not around. He tries, and that's what matters. So, it's okay." Meili blushed and smiled.

"I admire your spirit," Xiuying praised her.

The sky soon turned purple as the sun was almost gone.

"Ready to go, Xiuying?" Hua asked, and Xiuying nodded.

"See you tomorrow at school?" Meili asked.

"I thought you never wanted to go back," Xiuying replied with a smirk.

"I think I changed my mind." Meili smirked back and waved goodbye.

CHAPTER
SIX

"So, how was it?" Hua asked with curiosity as they walked toward their home.

"It was overwhelmingly awesome. I love Meili and her family! I finally have a friend!" Xiuying exclaimed and jumped to show her excitement.

"I knew you'd love them," Hua added.

When they arrived home, Xiuying lit the house with candles while Hua prepared dinner. Xiuying hated the dark, and she insisted on lighting up the entire house. The dark suffocated her. She'd moved on, but the memories were embedded in her mind like a brand.

During dinner, Hua told Xiuying stories of her childhood, how she met her husband, and how they fell in love.

They met and instantly connected when she was the only one who could replicate his famous cookie recipe during a competition that he held. They resented each other at first, always in competition, but soon, they fell in love.

Later that night, Hua tucked Xiuying into bed before climbing into her own bed. However, something kept the child awake. She struggled to fall asleep, but she didn't know why. She had a perfect home and the perfect life now, so why was her heart not at peace? The fact that she told Meili that her parents had died was now eating her up. She could have a perfectly normal life, but the memories of her scars were not going away. It wasn't the love for her parents that came back to haunt her. It was the hurt that the love brought, the fear of abandonment, the self-doubt, and the pity.

Xiuying soon found herself struggling to breathe, her own words and thoughts suffocating her. She stepped outside, and the street was empty. The air was foggy, but also so cold that it made her shiver. There were lanterns put on high poles, and Xiuying stood by the Tree of Hope.

"You know, sometimes I wonder how easy it was for people to abandon me, forget about me. I never mattered to anyone I cared about. I've been forgotten, rejected, abandoned. All of my relationships seemed one-sided, my existence unimportant to them. Sometimes it makes me wonder if maybe the problem lies within me. Maybe I'm just not likable," she whispered to the tree and held onto a flower.

Suddenly, her heart started to race again. She could feel her heart beat faster and faster with each passing second. The tingling sensation in her fingers was back, and then she realized that the flower she held was glowing. One after another, all the tiny yellow flowers around her started to glow with a golden light, and specks of dust from them fell onto the ground. The moment the golden dust reached the ground, it started to convert the dry soil into grass, the greenest she'd ever seen.

After a few seconds, the glow from the tree faded, but the grass stayed.

"That's it! That's it!" She beamed and cheered. "I have found my magical power. I can control nature with my emotions. That's what this place needs, greenery! I can't believe this! I can pay Hua back for her taking me in. I can help the island!" Tears of joy started to roll down her face. She looked up at the sky and whispered, "Thank you. The emotions I feel might hurt my soul, but they're going to help others."

She touched the grass, and it felt as soft as wool. She couldn't believe what had happened, as if it was beyond anything she had ever experienced.

Even though she was from a magical kingdom, nobody except Huizhong told her about the powers that she or her ancestors had. Hua believed that things would turn around for this island, and then the universe sent her Xiuying. Xiuying had wanted to help this island, and maybe becoming a tiny speck of hope would help her bring purpose back to her life.

Maybe now, she could justify to herself why she had gone through all the hardships in her life, why she was different, why she understood more than the other children her age. She tucked herself back into bed and closed her eyes. She didn't know how the villagers would react to what had happened when they woke up in the morning, but she was excited to find out.

THE NIGHT FLEW BY IN A BLINK. XIUYING WOKE UP TO VOICES OF chatter all around her. It was early in the morning, and the voices felt like a crowd had gathered. She got out of bed and rushed outside. Hua was nowhere to be seen, so she opened the front door to find about forty people gathered around the tree. Hua was standing right in the center of the crowd, and Lifen, Yilin, and Meili were also there. And the head of the village, Jifae, was standing right beside Hua.

"What's happening? Is this a gift from God?" Questions were whispered throughout the crowd.

The island had seen only sand, not even proper soil. It had bushes that were too dry, plants like cacti that one could only find in the depths of a desert, so seeing grass around the tree seemed like a miracle for the villagers.

"Does this mean our island is going to become green again, as mentioned in the myth?" someone from the crowd questioned.

"There, there. Over several decades, our island has been deprived of the gifts that Mother Nature bestowed, but we hoped, and we kept believing. We took care of what was left and saved it from depletion. I believe our time of worry is now over, and Mother Nature is taking back control, just like it should be. This occasion is a cause for celebration, and it should be celebrated. This is just the start. This will create a difference for generations ahead. Don't let your worries take over. Take a deep breath, and let the moment of change sink deeper within your heart," Hua explained, and as she finished, everyone cheered.

The moment felt like a festival. It felt like something that had been yearned for and was now given back to them.

"If this continues, my father would not have to go on those week-long traveling trips. Wouldn't that be great?" Meili exclaimed as she stood beside Xiuying.

Xiuying smiled and looked at her friend, seeing pure joy in her eyes.

"Maybe this is because of you," Meili said, and the words, yet again, made Xiuying's heart race.

"What do you mean?" Xiuying asked, thinking that Meili might have seen her last night.

"I mean, you are the lucky charm," Meili answered and chuckled.

"Oh, I'm sure I'm not. This is all because of the hope the village had. Hua told me all about it," Xiuying answered, trying to remain calm and innocent.

"In light of today's event, I announce a feast of celebration. This day shall be celebrated and remembered," Jifae commanded above them all. "Let the preparations begin; we feast at sunset!" he added, and everyone cheered.

"This is so exciting. Father is also coming back today. This means we have much to do, Xiuying! See you tonight!" Meili waved goodbye and headed toward her own home, accompanied by Lifen and Yilin.

The crowd dispersed within seconds. Everyone had things to do in such a short period of time, and Xiuying was left alone with Hua.

"Oh, Xiuying, my dear. Did you see the miracle? Honey, you brought luck to us!" Hua came over and hugged her.

They walked into their home, and Xiuying felt guilty for not telling Hua the truth. "Hua, I need to confess something," Xiuying muttered.

Hua smiled and sat across from her on a wooden chair. "I know, my dear," she replied.

Xiuying felt confused. "What do you know?"

"Huizhong told me about the magical power you might have because of your family. When you were looking around your new room, he gave tiny glimpses of what you have been through, and I know about the wonderful power that you have within you, my love. Use them for good, and use them wisely," she concluded.

"I'm so glad you know. I didn't know how to tell you," Xiuying said with a sigh of relief.

"I am honored that you wanted to tell me," Hua responded.

"Hua, can we keep this between us for now? I don't have control over my emotions and my power yet. It's all so overwhelming."

"Of course, my dear. It's your life and your decision. My lips are sealed until you want to disclose the gift you have, all on your own. But I hope you do one day. You are a miracle for our village."

"Hua, you are too kind. Thank you," Xiuying replied and beamed.

"Alright, my dear, we have a lot to do! Let's get to work, shall we?" Hua snickered.

"I will start when I understand what's going on. It seems like everyone's in a hurry and has something to do." Xiuying laughed.

"It's been a very long time since we last had a feast of celebration. What happens is that each household has a responsibility. Some bake bread, some prepare the curry, some bake cakes, some bake cookies, some are responsible for the decorations, and some are given the responsibility to entertain. Everyone plays a part that matters, and no one is left behind. Everyone gets dressed up, and we celebrate—laugh, dance, sing, and eat around the bonfire. It's all in pure joy, my child. It's about spending every moment in gratitude and with the people you love and care about." Hua explained and continued, "So, all you have to do for now is find the prettiest dress in your closet and focus on yourself, whatever you need to do."

"Don't you need help?" Xiuying offered.

"Oh, no. I have been doing this since forever. I can handle it!" Hua replied, and Xiuying went into her room while Hua prepared the dozen cookies that were needed for the feast.

Xiuying's heart felt at peace. There were moments when she felt like her past was taking over her thoughts, but the present pulled her out of despair. She now understood that her power was channeled by her emotions, but was it only from the feelings caused by distress, or could it be channeled by other emotions like happiness, fear, and excitement?

As these thoughts crossed her mind, her hands started to tingle again. She looked around and saw the flowers in her room begin to glow. The specks of dust mixed with the air and escaped through the window, and then suddenly, the grass started to spread faster, around the sides and toward the neighbor's place. A beautiful tree with pure green leaves and tiny pink flowers all over it wrapped the fence on the side of the house.

Xiuying looked out the window and saw only content faces. The villagers were amused, grateful, and now Xiuying felt even more excited because this assured her that the miracle was here to stay.

"So, it *does* work with other emotions!" Xiuying whispered to herself and smiled as she threw on the prettiest dress that she could find in her closet.

THE CELEBRATION WAS ON THE VERGE OF PERFECTION. A CLUSTER of pink flowers had covered some areas of the village, including the center of town where the feast was taking place. The merchants arrived and were shocked. It was hard for them to wrap their heads around what had happened. The entire village was lit with lanterns, colorful flags were displayed all around, the air was mixed with fresh fragrances and delicious aromas, the children were all dressed up, and every woman in town now had a pink flower in their hair. It was as if Xiuying had come to an entirely different place.

Youkai, Meili's father, was the head of the merchants, and they had come back with things needed for the village after a voyage of ten days. They were tired and overworked, but the feeling of helping their own community and bringing them back what they needed kept their minds going even as their bodies were giving up.

Youkai came home and received a heartwarming welcome from his entire family. They, too, were all dressed up and asked Youkai to do the same.

Meili explained to her father everything that had happened. The miracle. Xiuying's arrival.

"So, you think this new girl is the lucky charm?" he questioned suspiciously with a grin.

"I don't think. I *know* she is. And you know what? She's my best friend," Meili replied with enthusiasm.

"Well, I am looking forward to meeting her." Youkai pulled his daughter into a long overdue hug.

Youkai, Yilin, Lifen, and Meili left their home and headed for the center of town. The celebration had already begun, and each family was setting up what they had brought. The bonfire had turned the chilly breeze into warmth.

Hua was already ready and waiting for Xiuying outside her room. The door opened, and Xiuying stepped out. Hua was in awe because Xiuying looked so beautiful. She was wearing a royal pink gown that had bell-shaped sleeves and sparkles all over it. She tied her hair up in a bun and tinted her cheeks a rosy pink.

"You really *are* a princess, my love!" Hua exclaimed, and Xiuying beamed.

This was Xiuying's official public appearance. She was going to introduce herself to everyone as Hua's adopted daughter. As she walked toward the center of Naje, she bit her nails and fidgeted, nervous energy racing through her. She had never been to such a gathering before.

"It's okay, Xiuying. Everyone's going to love you. What's not to love?" Hua comforted her as she held tightly onto her hand and walked to the center of town.

The center was where all the streets met and formed a circle big enough to host a gathering for the entire town. As Xiuying strode in, everyone turned their heads to look at her. She was breathtaking, and her beauty was blinding. The music was loud and getting louder; drums, violins, and guitars all played at once. People were dancing around the bonfire and enjoying the delicious treats that everyone had brought.

"Rumor has it, you're the lucky charm." Jifae came over and greeted Xiuying officially.

Jifae was in his late teens and given the responsibility of the town after his father passed away. He was tall, had black hair, fair skin tone, light blue eyes, and a humble smile. He was known for making wise decisions that bene-fited the town.

"You and everyone else must be mistaken," Xiuying replied jokingly.

Meili rushed toward Xiuying and gave her a big hug.

"Hello, Gorgeous!" Meili was prone to spontaneous bursts of energy.

"Same to you, Meili." Xiuying complimented her back as she returned the hug.

Xiuying couldn't even finish her conversation with Jifae before Meili dragged her over to the table of freshly-baked buns. Like every other villager, Jifae was also stunned to see the pure beauty of Xiuying. Even Youkai was delighted to meet her, and he was even happier that Xiuying and Meili were getting along so well.

"I'm predicting that they will become the next Hua and Lifen." He laughed.

The rest of the family laughed alongside him while Xiuying and Meili danced around the bonfire. And for the first time, Xiuying felt loved, seen, and most importantly, she felt happiness like she had never experienced before. She knew she had found her home and her people. She promised herself that she was going to do everything in her power to help them and protect them, forever and always.

SEVEN

Twelve years had passed since Huizhong left Xiuying at the island, bringing soothing change into her life with the passing of time. She was taller now, had longer hair, and an alluring beauty that drew everyone's attention. However, even her appearance was overshadowed by her irresistible nature and talent. She was known for her forgiving and humble persona, kindness and perfection were her specialty, and her paintings were bought by every household in the village.

Her knowledge had grown with time. She knew everything and had read every book that the village owned, and now with Hua, she, too, advised Jifae with important matters of the village. After all, everyone *did* really believe that she was their lucky charm.

The island was now completely independent. The soil had changed and could now grow all sorts of fruits, vegetables, and wheat. There were grass and trees everywhere, and colorful flowers on every corner of the island. It was safe to say that the island had stopped mourning for the noble warrior and had started to celebrate new life.

Naje was flourishing, but it remained sworn to secrecy. The merchants stopped going on their voyages and started to spend more time maintaining the island itself. It was all working out, socially, economically, and most importantly, environmentally.

And Hua wasn't getting any younger. She was growing weaker with age, but she still had the will to stay active. She and Xiuying bonded over baking her famous cookies, and Xiuying would paint while Hua told her stories about her past.

Lifen passed away peacefully last year, and her death caused Hua great pain. She felt like a part of her soul had been taken away from her. They used to always be inseparable, and now Hua felt like her time to leave was close, too. Hua would often tell Xiuying that after she's gone, everything she had here belonged to Xiuying because her own children never came back to see her.

The thought of losing Hua sank Xiuying's heart. She wasn't ready to deal with yet another loss in her life, and she would always change the topic whenever Hua talked about herself passing onto the next world.

Meili had become a professional writer. She wrote stories for younger children and planned on pursuing a degree in literature in a city an ocean away. Lifen's passing weighed on their family. They missed her, but Youkai's presence made it better. He was now the head of the merchant market, where people traded within the island. Yilin had become a teacher at Meili's old school, and she spent long hours teaching children how to read and write. Meili was still unapologetically cheerful herself, the happy child inside her still alive, but sometimes, the silence inside their home ate Yilin alive. Lifen had taken all the joy with her when she passed.

Xiuying and Meili's friendship had grown stronger as the years went by. They shared secrets, tears, and laughter. They had truly become the next Hua and Lifen, but Xiuying still held secrets of her past that she never shared. She hid them from Meili, just as she hid her magic from the rest of the island. Meili would often ask questions about Xiuying's past, but she never opened up. Instead, she created her own stories and happy versions of her past life, where she talked about Mei as her mother and Huizhong as her father. She would tell Meili stories of how great they were, and the times she'd spent with them.

She was running from her past and using her imagination and dreams as coping mechanisms. She knew that. Her dreams had gotten to the point where they now felt like true memories that she'd experienced, and she would spend hours upon hours imagining how things would have been if they worked out as they did in her stories. Every time her parents crossed her mind, she would trick herself into thinking that they weren't real. But how long could she continue that? The truth would come for her eventually.

Jifae often visited Hua and had gotten closer to Xiuying. He saw her as a younger sister and valued her opinions and advice.

Xiuying made her way quietly down the hall and knocked on Hua's door one day.

"Hua, can we bake some cookies? You have been in bed for the past two days," she said and sat down beside her. "You are the amazing Hua. Even the walls miss the smell of your cookie dough," she said again, quieter this time.

Hua smiled and held Xiuying's hand. "Xiuying, my dear. I wish I could, but I can't," Hua replied in a faint voice. "I'm afraid I'm much too weak."

Xiuying was worried because Hua's health was depleting day after day, and she feared it would bring a loss that she could never move on from.

"Okay, then. Xiuying, the baker, will be taking over today, and I shall bake the most delicious cookies you have ever tasted. It is *my* time to steal the recipe from *you*, the one you stole from your husband!" Xiuying chuckled at herself.

Hua smiled again and pointed toward her books, letting her know where the recipe was kept.

"Alright, then! Time for me to show what I'm capable of. The best baker on this entire island!" Xiuying claimed and marched toward the kitchen.

"Good luck, my dear," Hua whispered behind her, her voice hoarse.

Xiuying gathered all the ingredients and started to experiment. She didn't know what she was doing, but she was going to at least try. She followed the instructions written and mixed all the ingredients with a keen eye on proportions. She was going to give it her best and do every-thing she could to make Hua feel better.

Spilled milk, chocolate, and baking powder were sprin-kled all over the kitchen counter, but the dough had the same smell as Hua's used to have.

"Yes!" Xiuying danced with joy.

The kitchen was in a state of disastrous chaos, but the

cookies came out perfect. She placed the cookie dough in circles on a tray and placed them into the oven for twenty minutes. She had a bit of time on her hands, and instead of cleaning the mess that she had created, she went to check up on Hua.

"Hua!" Xiuying cried in excitement. "You're going to experience the ravishing taste of chocolate chip cookies made by yours truly. This is a once-in-a-lifetime opportunity that you, and only you, will get to enjoy," Xiuying added with a laugh.

Hua drew a light grin onto her face and called Xiuying over to her side. "Xiuying... thank you," she whispered. "You are the best thing that life has ever given me. I will always be filled with gratitude for the amount of love that you have given me, and for the memories that we have created over the years." Hua's voice suddenly broke as she gasped for air. Xiuying stood still, and tears started to slowly stream down her face. But Hua wasn't done. "Always remember that I love you, and I always will, even when I'm not around, o-okay?" Hua stuttered.

"You don't have to say all this, Hua. I know!" Xiuying sobbed, holding onto Hua's hand.

The silence in the room took over, and then suddenly, the oven timer dinged.

"It's time," Hua whispered again, and Xiuying nodded in tears.

She released Hua's hand and left the room to grab her some cookies, only to come back to a lifeless body.

"Hua?" Xiuying whispered. But when no one responded, she dropped the plate and rushed over, placing her ear over Hua's heart and realizing that she had stopped breathing.

"No!" she cried. "Please, Hua, don't leave me," she sobbed.

The world came crashing down onto her shoulders at that moment. It was an unbearable pain that she couldn't handle. Her body shook, and everything around her swirled.

Hua had died, leaving Xiuying all alone in the home that now belonged to her. The other villagers were saddened by the news, and people started to approach the home to offer their condolences. They considered it to be a great loss for all of Naje, the death of someone whom everyone respected. Xiuying had grown quiet, choosing not to communicate or talk about her feelings to anyone.

The funeral took place at the center of town, the place once celebrated with a large feast and party decorations now covered with flowers of every kind. The entire town gathered there, lit candles for Hua, and said their prayers, wishing her luck in the afterlife.

Xiuying stood by Hua's silent, pale, and lifeless body. Hua was dressed in her wedding gown and had yellow flowers surrounding her. *Sweet*, *kind*, and *considerate* all started to chant in Xiuying's mind and repeated themselves in a loop. She couldn't understand the emotions that she was feeling, and she didn't have time to process any of them before she broke down in front of the entire town. She fell onto her knees, and tears started to drip onto the ground. She had forgotten everything just then, especially the fact that she had magic that was channeled by her emotions. The tears touched the crowd, and all the flowers around her started to glow. The glitter dust fell from them and mixed with the air, traveling to where they were needed.

Everyone witnessed what happened, and they were left

in shocked surprise. But in that moment, they understood that it was Xiuying helping their island all along.

The crowd started to whisper, "Is this magic? Did you see that?"

But Jifae interfered. "Alright, everyone! It's time to let Hua go to her resting place."

Xiuying remained frozen on the ground. Meili came to her aid and slowly lifted her up.

"It's time to say your last goodbye," Meili told her, and she looked at Hua one last time.

The villagers buried her in the island's cemetery, and slowly, things returned back to normal, except Xiuying was now seen as a Messiah, a savior. They adored her and worshiped her for her power. But even so, they didn't pester her or ask her to show them more. They knew she was grieving, and they gave her space.

Meili and Jifae took Xiuying home. She sat down in silence and looked around at the mess she had created in the kitchen that morning when she was baking cookies for Hua.

"She didn't even get to taste them," she sniffled.

"Are you okay, Xiuying? We're here for you," Meili said, and Jifae nodded.

Xiuying shook her head but didn't say a word.

The night soon took over, and the clock struck midnight. Jifae left to go home while Meili stayed with Xiuying. She was worried for her friend and didn't want to leave her alone. She joined Xiuying in Hua's room and sat down on the bed with blankets wrapped around them. Meili made a cup of hot cocoa and handed it over to Xiuying. She took it, feeling better than she did before, but was still heartbroken.

"How are you holding up?" Meili asked.

"I don't know," Xiuying replied with a sigh.

"Hey, can I ask you something?" Meili asked, and Xiuying knew what she was going to ask.

"Sure."

"Why didn't you tell me that it was you this whole time? Helping out our island?" Meili paused, took a deep breath, and continued, "That you had a magical power?"

"I never wanted that to define me, and I never wanted you to look at me as a savior or anything." Xiuying started telling her friend how she had gotten her power, and what her life was *really* like before she came to Hua.

"But you left out your whole history. Your family, your rank, your identity—you kept *everything* from me, Xiuying. And here I thought I knew you better than anyone else."

"Not everything. I'm still me. I'm still Xiuying, and I'm still your friend. The only thing that I left out were my... parents."

Meili sighed, defeated. "I can see why you wouldn't want to talk about them. What they did to you was awful and unforgivable."

"Exactly—"

"But," Meili cut her short, "your past is part of who you are today. And after everything we've been through and the life we've made here, you left out that crucial information."

Xiuying's eyes watered. She knew her friend was right, but she couldn't have imagined doing anything different if she had the chance to do it all over. She'd made a fresh, new life with a new family and friends of her own. No matter her parents or her rank, she had been exiled, and her past life ended. She wanted to move forward. But clearly, it had come at a cost.

Meili watched her friend's thoughts race across her expressions. She wanted to be angry, she wanted to stomp her foot and leave, and she wanted time to think this over and ask Xiuying what she was thinking all along. But the tears on her friend's face made her anger melt away. She knew Xiuying hadn't wanted to hurt her. She just wanted a new beginning from her awful past. Meili couldn't forgive her right this second, but she also couldn't stay angry at Xiuying when she had not only lost her past life but had lost Hua, too. She pulled Xiuying into a tight hug and stroked her back.

"It's okay, Xiuying. Thank you for sharing all of this with me," she smiled tightly, whispering into her hair.

Xiuying hesitated at first, but she was quick to hug her friend back. She was thankful beyond belief that Meili had accepted her even after her lies. And even though she knew this wouldn't be the end of this discussion and that this day was going to change everything for her, this hug, this moment with her dearest friend, was enough for now.

BACK AT THE KINGDOM, THINGS HAD TAKEN A TURN. QIANFAN spent the past twelve years pretending to love and protect Xiaofan, all in hopes of bearing a son as his next child. Daiyu was living a blissful life with a perfect daughter and a husband who adored her. She was active in the kingdom, holding galas and listening to the demands and needs of their people. She felt like she was doing it all, being a wonderful mother, a loving wife, and a queen of the people's hearts.

Xiaofan wasn't given the title of a princess, but she was given everything else. She had a room right next to her parents, was treated like royalty, and was sent to the most prestigious school that her parents could find. During her free time as a child, she would spend time with her mother, having tea parties and playing dress-up. She was kind, caring, but a little stubborn, just like her father. Her power was being able to manipulate the wind, for which she was getting trained. She had to learn how to control it and use it in the best way possible.

Even Xiaofan's bond with Qianfan was strong. They played chess together and talked about topics that suited both of their interests. Qianfan hated to admit it, but he also loved his conversations with Xiaofan. Every now and then, he would join Daiyu and Xiaofan's tea parties as well. He was giving his very best. After all, he knew how to put on a show and fool the audience. Only Qiang could decipher his true intentions.

The past twelve years had been torturous for Huizhong and Mei. Huizhong was considered Qianfan's most loyal soldier, but he was caught handing Xiuying's letter over to Mei, and as his punishment, was thrown into prison for life. On the other hand, Mei, too, was sentenced to life, their prison cells facing each other, and every now and then, they would have meaningful conversations over their experiences with Xiuying. They began to grow fond of each other, and that made their solitary life a little easier. They were being punished for caring, and they were paying the consequence together.

If things had been different, they might have gotten married and had a family of their own. Maybe the imaginary life that Xiuying had wasn't quite far from reality. She was obviously oblivious to what had happened to them, and she often wondered why Huizhong never visited her.

Qianfan had found new ways of torturing them, ways he found enjoyable and pleasurable. He'd starve them of any food or water for days on end. He'd leave them in a cold storage room for hours without any warm clothes. He was eager to punish them, torment them for disobeying him. After all, it was his hatred for Xiuying that brought the worst version of him out.

When she could, Mei always prayed for Xiuying. That was what kept her going, the will to pray for the girl she'd loved. Daiyu was expecting her third child after twelve years. It was the last month of her pregnancy, and she was already past her due date. This time, she was confident that whatever gender the child might be, it would be loved and accepted.

"It's a boy!" the nurse shouted after ten hours of intensive labor.

Qianfan took a deep breath and sighed with relief. "It's a boy," he repeated, and then chanted again. "It's a boy! We have been blessed with the prince and future king!"

Everyone around them cheered and congratulated Qianfan. He rushed toward the room and grabbed onto his baby boy, cuddling him in his arms. Daiyu's face lit with bliss. She, like Qianfan, also longed to have a son.

"We shall name him Jinhai," Qianfan stated.

"Jinhai," Daiyu repeated and smiled at the newborn.

This time around, the celebration was completely different from when Xiaofan was born. Celebratory galas were going to be held for an entire week. Each household in the kingdom would be sent a box of sweets, and golden coins and free food were to be distributed amongst the less fortunate. Qianfan looked after the preparation himself. Everything had to be *perfect* because, finally, he was blessed with a son.

Xiaofan, staring at all the commotion from a distance, felt the wind change. Her father suddenly turned his attention from her to her brother, and she couldn't understand why. Daiyu, too, didn't visit Xiaofan for three days after her son was born. She missed them and blamed the birth of her little brother for their lack of attention to her.

The first gala soon began, and piles of presents were brought. Kings and queens from all the other kingdoms came to visit the new prince of Jinu.

"Mother, can I come with you to tonight's gala?" Xiaofan asked.

"Sweetheart, of course you're going to be there, but I will have to stay with your brother. He's going to get marked with the stone today, just like you did," Daiyu answered.

"Were things like this when I was born, Mother?" she asked.

"Of course, how could they not be? You're equally special to us," Daiyu told Xiaofan and hugged her.

The ballroom was decorated with flowers, lit candles, and dark blue silk drapes. There were over a hundred main courses prepared, accompanied by several desserts. Xiaofan wore a light blue gown and was escorted by one of her nannies to the gala.

"It was never like this for your birth, or for your sister's," the nanny whispered.

"My sister?" Xiaofan questioned in shock.

"Yes, your father sent her away many years ago. Her name was Xiuying."

Xiaofan stayed silent, trying to understand the reason behind her father's decision, and she wanted to comprehend his change in behavior toward her.

At the end of the party, Jinhai was marked with the stone. Everyone in the kingdom praised the prince and the future king of Jinu.

Everyone except Xiaofan. Her mind was cluttered with

thoughts. She'd just found out that she has a sister she never knew about. Her parents never mentioned her either, and now she was being neglected for her little brother.

Fuming, she marched up to her parents and asked, "Why didn't you ever tell me that I have a sister?"

"Xiaofan, know your place. And it is not important for you to know," Daiyu replied with such an apathetic tone that Xiaofan was thrown back in shock.

"And why is Jinhai a prince, but I'm not a princess?"

Qianfan walked toward her slowly, his footsteps hitting hard on the floor. "Because he is a boy. He is a boy, and he is superior to you, a girl. There's no such thing as a princess."

Xiaofan stepped back; the rage she saw in her father was different than what she'd been used to.

"Where is Xiuying?" Xiaofan demanded. "I want to meet her."

"She's probably dead by now. I sent her away. Hopefully, for good. She has done *nothing* but destroy our family and hurt your mother," Qianfan answered. "And if you don't agree with the decisions I have made, maybe it is time for you to go, too."

"Sweetheart, just go to your room," Daiyu stepped in. "There's nothing for you to worry about. Don't question your father."

Xiaofan nodded in fear of what her father might do to her and left the room with a broken heart and shattered hope. She was living in a glass castle that was bound to break... by someone she loved.

Two weeks had gone by since Hua passed away, and Xiuying had felt alone ever since. Meili and Jifae would come to visit her every now and then, trying to start up conversations and pretending that things were normal, but they weren't, and Xiuying knew that. The villagers were now treating Xiuying like some sort of miracle maker. They'd greet her and thank her every time she went out, and that aggravated her. Their gestures were sweet, but she didn't think she deserved them.

Meili was trying her best to cheer Xiuying up. She'd bring her food and make her coffee every morning. She was there for Xiuying whenever she needed a shoulder to cry on, and she'd listen to Xiuying tell her stories about Hua, but their relationship began to strain. Xiuying had kept so many secrets from her, and Meili felt like she never really knew who Xiuying was, and she was struggling to understand where she stood in her friend's life.

Jifae, on the other hand, was taking care of all the finances. All of Hua's assets were given to Xiuying—the house, the bakery, and everything Hua had owned. People around the village would randomly drop by with knitted clothes or gifts, anything they could give to help out. Xiuying was grateful, but she felt like the people of the island thought they owed her something, and she didn't know how she could change that.

Hua's death made her relapse, memories of her old life and past trauma returning. With each day passing by, she was losing more and more of herself but still trying to remain strong. She knew Hua would want her to thrive and not remain stuck in her memories. And so, to save herself from self-destruction, she decided to volunteer at the local school... just to come home and fall apart right after. She was starting to feel hopeless, but one day, she heard a tiny whisper.

You can always write to me, even when I'm not there.

The thought of Mei and Huizhong hadn't crossed her mind for quite some time, but she knew what she needed to do. She sat on her bed and took out a quill to write a letter that she might never send.

Dear Mei,

It's weird how time just stops when you get home after a busy day. You tuck yourself into bed to finally rest, but your thoughts won't let you put yourself at ease. The buzz, the commotion, the worries, the chatter, letting all the memories from the past just pour in. The worst part is, you're there all alone with them, unable to escape.

I've recently lost a loved one to this universe, and now I feel like everything I've ever loved has been taken away from me, but maybe that's just life.

The secret that I'd been hiding my entire life is now out, and I'm trapped in a chamber of reflections. Reflections created by the people around me, and I don't know if they represent the real me or who they want me to be, but that's all I see because maybe, it's easier to believe in what others see in you than what you actually are. What do I represent? Abandonment? Betrayal? Unrequited love? Because if I look within, that's all I find, so maybe it's not that bad to see my reflection through someone else's eye.

Sometimes I feel like I am going insane. I dream about people, things, and situations that never happened. In reality, the people I care about don't return the favor, but they still mean something to me. That's something, right?

These dreams keep me going. They keep me happy. They make me look forward to what's ahead in life. I can't experience happiness in reality, but at least, I can imagine it. It's all a lie, I know. My dreams make me feel like the people present in them and their emotions toward me are real, but they're all figments of my imagination. One day, I'll have to accept them for who they are and not the versions I've created in my mind, just not today. For now, this is my coping mechanism, a subtle escape from the harsh realities of life.

It's all a little too much to take in, isn't it? And the worst part is, I can't say any of this out loud. I don't know who to turn to, even though I have some of the most caring people around me. I'm not able to open up to them because I feel like I've betrayed them somehow by hiding the truth.

Pray it gets better from here.

Yours,

Xiuying

Marking her full name brought her some peace. She had felt a lot of emotions at once, but at least now, she had written them down and turned them into words. She felt a sense of ease as she folded the sheet of paper, almost feeling like Mei had heard what she had written. Then she smiled, the yellow flowers on the Tree of Hope glowing and showering dust, bringing her a sense of relief. Xiuying was alone, but Hua was still looking over her shoulder from another life, and Mei was praying for her, wherever she was. And Meili and Jifae were showing up for her nearly every day, cheering her up.

How could things *not* work out in her favor?

EIGHT

Hua always used to say, "Your paintings will help you express more of who you are, and your ideas, values, and morals in a better way. Don't let the artist in you die," and Xiuying remembered.

It had been a month since she stopped painting, and now was the time to get back to it. It was early morning and a rather rainy one. Dark clouds had loomed over Naje, and they were pouring rain nonstop. Meili had come over to Xiuying's place with a thermos of hot cocoa and some freshly-baked bread.

"Hi, Xiuying. How are you? You're in a better mood today," she said with a sigh of relief.

"Yeah, hey, Meili. I do feel better. Much better. How about you?" Xiuying asked and pulled her into a warm hug.

"Just happy to see you happy!" Meili replied with a smile.

They sat around the coffee table and watched the rain pour.

"It's bad, right?" Meili asked.

"What's bad?"

"What else? The weather!" Meili exclaimed.

"Yeah, I guess it *is* pouring pretty hard." Xiuying then paused for a second. "And that reminds me. I have to apologize. I'm sorry I hid my secret from you. I know you're hurt. You don't have to hide it from me anymore, and I truly regret not telling you sooner. I feel guilty for hurting my best friend. You've always been there for me, regardless of the situation."

Meili was quiet before she cleared her throat. "Thank you, Xiuying. I was disheartened, but our friendship can overcome any obstacle. Besides, you had a valid reason for it. I can't blame you," Meili replied as she looked at her friend with a grin.

"Well, that's settled then," Xiuying agreed and offered Meili some cookies that she had just baked.

"I got accepted into the university I applied for, by the way—the literature program!" Meili suddenly spat out.

"That's so great. Congratulations!" Xiuying screamed with excitement and pulled her friend in for another hug. "You're finally getting what you have always dreamt of. I'm so proud of you. Your grandmother would've been proud, too. So, what's next?"

"I don't know yet, but I start in a month," Meili said hesitantly.

"You're leaving? Already?"

"Only for a short while! And I'll keep visiting, Xiuying. Naje is my home and always will be."

"Well, then, I guess the question now is, what shall we do until it's time for you to go?" Xiuying asked with a grin.

"Literally everything we can possibly think of. I *can't wait* to start creating memories!" Meili laughed.

"I like the sound of that," Xiuying replied and shoved a warm cookie into her mouth. "I love this, too," she mumbled and held the cookie up.

Their conversation was soon interrupted by cries of help coming from outside, and they rushed out the door. The villagers were bringing in injured people, who were all dressed in military uniform and bleeding.

"What happened? Who are these people?" Meili stammered.

"A ship of a royal kingdom has crashed onto our island. The ship has been badly damaged, the waves are wild out there, several people are injured, and they need our help. We can't leave them out there to die!" one of the villagers answered and rushed back out to grab more.

The rain stopped, and Xiuying and Meili were standing together beside the Tree of Hope, watching the disaster unfold.

Hours later, the storm passed, but the aftermath brought a worrisome weather over the villagers. The entire village had come together to aid the injured. Medications and homemade remedies were being collected, the local doctor was working tirelessly, and warm meals were being prepped by several households. There were fifteen soldiers and three maids total, all injured, most with bloody wounds that needed to be stitched up. The incident had warped the village into chaos. All the villagers were in great distress, like their own had gotten hurt. They began praying, concerned, and did everything possible to bring comfort to the ones affected. Jifae had ordered each household to take in one injured person and be responsible for providing them with everything they needed, nurturing them until they got better.

"Is there anything I can do?" Xiuying went up to Jifae.

"No, Xiuying. You just take care of yourself."

"Are you sure?" she asked again, and before he could reply, their conversation was interrupted by a young man.

"Are you Jifae?" the man asked, his voice heavy yet collected.

Xiuying turned around and saw a tall man with broad shoulders standing behind them. He had dark eyes, long black hair, defined cheekbones, and a sharp jawline. He was wearing a white robe with a golden dragon embroidered on it. As soon as Xiuying saw the dragon on his robe, she realized that he was royalty. Dragon embroidery and dragon-related patterns were *exclusive* to the emperor and the royal families of China.

"Xiuying, meet Prince Zhang Wei from the Baoshu Kingdom. His ship crashed onto our island as he was headed home from a voyage," Jifae introduced.

"Nice to meet you," Xiuying murmured in the lowest tone possible, and then started to walk toward her home without waiting for a reply.

Zhang noticed the woman walking away in distress, like something was clearly bothering her, but he chose to ignore it and continued his conversation with Jifae.

"My kingdom will forever be in your debt. You have

helped us during a time when we had lost our hopes of survival. Thank you," Zhang thanked the head of Naje.

"It was our pleasure, Prince Zhang. Our village is all about helping one another. We would have done the same for anyone." Jifae smiled as they walked through the streets of the village, taking it upon himself to show the prince around.

Zhang was among those with only a minor injury. He was amazed by the wholesome ambiance the village had and their will to help. He also noticed how green the village was, with colorful flowers surrounding the small cottages.

"So serene," he whispered. "I wasn't aware that this village existed on the island. We thought it was deserted. To see so much greenery behind the mountains..." Zhang drew out with his hands behind his back.

"It is a miracle. We have kept our island a secret for as long as our history goes back. It saves us from all the politics and power plays, and keeps our community together, strong, and most importantly, happy," Jifae replied.

"The greenery around here is beyond anything I have ever seen. It truly feels like a miracle on a rocky island," Zhang commented.

"Oh, this is all because of Xiuying and her power. She can control nature, and I'm not sure how or why, but she helped our island flourish," Jifae replied.

As soon as Zhang heard about the power, he knew that Xiuying belonged to royalty but was hiding it. He knew that there was only one kingdom in all of China that had control over the four elements, but he chose to keep the information to himself. He was now more intrigued than ever to know about the beautiful woman he had seen earlier and why she had walked away.

Xiuying, on the other hand, felt anxious. The way she

felt when she was around the prince, the way she looked at him, as if time had suddenly stopped. She was back at home, but she couldn't stop thinking about him.

"He is royalty, Xiuying," she told herself as she slammed the door to her room shut, and that thought reminded her of how royalty had treated her in the past.

She leaned against the wall and looked across to the window. The yellow tree was shining bright, the brightest she had ever seen. What was she feeling? Was it anger? Confusion? Or something else? She didn't know what it was, but one thing she knew for sure, was that she felt something toward the prince.

Before long, the moon replaced the sun, and it became dark outside when she heard a knock on her door.

"Who is it?" she asked.

"Your favorite person!" Meili sang and entered. "Do you always keep this unlocked?" She plopped herself down onto Xiuying's bed with two cups of hot chamomile tea.

"Only sometimes." Xiuying smirked and grabbed her cup.

"Thankfully, everything went well. All the injured soldiers and maids are treated and resting. And no one is in critical condition." She then hopped up and started pacing back and forth in Xiuying's room.

"That's good, right?" Xiuying asked, but Meili was silent in her pacing. "Um, is everything okay, Meili?"

Meili sighed with a frown. "No," she finally said. "Jifae asked for my hand in marriage."

"That's great!" Xiuying laughed. "Jifae is a wonderful person, and I'm sure he'll treat you right."

Then suddenly, that frown slowly turned into a smile. "I know... because I already said yes!" Meili screamed.

"You tease!" Xiuying threw a pillow over at her, but

then hopped up to give her a long hug. "I'm so happy for you. You two are going to be great together!" She looked over at her friend, who was now deep in thought. "What's wrong? Aren't you excited?"

"I am, I am." Meili shook her head. "But we were just children not that long ago. And now I'm getting married? How did life fly by so fast?"

Xiuying shrugged. "I don't know. Sometimes I wonder that myself."

"Hey, Xiuying, did you hear about the prince?" Meili asked. "I met him today, really don't know what to make of him."

Xiuying replied, "Seems like all the women in town are gushing over him."

"I hear he's single, and he's looking for someone to sit beside him when he replaces his father as king." Meili looked at Xiuying, batting her eyes.

"Why are you looking at me?"

"Because! You're both royalty!"

"Not anymore. I left that all behind, and I intend to keep it that way." Xiuying paused and started to light some candles. "And besides, I'm sure he isn't interested in me or our little town. He's privileged, and I know privileged people. They don't care about people like us."

"Well, just think about it. I think you two will make a cute couple!"

"Yeah, yeah, sure." Xiuying followed Meili to the front door as Meili got ready to leave.

"And remember to lock your door! You don't want anyone sneaking in here in the middle of the night!" Meili yelled behind her.

THE NEXT MORNING, XIUYING WAS PROVEN WRONG. ZHANG HAD requested to meet with all the villagers and was interested in getting to know more about their lives. He toured the village alongside Jifae and met with the villagers who were hosting his soldiers.

Within a few hours, the entire village was singing songs of praise. Everywhere Xiuying went—the bakery, the school, and even Meili's home—all she'd hear were compliments to Zhang, how intelligent he was, how charming he was, and how they all wanted to marry him. So much so that she started to grow frustrated and annoyed with the prince, locking herself in her home until they all left. For good.

As Zhang toured the village, all he could think about was getting a chance to see Xiuying again, *the lucky charm* as people called her. His eyes looked around for her, for the beautiful girl he'd met on that very first day, but he couldn't find her. Everyone around him was handing him bouquets of flowers, large and small, to welcome him to Naje, but those flowers only made him think of Xiuying even more.

"I see why you kept this place a secret," Zhang said to Jifae. "It needs to be preserved. The people here and the love they have for each other are rare, and trust me, I've been to many, many places."

Jifae beamed. "Thank you for your kind words and for understanding why things are kept the way they are."

"I assume we have met with everyone on the island?" Zhang questioned in hopes that Jifae would mention Xiuying.

"Yes, I believe you have," Jifae replied, and Zhang's tiny hope began to fade.

"Oh! I almost forgot! You are invited to dinner over at Meili's place tonight. She will soon be my wife, and we would love to have you over, as our gesture of courtesy."

"Of course, Jifae. I would love to attend," Zhang replied.

Zhang and Jifae grew closer and closer with each conversation, almost like they were becoming close friends. He was staying with Jifae for a couple days, and they were beginning to find that they had a lot in common.

On the other side of town, Meili came rushing into Xiuying's home.

"Quick! I need Hua's fruit cake tonight!" she shouted as she slammed the door like she always did, and she took a deep breath before speaking again. "Can you help me make one? Please?!"

Meili continued to plead, getting down on her knees and whispering "say yes" over and over.

Xiuying crossed her arms and stood in front of her friend.

"What's the occasion?" she asked, raising a brow in skepticism.

"Oh, nothing much. Jifae and I invited Prince Zhang over for dinner tonight, to welcome him to our village."

"I hope you know I'm not going," Xiuying stubbornly said.

"Not even for me?" Meili asked. "Not even for your best friend who is leaving in a month?"

"I don't know..."

"Come on! You said we'd make new memories! And this is a new memory!"

Xiuying rolled her eyes and hesitantly agreed, "Fine, but the emotional blackmailing stops here."

"Your wish is my command! See you at eight!" Meili cheered and walked back out the door.

Xiuying groaned as she closed the door behind her, locking it. Even when she tried her best to avoid the prince, it seemed like something was trying to pull them together. The universe, maybe? She thought to herself and scoffed before turning on the oven.

A few hours later, the cake was ready and packaged neatly, her home filled with the delicious aroma that reminded her of Hua.

"What am I going to wear?" she asked herself and walked toward her room. "What do you even wear when you meet a prince?" Her eyes looked around her closet of dresses, rejecting one after another.

She emptied her closet and finally found something that Hua had made for her. It was a long pink robe with ribbons on the sleeves and tiny embroidered white flowers.

"Perfect!" she heard herself say, stopping herself when she realized that she was indeed trying to impress the prince.

She was already drawn to him, whether she liked it or not.

It was nearing eight when she got ready to leave. She slipped on a pair of glass-like heels that Hua had gotten for her from another island when she went traveling, and she undid her hair, letting the long strands flow down her back. She then walked over to her mirror and applied a bit of color onto her lips, and she topped it off by placing a small pink flower in her hair.

"It's not for him; it's for me," she repeated several times and tried to make herself believe in her own words.

The clock soon struck eight, and it was time to leave. She picked up the cake and started to walk toward Meili's house. It was dark now, and the lanterns were lit. The breeze felt chilly, and for the first time in forever, she felt like herself. She felt happy, and deep down, she was eager to meet Prince Zhang.

Xiuying knocked on the door, and when it opened, Meili was standing there, a smile glossed over her face.

"You came!" Meili announced and gave her a kiss on both cheeks.

Xiuying stepped inside and saw everyone seated around the wooden dining table. Meili's home looked unrecognizable. There was a huge vase with flowers and slender candles on beautiful stands that looked like shining stars.

"My dear, you look ravishing!" Yilin greeted as soon as she saw Xiuying.

"Thank you, so do you," Xiuying replied with a smile.

Her eyes moved across the room, and she saw Zhang staring at her. She quickly looked away, but Zhang continued staring. He *couldn't* look away. He almost felt like he never wanted to take his eyes off of her. She looked so beautiful, the vision of perfection. And he suddenly felt speechless.

The feast was soon served. Two roast chickens, pork belly, Yilin's delicious ginseng soup, and the fruit cake that Xiuying had made, served alongside tea and wine.

"Everything looks so good. Thank you for inviting me," Xiuying said as she took a seat at the table... right in front of Zhang.

"Yes, I agree. Meili, you are an amazing host, I must say. You went beyond my expectations," Zhang chimed in.

"Oh, it's nothing. We love a good dinner with our friends," Meili replied and told everyone to start digging in.

Xiuying didn't say a single word during the entire dinner, focusing on her plate and nodding with a smile every now and then. She could sense Zhang staring at her, and she didn't want to say or do anything that she'd regret.

"Who's ready for cake?" Meili sang as she walked out of the kitchen with a knife. "Xiuying is the *best* baker in this town. Chef's kiss!"

When she served Zhang his piece, he took a large bite and grinned. "This is delicious! I could eat this every day for the rest of my life." He'd hoped that Xiuying would respond to him, but all she did was give him a soft smile. "I'd love to know the recipe and make this myself," he then added.

That did it.

"You bake?" she asked.

"Of course, I do. In fact," he leaned in closer, "I bet I can outbake you any day."

"I'd love to see that," she jabbed at him.

Then he leaned back and chuckled. "Alright, you got me. I don't know the first thing about baking or cooking."

"I figured."

"So, why'd you run away the other day? When we first met?" he asked, taking another bite.

Xiuying shrugged. "I didn't. I just had things to do." She blushed, hoping he wouldn't catch her bluff.

"What a shame. I was going to introduce myself, get to know you a bit."

"Xiuying paints, you know? She's really good," Meili interrupted before turning back to Jifae.

"Really?" Zhang's eyes settled on her again, soft and dancing with his gentle smile. "Well, I'd love to see some of them one day."

"Maybe. Listen, I should really get going. It's getting late, and I have to walk home alone."

"How about I walk with you? It's not safe for a young

woman to walk around alone at night," Zhang offered and started to stand up.

And just in time for Meili to step in again. "That's a wonderful idea! You can keep Xiuying safe, Zhang. Let me pack you two some leftovers to take with you."

Xiuying gave Meili a death stare, to which Meili smiled and winked. As much as she tried to stay away from the prince, Meili seemed to be conspiring to bring them together, like some sort of fantasy. And Zhang *definitely* seemed excited, unable to stand still beside her while saying his goodbyes to the rest of the group.

After Xiuying said her own goodbyes, Zhang escorted her out the door. The sky looked like it had stardust sprinkled in it. The moon was in full bloom, casting their shadows on the ground where they walked. The air was chilly but filled with the scent of cherry blossoms.

The silence between them broke when Zhang asked, "So, why did you *really* run away when we first met?"

Xiuying took a deep breath and replied, "I don't get along with royalty. The first time I met you, I assumed you were just like all the others—privileged and self-centered."

"And now? Do you still think that?"

"No, you're actually quite the opposite." Xiuying shook her head.

"Whew! That's a relief. It means you won't run away the next time I see you, right?" he asked.

"*If* you see me," she corrected him.

"Oh, I'm sure I will. If not, I can *always* find a way." He chuckled.

"Don't you have to go back to your kingdom?" Xiuying asked.

"I do, but I think I'd like to stay here for a few more days, cherish the beauty of this little island a bit more."

When they reached Xiuying's cottage, his fingers briefly touched hers. "You have a beautiful home, just like yourself."

Her cheeks turned a rosy pink. "Thank you, Zhang Wei." She opened her front door and let herself inside. "And thanks for walking me home."

"I'll see you around, Xiuying." He waved as she closed the door behind her.

THE SUN ROSE OVER THE HORIZON, AND SO DID XIUYING. IT WAS the next morning, and today was her first day teaching at the local school. She looked forward to meeting all the children. She adored children, and she absolutely *loved* teaching. Meili offered to join her. She'd sit in the back of the class, writing her stories, while giving Xiuying emotional support.

Xiuying quickly scarfed down her breakfast of congee with fish and got dressed, putting in extra effort on her appearance. She wore a simple dress with ruffled sleeves and a high neckline, then she tied her hair into a ponytail with a pink floral scarf. Almost everything she had in her wardrobe was related to flowers. Hua loved the fact that Xiuying could control nature, and she always wanted that to be a part of Xiuying's appearance, so Hua made all her clothes with embroidered floral patterns.

Last night's walk hadn't left Xiuying's mind even as she scurried around her house. She had a grin on her face, and it wasn't going away. It was like she had met two completely different people. The Zhang she met on the first day was a prince, someone she hadn't gotten a chance to know, and the Zhang she met last night was charming and friendly, and deeply cared about her village.

There was something different about him. He was royalty and came from a background of privilege, but he seemed so humble, someone who enjoyed going on long walks, someone who liked eating with commoners on simple floor mats, someone who adored the colors of the sky and flowers, someone who appreciated all the little things that people did for him. He thought about others before himself, he was a leader, and he *acted* like one. He was empathetic, his care for his own people not a fabrication, something that was rare for royalty. His aura radiated pure light, and Xiuying knew that she liked him.

She was being drowned by her own thoughts as she started to walk toward Meili's place so they could walk to the school together. She reached out and knocked. Yilin opened the door and welcomed Xiuying with open arms.

"Good morning!" Xiuying cheered.

"Good morning to you, too," Yilin replied as Meili came running out of her room.

"Do you ever walk like a normal person?" Xiuying asked.

"Sometimes, maybe," Meili huffed out of breath. Xiuying chuckled.

As they walked down the streets of the village, Meili spoke up, "You seem happy today."

"Why do you say that like it's a bad thing?" Xiuying asked.

"It's not, but I haven't seen you like this ever since, you know, Hua died."

"I guess I finally feel like myself again. I still miss Hua, but I'm sure she wouldn't want me to be sad all the time."

Meili stopped walking. "Something tells me this is

about more than just Hua." She caught a glimpse of Xiuying's blush. "Is it Zhang? Are you falling for him?!"

Xiuying shrugged. "I don't know. Maybe."

They arrived at the school, and the wooden door creaked open. At first glance, she saw Zhang sitting at one of the desks alongside her students.

"Zhang! What are you doing here?" Xiuying gasped.

He stood up and smiled at her, his pearly whites twinkling under the fluorescent lights. "Just volunteering. Getting to know the children of the village."

"Aren't you just a saint?" Meili laughed.

"Some might say that," Zhang replied, followed by a chuckle.

Xiuying began her lesson on gratitude and hope while everyone listened keenly as she spoke about the importance of showing gratitude toward even the smallest thing. She even told the children about the wonders of Hua and the Tree of Hope.

"It was hope that brought greenery to the island," she said and concluded her lecture.

Following her lesson, she asked the children to write about all the people and things that they were grateful for. And when the children handed in their assignments, so did Zhang. Xiuying looked down at his paper, and he'd written, *I'm grateful for the village's lucky charm.* Xiuying giggled and looked up to see Zhang standing in front of her.

"Care to join me for a walk?"

Xiuying agreed, and then turned toward Meili, who had her head buried in a pile of books, her hands covered in ink.

"Meili, care to come along?" Xiuying asked.

"Nah, I'm sure you don't want me to." Meili laughed, and then added, "Besides, I have a lot of writing to do. You two have fun! Why don't you show Zhang our spot?" Meili suggested before lowering her head back down.

Zhang and Xiuying quietly walked toward the opposite direction of the village, to the forest that led up a mountain.

"What exactly is *the spot*?" Zhang curiously asked.

"It's just a place a few miles up. You can see the entire village from up there, plus the sunset and the ocean. Meili and I always go there to take a break from the realities of life. She calls it *our spot* because no one else knows about it," Xiuying explained.

"Well, I'm honored that you're taking me there."

They walked through the forest and followed a rocky path to reach the spot. The sun was setting, and the sky was changing colors. It had turned into shades of orange and pink, with a little blue. The ocean was mirroring the sunset, and lanterns were being lit up in the village one by one. The tiny lights were appearing slowly, and the village was covered with flowers from one end to the other.

"This is beautiful, Xiuying," Zhang whispered as they sat on the edge of the cliff, taking in the fading sunset and the twinkle of the village.

"It really is." Xiuying looked at him, admiring the view in front of her eyes.

"This is all because of you. Jifae told me about your magic."

Xiuying stayed quiet when he said that. She didn't know how to respond to something like that.

Zhang continued, "He also mentioned how you helped the village without even letting anyone know about your power. A lot of people wouldn't have remained so silent. You're humble. I like that." Then he turned to her. "So, what's your story? How did someone born into royalty end up on a small island like this?"

"How did you know?" she asked and turned to face him, staring into his eyes.

"Your power. It's pretty obvious that you're from Jinu, the only magical kingdom in all of China."

Xiuying breathed. "I *am* from royalty. My father, Qian-fan, sent me away because I wasn't born a boy. He never accepted me, nor did my mother. And according to him, I'm already dead."

"Gosh, I'm so sorry. If I'd known, I wouldn't have pried. Forgive me."

"It's okay. I do feel a little better getting this off my chest. I've been keeping this to myself for years, and it's been such a burden."

"Why don't you just tell everyone the truth so you have someone to talk to?" Zhang asked.

"There are a lot of layers to the truth. The people here love me for who I am, and I don't want them to see me as a walking tragedy. The horrors I'd faced in my past were unlike anything else, and I want to forget about all that, move on." She took a deep breath. "Besides, it doesn't matter if I'm a royal or not. I was abandoned by my family, *forgotten*."

"But that doesn't mean you should just forget about your past. You deserve better than to be treated like a nobody." He leaned over and kissed her on the cheek.

Her heart sank. She felt a tingling feeling inside of her that she didn't know how to explain. Was this love?

The walk back to the village was silent, but Zhang held on tightly to her hand. When they reached her cottage, Zhang told her, "I won't ever let go if you allow me to stand by your side."

Xiuying nodded, and he smiled, giving her another kiss on the cheek before leaving for his own cottage. She opened the door to her home and found Meili sitting in the living room, munching on some leftover cake and sipping a cup of tea that she had just made.

"About time! I've been waiting for you for hours!" she yelled, and then jumped up in excitement.

Xiuying closed the door behind her and walked over to join her friend.

"Have some tea, and then *spill* the tea." Meili laughed and leaned over to hand her a cup. "Come on, say something! What happened with Zhang?"

"We just talked." Xiuying placed her cup of tea on the wooden table in front of her. She wanted to keep all her feelings hidden deep within herself, just as she had with her past all this time. But Meili looked at her with love and hope, and after everything, Xiuying *had* to tell her the truth. "He's so perfect in every way, and I don't know if I deserve to be in his life. Everyone I love seems to always leave me. All I've ever known was unrequited love."

Meili set down her own cup and scooted closer, her voice lowering to a reassuring drawl. "Xiuying, you're over-thinking this. He likes you, and it's on *him* if he wants you in his life or not; that's not for you to decide. The only decision that *you* have to make is whether you like *him* or not, whether you want *him* in your life or not. And don't you *dare* say that the only love you have known is unrequited. *I'm* here for you; the *whole town* is here for you. Hua gave you everything, Xiuying." Meili reached out and hugged her. "Let him in your life. I promise you won't regret it."

"You're right; it's time I give myself a chance at love."

CHAPTER

NINE

A WEEK HAD GONE BY, AND XIUYING FOUND HERSELF HANGING OUT with Zhang almost every day, teaching together, baking together. He even kept her company and entertained while she painted. Even the other villagers were growing fond of seeing the two of them together, seeing them as the perfect couple.

And the more time Xiuying spent with Zhang, the more she realized that she was sharing things with him she had never said out loud. In just a few days, he had become someone she could rely on. She told him all about the struggles she'd dealt with as a child, how her parents hated her, how Hua took her in before she died. She even mentioned Mei, Huizhong, her dreams, and the letters.

He knew it all, and most importantly, he understood her. He believed her troubles were all justified, and that she needed to heal, recover from her past trauma. And he promised that he'd help her, bring comfort to her life, and ease her raging thoughts whenever they crept up. The more time she spent with him, the more she found herself letting go of the past.

But the soldiers and maids had now recovered from their injuries, and they were preparing to leave the village soon. After all, Zhang had a life outside of Naje that was unbeknownst to Xiuying.

Jifae and Meili were getting married in just a few short days, the festivities already beginning. And Xiuying wanted to be there for Meili as she picked out her dress, flower bouquets, and wedding cake, but she couldn't stop thinking about Zhang. How he was due to leave the island right after the wedding. She'd gotten so close to him over the past few days, and she didn't want to watch him leave. She couldn't deal with the pain of watching yet another person she loved leave her, abandon her. And even though he was still here with her now, she felt as if her world was already falling apart. What would become of her and Zhang? Did they even have a chance at a future together?

Red roses were scattered everywhere on the day of the wedding. The ceremony was going to take place at the center of town at sunset. Meili was wearing the traditional Chinese wedding dress, a red one, and her face was covered with a matching veil. She looked ravishing, the happiest that Xiuying had ever seen her, and it was showing on her face. Jifae wore a traditional outfit in the same color.

Xiuying wore a magenta silk robe with her hair tied up in a bun, flowers from the golden tree around it. She reached the venue and was left in awe. The entire town had gathered together, holding gifts and presents for the soon-to-be newlywed couple, and Jifae was waiting at the altar. There were numerous lanterns lit, and the walkway down the aisle was covered with red petals, the air fresh and fragrant. The place looked magnificent! And while she was admiring the decorations and ambiance, she felt a tap on her shoulder. She turned around and saw Zhang standing behind her, wearing a white robe with tiny dragon patterns on the sleeves.

"You look beautiful, as always," Zhang whispered, pecking her on the cheek before grabbing her hand and walking with her to their assigned seats.

"You don't look so bad yourself."

Zhang laughed. "I tried my best."

They sat beside each other and waited for Meili to walk down the aisle with her parents.

"Weddings are the best, aren't they? They remind me of how strong love can be, and how important it is," Zhang said, to which Xiuying nodded in agreement. "I've also been thinking about us. I have to leave tomorrow, but I don't want to leave you," Zhang added, looking down at his foot, which was tapping against the ground. "Xiuying, I want you to come with me. There's so much more beyond this place, and I want to live my life with you." He was now looking at Xiuying, hoping for a reply that would make his day. "And I know you have your life here. You're here for a reason, and you've helped this island so much. But think of how many more you can help *outside* of this island. Our kingdom would be honored to have your presence." He paused and held Xiuying's hand. "And I'm not just saying this because I've fallen in love with you. I'm saying this because the talents you have are unbelievable, and you owe it to yourself to share it with the world."

Their conversation was interrupted by Meili's entry, and everyone stood up for her. She walked down the aisle toward Jifae, Youkai holding onto her arm, and Jifae drew tears of happiness while watching his future wife approach him. They stood in front of each other, holding hands and looking into each other's eyes to say their vows.

"I promise to keep you happy in times of sickness and health. I promise to wipe your tears away every time they meet your eyes. I promise to protect you from every problem that life throws our way. I promise to give all of me to you from this day on. I trust you and appreciate you. I love you, Meili. I always have, and I always will," Jifae concluded as he sniffed and wiped his tears.

Meili looked at him with a sparkle in her eyes and said her part next. "You have helped me understand love in a way that I never understood. You have proven to be by my side always and have helped me shape myself into a version that I can be proud of. When we first met, I never imagined that this day would come, but little did I know, I had fallen for you. You have always looked after this town and its people, but I promise to look after you. I love you, too. I always have, and I always will."

The audience was left in tears, moved by the speeches. It felt like everyone could experience them, understand them. The couple was pronounced husband and wife, and after that, the festivities began. The music played, and traditional Chinese cuisine was offered.

But Zhang was worried that he had said too much to Xiuying earlier, that he might've scared her away by coming on too strong. He feared that she'd turn him away and not want to be with him anymore.

When the night fell, and the party ended, everyone retreated back inside their homes, leaving Zhang and

Xiuying all alone. They finally had a chance to talk after hours upon hours of chaos and celebrations. They sat around the bonfire that was still lit in the center of town, and Xiuying snuggled close to him, intertwining her fingers between his. Zhang stayed silent, but he held onto her hand. He hadn't stopped ever since he told her he wouldn't let her go.

"I've fallen in love with you, too," Xiuying whispered quietly. "But this is my home, and I'm not sure if I can leave it."

"I promise you that we'll come back here anytime you want, Xiuying," Zhang assured her. "I want to build a life with you... in my kingdom. We can even open up a gallery to showcase all your paintings, build our legacy. Together."

"I'll sleep on it. Let's talk tomorrow." Then she stood up. "I have to go."

But before she could walk away, she felt a tug on her arm. She turned around and felt Zhang's lips press against hers, sending a shiver of warmth up and down her spine. She didn't know what she was feeling, but she also didn't want it to stop. And Xiuying returned the kiss, allowing Zhang to pull her in even closer.

"I love you, Xiuying. And when I say that, I mean it," he said, pulling slightly away.

"I know, Zhang. I know."

BACK HOME LATER THAT NIGHT, XIUYING THOUGHT ABOUT THE KISS as she tossed and turned, trying to make herself fall asleep. She was torn between her love for Zhang and her love for Naje.

"How can I leave the home that Hua left me? Raised me

in?" she asked herself. "Naje has given me so much. Hua is here, and everything that connects me to her is right here. I can't do it!"

She threw the sheets off herself and got out of bed. She stood by the door to Hua's room, her things still preserved and organized. Her eyes moved across the room.

"What if I'm not welcomed at Baoshu? Zhang is different, for sure, but there's no guarantee that his family will welcome me. They are royalty, after all."

She stepped inside the room and stood in front of the painted portrait that she had made of Hua. Hua looked so happy, her eyes sparkling like they always did, her smile brighter than the glow of a full moon; the painting felt alive. Xiuying then noticed a little note, written on the right corner of the painting.

Home is where your heart is.

Tears began to roll down her cheeks as she read the sentence that Hua had clearly written. Ever since Hua passed, this place felt a little less like home. Everything that Xiuying had associated with *home* was now gone, only fragments of memories left over. The stakes of leaving this place and starting somewhere new were too high for Xiuying. The thought of not feeling welcomed or accepted made her make a decision that she knew she was going to regret later on. But nonetheless, she was bound to it by fear.

"Zhang has to go without me," she said, looking at Hua's painting, and after a few minutes, she tucked herself into Hua's bed and fell asleep.

Hours later, her sleep was interrupted by loud bangs on the front door. Xiuying's heart started to pound. *I can never catch a break*, she thought to herself as she hurried to open the door.

"Guess what?" Meili bolted in with clouds of exhilaration surrounding her, always interrupting at all the wrong times.

Xiuying felt like her head was throbbing with pain from the lack of sleep, and from the fact that she was debating on walking away from something that felt like a fantasy.

"What?" Xiuying asked, showing no interest whatsoever.

"I'm staying!" Meili yelled.

"Staying? In Naje?"

"Yes! I've decided not to go to university!" Meili announced, leaving Xiuying stunned.

"But you've wanted that for so long. Why are you backing out? Did Jifae tell you not to go?"

"No, no, no," Meili repeated. "He has nothing to do with this. This is *my* decision. My wedding yesterday made me realize that I belong here, that my heart belongs here. Even if I leave, my soul will stay. So, what's the point? I love Jifae and my parents. I can't imagine leaving them." Meili grinned. "This is my *home*, Xiuying. I *have* to stay."

"Are you happy?" Xiuying asked.

"The happiest I've ever been," Meili replied.

A sense of realization suddenly struck Xiuying. Meili was taking a leap of faith and trusting the ones she loved. That's what she needed to do, too.

"I love him," Xiuying whispered. "Zhang. He wants me to go with him," Xiuying continued, looking at Meili for a sign.

Meili turned red with excitement for her friend. "Well, what are you waiting for? Do it! Go with him! You two belong together. And when you love someone, you don't stay an entire ocean away from them."

Maybe Meili was right. Maybe the right decision *was* to leave with Zhang. All Hua ever wanted was for her to live her life to the fullest, to chase after what she loved. And who she loved was *Zhang*.

"So, are you going?" Meili asked.

Xiuying took a steadying breath. "I am."

THE MOMENT ZHANG LEFT XIUYING'S COTTAGE, THE POSSIBILITY of losing her kept him awake all night. All he could think about was Xiuying's answer and the possibility of her rejecting him.

The next morning after breakfast, he went to go see her, eager for an answer. He knocked on the door, only to find Meili inside.

"Where is Xiuying?" he asked, and Meili pointed him in the direction of Hua's room. "In there," Meili calmly said and left to go home, just in time for her first ever breakfast with Jifae as his wife.

Zhang walked across the living room and knocked on the door.

"Who is it?" He heard on the other side.

"It's me, Xiuying." There was shuffling in the room before the door opened. Xiuying looked up at him with damp eyes. She started to speak, but he shushed her.

"I just want to say something before you make your decision," he said, moving closer to her. "I know this decision is hard for you, to leave your home behind and all the memories that you've made. I know you're afraid because of what you've been through before, but I promise you, my love, that I will *never* let your past repeat itself. I'll protect you, from anything. Always." He paused with a lowered gaze, and held her hands. "We're all searching for someone who grounds us, someone who sees us, someone who is always by our side at the end of the day. *You* are that someone to me, Xiuying, and I don't want to lose you."

Xiuying blushed. Seeing her smile made Zhang feel a little spark of hope.

She finally whispered, "Hua once told me that home is where your heart is, and my heart is with you, Zhang."

"That means you'll come?" Zhang asked as he leaned in to give Xiuying a kiss.

"Yes," she whispered, and just as she did, the flower mural painted on the walls of Hua's room started to glow and shower pink dust that sprinkled over them.

"Wow, that's incredible," Zhang whispered, seeing Xiuying's power for the very first time.

"You better get used to this." And they both started laughing.

Later that night, everyone whom Xiuying loved came over to her home for her farewell dinner. Zhang, Meili, Yilin, Youkai, and Jifae were all gathered in the kitchen.

"I can't believe this is it. Your last night here," Meili lamented.

"I know," Xiuying replied. "It feels unreal. After living in Naje for so long."

Xiuying had prepared a hefty serving of rice, served with chicken and chestnuts. And for dessert, she made her famous fruit cake. The dinner went by with everyone reminiscing and in tears, sharing memories from when Xiuying first arrived on the island. Yilin and Youkai left after dinner and hugged Xiuying goodbye, promising to see her again in the morning before she left.

Jifae and Zhang also left to go home, leaving Meili and Xiuying alone. Saying goodbye to a best friend wasn't going to be easy for either of them. The house was quiet now, the laughter in the air turned into silence. Meili was throwing sheets onto the furniture to preserve them from dust after Xiuying was long gone, and for once, was—quiet. Xiuying walked over to her, and they sat in front of the fireplace.

"This feels so weird," Meili mumbled. "Just last week, *I* was the one leaving. And now it's you. The universe can be very indecisive sometimes." She scooted over to her friend and squeezed her tight into a hug. "I'll miss you, Xiuying. It feels like I'm losing a sister."

Xiuying took a deep breath, trying to take it all in. "You're not losing me, Meili. I promise I'll come back and visit. You know, I used to think that friendship was all about playdates and sharing secrets, but that changed when I met you. It's as if you are the missing piece of my heart, Meili, like we fit perfectly together. You've always been there for me, even during times of despair, and for that, I'll always remember you. Thank you for always being there for me. And because of that, this has been one of the hardest decisions I've ever had to make." Xiuying cried as she curled up her toes in front of the fireplace.

"Oh, look at you getting all sentimental," Meili remarked as she wiped her own tears away. "I don't think I'll ever find anyone else who can tolerate my constant outbursts." She laughed, and Xiuying joined in.

Silence soon took over again, and the two of them stayed quiet, observing the flames of the burning fire that left a trail of burnt ash behind. The bond they both shared was rare. They were inseparable ever since they were just children, and now they were parting ways as adults.

"I guess it's time for me to go now. Jifae's probably all worried, still waiting up for me." Meili tried to put a smile on her face as she stood up. "See you tomorrow?"

"See you tomorrow," Xiuying answered with her own wobbly smile.

Xiuying looked around the place that she'd called home for the past twelve years after she closed the door behind Meili. It felt so empty, so different. The house didn't even seem alive anymore, with all the furniture covered and wooden boxes packed. She was leaving most of her things behind. The only thing she knew she had to take with her was Hua's book of recipes and the painted portrait of Hua herself. She wanted to keep this place sacred and preserve it for as long as she could.

She toured the rest of the house and stopped by the Golden Tree of Hope, the same tree that had made her power and her identity visible to her, the tree that changed her. She knew that despite whatever life had planned for her, she was *never* going to lose hope. She took a deep breath and sat under the tree with her eyes closed. The tree began to glow, and the flowers showered her with glitter dust. When she opened her eyes again, she saw many more trees, bushes, and flowers surrounding her. Sure, she was leaving Naje, but her presence was going to stick around forever.

THE NEXT MORNING, HER LAST MORNING ON THE ISLAND, SHE threw on a white dress that Hua had made for her. Like every other dress of hers, it had embroidered flower patterns on it. She then threw on a pair of matching slippers and pinned a clip onto the side of her head. She heard the door knock, and she hoped that it was Meili. But when she opened it, she found Zhang and his army of soldiers standing in front of her.

"We are here to get your things, Xiuying. The ship is being loaded, and we should really get going," Zhang informed her and walked in, only to realize that Xiuying hadn't responded. "Are you okay, my love?"

"Yes, yes, I am. I think I've made my peace," Xiuying assured him and stepped outside. Then she turned around and whispered, "Goodbye, Hua," and she locked the cottage door behind her, holding onto the key tightly.

As she made her way to the cove, she noticed the empty streets. Silence. Not a single villager walked around. Even Meili, who had *promised* to come see her, was absent. She felt betrayed, forgotten, like no one cared that she was leaving, possibly for good.

But when she arrived at the ship, she saw the entire village standing there. Everyone—from her students, to the doctor, to her neighbors—were holding onto bouquets of flowers. Even Meili, who had the biggest smile plastered on her face. Yilin walked up to her and gave her a long hug.

"Don't forget about us," Yilin whispered.

"Never," Xiuying answered as she moved on to Meili, who was already in tears. "Oh, Meili!" Xiuying whimpered. "I promise I'll come visit."

"Take care of yourself," Meili sniffled inaudibly. "And be yourself, okay?"

"I will, I promise. What will I ever do without you?"

As Zhang watched the tears unfold, he felt slightly guilty for being the reason that Xiuying had to leave behind those she loved. He felt like he'd asked her to give up too much, but he also knew that he needed to. He was going to ask for her hand in marriage as soon as they reached the kingdom. He was going to ask her to be his wife.

Xiuying knew she had to trust the uncertainty ahead and hope for the best. On the walk to the ship, she realized how far she had come, how she had met people whom she could finally rely on. And for once, it was *her* choice to leave.

The villagers watched as she stepped on, clapping their hands to wish her the best of luck and waving goodbye as she stood on the deck. And when the ship began to sail, Xiuying rushed to the edge and watched as the people she loved began to shrink, smaller and smaller until they finally disappeared.

Zhang was standing beside her, admiring her for her strength, her beauty, and her love for him.

"How did I get so lucky to meet you?" he asked as they both watched the rushing waves.

Xiuying beamed and leaned her head on his shoulder.

"To new beginnings?" he asked again.

"To new beginnings," she whispered and closed her eyes. She wanted to remember every second of this moment.

Xiuying trusted Zhang, but she still had her doubts about returning to a kingdom and interacting with people from royalty. On the ship, she was already being treated like royalty. Zhang had appointed two maids to cater to her needs, and the cook was instructed to make anything that Xiuying wanted. She was given the biggest room on the ship, with off-white velvet sheets on a king size bed. There were glass vases filled with flowers, and a small wooden table that was accompanied by two chairs. The room smelled of jasmine flowers, and that, Xiuying adored.

But as much as she appreciated the efforts that Zhang was making, she wasn't used to this kind of treatment. And she didn't want to tell him. She didn't want him to think that she didn't want to be with him. She didn't want him to think that she was still afraid.

CHAPTER
TEN

TIME WAS RACING AGAINST THE WAVES OF THE OCEAN. XIUYING had seen all shades of blue that had ever existed in the sky, the ocean, and soon, four days had passed with just the blink of an eye. Xiuying spent the journey enjoying all her favorite meals and conversing with Zhang, sharing laughter and moments of sorrow that came from stories about their past. The trip helped Xiuying understand Zhang more. She understood that even though he was royalty, a person who spent his entire life in comfort and with the highest level of prestige, he never let that affect his behavior toward others. He understood that he had a responsibility, that he had to take his father's place on the throne, but he wanted to do it with empathy and by winning hearts.

Xiuying felt her fears beginning to fade, and she was ready to embrace whatever laid ahead because she had Zhang by her side. Zhang, on the other hand, felt like he could tell Xiuying anything. He felt like he could be vulnerable around her, and that's what he cherished. He promised himself to never let her down, to never let anyone question her position, place, or worth in his life. He was ready to tell his family and his kingdom about his future wife.

The ship eventually reached the harbor, and the anchor dropped, followed by a loud bang as it met the edge of the ocean. The wooden crates were gathered and loaded onto horse carriages.

It was a big day, and Xiuying was feeling all levels of nervousness. How could she not? She was about to be introduced to Zhang's *entire kingdom* as his lover, some girl he'd picked up from a stranded island.

How would the kingdom react to the news? What would his family think of me? she thought while she combed through her hair with her fingers and tied it with a pink ribbon. She knew she had to make an impression, and a good one at that.

The door to her room opened with a knock. Xiuying turned to find Zhang standing before her.

"Beautiful, as always," he whispered when he caught sight of her. "Ready for the big day?" He was wearing the same white dragon robe that he had worn when they first met.

"I think so," Xiuying mumbled. "Do I look okay?"

"Okay?" he repeated. "You look stunning, Xiuying. Don't worry, everyone's going to love you, I promise," he consoled her and leaned in for a kiss. "I love you. Remember that. And they will, too."

Xiuying nodded with a smile and grabbed onto his arm. "I hope so."

When they got up to the deck, Xiuying could see a crowd gathered to welcome him. "Are you sure you want me to accompany you like this?" she asked, having second thoughts about making an appearance in such a spontaneous manner.

"I have never been so sure about anything else in my life. You're here because of me, and I will never forget that. I won't leave you behind," Zhang replied with a meaningful gaze.

There were hundreds of people in the crowd, all there to welcome the prince whom everyone thought had disappeared for good. The soldiers and maids walked out first, and they were showered with flowers and cheers welcoming them back. Zhang made his way off the ship with Xiuying beside him, and the crowd cheered even louder. Their walk from the ship to the carriage was filled with prayers and blessings, and Xiuying felt a little more at ease. He opened the carriage door for her and helped her get in. He then followed suit and sat beside her.

"So?" Zhang looked at her. "What do you think?"

"What do I think?" she repeated. "Baoshu is divine!"

She looked out the window and observed her new kingdom. It was much prettier than she'd imagined. It was decorated with red lanterns and dragon paintings on the walls. There were cherry blossoms everywhere in full bloom. And the streets were lined with trading posts, small eateries, and amazing architecture, exemplifying shades of maroon and beige.

The ride to the castle was tranquil as Xiuying continued to study her new environment, adoring Baoshu. When they reached the castle, the main gates opened, and the carriage traveled along a pristine stream full of water lilies and koi fish before reaching the grand entrance. The castle was huge, larger than the one that Xiuying had grown up in, with temples, galleries, gardens, and even a courtyard. The pointed rooftop was a nice shade of dark green, and the main corridors were a combination of white and maroon. Behind the castle were tall and rugged mountains covered with greenery. It all felt so real, yet Xiuying felt like she was dreaming.

Zhang's family was enthusiastically waiting to see him, and they were all standing by opened doors, ready to welcome him. The wheels of the carriage stopped right in front of the staircase that led to the grand entrance of the castle, all eyes on the carriage as the door opened. Zhang stepped out first, and he held the door open for Xiuying. Her heart was now racing faster and increasing with every step she took. She strolled out, and Zhang offered his arm, to which she held onto and beamed.

"It's okay," Zhang whispered to her, and they walked up the steps, soldiers standing on each side with silver swords in their hands.

Zhang's family was looking at them with raised eyebrows as they approached them. Zhang had two sisters —both adopted and from different families who had abandoned their daughters due to the one-child rule—who lived inside the castle. The Baoshu Kingdom was one of the only kingdoms in all of China who defied the one-child rule, refusing to partake in such a horrible tradition. This was also the reason why many other kingdoms hated, yet still respected, them.

Kyrie, the youngest, the light of the castle and adored by everyone, had a fair skin tone, light brown shoulder-length hair, and rich brown eyes. Kamari, older than Kyrie but younger than Zhang, was known for her confidence and strong political opinions. The king would always call her in for consultations. She was taller than Kyrie, had long, straight, dark hair, black eyes, and a complimenting skin tone with reddish cheeks.

The queen of Baoshu, Huiqing, was known for her empathetic nature, which kept her family together. She was shorter than Zhang, had silver strands in her dark braided hair, and a smile that could brighten up anyone's day. The king, Ming, was someone whom people drew inspiration from. He loved his family and prioritized them over everything else. He was tall, had long hair that was always tied in a bun as their tradition preferred, and a muscular figure.

Zhang and Xiuying reached the entrance to see Kyrie running toward them, throwing her arms around her brother.

"Welcome home, Zhang!" she cheered. "I'm so happy to see you! We were all so worried about you!" She grabbed his hand and led him to the front door.

"I'm happy to be home, too," Zhang replied.

"My son!" Ming greeted him in a loud tone.

"You're home!" Huiqing gushed and gave him a hug.

"Glad you're back." Kamari smiled, also leaning in for a light hug.

"Everyone, I'd like you to meet Xiuying," Zhang declared with a spark in his eyes. "We met on the island where the boat was stranded. She's very special to me."

"Oh, really?" Kyrie teased. Kamari giggled.

"Welcome to Baoshu, Xiuying. We're happy to have you here. If you bring Zhang joy, then you bring us joy as well," his mother welcomed her.

"Thank you for having me. I hope I'm not intruding," Xiuying replied with a soft tone.

"Not at all!" Huiqing led them both inside and told her to get settled in the royal wing of the castle, next to Kyrie and Kamari's room.

The two girls showed her the way while Zhang went into his own room, accompanied by his parents.

"Don't worry, you'll see him soon," Kyrie assured her.

"I love your dress. It really suits you," Kamari added as she opened the door to the room. "Here's your room. Dinner is at six!"

"Thank you for escorting me," Xiuying replied, and Kyrie and Kamari left her to gather her thoughts.

Xiuying closed the door and looked around the room. It was so elegant! The walls had drawings of traditional cherry blossom trees, the bed had silk light pink sheets and matching drapes, wooden dragons were carved on all four corners of the room, and the windows opened to a huge balcony that had a view of the entire kingdom. Xiuying took a deep breath and felt a wave of instant relief. Everything was beyond perfect so far. The kingdom was more than welcoming, Zhang's family was already treating her like one of their own. There wasn't a single thing that she could complain about. But still, she feared that it was all too good to be true.

While Xiuying was settling in, Zhang had an earnest conversation with his parents. He sat down with them and told them everything, who Xiuying was, her power, how he'd met her, and how he'd fallen for her. Ming and Huiqing were impressed that their son had found not only a woman of royalty, but a magical one at that.

"I want to marry her," he continued. "I cannot imagine myself with anyone else."

His parents looked at each other, and then his father replied, "If that's what you want, then you have our blessing, my son." Ming granted his approval, and Huiqing nodded.

She gave Zhang a kiss on his forehead. "Look at you, all grown up and talking about marriage. You've found a lucky one. Love her and cherish her."

Dusk had taken over the kingdom. Lit red lanterns and tiny oil lamps were placed on every window. Tiny lights twinkling were heard from Xiuying's room, and she woke up from dozing off to find herself still in the room that had appeared in her dream.

"It's real. It's really real," she whispered.

She forced herself to get out from under the comfort of silk sheets on her bed, and browsed her wardrobe to find something suitable to wear to dinner, but she failed to find one that would work.

"What am I going to do?" she asked herself in distress and sat by the window. "If only Hua were here to help me, or Meili to give me advice. I wish you were both here."

She looked out the window and gazed toward the ocean that had almost disappeared into the darkness. Suddenly, the door opened, and two maids came in with a box in their hands.

"A present from Prince Zhang," one of them said, handing the box over to Xiuying and then leaving.

On it was a note saying, *For my one and only, Xiuying.*

Xiuying couldn't help but smile when she opened the box. Inside, was a beautiful magenta gown that had flowers embroidered on it, but with jewels. It was something a princess would wear, but at the same time, it was minimal, something Xiuying could see herself in. She realized that even if Hua and Meili weren't here to look after her, Zhang was here for her, giving her everything she needed. She hadn't seen him since they'd reached the castle. He had responsibilities, things to look after, but Xiuying obviously didn't leave his mind, not even for a second.

She got dressed and looked in the mirror. The Xiuying she saw was much different from the Xiuying she'd been at Naje, but in a good way. She was stepping her way back into royalty, as if the universe was giving her back something that was once stolen from her. She then tied her hair into a low ponytail, dabbed a little blush on her cheeks, and put on some lip balm to match.

Suddenly, there was a knock on the door, and she was surprised to see Zhang on the other side.

"Were you expecting someone else?" Zhang asked as he walked in and sat on a wooden chair that was placed by the window.

"Not at all." Xiuying chuckled and added, "I just didn't know whether I was going to see you before dinner."

Zhang offered her the seat next to him. "I also thought that, but I couldn't wait any longer to see you, so I came." He paused, and then continued as he held onto her hand. "And there's actually something that I want to ask you. I know this may come as a surprise to you. This might even feel like I'm rushing into it, but I simply cannot wait anymore." Zhang got down onto one knee before her. "Will you give me the honor of being your husband? Will you marry me, Xiuying?"

Xiuying knew what was ahead when Zhang held her hand and said that first sentence. She was flattered but also cautious. It was only her first day here, after all.

"I want to, Zhang. And I wouldn't want to be with

anyone else, but I don't know if I'm ready yet for something so big. What if your family doesn't like me?"

"They love you already, Xiuying. I talked to them, and this isn't about them. It's about us. And your decision depends on how you feel about me; that's all that matters."

Xiuying's heart thumped. His words made her realize that she was the only one holding herself back, not because of anyone else stopping her.

"Then yes, Zhang. Yes, I will marry you."

Tears of joy began to creep from his eyes, and he picked her up and spun his fiancé around the room before planting a passionate kiss onto her lips.

"But I don't want anyone to make a big fuss about it. Not until I've settled in."

He nodded. "You have no idea how happy you've just made me."

Zhang escorted her into the dining hall. There was a long wooden table on the floor in the center of the room, with handwoven carpets to sit on. The people of the Baoshu Kingdom were humble, not only Zhang, but his entire family kept their lifestyle similar to the common people.

The table was decorated with vases filled with flowers, and mats that were made from bamboo. But even though the setup was down-to-earth, the menu was not. It had all sorts of dishes, some that Xiuying had never even heard of. There was Peking Duck, fried rice, stinky tofu, chow mein, congee, kung pao chicken, and for dessert, a platter of moon cakes. The room was lit with oil lamps and candle-sticks, with a scent of cherry blossoms in the air.

Kyrie and Kamari were already in the room when Zhang and Xiuying arrived.

"Oh, look at you two!" Kyrie sang.

"Come sit with us, Xiuying," Kamari invited her.

"We're going to tell you all of Zhang's embarrassing secrets!" Kyrie declared.

"Yeah! You're going to love this," Kamari added, and Xiuying laughed as she sat in between Kyrie and Kamari.

Kyrie started telling stories from their childhood. She told Xiuying how Zhang wanted to become a cobbler when he was younger and had a habit of shining shoes that people were still wearing. Xiuying laughed while Zhang gave Kyrie a death stare. Kamari told stories about how he was too afraid to sleep in his own room alone, even when he was in his late teens; he'd always get his mother to sleep next to him.

"You used to be such a scaredy cat!" Kyrie teased.

"It was just a phase," Zhang retorted, and everyone laughed. "This is supposed to be a family dinner, but apparently, it's turned into a story session at my expense."

Story time was put on hold when the king and queen entered the room, and everyone stood up in respect to welcome them.

Huiqing came over and hugged Xiuying. "You look wonderful!" she complimented.

Ming and Huiqing took their places side-by-side at the center of the table.

"I'm so glad to see all my children together," Ming remarked. "Your disappearance made us very worried, Zhang."

"But I'm here now! So, let's eat. I'm starving!" Zhang exclaimed.

"You're always starving. How do you eat so much?" Kamari asked.

"Seriously!" Kyrie chimed in.

"Okay, girls, let him eat in peace." Huiqing laughed, and they all dug in.

Xiuying was surprised to see the connection that they all had. It was rare and pure, and something that many royals lacked. But the Wei family was different.

"So, Xiuying, Zhang tells me you're a bit of a painter?" Huiqing asked.

"I'd like to think so," Xiuying answered, nodding her head.

"I'd love to see some of your work," Ming added.

"But... I left all my paintings back at the island."

"We can get you some supplies. Anything you need!" Huiqing insisted.

"I was actually thinking we could set up a gallery for her, showcase her work to all of Baoshu," Zhang suggested.

"That's perfect! I can help you!" Kamari offered her hand, and Kyrie added, "Me, too!"

Ming intervened, "Will you all please let the girl breathe?" Then he turned to Xiuying. "What do you say? Interested?"

They all looked at her, impatiently waiting for an answer. "Of course, that sounds fantastic."

And they all cheered.

When dinner ended, and it was time for bed, Huiqing pulled her son aside. "Remember, Zhang. You must keep your distance from Xiuying until *after* you are married. It's tradition. An honor of respect."

"That's not fair!" Zhang protested.

"Everything is fair in love and war!" Kamari called out with a laugh.

Then he turned to Xiuying. "Well, I guess I'll have to say goodnight to you here," he whispered to Xiuying and squeezed her hands tight. "I'll see you in the morning?"

"In the morning," she repeated, reassuring herself yet

again that she'd made the right decision moving in with Zhang.

Xiuying woke up the next morning to the birds chirping outside her window. The golden light from the sun was coming in through the glass, and the room looked so serene. She got up and realized that the tree in front of her window had suddenly sprouted pink flowers, her emotions causing them to blossom from the immense love and affection that she felt. She exhaled, relieved that Zhang's family knew about her power and still accepted her for it.

But soon, Kamari ruined that peaceful moment by rushing into her room with a platter of food. "Rise and Shine!" she yelled as she came in unannounced.

"Do you ever knock?" Xiuying asked Kamari, reminding her of Meili.

"You should get used to this. I go into everyone's rooms unannounced. That's how I show my love."

Xiuying chuckled. "It's okay. You remind me of a friend I had in Naje who always used to do the same thing."

Kamari smiled. "I'm your friend, too! Let's eat! I want to show you your gallery after."

Xiuying agreed, and they sat together on the balcony with their bowls of congee.

"I love what you did to the tree," Kamari pointed out.

"Honestly, I didn't do anything. It just... happened."

After breakfast, Kamari went to get dressed. She was planning on giving Xiuying a tour of the kingdom before heading over to the gallery. Xiuying was excited to meet the rest of Baoshu. The villagers of Naje had been nothing but kind, and she had no doubt that the people of Baoshu would be the same.

Xiuying, Kamari, and Kyrie soon boarded the carriage and started their journey toward the market square, the busiest area in the entire kingdom. From the sound of it, Xiuying imagined it to be chaotic, but it was quite the opposite. The streets were wide, clean, and decorated with plants, flowers, and artwork. There were also tall poles that held onto large oil lamps lining the streets.

The square was huge and had tons of different shops, with separate streets featuring a different theme—one for clothes, one for produce, one for poultry, one for crafts and handmade décor, and finally, one dedicated solely for artwork.

"This all seems so calm," Xiuying commented as they stepped out of the carriage and walked toward the art.

The gallery designated for Xiuying was located right by the front gate. It looked like her cottage at Naje but smaller, and it had an arched wooden door and a bay window.

"So? How do you like it?" Kamari asked with Kyrie leaning on her shoulder.

"I love it!" Xiuying exclaimed, still in disbelief that she was here at all. This was hers. This was *her* place to make art, showcase it, and show everyone a sliver of herself. Something warm bubbled in her chest, and she couldn't stop her smile from growing.

"Alright, let's get started! I'm a bit of a designer myself," Kyrie claimed. "I can help you set up!"

"And I will go and order some supplies for you, Xiuying. Some furniture, canvases, paints, and wooden paintbrushes. Anything else?" Kamari asked.

"Maybe some plants?" Xiuying suggested.

"Oh, how could I forget that? Flower Queen!"

Kyrie and Xiuying spent the entire day setting up the gallery. They painted the walls white, covered them with paintings and posters, and then they arranged for a corner bakery to serve coffee and moon cakes for their customers. They set up wooden tables and some chairs in a corner, placed oil lamps on the tables, and gave the gallery a finished look by hanging plants by the windows.

When the night fell, they headed home. Xiuying looked out at the houses that raced by as their carriage skipped down the streets. She admired a kingdom that was unlike the rest. It was beautiful, welcoming, and peaceful, yes. But it had shown her in such a short time that it actually respected their daughters. Women were celebrated here, and Kyrie and Kamari were given permission to break the barriers of being a royal. In Baoshu, they were respected and honored, but at the same time, treated as normal people.

When they reached the castle, Xiuying walked into her room to find her closet filled with new gowns and robes that Zhang had sent over. And on her bed, was a note. *You're already beautiful, but maybe these will remind you how beautiful you actually are.*

Xiuying beamed. She always did when he went out of his way to make her feel special. Her heart felt at ease, and she knew it belonged to him. She changed into one of the dresses in her closet and went to join the family for dinner. Everyone else was already present and waiting for her. Xiuying apologized and sat next to Zhang, who lightly touched her hand and smiled.

"Xiuying's gallery is all set up and ready to open in just two days," Kyrie told everyone.

"That's wonderful. We'd love to see it," Ming declared, and Huiqing bowed beside him.

"I have to give the credit to Kyrie," Xiuying answered. "Her decorating skills are impeccable."

While Xiuying, Kyrie, and Kamari went to the market, Zhang had been occupied with the merchants and soldiers. He attended training sessions with them and went over the security checks of the kingdom. They took their kingdom's safety very seriously and were always ready to fight back if ever needed. Their kingdom was powerful, even without having any magical powers. They were respected, looked up to, but mostly, envied by many. Zhang briefed his father on the details, and then after dinner, he asked Xiuying to join him for a walk.

He held onto Xiuying's hand as they walked slowly through one of the gardens of the castle.

"I think some of these plants need your magic touch," Zhang said.

"Zhang, I've been thinking a lot about the other day."

"Hm?"

"About agreeing to marry you."

"You're not going back on your word, are you?"

Xiuying shook her head. "No, I've been thinking more about it, and I'm actually really glad that I said yes. And not just because you're a prince. Because the more I spend time with you, the more I never want to leave your side."

Zhang came to a stop and pulled his fiancé closer to him. "I, too, never want to leave your side. You have my heart and forever will."

Against his mother's words, he leaned down and kissed her, his soft hands roaming up her back, his lips kissing her neck and shoulders.

"I am a man of tradition, but sometimes, I wish I weren't." He breathed heavily into her ear before stepping slightly away.

Xiuying blushed, and suddenly, all the flowers around them started to glow, glitter dust falling on them before dispersing into the air.

"There it is!" Zhang exclaimed.

"I can't wait. I can't wait!" Kyrie jumped in excitement the next morning, ready to start decorating for the wedding.

"There's so much to do! Where do we even start?" Kamari asked.

"The decorations, the color palette, the dress, cake, menu," Kyrie mumbled and yelled at the same time.

"Alright, tone it down, you two!" Huiqing laughed.

"Don't worry, Xiuying. We will handle everything," Ming assured her. Then he turned to his son and continued, "Zhang, remember, you must go and meet the king of Liaoshan as soon as possible. This is something you cannot postpone."

The room fell silent. During Zhang's last voyage, his ship ended up crashing, and everyone feared the same thing happening again.

"Yes, Father. I will leave tomorrow after Xiuying's gallery opening," Zhang calmly replied.

"We can work on the wedding preparations until then!" Kyrie commented to disrupt the silence, and after a while, everyone dispersed.

Xiuying went into her room to finish up the several pieces that she was going to showcase in her gallery tomorrow, but the thought of Zhang leaving for a voyage wouldn't stop bothering her. She took a deep breath and went onto the balcony.

"It's not like he's going away forever," she told herself.

She stared out at the ships that slowly vanished into the depths of the ocean, how tiny they seemed from where she was, but the weight they could carry was incredible. Then she felt a tap on her shoulder and spun around. It was Zhang.

"There's a Japanese phrase that I read before coming to your island. It's called *koi no yokan*, and it's the feeling when you first meet someone and inevitably fall in love with them. Maybe you don't love them right away. But you will." He took a deep breath and looked at her. "I didn't think I'd be standing here with you right now when I first saw you. I thought you were just some girl on a random island. But as I got to know you more, my heart started to open up, and now I can't imagine a life without you."

Xiuying was listening, but continued to watch the ships leave, one after another.

"Even if I am away, my heart will always be here with you," he whispered.

"How do you *always* know the right things to say?" she teased.

He shrugged, a smirk on his lips. "It's a gift, I guess. Anyway, I should let you get some rest. After all, you have a big day tomorrow."

After he left, Xiuying went back to her canvases, her fingers moving the brushes in a circular motion, mixing the paints and her emotions together. She felt joy and sorrow at the same time, and was confused as to which one she should follow.

It was the night before the opening of her gallery, and she struggled to fall asleep. The only thing she knew how to do that would bring peace to her mind was to write. Write to one of her loved ones whom she could no longer talk to. She had talked herself out of happiness so many times before, and she feared doing that again. Writing seemed to always clear her mind, so she wouldn't make a decision that she'd regret.

Dear Hua,

I'm the happiest I have ever been, or at least, I'm supposed to be. I have found my significant other, the love of my life. He's everything you would have wanted for me. He listens, makes me feel special, his smile and jokes light up my day, he believes in me, but most importantly, he accepts me for who I am. I finally feel seen. I no longer have to dream or trick my mind into thinking that life is beautiful... because it is.

I'm getting married, Hua, and I have my own gallery, with all my beautiful paintings, but something in my heart fears what's ahead. I have trusted uncertainty for the longest time, but this time, it feels different. It feels like the uncertainty is going to bring back some dark times. The possibility of things not working out is suffocating my happiness. Every time Zhang leaves, I fear for his well-being. Every time I take the next step, I fear I might fall on my face.

I am the happiest I have ever been and surrounded by people who adore me, but I wish you were here. I wish Meili, Huizhong, and Mei were all here.

Your daughter,

Xiuying

CHAPTER

ELEVEN

The next morning, Xiuying woke up to her room filled with all kinds of flowers in different colored vases.

"Surprise!" The door to her room opened with a *bang*, and in rushed Kamari and Kyrie.

"Mother also sends her best wishes. She's going to be there at the opening," Kamari added.

"Do you like our present?" Kyrie asked with excitement.

"Wow, I do, but you didn't have to do all this," Xiuying replied sleepily, barely out of bed, and definitely not dressed and ready to engage with the vivacious sisters.

"Nonsense! Of course, we had to. It's a big day for you, and we *are* your family!" Kyrie exclaimed. "That's what families do. They support each other."

Xiuying felt her heart warm. She thought the flowers were from Zhang, but the fact that Kamari and Kyrie did this made her even happier. Zhang wasn't the only one in the household who cared, and the sisters were quickly becoming irreplaceable in her life.

But her thoughts were cut short when footsteps approached from the hall. Zhang stepped into the doorway, his face bright with shock and a small bouquet of flowers in his hand.

"What's going on here?" he asked, examining the room, which was now filled with a concoction of fragrances from the different flowers, the floor partially covered with colorful fallen petals.

"Nothing, but it looks like we outshined you this time," Kyrie sang while Xiuying and Kamari chuckled.

"You got here too late, I suppose," Kamari teased.

Zhang walked in and handed the bouquet over to Xiuying. "It's not about the quantity; it's about the amount of love put in," Zhang said with a curling smile.

"If that makes you feel better!" Kamari poked. "Denial truly *is* your best friend."

"Alright, alright. This isn't a competition." Xiuying laughed. "But thank you," she added, looking from Zhang over to the girls and back. "I can't tell you how much this all means to me." Her eyes watered before she could stop them. She sniffled, wiping her sleeve across her eyelids to muffle her uncontained happiness.

"Aw, don't cry!" Kyrie wrapped her arms around her.

"It's happy tears," Xiuying whispered as Kamari joined in. The sisters squeezed her tight, and Xiuying couldn't hide her warm smile before looking up to find a similar expression on Zhang's face.

The opening of the gallery was beyond anything that

Xiuying had ever expected. The king, queen, Zhang, everyone in Baoshu had showed up to admire the paintings. Within two hours of opening, all her paintings had sold out. Xiuying was introduced by Zhang to everyone who came in, and they all praised her for her artwork. Xiuying made new friends, and people adored her. They all knew about her magical power; everyone in Baoshu, much like the villagers of Naje, knew about her and her ability. They even praised her for being some sort of goddess who had blessed them. But even so, her paintings continued to speak for themselves.

The sun was setting over the horizon, the sky changing colors from blue to orange, and the cold breeze making saying goodbye hard as Zhang prepared to leave for his voyage. All the family members were gathered at the entrance to wish him a safe journey. Xiuying was standing beside Kyrie and Kamari while their parents were talking to Zhang. He was wearing his army's royal suit and carrying a mid-sized silver sword.

Xiuying's heart started to thump harder and faster in her chest, her shoulders, her arms, her fingers all tense with anxiety. She wanted to stop Zhang from going on this journey, but how could she do that? How could she stop him from pursuing something that he loved? Especially when he was always her biggest supporter.

He walked up to her and whispered, "I promise, I'm going to return in three days. Remember, you are safeguarding the most precious thing I have or will ever own."

Xiuying's stomach dropped, but she forced herself to nod her head. "Stay safe," she whispered back with a grin.

"Don't worry, she's in good hands," Kyrie assured Zhang as he bid farewell and climbed aboard, followed by a group of soldiers. The group resembled an army to Xiuying. She couldn't shake that image.

The king and queen soon walked away, and Kyrie accompanied them. Xiuying just stood there, watching Zhang's carriage fleet outside the castle doors. The time had come faster than she thought it would. Maybe he really *would* be back before she expected. Maybe.

"He's going to be back in no time, Xiuying. In the meantime, we can continue preparing for the wedding," Kamari said from beside her.

"You're right. I should keep myself occupied," Xiuying answered, forcing her fingers to loosen from clenched fists.

"That's the best thing you can do for yourself." Kamari smiled and started to brief Xiuying on the infinite things that they had to do over the next three days. But even with the seemingly endless tasks, Xiuying couldn't seem to shake that tight, uneasy stirring in her stomach.

OVER THE COURSE OF THE NEXT FEW DAYS, XIUYING HAD MUCH TO do, including deciding on a wedding dress, the decorations, the menu, the cake, the flowers—Kamari helped her decide on the hairstyle and jewelry that she would wear. Huiqing also brought some of their family heirlooms for Xiuying to wear and use, as she was going to become the next queen.

The only thing that Xiuying struggled to decide on was the venue. She wanted to wait for Zhang before making that decision. So, in her spare time, she prepared more paintings for her gallery and met with some of the community groups in the kingdom. She was going to donate all the proceeds she made to those in need, as one should. *A true queen at heart*, people would call her.

Finally, on that third day, a day Xiuying thought would never come, Zhang returned home. As his family welcomed him, he walked up to Xiuying and told her to close her eyes.

"Why?" Xiuying laughed.

"Just do it," he answered. She closed her eyes and patiently waited, anxious for what she was going to see when she opened them again. "Okay, you can open your eyes," Zhang whispered. And when Xiuying did, she was shocked to see Meili and Jifae standing in front of her.

"Surprise!!!" Meili yelled at the top of her lungs.

Xiuying jumped and rushed over to hug Meili. "I'm so happy to see you!" she said. "I had no idea when I was going to see your face again."

"Are you kidding? No way was I going to miss your big day!" Meili answered, and Jifae added, "Also, Zhang wanted to surprise you."

Xiuying looked over at Zhang as he beamed at her. "Thank you," she whispered.

But before she could say anything else or fully welcome Zhang home, he was summoned by his father. Meili and Jifae were shown to their guest room and were invited for dinner later with the entire family.

Meili and Xiuying spent the day catching up on what had happened ever since she left the island. Xiuying told her all about Zhang and his family, the kingdom, the gallery opening, and now she felt like her life was complete because everyone who mattered to her was here with her.

"I'm so happy for you, Xiuying. Coming here was the right decision for you. I mean, you're about to become a queen!" Meili exclaimed.

"Just like you're the Queen of Naje."

"You bet I am."

Xiuying brought Meili to her room and showed her the

wedding dress and the heirlooms that she had received from Huiqing, and they continued to talk for hours over tea and moon cakes.

Later that night at dinner, they were joined by Kamari and Kyrie, who both befriended Meili quickly. All four of them got along well enough, throwing jokes out, laughing, sharing stories, and teasing each other like they had been close friends all along.

With everyone gathered for dinner, it felt like the place was alive. There were only two days left before the wedding. The preparations were on the verge of completion, and the guests from other kingdoms had started to arrive. For the venue, Zhang and Xiuying decided on the gardens of the castle because they wanted an outdoor wedding, and the gardens were the *perfect* sentimental place. After all, Zhang held the most pleasant of his childhood memories there, and it was also the place where he asked for Xiuying's hand in marriage. There could be no venue *more perfect* for them than the gardens.

Once it was decorated lavishly for the wedding ceremony, Xiuying and Zhang couldn't wait any longer to move forward and spend the rest of their days united together. When the day finally came, they were more than ready.

The entire kingdom was decorated with flowers and lanterns. The gardens were lit up with oil lamps as the sun dipped. The wedding was happening after dusk, there were cherry blossoms everywhere, the decorations were white and pastel pink, there were stick candles on every table, and the menu had more than twenty-five main dishes and ten desserts.

The small list of invited guests soon started to come in and take their places for the intimate ceremony, while the entire kingdom were invited to attend the ball afterward.

This created a rumbling wave of talk about the wedding. Gossip and excitement flowed throughout the kingdom. And not only in theirs, but among the citizens of every other kingdom that was invited as well. Soon, the news reached all the way to Jinu, Xiuying's kingdom, one that wasn't invited to the wedding but cared about the news very much. Qianfan and Daiyu were shaken to find out that the prince was marrying the daughter they'd abandoned.

Xiuying walked in, wearing a long and form-fitting cheongsam. It was red with flowers and dragon patterns embroidered on it with silver and gold thread. Meili and Jifae walked Xiuying down to the aisle. She was the prettiest person present, and like always, all eyes were on her. People gasped and sighed contentedly as she slowly walked toward Zhang. He was standing at the front, wearing a long silk white traditional robe that had patterns nearly matching Xiuying's. Even their outfits complimented each other.

As soon as Zhang caught sight of his bride, he could not believe his eyes. How did he get so lucky? To have someone so compassionate, so loving, and so empathetic. Xiuying reached for him, and he held onto her hands with a smile. The ceremony was small, intimate, and was performed in a strictly traditional manner.

After it was over, the *real* celebration began. Zhang and Xiuying were now husband and wife, and while it was their happiness, the entire kingdom celebrated with loud music, fireworks, and firecrackers. Their wedding was like a traditional festival. The ball that was hosted at the castle was divine, and there were kings, queens, princes, and princesses coming up to meet and congratulate the happy couple.

From a distance, Xiuying could see everyone celebrating

and dancing in joy—Kyrie, Kamari, Meili, and Jifae. These were *her* people, and this was *her* happy place. A place she could call *home*.

The ceremony ended around midnight, and finally, Zhang and Xiuying got a chance to relax when they got to their new royal suite. It was large—unbelievably *large*. Wardrobes sat at opposite ends of the room, and huge windows lined the walls and opened in one spot to a large balcony that overlooked the entire kingdom. The walls were painted light brown and had paintings of dragons on them, similar to the patterns on their wedding attire. And the oil lamps placed in every corner of the room created slick glowing shadows on the red silk sheets on their bed. This room felt like it was *made* for a king and queen. And now the room—and soon the titles—were theirs.

"I know this is all a little too much, but it's not going to be like this forever. You can change anything you want," Zhang replied.

"Alright." Xiuying nodded.

"Thank you for letting me be your husband for life," Zhang told her, holding onto her hands.

"And thank *you* for letting me be your wife for life," Xiuying replied, and they both laughed.

"You have never looked prettier. I couldn't even get my eyes off of you," Zhang claimed.

"You didn't look so bad yourself," Xiuying teased.

"Okay? That's all I get?" Zhang laughed. "So unfair," he teased her right back, poking and tickling her as she slid under the silk blankets on the bed.

Xiuying giggled, swatting away his hands before he tucked her in to sleep. He scooted in behind her and pulled her close. She curled into him, soaking in his warmth and reassurances. This would be *their* future. This would be their routine every night. She beamed, warmth spreading through her body until she drifted off to sleep.

Xiuying woke up before Zhang the next morning. Her eyes opened, and she could see his face on the pillow right next to her. His eyes were closed, dreaming of all the things that he wanted to achieve. He held onto her hand even while he was asleep, the golden sunlight touching his face, making the tiny freckles on his cheeks visible. Xiuying got up to push the drapes down so that Zhang didn't get disturbed, when suddenly, she heard a knock on the door.

Who could it be, so early in the morning? she thought.

She opened the door to find a maid standing with a scroll in her hand.

"This came for you in a manner of urgency," she said.

"Is this for Zhang?" Xiuying asked.

"This is for you, my queen," she replied, taking a bow before she turned around and left.

Xiuying held the scroll tightly in her hands. She went to the balcony that faced the kingdom, her heart pounding in her chest. She looked down in her hands and turned the scroll over, and there was the royal seal of... *her family*. A scroll from the parents who abandoned her. A scroll from the father who left her to die. A scroll from the mother who didn't stand up for her own daughter.

Why now? A part of her wanted to throw the scroll away and forget about it forever, but another part of her wanted to rip it open and read what they had to say. It had taken her a decade to forget the memories that caused her pain. Was she going to let them all rush in again? She took a deep breath and gathered her waning courage before tearing the seal apart.

There were two letters inside. One was an invitation, inviting her and Zhang to a royal dinner to strengthen the ties of the two kingdoms. The other was a long note written by Daiyu, addressed only to Xiuying.

Dearest Xiuying,

I know that it has been ages, and you must hate your mother for giving you away and for never being there for the little girl you were. The chains of my marriage and royal responsibilities never allowed me to be the mother you needed, never allowed me to stand up for you, never allowed me to wipe your tears or see you smile. You have fought many battles from a young age, and that, too, was all on your own.

I am sorry, my daughter. I am sorry, Xiuying. I have failed as a mother for both you and your sister. I know there's nothing I can say or do to make you forgive us, but consider the thought of letting your mother see you once more, my daughter. I tried to look for you, but I couldn't find you anywhere. There were no records of you, but you found yourself in royalty once again because that's where you always belonged.

You must be a married woman by the time this letter reaches you. I am sure you must have been the most gorgeous bride that the kingdom has ever seen. Zhang is one of the best in our country, and you are lucky to have each other. I've even heard that you possess one of the rarest powers—emotions that control the environment, and I have never been prouder. I always knew you had something special in you.

Your father asked me to contact you and welcome you back, Xiuying. I hope you find it in your heart to forgive us. I hope your heart is open to letting a little love back in.

Waiting for you,

Your mother and father

Xiuying found herself in rage and tears.

"The audacity!" she screamed.

It was unfair, and she knew they only reached out to her because she was going to become a queen. And the mother of all ironies was that the woman who let her child go—let her die—was now hoping that Xiuying had not turned her heart against them.

How could she? She fell to her knees and started to sob, her eyes turning all red and her body shivering. Zhang woke up to Xiuying crying, and he rushed through the entrance of the grand terrace to find her on the floor.

"Hey, hey, hey," he repeated as he gathered her into his arms. "Xiuying, what happened?" But then his eyes flickered, and he caught sight of the abandoned scroll with her family's seal. He let out a sharp breath.

"It's okay, Xiuying," he whispered. "I am here."

His warmth enveloped her, but her breaths would not slow; her heart would not cease its rampant race. She was choking on her own lack of air. She couldn't get a deep enough breath—she couldn't stop. Zhang repeated his phrase three times before her head grew light, and she collapsed into his arms without even replying. He picked her up and carried her to their bed. He set her atop the blankets and sprinkled a few drops of water onto her face in a rush to make her gain consciousness again. When she jolted awake, he assured her that he was by her side, and she slept unsoundly.

Once Xiuying was asleep, Zhang went back to the balcony and read the scroll that had been sent to Xiuying. His fingers tightened on the parchment paper, tearing a piece off one edge. He understood why the letter bothered her the way it did, and he felt nothing but pure rage and anger for Qianfan and Daiyu. After all, Xiuying had a family now, and a husband who was willing to do and go anywhere to protect her, to make her happy. This was the first time that Xiuying had shed a tear inside their castle, and he *did not* like it.

The day passed by, and everyone in the family soon heard of what had happened. They were concerned for Xiuying more than anything else and wanted to bring her remedies and food that could help with her distress. But when Xiuying awoke again, she only wanted to talk to Zhang.

"I want to visit them," Xiuying whispered as Zhang came over and sat next to her on the bed.

"I don't think you should," he said honestly. "Look at what one letter did to you. Seeing them would only make everything worse, Xiuying," Zhang replied.

"I just want to see their faces. They are blurred fragments in my memory. I know that her letter is not sincere, but she mentioned that I have a sister, and she wronged her. I want to be there for her when no one else has been her whole life. Please, let me do this, Zhang."

Zhang was not fond of the idea, but he knew his new wife was stubborn. He knew the fight in her was far from extinguished. And if she felt that she needed answers and closure for herself and for her sister, then he would be there, too, right by her side.

"Fine. We leave at dawn," he said.

"Thank you," Xiuying whispered.

He smiled and soothed her until she felt ready to face the world again. Meili and Jifae were leaving for Naje the same day, and the goodbye this time was even more distressing than before. Her dearest friends were leaving her side again, and she felt her own limbs being pulled away.

Xiuying cried her heart out later that night, but she put on a brave face in front of her most beloved friends as she watched them depart.

Soon after their friends' departure, Zhang had preparations made for the trip. Three ships were leaving with them —one for themselves, and the other two filled with weapons, soldiers, and presents. They wanted to be prepared for any possible circumstance, and they *never* visited a place empty-handed.

Xiuying and Zhang left, and after a day of traveling through the ocean, they reached the kingdom of Jinu. Their ships were the largest ones on the harbor, earning them even more attention as they exited. Zhang and Xiuying scurried into a carriage that was heavily guarded by ten soldiers. It lurched forward, just as Xiuying's stomach did.

"We can still turn back, Xiuying."

"We have come so far. I cannot just go without knowing about my sister." Xiuying squeezed Zhang's hand.

Zhang had spent the entire day worrying about her health and had tried his best to make her feel comfortable and happy.

They reached the castle, and all the memories of her leaving rushed back to Xiuying's mind. She had been thrown into a carriage and sent away before, but now the glory she entered in was unmatched and something the kingdom had never seen.

They got out of the carriage after a bumpy ride and were escorted to the grand hall for dinner. It all seemed so dead, so dry, as if the joy from the castle was taken away. Xiuying struggled against the lingering silence, especially after her experiences at her new kingdom.

Footsteps were then heard from a distance, echoing from afar, and after a moment more, Qianfan and Daiyu came into view.

"You came—Oh! My daughter!" Daiyu gushed.

"I am *not* your daughter," Xiuying hissed, clenching her fists. Zhang stood next to her, guarded by soldiers.

"We have brought you gifts," Zhang said evenly, cutting into the tension like a knife.

He asked the maids to bring the gifts in, and they all waited and watched each other as several women scurried in with boxes of fresh fruits, gold coins, and silk cloth. Qianfan was quiet and watchful, but as the final box was set down, Xiuying couldn't hold herself together any longer.

"Where is she?"

"Where is who?" Qianfan raised a brow.

"My sister." Xiuying gritted her teeth.

"What makes you think she's here?" Qianfan laughed. "We sent her to a concentration camp," he declared.

All the blood in Xiuying's veins froze over. All the heat, all the fire, all the fight that had burned brightly inside of her froze over like a pond in the heart of winter.

"What?" Xiuying whispered, but her voice steadily rose. "What did you say?"

Her father smirked.

At the curl of his thin, chalky lips, she exploded.

"How could you?!" she screamed. She turned to her mother.

"Your f-father—" Daiyu stuttered. But Qianfan interrupted her.

"You have no right to speak to her in that tone."

That was when Zhang finally stepped in. "And you certainly cannot talk to Xiuying in *that* tone."

Qianfan glared at him. "Get out."

"Where's Mei?" Xiuying's cries echoed down the empty hall. But she couldn't calm herself; she couldn't lower her volume. Something curled and crawled and wriggled up her throat, threatening to choke her again. "Where's Mei?"

"She's dead!" Qianfan yelled, his voice overpowering hers.

Xiuying stared at him, her eyes wide and disbelieving.

"She died in that bloody prison cell. She never saw the sunlight after you left the castle." Qianfan sneered, that dark, festering hatred lining every crease, every wrinkle, on his face.

Xiuying shook in her shoes. Her legs wobbled underneath her, and she couldn't... breathe.

Mei had *died*.

Hua had *died*.

Zhang took Xiuying's hand and led her away from the festering dark stares of her parents. Her father watched with that devilish smirk as Zhang pulled her away while her mother dropped her gaze to the floor, unable to meet her eyes. Zhang dragged the shell of Xiuying to the carriage awaiting at the front of the castle, and he whisked her away as quickly as he could.

Xiuying sat quaking in her seat. Once again, she was boarding a ship from the same place, leaving the castle with the same heavy heart. But this time, she *really* had no tie left to her home or to her family. They had taken her—they had taken Mei. And she would *never* see her sister again.

The trip back to Baoshu was silent and tense, but Xiuying barely recognized what was happening. At one point, she was watching the castle gates to her parents' kingdom disappear in the distance, and then the next thing she knew, Zhang was escorting her to their room on the ship. Once she was surrounded by the silence of the cabin, her legs collapsed under her, and her throat let out a muffled cry before she toppled to the floor in a heap.

She woke up again after a few hours and found Zhang waiting by her side. He held her hand firmly in his own, and his foot tapped on the wooden floorboards. She squeezed his hand lightly. Zhang's gaze whirled on her, relieved.

"Hey," Zhang whispered. "We're almost home."

Xiuying sniffled. "I'm sorry, Zhang. You told me not to go, but I did anyway. I should have listened to you."

"It's okay. But you must know, Xiuying, that they don't deserve *anything* from you. Not your attention, not your love, and certainly not the kingdom that they have. I am going to make sure that they pay for how they treated you." Zhang's eyes darkened. A chill rushed across Xiuying's skin, but with it, the fire inside flickered to life.

She went over her father's words again and again and again, but with them, she found herself doubting. When had he *ever* been truthful to her? When had he *ever* respected her or cherished her? Something *wasn't* right, and as much as she wanted to be done with her parents and their delusional games, this one wasn't over yet.

"You're right," she whispered. "They cannot get away with this. And I am going to find my sister and make sure she's okay," Xiuying mumbled.

Zhang looked at her, a thread of doubt passing through his eyes. But he trusted her more than he trusted anyone else. He would follow her to the abyss and back if it meant she would be safe in this life.

"We'll find her, I promise," Zhang assured her.

With that, the ship rocked forward, and the voices of the crew called out their arrival. They had returned to their kingdom—their home.

The return home marked a new journey.

A week later, Zhang and Xiuying were crowned king and queen of the Baoshu Kingdom. Immediately, they started making decisions for the betterment of the kingdom, which flourished even more than Zhang's parents' era. But not all was bright and cheery for the new royal pair.

Zhang was determined to take over the kingdom that insulted his wife. He wanted to bring Qianfan and his empire to their knees. On the other hand, Xiuying was on a search to find her sister and bring her home. Revenge was all she wanted from the kingdom that she was born into, but she couldn't achieve that until she had her sister safe and sound at her side once more.

The future was once again unsteady and clouded by fog for Xiuying, but one thing was for certain—Zhang. Their marriage and her love for this kingdom were real. Xiuying was finally safe and had finally found a place and a person to call *home*. Now, she wanted the same for her sister.

To be continued...

THE BROKEN DAUGHTER

THE LOST DAUGHTERS TRILOGY
BOOK TWO

The Broken Daughter

THE LOST DAUGHTERS TRILOGY BOOK TWO

VIOLA TEMPEST

CHAPTER
ONE

THE RIGID WINTERS AND OPACITY OF THIS TOWN WERE SOMETHING a person could *never* escape from. It transferred from one person to the next, killing the smallest speck of light and hope within a soul.

There she was, standing at a distance, radiating light with all her glory and prestige, looking elegant as one could ever be while surrounded by an army of soldiers.

"Xiuying?" Xiaofan heard herself say. "The queen?" she questioned herself. "How?" she muttered. The sister her parents had abandoned was now a queen? She failed to understand what had happened as she peeked from the tiny window of her room, hearing chants of people praising the queen.

The town hadn't had a visitor for ages, or ever since Xiaofan was sent here, and what were the odds? The only time the town ever got a visitor, and it turned out to be her long-lost sister?

She forced herself to understand that this was just a sheer coincidence and had *nothing* to do with her very existence, and she climbed under her sheets and let all the memories sink in. The child who was once loved, admired, and cherished in a wealthy kingdom, served by hundreds of servants, maids, and soldiers, was now taking shelter at an orphanage that had nothing to offer but dismay, oppression, and dampness.

Xiaofan now found herself deprived of everything that her parents had once promised her. She was the second daughter of Qianfan and Daiyu, the king and queen of Jinu. Parents who had once abandoned their firstborn daughter in spite of not having a son, accepted Xiaofan, celebrated her, and gave her all the love that a child deserved. The early years of her childhood were spent in pure bliss, admired by her father, treasured by her mother, and respected by the entire kingdom.

She was the most respected in political and educational trials. From a very young age, she had a better understanding of complex matters than those around her, her comprehension levels above and beyond those of the local adults. She was proud, and rightfully so. She had *everything* —status, wealth, power, and rank. Though these things made it difficult for her to make friends her own age.

She never got along with other girls her age; she always thought they were below her, and she was superior to them. The love and power surrounding her daily life had taken over her mind and soul.

However, the oblivious child in her didn't know that

pride wasn't enough, and *her* pride eventually fell. She saw her future in the kingdom among rulers, but her father had other plans for her, and her mother never questioned his decisions.

It had been eleven years since she was sent here, and she still remembered the warmth of her mother's love, her voice, and her touch of affection. She still remembered the conversations about politics with her father, their friendly chess matches, and him telling her how much she reminded him of his younger self. The memories were still embedded in her heart and mind, especially the harsh ones and the series of events that led her here.

She tried to turn a deaf ear to the chants coming from outside and closed her eyes to sleep, allowing all the events to reoccur in her mind.

Eleven years ago...

On a balmy morning during the rich season of spring, eight-year-old Xiaofan woke up in her enormous room that was right next to her parents' room. The room had been painted a shade of lavender and decorated with painted portraits of her family. She had a large wooden desk in the corner that had every quality of paper and ink that ever existed. It was her *favorite* part of the room as she *loved* creating stories.

Next to the desk was a shelf that had books with all her writings and also some works by famous literature writers. Her space was *always* lit up with oil lamps and scented candles, the fragrance of vanilla essence constantly lingering in the air.

She managed to get out of bed, her sheets smoother than silk and her pillows soft like clouds. Her bedroom had two huge windows on two different walls—one showed her the view of the entire castle, and the other allowed her to look over her kingdom. She walked across her room and stood in front of the window that allowed her to see her kingdom and the tiny homes that people lived in.

How do they live in such tiny homes? she would often think to herself.

As much pride as she had, she *did* try to stay humble. She was lucky to be here, she knew that. She was fortunate to have the wisdom to understand worldly matters, and she made a vow to herself to work hard so she could help the people of her kingdom and raise their living standards.

The door to her room suddenly pushed open, pulling her out of her thoughts. It was one of her maids.

"The queen has birthed a son," the maid revealed. "Congratulations, you have a baby brother."

Xiaofan turned with her answer. "Prepare my dress. I shall go see him."

The maid paused before replying, "The king *forbids* anyone from seeing the queen and the newborn for the next three days, and he expects you to understand."

Xiaofan took a step back. *Why? Why would he forbid me from seeing my own brother?* She failed to understand the decree, but she could do little to argue against her father's orders.

Three days went by, and Xiaofan was excited to finally meet her new baby brother. She ordered her maid to bring her the best dresses that she had. She shook her head and smiled as she left, only to return with ten different options for her. Xiaofan chose one and started to get ready.

What will it be like to have a sibling? she thought to herself as she combed her long locks, oblivious to the fact that she already had a sibling.

Xiaofan tied her hair back and took a look in the mirror. Her fair face with rosy pink cheeks was glowing, and her hair tied back looked elegant. She'd made an *excellent* choice with her dress, choosing to wear a lilac dress with ruffled sleeves. She looked divine, like a princess should.

"Perfect," she complimented herself and swirled. She then left her room, followed by two soldiers and three maids who accompanied her everywhere.

Her parents' room was at the end of the royal corridor. It was right next to *her* room, but it took at least five minutes to walk there, and Xiaofan *never* left her room without her army of soldiers and maids, even if it *was* for just five minutes.

The maids knocked on the door to the king and queen's room and announced Xiaofan's presence. They allowed her to enter, and when she stepped in, she saw a small baby boy wrapped in a dark blue blanket that had dragon patterns embroidered on it. Daiyu was holding him close to her while Qianfan was sitting right next to her. Xiaofan came running in to see her brother, but she was not allowed to touch him.

"Stop right there!" Qianfan yelled as he saw Xiaofan leaning in to hold the boy. "Are your hands clean?" he questioned. "We cannot take *any* chances with the newborn."

"Yes, Father, they are," Xiaofan whispered.

"You can just watch him from afar," Qianfan declared, now standing up on his feet and looking down over the boy.

"Honey, give it some time. You will get a lot of time to spend with your brother," Daiyu whispered in a low voice with her eyes still on the boy. She didn't even look at Xiaofan for a second.

"Okay," Xiaofan murmured.

"Now that you have seen the newborn, you should head back to your room," Qianfan ordered.

"Yes, my dear. The ball is tonight, and there are still so many things to do in preparation," Daiyu added.

"Can I come to the ball, Mother?" Xiaofan asked, looking up at her mother with glowing eyes.

"Yes, of course, but for now, you need to get going."

Xiaofan shook her head, indicating that she understood, but her inner monologue was failing to understand why Qianfan and Daiyu were treating her differently than before. She slowly left the room, and her army escorted her back to her own room.

She marched in and slammed the door shut behind her. Something had changed; she could feel it in her bones and in the air. She felt like her place was being taken. She was being *replaced* by someone better, even if that someone was just an infant. The anger in her was something that she had inherited from her father, and *that* was what channeled her magical power the most. She had control over wind and fire, and she was being taught by the wise wizard of the castle how to control them.

After hours of envying her new baby brother, Xiaofan decided to get ready for the ball. The festivities had begun, and the castle looked like a completely different place. It was decorated from one corner to another with flowers and silk drapes, and guests were arriving with presents and treats.

Xiaofan could see all the glory from her room. This was something that she had never experienced, she had *never* seen something being celebrated to such transcendent extents at the castle.

The maids knocked and entered her room, bringing a gown with them that was specifically made for her and sent by her mother. The dress was a pastel purple silk dress with long bell sleeves and traditional flowers embroidered onto it with jewels.

"The queen has requested that you wear this," the head maid said, and Xiaofan nodded as a sign of assurance.

Xiaofan was a little relieved after receiving the dress. "She didn't forget about me," she muttered to herself and started to get ready for the ball.

As much as Xiaofan was fond of the perks of being a royal, she hated gatherings; she hated meeting people and pretending to be nice to them. A royal ball was the *last* event that she looked forward to, and this time, she was already annoyed. In spite of the newborn, her mood swings were already unpredictable, and they would only get worse during the celebration.

The ball had begun, and the main hall was filled with royal families from all around the country. Xiaofan arrived an hour late and greeted everyone with smiles and hugs.

Oh, the misery, she thought every time she had to sweet talk another elderly person.

After twenty minutes, the guards announced the arrival of the king, queen, and the prince. They walked in with all the grandeur of a happy and powerful royal family. Daiyu was holding the newborn, and Qianfan walked by her side. He was prouder than he had ever been his entire life. They came upfront while everyone showered them with flowers.

"After years and years of waiting, we have finally been blessed with an heir, a prince. A boy who is going to continue our legacy, just like I did, just like my father did, and just like our ancestors did. Today is a blessed day that needs to be celebrated with all our hearts," Qianfan announced in a loud, strong, and firm voice, silencing the crowd before them. "We name him Jinhai, for he is the golden sea that is going to bring in enlightenment."

Qianfan then took the magical stone to mark Jinhai's wrist as per tradition. The packed hall started to chant, "Long live Prince Jinhai! Long live Prince Jinhai!"

Daiyu broke into happy tears as she watched the scene unfold before her while Qianfan held onto her hand tightly and grinned. Xiaofan watched the events from where she stood above them.

Why am I here and not down there with them? Am I not a part of the family? Questions started to boil in her mind one by one, when suddenly, she heard a whisper.

"It was never like this when you or your sister was born."

Xiaofan paused, and then continued in a low voice, "When I was born?"

"It was a little like this, but *this* is a *lot more*." One of the maids revealed herself. "But at least you were welcomed. Your elder sister was not."

"What are you saying?" Xiaofan asked as shock and disbelief sparked under her skin. "*I* am the firstborn; I don't have a sister."

The maid, who was known as Fang, suddenly realized how big of a mistake she had just made. She tried to take back her words, but it was too late. Xiaofan left the crowded ball and took Fang to her room, where she had no choice but to come clean to Xiaofan. While her parents and their guests were enjoying the ball, eating and drinking their hearts out while they celebrated, the somber truths of the castle and her parents were exposed to Xiaofan inside her room.

Fang told her everything—how Xiuying was born, how she wasn't accepted by Qianfan, how she was abandoned and raised by Mei, her attempted suicide, and her eventual expulsion to an abandoned island to die. Xiaofan just stood there while absorbing all the tales, staring at the kingdom in blissful hysteria from her room's window.

Her heart pounded in her chest as tears started to roll down her cheeks.

"Please, don't tell *anyone* that you heard this from me. They will incarcerate me, just like they imprisoned Mei," Fang pleaded.

"I won't tell anyone, I promise." Xiaofan sobbed. "I would like to be left alone now."

"Are you sure?" Fang asked, and Xiaofan nodded.

As soon as Fang walked out, Xiaofan fell to her knees, struggling to breathe. "It has all been a lie!" She shook her head but failed to understand. "It has all been a lie!" she screamed again and cried.

How can this be true?

How can they just abandon my sister like that?

Is their love for me even real, or is it all just a lie?

My entire life has been a lie, a false reality.

She could not contain herself any longer. She felt neglect and rage, so she decided to confront the source of all this... her parents. After all, she *was* her father's daughter.

The ball had now ended, and no one noticed that Xiaofan wasn't there.

Without asking for permission, she stomped her way over to her parents' room and slammed open the door, yelling, "Why didn't you ever tell me that I have a sister?"

Her father didn't even look surprised to see her standing there, her face fuming red. Her mother, at least, had the nerve to be a little shocked at her appearance.

"Because it is not important for you to know," Daiyu replied in polite disbelief at Xiaofan's outburst.

"And why is *he* a prince, and I'm not a princess?" Xiaofan pointed over to the newborn and back to herself.

Qianfan walked toward her slowly, his footsteps hitting hard on the floor. He gripped her shoulders tightly, in a way that sent a sharp ache through her joints.

"He is a *he*," Qianfan stated firmly. "*He* is a boy, and *you* are a girl. There's no such thing as a princess. He is superior to you."

Xiaofan stepped back, and the rage she saw in her father today was different... scarier.

"Where is Xiuying?" Xiaofan mumbled as fear took over, and her anger shifted toward despair.

Qianfan tied his hands back, started to walk toward his newborn, and chuckled. "Oh, Xiuying! She's probably dead by now." Xiaofan gasped, but that only made his wicked smile widen. "I sent her away. She *destroyed* our family and your mother." He paused, giving her a long look before he opened his mouth again. "We treated you right, and look how karma repaid us. We have been blessed with a boy *only* because we gave you everything you needed."

Xiaofan couldn't believe the words that she was hearing from her own father's lips. All this time, he hadn't loved her. He had done what he needed to do in order to obtain what he *really* wanted—a son. She meant *nothing* to him. Xiuying had been a victim of his hate, and though Xiaofan thought she was different, clearly, she had been wrong, too. But her father was not content with stopping there.

"If you don't agree with the decisions that I have made, maybe it is time for you to go, too." He scowled at her.

Xiaofan shuddered and took a few steps back. Was the person standing in front of her *really* her father? The one she played chess with and had conversations with about politics? Her eyes were red with tears.

Daiyu interrupted at that moment, sensing the tension in the room. "Sweetheart, just go to your room. There's nothing for you to worry about or know about. Don't question your father."

Xiaofan stared at her in disbelief. After the lies, the hate, the threats from her own father—her mother would not stand for her, either. She nodded in a shaken state of horror at what her father might do to her. The possibilities were limitless.

She ran toward her room with a broken heart and shattered hope.

CHAPTER
TWO

XIAOFAN COULD NOT STOP SHIVERING WHEN SHE GOT BACK TO HER room, her shoulders aching from her father's grip. She felt like someone had crushed her bones, and her soul had left her body. She sat down on her bed with her arms wrapped tightly around herself.

"It'll be fine," she comforted herself, now understanding that she was living in a glass castle that was bound to break by someone she loved the most. The king was only going to be a father for a *boy*. That was loud and clear.

A few days had gone by, and the weather was changing. The subtle spring had transformed itself into worrisome winters for Xiaofan. She had not seen her parents or heard from them, but she would hear from her maids about their affection toward the newborn. The efforts that they were making to mark his name in the kingdom and its history were great already.

Every day, Qianfan would distribute golden coins and food amongst the underprivileged people of the kingdom to show his gratitude, to show love to his people. But Xiaofan knew now that it's all just a show, an act of pretense to care for everyone in his kingdom.

Rumors and whispers floated around the castle, questioning the presence of Xiaofan. From maids to soldiers, everyone was debating over what Xiaofan's fate would be while she locked herself in her room, isolating from the world and praying that this was all just a horrible nightmare.

Qianfan, on the other hand, was planning to get rid of her.

"Karma has spoken," he told himself. "There's no need to deal with her anymore, especially after she dared talk back to me. How *dare* she?" he whispered to himself.

His mind came up with ways to send her away, but what would he say to Daiyu? How would he convince her to send Xiaofan away, especially after Xiuying? The only person he ever held in high regards after himself was Daiyu. He loved her, but not the girls, even though they were smaller versions of his beloved. How unfortunate was he to not understand the worth of having girls born into his family?

Xiaofan's attitude toward other people had changed. Suddenly, the contentment, the reliance on the kingdom, and the trust in her parents had all vanished into thin air. The experience had somehow made her humble, humble enough to have normal conversations with the maids who looked after her growing up. Humble enough to make her understand the harsh realities of life and how quickly people can change.

This was the first time she didn't feel like she was in control. She felt feeble, yet she understood how the people of the kingdom lived—without any control and under a ruler who worked only for himself. How naïve she was to think that she would be able to help the people of the kingdom out of their mediocre miseries. She, too, was stuck behind the walls of false affection and sheer simulation.

Maybe I deserve this, she thought to herself. *This is what I get when I think I'm above and beyond everyone and everything.* Her thoughts spoke while she admired the tiny homes that she could see from her room's window. All was quiet, all was dark inside her, when all of a sudden, the door to her room swung open, and she was surprised to see her parents walk in.

"Oh, I'm so happy to see you!" Xiaofan gushed and rushed over to hug her mother while Qianfan stood next to her with a dreadful face in silence.

"I am afraid I am here with unsettling news, my darling," Daiyu muttered as she held onto Xiaofan's hand. "Your father thinks it's best that you go to training school, a place where you can learn how to behave like a royal and gain better control over your power."

"And your mother agrees," Qianfan added. "We both think it'll be best for you to move away from here. All the arrangements have been made, and you will leave today."

Xiaofan's heart sank deep into the depths of dismissal.

What's happening? They're choosing the newborn over me, and I'm going to end up like Xiuying.

"No!" she shouted and took two steps back. "No! This is my home. I am *not* going anywhere! Don't send me away," she pleaded, trying to get Daiyu to understand. To stand up for her.

"Sweetheart, this is only temporary; you will come back. But for now, you will have to go. This is what's best for you," Daiyu casually responded, barely meeting her daughter's teary gaze.

"You leave in two hours," Qianfan stated firmly. "Pack your things, everything you need, and *don't* leave anything behind," he added with a smile creeping onto his face that only showed how his plan was working out.

"This is goodbye, Xiaofan, but only for a little while," Daiyu told her. She hugged her daughter quickly and left the room, leaving Xiaofan behind in a state of hysteria.

"This is goodbye... forever," Qianfan hissed after Daiyu was gone. "You are going to pay for the rest of your life for questioning me." And then he left the room without any regret.

Xiaofan broke down completely once she was left alone once again. "Why? Why? Why?!" she cried out. "I'm sorry. Let me stay! Let me stay!" she screamed, but all her cries fell on deaf ears. There wasn't a single person in sight who would stand up for her against Qianfan.

The maids started packing her things, putting them all in wooden crates. In a matter of minutes, her room was no longer her home. It felt empty, just like her soul. She quietly sat in the corner, watching all the boxes get carried out by the soldiers.

"It's time to leave," Fang whispered in a low voice. "I'm sorry. I wish I could help you, but my hands are tied."

Xiaofan stood up with no expression on her face and started to walk out of the room. She was escorted to the grand castle door and was told to wait. After a while, Qianfan appeared.

"Farewell!" He waved with a laugh. "I'm sure you wish that you stayed within your given limits because that's where tiny dolls like you belong. The consequences of questioning me are going to weigh over your little wish of being treated equally to your brother." He paused, and then added, "Oh, apologies. Not your brother—the prince."

Xiaofan stood there in silence. She didn't reply; she didn't cry; she didn't plead to let her stay. She just accepted her fate, and after a while, the royal carriage took her to the harbor, and she boarded the ship without any hesitation.

AFTER A JOURNEY OF ABOUT TWO DAYS, FEELING AND SEEING ALL the blues, Xiaofan reached a small town. The steps ahead were only going to take her further away from her past self. She stood up straight on the deck, her body stiff, and she looked over at the wooden boxes that contained her life, which were now being transported from the ship to a black carriage. She turned around and saw the flag of her kingdom waving against the strong winds, the colors prominent over the background of dark gray clouds. This was probably the last time she would experience something that made her belong to royalty. This was probably the last time her eyes would look at the flag that once represented her home.

It was time to leave and board the carriage. She walked down the steps to the wooden harbor that looked like it would sink into the sea any minute. She sat inside the carriage, and it started to move toward a dark alley. The roads were not built properly, and the wheels of the carriage kept hitting against the loose rocks. There were no lights or lamps in the streets, there was an unbearable stench that felt like it was coming from a rotten corpse, and the hair-raising vibes and eerie atmosphere were making her fear what was ahead.

After an hour of traveling on a pathway that felt like it was never going to end, they reached a building that was in the middle of nowhere. And surrounded by a brick wall was a two-story cottage that was painted gray with black windows, and a chimney that had smoke billowing out of it. There was no greenery in sight, the grass had turned brown, and the trees were barren with dark black crows sitting on them.

Xiaofan stepped out, and her heart started to beat faster and faster with every second. She looked around and saw a few single-story shops around the borders of the cottage with rotten fruits and vegetables on display.

The gates opened, and she walked in, the soldiers carrying the wooden boxes behind her. The maid rang the doorbell, and the back door opened. A tall, stocky woman stepped out, standing straight. She was dressed in a black gown, her dark hair was tied in a braid, and she had a round face with tiny eyes that were covered by the glasses she was wearing.

"Look at this! The *princess* is here," she mocked in a sarcastic tone. "Come in, come in!" she whispered, and Xiaofan stepped in the house, taking small steps. The soldiers were told to bring the boxes into her room upstairs.

The cottage was an orphanage for young girls who had no one to look after them, all living under one roof. The wooden floor creaked with every step Xiaofan took. There were paintings of the founders hanging on each of the gray walls, the furniture was old and rusty, a huge wooden staircase led to the upper floor, and there were a few oil lamps lit up that looked like they were about to run out of juice.

Xiaofan was numb. At this point, she didn't just blame her father. She blamed herself for letting her anger cloud her mind, for letting pride take over her. Karma was performing an act of revenge, and she's its latest victim. She stood silent by the staircase as the soldiers placed all her things inside, and then they left without saying a single word to Xiaofan, leaving her there all alone with the woman wearing glasses.

"So, you are the princess whom Qianfan got rid of," she commented, and then continued in a harsh tone, "I am Liling, the headmistress of this orphanage. Now that you are here, you will have to live by *our* rules—eat what we eat, wear what the other girls wear, and have the same lifestyle as every other orphan girl here." She paused, studying Xiaofan's small form dressed in fine clothing made with royal fabrics and jewels. She scowled before continuing, "Forget about the castle because you are *never* going back there. I only agreed to keep you here because the king has offered me a generous donation. Now off you go! The first room on the left upstairs is yours."

Xiaofan bowed and silently went to find her room.

She could hear every step she took; the silence in this place was deafening. The door squeaked as she forced it open. It was a tiny room with simple gray painted walls, a small window with no curtains, and a single bed with plain white sheets and one blanket. The place was not only dark, but it was cold as well. It made her feel like she was being buried alive, her new home suffocating her.

She entered the room and closed the door behind her. The tiny room was filled with all the wooden boxes that contained her life. She sat down on the bed, took a deep breath, and started to sob without even realizing that her eyes were pouring tears. She curled up under the blanket with her arms and knees folded to her chest, questioning her very existence, questioning her life ahead, her future. She felt lonely; she had no one.

A heavy knock on her room's door disturbed her silence, and she sprung up, startled with dried tears on her face and an aching body. She struggled to get out of bed, but somehow managed to reach the door and open it up… finding herself face-to-face with a little girl her age.

"Hey," the girl said in a sweet and gentle tone. She was dressed in a long off-white gown that had a little touch of black embroidery around the neckline. She had a thin face with round eyes and long dark brown hair.

"Hi," Xiaofan responded, her voice a choked croak from all her tears.

"Can I come in?" the girl asked.

"Sure." Xiaofan opened the door wider.

"Are you okay?" the girl asked, stepping inside. "We all heard you crying."

"I'm okay," Xiaofan answered awkwardly, avoiding the girl's eyes. But then something struck her. "We?" she asked.

"Yes, all the girls—they're worried about you. We look out for each other here, and you are one of us now," the girl replied, sitting on the corner of Xiaofan's bed.

Xiaofan hesitated. "That's very thoughtful, but I'm okay." She'd never made friends and never interacted with children her age before, especially when she was at the castle, and now when they were trying to bring forward a hand of friendship, a hand of support, she hesitated.

"Alright." The girl stood up. "I understand that you are overwhelmed right now, but we are here if you want some company." The girl smiled and moved to leave, but she stopped in the doorway. "Oh, and my name is Fia."

"Xiaofan," Xiaofan mumbled, and Fia nodded and left.

Part of her wanted to follow the girl, to have someone—something—to stick to in her time of confusion and despair. But the larger part of her wanted nothing more than to be left alone. So, she closed the door to her room, encasing herself in silent darkness, and she sat down on her bed again.

This place was soaking every tiny bit of hope and life that she had left in her; darkness was all around her and affecting who she was. The girl who had ambitions, dreams, and hope was now broken, far too gone.

She was sitting alone, gazing at the moonlight shining through the tiny window when a quote that she had recently read crossed her mind.

Things get broken, and sometimes, they get repaired. But in most cases, you realize that no matter what gets damaged, life will always rearrange itself to compensate for your loss, sometimes wonderfully.

She chuckled over the fact that when she'd read it in the comfort of the castle, she believed every word of it. But now she felt like her soul was shattered into miniscule pieces that were impossible to put back together. She was broken in a way that could not be repaired.

Her thoughts were interrupted by a knock on the door… yet again.

Xiaofan stood up, got off the bed to open the door, and saw a group of bright smiles staring back at her.

"Yes?" Xiaofan asked, a bit annoyed.

"We brought you dinner," Fia answered. "And we thought we could all eat together."

Another girl added, "You should join us in Fia's room."

They waited for her to respond. How could she refuse a group of young girls who were only trying to be there for her? How could she tell them that she really didn't need any company? How could she tell them that all she wanted was to remain alone?

"So? Are you joining us?" Fia asked.

Without another second of hesitation, Xiaofan tried to smile. "Yes."

All the girls cheered after hearing her response, and they all ran straight to Fia's room. Xiaofan followed the group after closing her room's door behind her.

Fia's room felt different. She had two oil lamps that made her room bright, and she was an artist. Her room had a lot of colorful paintings on the walls, the colors making her room feel alive and joyful compared to the rest of the orphanage.

"We all usually have dinner together at the dining table in the main hall," Fia said. "But we wanted to make you feel more at home, so we're here." She smiled at Xiaofan just as the others nodded and did much of the same.

Xiaofan didn't know how to respond. "Thank you. I appreciate this, but I don't need it," she murmured.

"Of course, you need it. We all remember our first days, and they were horrible!" another girl, Xiang, added.

They all ate their dinner, and then started to share stories of their lives before the orphanage and how they ended up here. They didn't force Xiaofan to talk or share hers, but they shared their own anyway to make her feel welcomed. They seemed comfortable in telling their tales, Xiaofan noticed. There was no shame, no embarrassment.

Fia shared her story first. Her parents died in a carriage accident when she was only three years old, and her own relatives refused to take care of her. All they wanted was to get rid of her, so they sent her to this place, and she'd lived here for as long as she could remember. At first, this place was torture, but it got better after she started to make some friends. She was one of the first orphans here, and even from the very beginning, the staff never cared about the well-being of the children. They never invested in them, all their funds and donations used by the headmistress herself. Nothing came easy at this place.

Xiang was next to share her tale. Her mother died while giving birth to her, and her father blamed her for it. He refused to take her in or even see her face, forcing the nurse who helped birthed her to care for her. But after she started her own family, she also sent Xiang away, which was how she ended up here at the age of five. But she did experience love for a short while, even if it couldn't last.

Fia and Xiang were best friends. They had been there for each other ever since they'd met, and they started this tradition of welcoming new girls so that they wouldn't have to go through the same terrible experiences that they had. Xiang had experienced the worst verbal and physical abuse by the headmistress. She made Xiang do all the chores in one day—from cleaning the dishes to washing, drying, *and* folding all the clothes, from mopping the floors to dusting the rusty furniture. Liling made her do every-thing without any breaks, and at the end of the day, she was exhausted, aching, and had blisters all over her hands.

Liling also considered Xiang to be unlucky, and she made her realize that she was always going to bring bad luck for herself and everyone around her. For every bad thing that happened to Liling or to the orphanage, Xiang was blamed and held accountable, even if it had *nothing* to do with her. It was cruel, unfair, and Xiaofan felt her chest swell with anger at all the stories. The headmistress had been rude enough to *her* when *she* arrived. She couldn't even imagine the tortures that all these girls faced every day at her hands.

The next two girls to speak were sisters, Lanying and Luna. Both of them were very close to one another, sisters who were the best of friends. Their parents left them at the doorstep of this orphanage because they could not afford to feed them. And once again, Xiaofan was reminded of the little homes in her kingdom that she used to watch through her window. Her hopes, her dreams—her promises to help them. The underprivileged people had to give up everything, even their own children.

The sisters' parents left them last year, promising to return, and the sisters still believed that their parents would come back for them one day. But unbeknownst to them, that promise would never come true. Luna was a year older than Lanying, their ages eight and seven. They were both happy most of the time because they were together, even if most days were bad days inside the orphanage.

The rules to earn food were tricky; one mistake, and a child was without it for an entire day. Sometimes they had to share food or even go to sleep hungry. But the sisters made a pact that if one of them didn't get any, they'd always split what they had between the two, so neither of them would ever have to go to sleep without.

The last girl in the group seemed like a loner, not speaking or smiling as much as the others did. Her name was Suki, and she came to the orphanage willingly because her parents got divorced and remarried. Both of them created new happy families of their own, and after sweeping away their past, they swept their first daughter away with it. Neither of them wanted to keep her, and that left her with no other place to go. She came to the orphanage for shelter, food, and maybe a little bit of hope.

The group of girls inspired Xiaofan. All of them had different heartbreaking stories, but they managed to fight through all the odds and put their trust in life. Xiaofan could see it in their eyes, their smiles, and the way they told their stories with courage. This confidence, this humbling togetherness, put Xiaofan at ease. Her chest loosened, and her muscles relaxed. For the first time in days, the tears stayed away. She took a deep breath, and she decided to share her story as well.

She mumbled everything from start to finish, including how she'd treated people and looked at those who were less privileged than her. She explained what happened to her sister, the birth of her brother, and how her father sent her here to get rid of her. She even told them how she thought this was karma's revenge for how she'd behaved.

"Don't say that!" Suki comforted her. "There's always a plan for us, and things happen for a reason."

"Exactly," Fia agreed.

"And these circumstances are not the best, but at least you have us." Lanying smiled.

"Maybe," Xiaofan murmured.

They all became quiet as she thought about her past, her family, and what was to come. But then the realities of her new life in the orphanage took over. Fia broke the silence and started discussing the details for tomorrow. Chores were assigned to everyone, including Xiaofan, and in order to earn food for the day, she had to make sure that whatever she was assigned was completed with perfection. Xiaofan could think about her family, their betrayal, and her future later. For now, she needed to survive this place.

CHAPTER
THREE

The first morning at the orphanage felt like a living nightmare. Xiaofan woke up in a room that felt like a prison cell. She got out of bed, and shivers passed down her spine. And as her feet touched the cold marble floor, she gathered herself and went to wash up, only to pull her hands back when the freezing cold water touched her. There was no source of heat inside the orphanage, and the fireplace was only lit when the headmistress wanted to sit beside it, never allowing any of the girls to come near her.

Xiaofan's chore today was to clean all the bathrooms— all *eight* of them. This particular chore was supposed to be the toughest, and everyone knew that Liling was trying to torture her on purpose. But Xiaofan refused to back down from the challenge. She got dressed in the white gown that had been given to her—the same one that every girl was given to show that they belong to the orphanage—and walked down the stairs to find Liling standing at the base.

"Our tiny princess will be cleaning all the bathrooms today. Your tiny little hands are going to get all dirty!" She laughed while handing over a bucket of soapy water and a mop. "Get started if you want to save yourself from hunger. And make sure *everything* is sparkling clean. I will make you do it all over again if I see even a single speck of dirt."

Xiaofan silently took the cleaning supplies and nodded. She found herself inside the first bathroom, and the stench was making it hard to breathe. One look at the grime settled into every nook and cranny, and her tenacity crumbled.

"I can't do this. I can't do this," she repeated to herself, staring at the dirty walls and muddy floor. Never before had she had to clean. Never before had she thought she would. But now her survival banked on her ability to do it properly.

"Why?" she choked on a rising sob.

She sat outside the door and tried to calm herself as she realized how poorly she'd treated her maids at the castle. She had insulted them, taunted them, and now she was doing what they did every day—cleaning the mess that someone else had created.

"It's all karma," she whispered to herself. With that thought, she forced herself to understand that she had to go through all of this in order to reach the end, in order to make it to a better side. She stood up, gripped the mop tightly, and turned back into the bathroom.

"I *can* do this. I *will* do this," she kept whispering to herself as she started to clean. "This is all going to be over one day."

The first bathroom was spotless by the time she finished, and Liling couldn't point out any problems or faults. So, Xiaofan moved onto the next. One after another, Xiaofan eventually managed to clean most of the bathrooms, and Liling approved them when she finished. The entire day had passed, and Xiaofan hadn't eaten *anything* while the rest of the girls finished their lunch hours ago. She was tired, aching, and she desperately wanted sleep, but she still had two more to go. It took her an hour to finish cleaning the last of them, but when Liling found a speck—a tiny little piece of dirt—on the floor, she refused to feed her.

"But—I've worked the entire day!" Xiaofan pleaded. "Please don't do this!"

"Rules are rules. You have to *earn* your food with honesty and hard work," Liling firmly said as she mopped up the speck of dirt that she found. She set the mop head down with a wincing *clang*! "You don't get food when you don't work properly. Now go to your room!"

Tears started to roll down Xiaofan's face as she ran to her room and slammed the door behind her. Everyone heard it, but the girls knew that this was going to happen. This was something that Liling *always* did to the new girls. Luckily, they'd all saved small amounts of food from their own meals and were waiting for her to come upstairs to eat. Liling never checked on them, especially after sunset, so they didn't have to worry about getting caught.

Xiaofan was crying her eyes out on her bed when the girls knocked on her door.

"Not now!" Xiaofan yelled. "Leave me alone!"

The girls looked at each other with concern. They didn't take Xiaofan's behavior to heart as they all understood how taxing all of this was for her. They knocked again, softer this time.

"We have food for you," Fia said in a cheery voice. "You have worked really hard today, so come eat."

"We all saved a little bit of our own food for you," Suki added, hoping that it'll convince Xiaofan to open up.

The moment she heard that, Xiaofan lifted her head. It was in that moment that she came to the realization that she was repeating the same behavior that led her into this mess—the same behavior that made karma come after her. She was projecting her problems and emotions onto others, and she'd promised herself that she'd change. She gathered the little strength she had remaining and opened the door to all the smiling girls.

"I'm sorry," Xiaofan sniffled.

"It's okay; it's been a hard day for you," Fia reassured her. They all gave her a group hug as they entered her room.

"You don't have to apologize," Luna whispered.

Lanying agreed, "We have all been through this. Liling always manages to point out a fault."

Suki added, "Yes, and when she cannot find any, she intends to create them."

Xiang jumped in. "And most of the time, she plots them herself. Nobody gets the opportunity to eat on their first day. We've all experienced it, and that's why we're here for you."

"Thank you. This means a lot to me. I don't even know how I'm going to pay you back for all of this." Xiaofan wiped away her tears with a sleeve.

Fia waved her off. "There are no paybacks in this family."

After that day, their friendship tightened. Even though

every day at the orphanage was a pain, the wrath of Liling was never a surprise. It felt like it was her life's mission to make the lives of the girls miserable, but at the end of the day, they all had each other to lean on, to share secrets with, and to vent about their problems with. They'd created their own little family at a place that was known to be a shelter for those without one.

They'd found a family in each other.

Xiaofan slowly began to come out of her shell. She became more expressive and talked about things that bothered her or meant a lot to her. It was hard for her to leave the comfort of the castle and find a new home here, but her life before was a false reality, and what she had found here—in a group of young girls—was something that she could never have experienced in her old life.

TEN YEARS SOON PASSED IN THE BLINK OF AN EYE. THE GIRLS HAD all grown up, even though much of the orphanage hadn't changed. They were all still subjected to extreme lengths of physical and mental abuse, the living standards remained detrimental, and the structure of the orphanage had corroded. The town was always taken over by extreme winters, and there would be long, endless days without sunlight or blue skies. Most of the days at the orphanage were full of sorrow and remorse, only a small percentage being somewhat close to comfort.

The past decade had made Xiaofan learn a lot about the town, the orphanage, and their headmistress. She understood emotions that she never knew existed, half of them just extensions of melancholy. Pure happiness was something that she had forgotten about, and the only thing she cherished about that phase of her life was the friendship she had with the orphan girls.

They would often gather at night just to talk over saved food and stolen hot chocolate. They once decorated their rooms, but Liling marched upstairs unannounced one evening and ripped down all the artwork that they had made. They never tried to stand up for themselves because Liling held the power over their livelihoods. She could do anything she wanted to harm the girls. She refused to fix the nails coming out of the floorboards, and the girls would often end up getting injured. She also refused to fix the rooftops, causing freezing rain to pour inside.

Liling was coldblooded. It almost seemed like she had no humanity in her, no sense of empathy for the girls.

Xiaofan hadn't been in touch with her powers once since leaving the castle ten years prior. She almost felt like they didn't exist anymore because she had been nothing but numb for the longest time. She only felt sorrow, and in order to take control over her power, she had to experience *different* emotions. Here at the orphanage, nobody knew that Xiaofan had a magical power. She never mentioned or projected them because they were something from her past, and she didn't want to remember them.

On top of it all, even though Xiaofan was fond of the girls at the orphanage, she often felt like she was everyone's second choice. The girls had been together long before her arrival, and even though they welcomed her with open arms, she felt like a gap was present between them. A gap of time and things that she could not comprehend.

Maybe she was overthinking this. Maybe it was her insecurity taking control over her, but she felt like everyone prioritized others over her. She always felt like she was constantly the last one picked, and that always brought back painful memories. She remembered how her father chose her brother over her and sent her away. She often thought about how her mother never reached out, never wanted her back from the fake training school that she was attending. Perhaps she *did* know where Xiaofan really was and just didn't care. Maybe she only wanted betterment for herself, and standing up to Qianfan or coming to get her daughter would have only created problems for her.

"Good for her," Xiaofan would always say whenever she thought about her mother.

The town that she was in was known for its darkness and practices of black magic. They had a tendency to worship the evil spirits and let them roam free in this worldly realm. There were brothels on every street, drunk men lying on every corner. The town was not safe for *anyone*, especially young girls. Even if the girls *did* finish their chores early and were permitted to leave, they always confined themselves within the walls of the orphanage. Angry, evil spirits roamed there, and Liling was the center of it all.

Liling was the most wicked individual that Xiaofan had ever come across, and she *never* let the girls out of her sight. Xiaofan often thought about Liling's life before she became the headmistress of this torture chamber. Maybe, like her, Liling had also endured great extents of pain, and she was putting up a façade to hide all her scars.

Xiaofan, Xiang, Luna, Suki, and Fia were all seventeen now, while Lanying was just a year younger. The orphanage had five beautiful teenage girls residing there, and the place had become a hot topic of discussion in town. Drunk men would show up at the door, banging on it loudly to let them in. Strangers crept around the orphanage's grounds and lurked across the street. Liling would even receive invitations to events that would allow the girls to interact with the men of town.

But the headmistress always declined the invitations, even when she was being offered handsome amounts of money. The girls were still her responsibility, and despite how much she hated them, she still protected them from the darkness looming outside.

The girls woke up one morning to see complete darkness outside. The sky was covered with thick, dark gray clouds that were about to welcome a hail storm at any minute. They all came out of their rooms and assembled for breakfast.

"Something feels different today," Suki muttered while trying to light the oil lamps in the entrance hallway.

"Yeah, you're right," Xiaofan replied. "It feels like something really bad is ahead of us."

"Let's *not* let that thought ponder over us." Suki smiled and went to grab breakfast—boiled beans and black tea.

"Oh, how delightful!" Fia commented sarcastically as she filled her plate.

"At least we aren't being starved to death," Suki commented.

"Suki, take a break from all your positivity and gratitude for once," Fia muttered. "I just want to feel what I feel right now—ungrateful."

"I second that!" Luna chuckled with a mouthful of beans.

Xiaofan felt the air change, and she feared for something unknown. Most of the time, she stayed silent during their conversations. She kept her opinions to herself and only answered if someone asked her a question or spoke to her directly. The girls understood that about her and always respected her space.

After ten minutes, they all went to different corners of the orphanage to complete their chores. They had a rule—start early, finish early. But this rule never meant much because the chores usually took all day to complete, and after that, they had to study, leaving them exhausted.

The sky grew darker as hours passed by, the roaring thunder leaving the weak walls of the orphanage startled. After a while, it started to hail, and the ceiling inside their rooms started to leak.

"Wipe up the floors! There's water everywhere!" Liling demanded.

The girls looked at each other, all with no will to grab the brooms and wipe the floors clean. But they knew they couldn't go against Liling, so each of them grabbed their supplies to mop... except Xiaofan. Her stomach cramped and squeezed. Her arms sagged with fatigue. Her head spun from the dizziness and lack of nutrition. She couldn't do one more second of cleaning. She *wouldn't*.

"No," she whispered, looking down at the floor as her stomach growled.

"What did you say?" Liling took a step toward her, her face tight.

"I said, *no*. No, I am *not* doing this. I'm tired, and I'm hungry. I'm *not* going to spend another hour cleaning these stupid floors on an empty stomach!" she yelled.

"Watch your tone!" Liling spat before her lips curled into a snarl. "You are going to regret this."

"Bullshit! The only thing I regret is staying here under your supervision. You don't have a heart; you don't care. You never have!" Xiaofan screamed.

"Then what are you waiting for? Leave!" Liling suggested with a snicker. "You think *I* don't care? Wait until you go outside these walls. People will eat you alive. They're ready to hunt a pretty princess like you."

Xiaofan laughed in disbelief. "How can a monstrosity like you even *think* about talking about the evils of life? I would rather live on the street than under your command for one more second!" Xiaofan bellowed.

Liling could not accept the disrespect, and she had reached the verge of her patience. How *dare* she question her? How *dare* she call her a *monster*? After all she had done for the little ungrateful twit—how dare she?

Liling grabbed her by the shoulder and pushed her out of the orphanage into the pouring rain. The girls called out behind them, and Xiaofan fought against her grip, but nothing could stop the storm of the headmistress.

"Your wish is my command. Go die on the street for all I care," Liling spat as she kicked Xiaofan outside. She locked the door behind her when she came back in and ordered the girls to go to their rooms.

"Please, let her in! She'll freeze to death!" Fia cried out.

"Anyone who wants to advocate for her can go join her outside," Liling declared, thinking that threat would shut them up. But Fia took a step forward.

"Fine. I will go then. I will *not* leave her alone."

"I will, too!" Luna added, stepping up beside Fia.

"Me, too," Xiang murmured.

"Yes. Us, too," Suki and Lanying agreed.

They all unlocked the door without waiting for a response from Liling, and they marched outside. The door slammed shut behind them, but they didn't bother turning around to look. They searched everywhere for Xiaofan, but she was nowhere to be seen. The pouring rain had turned into a slight drizzle, but it was still very dark.

Liling stared at them from her room's window, hoping

they would come to their senses. She snickered to herself as she watched them wander aimlessly. Her mind already started coming up with a list of things that she could do to punish them after this.

After about an hour, Liling walked over to the entrance and opened the door, indicating that the girls were allowed back in. Xiaofan was nowhere to be found, and the freezing rain was beginning to send shivers throughout their bodies, forcing the girls to give up and retreat back inside.

"Where could she be?" Fia muttered.

"I don't know," Xiang whispered.

"I hope she's safe." Luna looked over her shoulder as they walked in, leaving the door open for Xiaofan to follow if she was still out there.

"Back already?" Liling chuckled. "Where's the rebel? Hiding behind you all?"

All of them just stared at her.

Fia broke the silence. "She's not here."

She's not—? Liling's mind repeated those words again and again. What if someone had taken her? What if she became a victim of something unspeakable? Questions started to cloud her mind, and she left for her room without punishing the girls, without saying a word.

Hours ticked by into the night, every second leading them toward the possibility of never seeing Xiaofan again. Fia paced back and forth in the hallway while all the other girls sat by the fireplace, something they were never allowed to do. The room was filled with silence, and the air was getting harder and harder to breathe as it soaked up their anxious thoughts.

"We should have said something," Fia mumbled and sat down by the fireplace. "We were too late. We should've said something when she stood up to Liling."

Nobody answered at first, exchanging glances with each other instead.

But then Suki spoke, "We *did* go after her; we were just too late."

Fia wiped her tears away. "Yeah, too late."

Lanying and Luna remained silent, sitting close to each other.

"This is on her; it's not our fault. Her ungrateful attitude went to her head. Girls like us don't have a choice but to compromise with reality," Xiang whispered quietly. "We can't blame ourselves."

"Well, we can't blame her, either. She stood up for us!" Fia argued.

"Yelling at each other isn't going to help bring her back! Get over yourself!" Xiang yelled, leaving Fia speechless. After a moment of silence, Xiang sighed, defeated. "I didn't mean that."

Fia mumbled, "I'm sorry."

Now it was Xiang's turn to let the tears fall. "I-I just don't know what's happening," she stuttered.

"It's okay," Fia replied and reached over to give her a hug.

While Fia and the girls were praying for a miracle, Liling was out looking for Xiaofan. She waited hours and hours for her to show up, and when she didn't, she went out to search for her herself. Maybe she really *did* have a heart.

Liling was also an orphan, still bearing the scars of a childhood spent inside an orphanage. She was subjected to harassment and abuse several times during her early teen years. And now, she was stuck running the very same orphanage that had done her dirty. The memories she had in here were not something she wanted to remember, and she only took her rage out on the orphans to protect herself. All these years, she tried to hold it together, tried to keep up that wall of apathy. But the moment that Xiaofan didn't come back in, she couldn't help but fear that she'd face the same tragedies that Liling had as a child.

She roamed the streets and knocked on several doors, asking if anyone had seen a young adolescent girl. After searching for several hours and coming up empty, her mind convinced her to give up and head back to the orphanage. Her steps toward the orphanage were slow, and her mind was filled with guilt. She entered the main gate and closed it gently behind her. Her eyes continued to look around but failed to detect anything that would lead her to Xiaofan.

But just as she reached the front door, she heard a strange sound coming from the back yard. She slowly walked around the building and closed her umbrella, ready to use it as a weapon in case someone or something jumped at her. Suddenly, she saw a piece of white cloth that looked very similar to what Xiaofan was wearing. She ran toward the cloth and found the girl lying on the ground, unconscious and with a high temperature.

"My child! My sweet, sweet child!" Liling whispered, thanking the sky for keeping her protected from the predators outside. She held Xiaofan's lifeless body in her arms and carried her to the front entrance.

Liling pushed open the door and rushed toward the fireplace. The girls quickly jumped up at her sudden appearance before moving aside when they realized who the headmistress was carrying. Liling was completely soaked from the rain, and with apprehension visible on her face, she placed Xiaofan on top of the warm blankets that Fia had laid down on the floor. The girls surrounded her after running to grab more blankets and some hot tea. They covered her and gave her everything that she would possibly need to fight a severe cold.

An hour later, Xiaofan woke up to find everyone settled around her.

"You're okay," Fia muttered with dried tears around her eyes.

"Here, get up. Eat some soup," Xiang ordered her.

"Liling made it for you," Lanying revealed.

Xiaofan felt too weak to get up on her own, so Suki helped her sit up and held her tight so she could focus on the bowl. "Is it poisoned?" she asked.

Everyone stared at each other.

"No," Liling answered politely, stepping back into the room.

Xiaofan gave her a look of uncertainty, but she sipped at the warm soup, nonetheless. It was too fragrant to ignore.

"Oh, it's very... good," Xiaofan whispered, and then a laugh bubbled out of her.

Xiaofan looked at Liling over the top of her bowl, remembering everything that she had heard while she was unconscious. She had heard *everything*—how the headmistress was worried about her and how she went out into the pouring rain to look for her. Maybe Liling was a different version of herself now. Xiaofan finished her soup, and gracefully thanked Liling for taking care of her.

The headmistress escorted all the girls back to their rooms for bed. When she got to Xiaofan's room, she sat down beside her after tucking her in.

"What happened?" she asked quietly.

"What?" Xiaofan looked up from above her thick blankets.

"When you were outside. Did something happen?"

Xiaofan paused. "No," she admitted. "After you left, I went to the back yard and slept."

"Okay, good." Liling sighed with relief, chuckling at the silliness of the whole situation and her long, unnecessary search. The girl had been in the back yard all along.

She went back to her own room after wishing the orphan a good night and turning off the lights.

But Xiaofan lied awake in the dark. She had lied to Liling and the others. Something *did* happen while she was out in the wild. But she wasn't ready to talk about it. Plus, she sensed that Liling change for the better because of this, and she would blame herself if the truth ruined it.

When Liling left her outside, she just stood there, regretting taking a stand for the girls and for herself. She was afraid, but a part of her was determined to prove her point. She saw the door close before her very eyes and heard Liling locking it, and that's when it clicked—there was no going back.

Xiaofan looked around and saw a group of men leering at her while smoking cigars and drinking from glass bottles. She always watched over this street from her room's tiny window, but standing here felt different. She felt eyes all over her, making her feel uncomfortable, something she hadn't felt in a very long time.

She started walking toward the left side of the street. The sky had grown darker, and it almost felt like it was midnight. The eyes followed her with every step she took, and after a while, she noticed that a trio of men were following her. There was no one else on these streets as Xiaofan's steps became quicker, but the faster she tried to walk, the closer the footsteps behind her got.

She started to run, her heart pounding loudly in her

ears. *Mother, protect me*, she prayed, when suddenly, she felt someone grabbing her by the waist.

"Looks like the little lamb has lost her way," one of the men whispered into her ear.

"Get your hands off of me!" Xiaofan screamed.

"Run! Run... *if you can*," the man laughed.

The other two men had disappeared, and Xiaofan knew she had to fight for herself; she didn't have much time. She screamed again, but there was no one around to hear her. Rage—that's all she felt, and after struggling to get out of the man's grip, her body started to grow warmer and warmer.

Suddenly, her hands turned into two flaming fireballs that burnt the man's wrists and his upper arms, which were wrapped around her. He screamed in hysteria and loosened his grip on her. She could see the fear in his eyes and felt herself smile.

"Who's the little lamb now?" Xiaofan yelled as she pointed her hands toward him and started to throw balls of fire. Seeing this, the man turned and ran for his life.

Xiaofan calmed down after she saw him disappear into the darkness. Her hands turned back to normal when her heart rate eventually settled. She smirked at her warm hands, feeling the magic within her pulsing and flowing with life.

She rushed back toward the orphanage, not wanting to attract any more attention on the dark street. Xiaofan was shivering, traumatized, even if her magic *did* just save her life. She stood in front of the door, but she didn't have the mental stability to confront Liling, so she went around to the back yard instead.

What just happened? A few minutes ago, she was covered in fireballs, and now she felt like she was going to freeze to death. With her thoughts racing, she started to feel dizzy, and before she knew it, she fell unconscious on top of the wet grass.

When she regained consciousness, she was back inside, surrounded by Liling and the girls of the orphanage. They offered her love and comfort; they prayed for her to get better.

The last few hours had slipped her mind, and she couldn't remember anything after she had fainted except for the cries of Liling. And the sight that she saw when she opened her eyes again was something she had never seen before in her ten years of living here. The incident had brought them all together and changed Liling for the better. There was no way she was going to ruin all that.

But in the quiet solitude of her own room, the trauma came flooding back.

CHAPTER

FOUR

THE INCIDENT HAD AN IMPACT ON EVERYONE AFTER THAT NIGHT, especially Liling. She completely changed the menu of the orphanage to meals that the girls liked, took away all their chores, and even hired someone to fix the roof. She started treating them better, splurging on them, and told them that the only thing they had to focus on were their studies.

Liling realized after that fateful night that she was never at peace, that she was only torturing herself by projecting her emotions onto the girls. She knew she had to make their experiences at the orphanage better so they'd never have to go through what she went through. She knew she'd only be at peace after she made things right for these girls.

The girls had also gotten stronger after that night, and they realized how much they loved each other after almost losing Xiaofan.

Xiaofan, on the other hand, did what she did best—put on a show. She claimed she was fine. She laughed and joked around, but deep down, she could still feel the hands wrapped around her, suffocating her. She would lock herself in her room for hours and cry, and she'd constantly have nightmares of men laughing at her replaying over and over inside her head.

Her emotions were all over the place, and she couldn't control them *or* her power. The dark shadows that used to loom over the orphanage were slowly being lifted, but they were all transferred to Xiaofan.

Three months passed by before the girls and Liling finally started noticing her isolation, but no one reached out to her. They just assumed it was something to do with her past, and they chose to leave her alone because that's what Xiaofan usually preferred.

One day, Xiaofan heard a noise coming from outside her room, a noise she'd never heard before. She peeked out the window and saw carriages passing by, all with royal guards sitting inside them. The carriages stopped at a distance, and the guards stepped off. They were dressed in formal black uniforms, and all of them had swords beside them. The guards cleared the street and took their positions on both sides, capturing Xiaofan's attention.

A few minutes passed, and nothing more happened, but when Xiaofan started to turn away, a much larger carriage —one led by white stallions—showed up and stopped right in front of the orphanage.

The guards tried to clear the surrounding streets, but their presence only brought in a larger crowd. Men, women, and children stood on both sides of the road, eager to know what was happening.

A man then walked out of the large carriage and loudly announced, "Make way for Queen Xiuying!"

"Xiuying?" Xiaofan heard herself say. "Queen? How?"

The sister her parents had abandoned was now a queen? She couldn't understand what was happening as she glimpsed from the tiny window of her room, hearing chants of people praising the queen. Xiaofan decided to ignore all that was happening because she knew that there was no way her sister would come all the way here just to see her. She told herself that this had *nothing* to do with her and forced herself to sleep.

Xiaofan woke up a few hours later to find Xiuying sitting on the side of her bed. She slowly opened her eyes and rubbed at them—she must still be inside her own dream. But Xiuying was really there, grinning down at her and holding her hand. Xiaofan sat up.

"Hi, Sister," Xiuying greeted gently.

"Hi...," Xiaofan replied with great hesitation.

Is she really here for me?

Was this all a lie?

Was she ever abandoned?

Xiuying stood up and took a deep breath, trying to think about how to start the conversation. "Xiaofan, I am your sister."

Xiaofan was now looking down at her hands and noticed that Xiuying had a tiny mark there, too. She stayed silent for a few seconds before whispering, "I know."

"How do you know?" Xiuying asked, raising a brow in question.

The flood of memories rushed back to Xiaofan—everything that had haunted her since she was eight years old.

She was a different person now, but with her sister standing right in front of her... she didn't feel so alone anymore.

"A maid from our castle told me about you, and when I questioned our father and tried to ask about you, he sent me here. He resented me for talking back, for disobeying his rules," Xiaofan replied with tears burning her eyes.

Xiuying sat down beside the bed, her eyes glowing with unshed tears of her own. "I'm sorry that you had to suffer because of me."

"No, not because of you," Xiaofan continued. "He finally has a son, what he's wanted all along. With a baby boy in his life, he no longer needed me. I just hope he becomes a true father for our brother."

"People like him can *never* become parents. I met him two years ago. And let me tell you, *nothing* has changed."

"What do you mean?" Xiaofan perked up.

"Mother and Father reached out to me when I got married to the Prince of Baoshu. The letter that they wrote to me mentioned you. I only went back to our kingdom to meet you, but you weren't there. Father told me how he'd sent you away, and I've been looking for you ever since. From island to island, from shelter to shelter."

Xiuying looked up at her sister, that warm smile blooming once more.

The words that came out of Xiuying's mouth calmed Xiaofan for the first time in months. Someone was there for her, someone who cared, someone who didn't give up on her. That's all she ever wanted, and Xiuying, the sister she'd never known, had given her that.

Xiaofan started to cry when she heard her sister explain her struggles of finding her, and Xiuying comforted her, assuring her that things were only going to get better from here on out. Xiuying sat beside Xiaofan on her bed with a warm blanket wrapped around her. She wiped her tears away as she finished her story, and they started to talk as sisters and friends. They had so much to catch up on.

Xiuying told her about her own life, how her birth was mourned as a death at Jinu, how she was brought up by a nanny named Mei, how she felt neglected and abandoned, how she survived suicide, and how Mei stood up for her.

She explained in detail her journey to the island of Naje. She talked about Huizhong and his letters, along with her new life on the island. She mentioned Hua, and the way she took her in and showered her with love and affection. She told her about her best friend, Meili, and how Zhang magically appeared in her life. Finally, she talked about her life at her new kingdom, her wedding, her visit to their parents, and how she ended up here.

Xiaofan was bewildered. Her older sister went through extreme measures just to reach her, and Xiaofan felt waves of guilt rush through her bones for merely suffering alone at the orphanage this whole time. It had consumed her life, but still, it seemed like nothing compared to Xiuying's life.

"I have dreamt about this day every night for the past two years. I'm grateful that I have finally found you, and from here on out, I will be there for you." Xiuying took her sister's hand and squeezed it gently. Xiaofan looked up from their embrace, only to meet Xiuying's serious gaze. "I won't let you stay here any longer."

This reunion brought a sheer sense of felicity for both of the sisters. Looking at the dreadful conditions of the town and the eclipse that it sheltered within, Xiuying refused to leave her sister in this filth. Even though the town itself was home to obscurity and sin, the orphanage felt like an escape from all evil. Xiuying was amazed to see the bond that all the girls and the headmistress had, and was completely oblivious to what had happened in the past.

After the heartfelt exchange, Xiaofan accepted Xiuying's offer to join her at her new castle and leave this nightmare behind. But the girls. She had made true friends during her stay, and whether she wanted to admit it or not, she was going to miss them. Their secret getaways, shared sorrows, and cheery chatters. They were a part of her life; they were her sisters before Xiuying showed up. They gave her hope and a family when she needed them the most. She would never forget that.

Xiaofan packed her belongings into a small wooden box, suddenly realizing how little she had. The orphanage had taken plenty from her, but it also made her understand herself in a better way. She was able to recognize her *true* self and grow into someone stronger. The town and its people made her take control over her power and helped her become humble. The prideful Xiaofan who walked in a decade ago was no longer there, and maybe *that* was the most valuable thing that she could bring with her.

The door to Xiaofan's room opened with a subtle knock. It was Xiuying.

"Ready to leave?" she whispered with a grin, and Xiaofan nodded.

This was the last time that Xiaofan would be in this tiny, damp room. The room had been home to bitter memories at first, but it also housed many good ones with the girls, and eventually, with Liling, who had turned into a loving caretaker. She stood in the doorway and gave it one last look before pulling the door shut behind her, leaving her past and her dark memories behind.

She walked down the staircase to find everyone standing there to wish her a happy farewell. All her friends were standing in line, holding presents that they wanted her to have. Fia handed over a painting that she had made of all the girls.

"So you don't forget us," Fia mumbled, sniffling.

"I'll *never* forget you guys," Xiaofan whispered.

Xiang gave her a knitted scarf that had all of their initials embroidered onto it.

"This is beautiful." Xiaofan took it gratefully, smiling at her friend.

Lanying, Luna, and Suki brought out a cake that they had baked for Xiaofan, with frosting on it that said, *You will always be family.* Xiaofan found herself speechless; it was the people that she was going to miss the most. Even if she didn't accept this place as her home, she still had a family here.

Liling hugged her. "You have changed things for the better. Thank you."

They all walked Xiaofan out to the main gate of the orphanage, and the girls called for a group hug one more time before Xiaofan stepped onto the carriage with her sister. Xiuying was surprised to witness all the emotions, but she was glad that Xiaofan had the support of these girls when she couldn't be there to support her sister. Her happiness caused her own power to stir inside her, and suddenly, golden shimmering dust appeared in the air, leaving everyone in awe.

Within a matter of seconds, the area surrounding the orphanage was covered with bushy green trees. The grass turned green, and flowers of all kind began wrapping around the walls of the orphanage. As a gesture of good will, Xiuying handed over two boxes filled with gold coins to Liling, and the headmistress promised that she would look after the girls and their well-being.

Xiaofan was stunned, speechless. The power that Xiuying had was simply... beautiful.

I wish I were like her, Xiaofan thought to herself, admiring the flowers around her and admittedly feeling a little envious at the same time.

Xiuying boarded the carriage after Xiaofan, and they were escorted by guards to the harbor. Xiaofan peeked from the door's window and noticed that nothing had changed about the town. It looked just like it did the day she came here—the harbor was in a horrible condition, and there were no boats around except for the three that belonged to Xiuying. History was repeating itself, and Xiaofan found herself going back to royalty, feeling the same emotions that she felt whenever she thought of that word.

The ship began to set sail, and the town started to shrink in the distance, but Xiaofan kept her eyes on it until she could no longer make out the buildings.

"Xiaofan?" Xiuying whispered as she stepped up beside her. "Are you okay?"

Xiaofan nodded but stayed silent, and Xiuying was starting to notice her sister's scars. The orphanage, the kingdom, their father—they had all ruined her. And it was time for Xiuying to heal those wounds and make it all better.

"Let me show you your room!" Xiuying turned, and Xiaofan followed her.

They walked down the deck to an enormous room, one that was way bigger than any of the rooms at the orphanage. It held a single bed with light pink silk sheets and drapes, there were pink roses placed inside a vase on a wooden desk beside some books, and the room was lit with several oil lamps.

"Y-You d-didn't have to do all this," Xiaofan stammered.

"I did, Sister. I did," Xiuying replied, beaming at her. "Now relax! I'll be back for you in a bit." With that, she turned toward her own room and left Xiaofan alone to gather her thoughts.

Xiaofan took a deep breath, closed the door, and sat down on the bed. All of this was so surreal! She stood up and walked over to the table, picked up a book, and flipped it over in her palms. It was thick and heavy, something she hadn't seen in ages. She remembered a time when she used to read books like a maniac, but now she couldn't find it in herself to concentrate. Her passions had been taken away by the wretched town over time.

She placed the book back in its place and walked back to the bed that felt foreign to her. It was so soft, so clean, nothing like her bed at the orphanage. It was... strange, and she felt like an intruder in her own room.

A BIT LATER, XIAOFAN WOKE UP TO A KNOCK ON HER DOOR.

"You may enter," she called out groggily.

Xiuying entered with a shiny silver tray in her hands. She hopped onto the bed with her legs crossed as she faced Xiaofan.

"Did I wake you?" she asked.

"No, I was already up," Xiaofan lied.

"Great! I baked some moon cakes for you," Xiuying revealed giddily as she uncovered the tray.

Xiaofan's eyes widened with delight. "They look delicious, but what are these again?"

"Moon cakes are a specialty in our kingdom, preferred

during moments of delight and celebration," Xiuying explained.

Xiaofan beamed and took a bite.

"This is amazing!" Xiaofan moaned against the sweet warmth of the cake coating her tongue. She took another bite. "I could have this every day!"

Xiuying laughed. "Well, I'm sure you're going to admire the kingdom and its people just as well."

Xiaofan looked down all of a sudden. She didn't know what to say nor what to expect. Xiuying paused, noticing her hesitation. She reached out and touched her sister's hand.

"I know this is scary for you. It's a big change, and I went through something similar, so I can understand the emotions that you're going through. I didn't believe Zhang either when he assured me that the kingdom was going to welcome me with open arms, but I saw it for myself. You *will* be welcomed, like you are coming home, Xiaofan. I promise you." She squeezed her hand, and Xiaofan's chewing slowed as she looked at her. "Everyone has been worried for you, ever since we found out about you. Even though they haven't met you, the people of Baoshu have been eagerly awaiting for your arrival. And I'm sure they are going to love you when they meet you in person." Xiuying smiled, but Xiaofan stayed silent for a few seconds.

"I don't know who I am, and I don't like who I was before at the kingdom. I was filled with uncontained pride, and that's what led me to my downfall. Like Father said, it's karma."

"What do you mean?" Xiuying asked.

Xiaofan took a slow, heavy breath. "Father believed that the way he treated you was the reason why his second child was a daughter, too. He deemed that the universe was punishing him for the way he treated you. He acknowledged that what he did was evil, but he felt no regret; in order to reverse the vengeance of karma, he tried his best to treat me right. He gave me everything that I wanted and acted like a loving father should. And then, after years of pretense, he was given a son. His third child was a blessing for him after all this time, and in his eyes, karma was on his side again. After our brother's birth, things changed. His attention shifted, and he abandoned me," Xiaofan paused and gasped for air.

"I wasn't an amiable person at the kingdom," she continued after catching her breath. "I treated people like they were debris. The grandeur, the pretense of love, and all the privilege had gone to my head. I lost count of how many people I've mocked, offended, and insulted. I was *not* respected; I was feared, and I looked at everyone like they were beneath me. Just like Father did. That's why karma did what it did to me—pride dragged me to the pits of despair. I don't want to be like that again, Xiuying."

"Xiaofan, maybe you're seeing all this in the wrong light. You are afraid that royalty is going to make you prideful again, but you are also forgetting that you can be proud *without* being vain. There is nothing wrong with being proud of yourself; it's something that human beings are particularly prone to. You need to understand that you *can* be humble *and* proud of yourself, all at the same time. You are no longer who you were at the kingdom, right?" Xiaofan's eyes flickered. "Time has passed, and you've grown to be a wonderful person. You were a child back then. You have learned so much, stayed humble, and made great friends. You are not who you were. People change, and *you* have changed."

Xiuying squeezed Xiaofan's hands tightly, and for the first time since they met, Xiaofan squeezed back.

Xiaofan finally felt at peace after such a long time. She had kept all this inside for years, and saying it out loud made her feel like a tumor had been removed. She had never seen her situation from the perspective that Xiuying showed her, but with it, the darkness in her heart lightened.

"Thank you," she whispered. "Thank you for everything. And thank you for listening to me."

"What are sisters for?" Xiuying joked, lightening the tension in the room. "You can *always* trust me, Xiaofan. You're the only blood family I have, and I will *always* look out for you. Got it?"

"Got it." Xiaofan grinned and began to munch on the moon cakes again. "These really *are* remarkably delicious."

Xiuying chuckled and poured some tea as they talked about the Baoshu Kingdom, Zhang, and the Wei family.

CHAPTER
FIVE

THE JOURNEY TO THE KINGDOM TOOK THREE DAYS, AND THE sisters didn't spend even a minute apart. Xiuying felt like she held the responsibility to make her sister feel at ease, to make her feel at home, just like Zhang did when *she* needed it. Xiuying realized that she was the backbone of the family, and she promised herself that she was *never* going to let her younger sister down, especially after everything that had happened in their lives.

Hours before they were due to reach the kingdom, Xiuying got ready. She wore a pink gown with long bell-shaped sleeves and tiny flowers embroidered onto it, tied her hair into a bun with a tiny tiara, and colored her lips with handmade rosy balm. After she was done, she rushed to Xiaofan's room with a dress that she had selected. It was a purple silk gown with tight sleeves and a collar embroidered with jewels.

"Here! I grabbed this for you when I was leaving the kingdom," Xiuying said with a grin.

Xiaofan blushed as she eyed the dress. "This is beautiful." She held the dress closer to her, but she couldn't ignore Xiuying's smile. "You're being so kind to me," she murmured, heat welling in her chest.

Xiuying laughed and waved her off. "Oh, stop it and get ready. We're about to reach the kingdom!"

Xiaofan's eyes sparkled as she stared at her new dress. She had never worn a gown like this, not even at her own castle. And it felt like such a relief to finally get out of the same rag that she's been wearing at the orphanage. She slid on the dress, let her hair down, applied the balm that Xiuying had given her onto her lips, and she brushed her cheeks with peach powder.

When she was done, she turned around to face the mirror and lightly gasped. She didn't even recognize herself! The last time she looked this pretty was when she was going to attend her brother's welcoming ball. That memory of such a dreadful day would have brought her down normally, but her excitement brushed the thought away. She would've never imagined her life turning out the way it did, and she owed it all to her big sister.

A loud bang sounded outside the ship, and Xiaofan turned away from her reflection.

"We're here," she whispered to herself with a mixture of trepidation and delight.

Her sudden urge to get a glimpse of the kingdom brought her toward the window of her room. One look outside, and she gasped. It was huge! She could see the castle from afar, and the landscape looked like someone had painted it in vibrant flowery shades. This kingdom looked like it came out of a fairytale and was the complete opposite of the town where she had spent a lifetime in.

She swung open her door and slowly went up the stairs to the deck, where she found Xiuying standing at the front of the ship, waving to the people who had gathered while the soldiers and maids transported items from the ship to the carriages. Xiaofan was about to walk up to her, but then something stopped her.

I'm nothing but a mere peasant compared to the great queen.

Xiuying turned her body slightly, and she saw her baby sister with the corner of her eye. She waved her hands abruptly, indicating for Xiaofan to join her.

Xiaofan stepped back, slowly moving her head from left to right. She knew she didn't belong up there in front of the public.

"Nonsense!" Xiuying whispered to herself and rushed to grab Xiaofan. "Come on! What's with all this formality?" She pulled Xiaofan by the wrist and brought her to the front of the deck. The moment she arrived, someone standing on the edge of the harbor loudly announced, "Let's all welcome Princess Xiaofan, sister of Queen Xiuying!"

With that, everyone cheered for her, and Xiaofan was taken aback. She never would've expected such an overwhelming response from people she didn't even know. Her heart was filled with happiness, and she started to cry as she squeezed Xiuying's hand. Her sister smiled at her.

"I told you," Xiuying lightly teased.

Xiaofan nodded while she waved at the people who were cheering for her, never wanting to forget this sight— the people throwing flower petals at them in celebration, the fragrant aroma lingering in the air, and being able to finally stand next to someone who loved her.

A guard informed them that their carriages were ready, and they stepped off the ship together. The harbor here was different from the one near the orphanage; it was well-constructed, massive, and strong. There were several ships docked on the harbor with huge flags waving the kingdom's crest.

Xiaofan got into the carriage, and her journey toward the castle began. Passed the harbor, she noticed the busy streets, the tiny homes decorated with dragons, red lamps hanging over every corner, and flowers of every kind that painted the town in rainbow colors. They even passed the market, and she saw how alive the place was with shoppers buying products left and right and kids running around freely. For the first time in years, she felt safe, comfortable, and at peace.

This felt like *home*.

Xiuying stayed silent to let her sister enjoy her moment. The carriages reached the castle soon enough and stopped right outside the grand staircase. Xiaofan and Xiuying climbed out and found armed guards standing on both sides of the staircase, which had a red carpet neatly laid out in the middle of it.

Xiaofan couldn't stop admiring the place as she took a few steps forward. Her eyes were on the castle and its details. The wooden dragon carvings on the doors were something that she had never seen before. Baoshu Kingdom was grand and luxurious, even compared to Jinu, and she found herself overwhelmed by everything in front of her.

They reached the main entrance and were welcomed by

Zhang's sisters and their mother. They all hugged Xiaofan and introduced themselves eagerly.

"We're so glad to finally meet you, my dear," Huiqing, Zhang's mother, greeted as she held onto Xiaofan's hands.

"Yes, this is a sight for sore eyes. Xiuying has looked *everywhere* for you," Kyrie declared.

"This calls for a celebration!" Kamari cried.

"Indeed, but where are Zhang and Father?" Xiuying asked, looking around.

"They went on a voyage three days ago to increase the security of the kingdom. They should be home tonight," Huiqing informed them.

"Zhang *did* mention it before, but I was unaware that they had to leave so soon," Xiuying whispered.

"He didn't know. It was *very* last minute. Don't worry!" Kyrie assured her.

"Yeah! Now let's get ready for that celebratory dinner! Come on, Xiuying, we have lots to do," Kamari added, tugging on Xiuying's hand.

"Alright." Xiuying chuckled.

"In the meantime, I'll show Xiaofan her room!" Kyrie declared and turned to Xiaofan with a beaming smile.

Xiuying, Kamari, and Huiqing went into the kitchen while Kyrie escorted Xiaofan to her room. The girls were both the same age, and a genuine friendship was bound to be born.

"Everything has been so out of place lately with all the wedding preparations and Xiuying being gone. I'm so happy that we found you before my wedding," Kyrie cheerily told Xiaofan.

"Congratulations! When is the wedding? Who's the groom?" Xiaofan asked with surprise and excitement.

"The wedding is in two weeks, and the groom is the

Prince of Umai. He's so handsome, and I still can't believe I'm actually getting married to him!" Kyrie squealed and opened the door to Xiaofan's room. "Here we are! And I'm *right* next door if you need anything. I'll let you get settled in before I tell you the rest of my love story." Kyrie winked.

"I can't wait." Xiaofan smirked before Kyrie closed the door behind her.

Xiaofan turned around to see an enormous room that was even more luxurious than the one on the ship had been. The room came with a walk-in wardrobe that was filled with gowns of every color, a tremendous bathroom that had handmade soaps and scented candles scattered about, and a wooden desk by the window with all the essentials.

"Am I in Heaven?" she asked herself and sighed with joy.

She spent the entire afternoon trying on the dresses that were hung inside her closet, and she treated herself with a long, long bath. It was clear that she hadn't forgotten how to treat herself like royalty.

Darkness swept over the kingdom soon enough, and Xiaofan got herself ready for dinner. She hadn't seen Xiuying ever since they entered the kingdom, but Xiuying was the queen of Baoshu, so Xiaofan understood that she had things to take care of. She threw on a lilac gown and tied a matching ribbon around her hair. She then used a little blush to polish her cheeks pink when a knock sounded on her door.

"Come in!" Xiaofan called.

Xiuying popped her head in and entered the room.

"You look so beautiful, Xiaofan."

"Thank you, as do you, Sister."

"Do you like your room? Clearly, you have seen the

clothes that I have picked out for you. Do you like them?" Xiuying asked.

"I love them! You have *exceptional* taste." Xiaofan twirled around in her dress to prove her point.

Xiuying chuckled. "I'm so glad that you like them. And you know, if there's anything else you need, just say it."

Xiaofan beamed. "I already have everything I need, thanks to my big sister!"

Xiuying laughed. "Okay, then. Ready to go?"

Xiaofan nodded, and the two of them left for the dining room.

The dining room at Baoshu showcased a beautiful wall with a cherry blossom tree painted on it. Candles were lit up in every corner that made the room shine, and the small flames looked like stars dancing around the large tree. Kyrie and Kamari were already sitting down when Xiaofan and Xiuying joined them.

"So? How does the place look to you?" Kamari asked Xiaofan.

"Amazing! I have never seen such elegance in a room before. Everything looks beyond perfect."

"Can we talk about the wedding now? It's just two weeks away!" Kyrie pleaded.

Xiuying snickered and whispered, "Someone's being impatient."

Kyrie huffed, and soon, they heard footsteps approaching them from behind. Xiuying spun around and saw her husband standing behind her.

"You're back!" Xiuying screamed with excitement and jumped up to hug him.

"I've missed you," Zhang whispered and kissed her on the cheek. He held her for a few minutes before pulling back, just enough to look into her eyes. "You're even more beautiful than when I left."

Kamari coughed to make everyone else's presence known, and then started to laugh hysterically.

"Oh, grow up, will you?" Zhang teased, still holding onto Xiuying.

"I found her," Xiuying whispered, and then Zhang looked around to find Xiaofan standing beside his sisters.

"You're finally here!" He stepped toward her, arms outstretched. "Your sister and I have looked *everywhere* for you. Welcome home!" He gave her a light hug, and while Xiaofan hesitated for a moment, she hugged him right back. "Oh, I almost forgot! I want to introduce you all to someone."

Kyrie glanced around, but no one else was there. "Are you talking about your shadow, Zhang? Or perhaps a ghost?"

The sarcastic tone in Kyrie's voice made everyone laugh, but just seconds later, a tall and handsome brown-eyed man walked into the room.

"Ah, here he is!" Zhang announced. "This is Prince Han Qin of the Shénhuà Kingdom."

Han looked around and smiled at everyone, his eyes on Xiaofan the longest. He was Zhang's oldest childhood friend, so Kyrie and Kamari recognized his face. When he was properly introduced to Xiuying and Xiaofan, Ming and Huiqing entered the room for dinner. The rest of the night was spent talking about Xiaofan's dream of becoming a writer, Kyrie's upcoming wedding, and Zhang's stories from his voyage. For the first time in her life, Xiaofan felt like part of a loving family.

"Women are the leaders of our future. You should join Kyrie when she visits the university," Ming suggested.

Xiaofan's intellectual side was praised by everyone at the table and secretly admired by Han. She didn't exchange any words with Han, but they learned a little about each other as others spoke. Xiaofan found out that Han was the only child born in his kingdom, was passionate about improving living conditions for the unfortunate, and he had come to Baoshu specifically to attend Kyrie's wedding.

THE NEXT MORNING, XIAOFAN FOUND HERSELF THINKING ABOUT Han as the sun shone through her window. They had just met, but for some reason, she found herself drawn to him, her heart wanting to pounce out of her chest and run over to him. She was so used to keeping to herself, but there was just something about him that made her want to go against her habit.

"Come in!" she called out when she heard a knock on her door, and Kyrie came skipping into the room.

"Good morning, Sleepyhead!" Kyrie exclaimed in a cheerful tone.

"Morning to you, too."

"Why are you still in bed? We have to visit the university today. Father instructed me to take you there as soon as we're up," Kyrie said.

"Oh, right. I almost forgot." Xiaofan quickly stumbled out of bed.

"Really? I wonder what you could possibly be distracted by." Kyrie winked.

Xiaofan felt her cheeks turn hot. "What do you mean?"

"Oh, please, I saw the way you were looking at Han!" Kyrie teased.

"I wasn't looking at him."

"Yeah, okay." Kyrie snorted. "You're totally in love!"

"I *just* met him, Kyrie. I *can't* be in love. But that reminds me, you still have to tell me *your* love story."

Xiaofan turned toward her wardrobe, hoping that Kyrie would get the hint and change the topic.

"Nice try, but get dressed. I'll tell you on the way."

Kyrie walked out and left Xiaofan alone to choose an outfit that would be suitable for her important day. She'd spent most of her life in a filthy orphanage that she'd almost forgotten how to dress.

"Ready for your big day?" Xiuying asked as she peeked inside the room.

"I think so," Xiaofan replied with a nervous smile.

"Best of luck, Xiaofan. I'm proud to be your big sister."

"Xiaofan, it's time to leave!" Kyrie came running into the room again.

Within minutes, they were inside the royal carriage, and Kyrie revealed that she met her fiancé, Zhao, at Xiuying and Zhang's wedding. It was love at first sight, and he asked for her hand in marriage a month later.

"I never thought I would end up with someone who makes me believe in fairytales. I knew what love was, but I never felt it before I met Zhao. I can talk to him about anything without feeling like he'd judge me. He supports me all the way, and I feel truly blessed."

"You certainly *sound* like you're in love. I'm happy for you," Xiaofan replied, wondering if she would ever experience what Kyrie was feeling. It felt so... genuine.

Xiaofan never expected herself to be with a man, especially not after her traumatic experience with men back at that ruthless town. It scarred her, and she had given up on the idea of love. But after last night, after Han, she wasn't so sure anymore.

When they arrived at the university, Xiaofan found it even more extravagant than the castle. Almost everything was intricately carved in wood, and pillars of spiritual animals lined every building. There were beautiful fountains everywhere she turned, and the blooming gardens were much, much bigger than her orphanage.

"You *must* see the library. It's the largest in the entire world." Kyrie pulled Xiaofan and started running toward the west wing.

"There's so much to see and so little time!"

"After a week, you'll be spending every day in here."

When they walked in, Xiaofan could see books lining every corner of the room, stacked from the bottom all the way to the top. She took a deep breath as she stood there and breathed it all in. The smell of fresh pages, ink, and old books always made her feel at home, and it'd been almost a decade since she stepped foot inside one.

"This is divine," she whispered. Xiaofan wandered around and gathered some books to take home while Kyrie sat down at a wooden desk.

"Han?" Kyrie asked loudly.

He lifted his head, which was buried inside the book that he was reading.

"Kyrie?" Han whispered.

Kyrie walked over to him and sat down beside him. "You *have* always been a nerd, haven't you?" she teased.

"I have. I'm surprised to see you here, though."

"You know me well. I've never been a fan of reading. But I wanted to bring Xiaofan here. She just enrolled."

"Good for her," Han replied, his eyes scanning the room in search of Xiaofan.

"She's right behind you."

"I'm not looking for her."

"I never said you were." Kyrie laughed, inviting Xiaofan over to the table. "Xiaofan, look who I found buried under a pile of books!" Kyrie yelled, directing everyone's attention toward them.

Xiaofan's heart started to pound against her chest as she heard Kyrie. A part of her hoped that it was Han, but another part of her was nervous to see him again. She gathered her books into her arms and walked toward the table.

Han turned as she approached and couldn't stop staring at her.

"Hey," he whispered with a smile.

"Hi," Xiaofan replied, placing her books onto the table.

"I have no idea why people read. It's so boring!" Kyrie remarked.

"Only people with a *stable* brain can read. I understand why this doesn't sit well for you," Han mocked, causing Xiaofan to chuckle.

"Oh, please!" Kyrie said with a sneer. "I just prefer not to. Why are you here, anyway?"

"I had some spare time on my hands. Don't worry, everything will still be perfect for your wedding."

Kyrie rolled her eyes. "Yeah, sure. Anyway, I have to run. Do you mind escorting Xiaofan back to the castle?"

Xiaofan shot daggers at her friend, but before she could interject, Han replied, "It would be my pleasure."

Silence had taken over after Kyrie threw a wink over at Xiaofan and disappeared. Han offered Xiaofan the seat in front of him, and they both started to read without saying a single word to each other. Xiaofan went through all her books, one after another, reading the pages with transcendent enthusiasm while Han was only pretending to read. He glanced up at her every now and then, and admired how passionate she was.

"Han?" Xiaofan murmured, waiting for him to respond. But her voice had gone unheard as his mind was busy thinking about her over a blank page in his book.

"Han?" she said a bit louder, and his head popped up.

"S-Sorry, did you say something?"

"Do you mind if we leave now? I have to reach the castle before sunset."

"Anything for the princess." He smiled at her as he got up from his chair and placed his book back onto the shelf. "Are you taking these books with you?"

"No, I'm done," Xiaofan replied and put hers back as well.

They silently walked out of the library and continued down the hallway.

"So?" Han asked.

"So?" Xiaofan repeated, failing to understand the question.

"You're quite the reader," Han commented. "I must say, I am impressed."

"I can say the same about you."

"I was hardly reading." Han admitted. "I was too busy paying attention to you."

"Why's that?"

"Because I find you fascinating, and I can't wait to learn more about you."

As he looked into her eyes and smiled, Xiaofan could feel herself blushing and quickly turned her head away.

I can't be in love. I can't!

CHAPTER

SIX

"You don't talk much, do you?" Han asked on their way back to the castle.

"What?" Xiaofan asked back.

"Well, we've been sitting in this carriage for the past thirty minutes, and you haven't said a single word."

"I do t-talk," she stuttered. "I just don't have anything to say right now."

"Let me help you out, then. I can't let this silence steal away my opportunity to get to know you better." He grinned at her. "But I feel like we already have so much in common."

"Indeed, we do."

With each sentence, Xiaofan found herself slowly

opening up to Han, and she even found herself falling for him more and more after learning about his love for politics and discovering the true meaning of life.

Maybe I shouldn't be so afraid of love after all.

They reached the castle just as the sun was beginning to set. The sky glowed all sorts of pretty colors—pink, orange, yellow, purple. Han stepped out first and opened the door for Xiaofan as the carriage came to a stop.

"I told you we'd be back in time." He smiled.

"You're a man of your word." Xiaofan smiled back.

"I hope I can see you again soon, Xiaofan."

"Maybe," Xiaofan whispered and started to walk toward the grand entrance.

Han found himself grinning from ear to ear as he stood there, watching Xiaofan disappear up the stairs and into the castle. His heart was pulling him in different directions. He wanted to be with Xiaofan as he couldn't stop thinking about her, but his parents—they wanted a different path for him. They wanted a different *girl* for him, a girl they had already chosen, and Han *had* agreed to this... *before* he met Xiaofan. He didn't want to disobey his parents—he couldn't—but after meeting *her*, he was torn.

He was drawn to Xiaofan; he was falling in love with her. Xiaofan felt like home to him from the moment his eyes met hers. However, he realized that he was losing grasp of the reality his parents had designed for him, and the only possible consequence for his affection toward Xiaofan would be unrecoverable heartbreak for them both.

The colors of the sky faded slowly, turning into a shade of darkness that reminded Han of himself. His heart was gambling with fate, and there was *nothing* he could do to stop it. He couldn't get Xiaofan out of his thoughts, his future and his parents' plan tossed to the wayside. The only thing that mattered to him now was seeing Xiaofan again.

Xiaofan's walk to her room was overwhelming. Her thoughts, emotions, and feelings refused to give her peace, and with every step, questions arose in her mind. Was she in love? Were her feelings for him even reciprocated?

She couldn't get his smiling face out of her mind. His voice was on a loop, saying her name again and again. It felt like home when he said it, along with the sparkle in his eyes. And whenever she closed her eyes, she saw his reflection. She opened the door to her room and entered to find Kyrie waiting for her on her bed. She met her eyes with that knowing smirk of hers as Xiaofan closed the door behind her.

"Where have *you* been?" Kyrie teased.

Xiaofan shook her head and chuckled, refusing to fall prey to Kyrie's antics. But Kyrie wouldn't let her get away *that* easily.

"I see that smile... and the light in your pretty, pretty eyes, Xiaofan." She poked and prodded, scooting closer to the edge of the bed. "Spill the beans already!"

Xiaofan sighed dramatically and sat beside her friend. "Alright, alright." After another steadying breath, she told her everything. "The ride back home was long, but it felt like it only lasted minutes. Han started the conversation by saying he wanted to know me, and I hesitated at first. But then—I don't know what happened, but everything shifted. I felt like I had known him my entire life. We talked about everything, and he made me laugh a lot. I don't remember the last time I was this happy. I just... didn't want the journey to end."

"You *do* love him!" Kyrie squealed. "I knew it! I knew it the first time I saw you two staring at each other." Kyrie jumped in excitement. "I'm so happy for you, Xiaofan. And you know, Han doesn't interact with people much, so the fact that he wanted to get to know you shows that he feels something toward you, too."

"Let's not get ahead of ourselves." Xiaofan held up her hands to slow down her friend. "Things usually come crumbling down whenever I hope for them to work out."

That sent a pang through Xiaofan's chest, but she ignored it. It wasn't untrue, but saying it out loud felt... vulnerable in a way.

"It's going to be *different* this time," Kyrie assured her, but then her eyes flickered to the clock on the wall. "Let's finish this later. We have to go!"

Xiaofan raised a brow at her. "Go where?"

"Tea! Kamari and Xiuying are waiting for us," Kyrie told her, and Xiaofan jumped up. She was eager to see the others, but especially Xiuying.

Evening tea was being served at the grand terrace, with a breathtaking view of the ocean, mountains, and the city.

"This is heavenly," Xiaofan whispered as her eyes glazed over the picturesque surroundings.

Xiuying brewed the tea herself and baked Xiaofan's favorite moon cakes, and Xiaofan couldn't get enough.

"I repeat, I could have these *every day* without getting sick of them." Xiaofan moaned with a stuffed mouth.

"Most of the preparations for the wedding are done," Kamari said.

"All that's left are the food and our dresses," Xiuying added.

"That's great! We had a rather... interesting day, too." Kyrie winked and wagged her brows at Xiaofan.

"Really?" Kamari asked.

"Tell us about it," Xiuying said, setting her teacup down.

Kyrie gave Xiaofan a look as if asking for her permission. Xiaofan rolled her eyes but nodded reluctantly. Kyrie quickly and eagerly told them everything—how they ran into Han, how she came up with the idea to leave them alone, and their conversation during the ride home. She took *all* the credit.

"They wouldn't have even said a word to each other if it wasn't for me." Kyrie pointed at her chest with a wide grin.

Xiaofan rolled her eyes again, but the other two laughed.

"Xiaofan, Han is an exceptional human being. You will be lucky to have him by your side," Kamari said, taking a sip of her tea.

"I also noticed him staring at Xiaofan during dinner, but I thought I was just seeing things," Xiuying admitted. "I still need time to process this because you *are* my baby sister, but I am so glad that this happened." Xiuying smiled over the lip of her teacup as she took another slow sip.

"I don't know... Maybe we're just friends." Xiaofan whispered with flushed cheeks.

"Let's hope not!" Xiuying exclaimed.

"We second that!" Kamari and Kyrie agreed while raising their cups.

"Either way, can we *please* keep this between us?" Xiaofan asked.

Xiuying blinked. "Of course, Xiaofan. My lips are sealed."

"What were we even talking about?" Kamari giggled.

"I'll never say a word," Kyrie said, and everyone laughed.

"Especially you, Kyrie." Xiaofan swatted at her friend.

Xiuying felt euphoric seeing how her sister had found a friend in Kyrie, just like she'd found a friend in Kamari when she first arrived. And she secretly hoped that Han would be the one for her sister.

The rest of the evening was spent discussing color combinations for the wedding dresses. But Xiaofan's heart was elsewhere. She felt like she'd left herself with Han inside the carriage and was longing to see him again.

Xiaofan walked back to her room after the evening team. She'd expected Han to show up, but when he didn't, she felt her heart beginning to ache. Her eyes were locked on the door the whole evening, anticipating his presence and hoping that he would walk in at any minute. She was impatiently waiting to see him again, and she continued to wait for him even after everyone else had left. But her hopes were left empty.

She reached her room with a sense of anguish. The room was darker than usual; only a few of the candles were lit, so she decided to light some more. The darkness always stifled her. She lit one candle at a time, and once she was satisfied, she sat at her desk and propped open a book from the collection in her room.

The Scripted Affection, the cover read. She opened the book and started to read the first page. "To feel estranged has been a constant state of mind for me. To belong somewhere or to a person is all that my heart has ever wanted. I'm always trying to get back to somewhere imaginary. My life feels like an eternity of long-lost longing." She closed the book. The fact that she could understand and relate to every word made her feel trivial, and she didn't want to read anymore.

She wrapped herself in a thick wool blanket and closed her eyes.

The Scripted Affection... was it a sign? Maybe the universe was telling her that she was scripting a tale of love that had absolutely no significance. Maybe she had misread Han's signs, and he really *did* just want to be friends. Her clouded mind whirled, spiraling deeper and deeper toward the darkness. Before she knew it, her body fell victim to that darkness, and her mind quieted.

Xiaofan woke up in the middle of the night covered in sweat and tears. The room had fallen silent around her, and all the candles were blown out by the force of brisk winds that came through the window. The only source of light was coming from the faint shimmer of the moon. Her hands were sweaty and aching; she kept rubbing them together, but the sensations didn't cease. Unable to breathe properly, she got out of bed and ignored the dizziness inside her head as she walked toward the window.

She just had a nightmare that made her re-experience the ill-fated event that transpired outside her old orphanage. Even after all this time, it felt so real, like she was there all over again. She could feel the hands grabbing her, she could hear the sinister laughter, and she remembered how feeble and alone she'd felt. It was something she *never* wanted to experience again, but here she was, struggling to forget. This was the one thing she kept to herself; not even her own sister knew. Perhaps that was the reason why it was weighing her down with iron fists that wouldn't give.

Xiaofan stood by the window but still struggled to breathe properly as thick tears started rolling down her cheeks. She didn't know what to do, how to escape her past and its dark memories, so she went outside. Maybe a walk around the garden would clear her mind.

She silently walked down the hall and out through a side door with a candle in her hand. She stopped when she reached a window that faced the town and showed her a view of the magnificent trees beyond. The atmosphere was still dark, covered by a little fog, but the lights lit inside the homes looked like tiny stars to her. Xiaofan felt too weak to walk any further, so she placed the candle on a step beside her, and she sat down with her head placed on her knees and her arms wrapped around her legs.

She sat there for a few minutes in solitude until she heard footsteps approaching. Her heart started to beat faster, and once again, she struggled to breathe. She was safe inside a guarded castle, but her experience had made her cautious of everything and everyone. She squeezed her eyes shut as the footsteps stopped.

"Xiaofan?"

Her eyes flared open as she heard a voice and recognized the softness in the tone. It was Han. The last thing she wanted was to let him see her in such a vulnerable state, so she lifted her hand and waved weakly. But Han's worried gaze didn't waver.

"What are you doing here? It's past midnight." He was standing behind her and was able to recognize her even in the dark because of the ribbon that she always wore around her hair.

"I j-just...," Xiaofan stuttered in a weak voice. "I just needed some air."

"Is it okay if I join you?"

Xiaofan wavered, but her voice came out in a quiet whisper. "Yes."

Han sat next to her on the staircase, not giving her a chance to hesitate again.

Xiaofan looked up toward the town, and Han noticed that her eyes were red but shining with the reflection of the town's lights. Her nose had turned pink, and the golden light of the candle was making her look even more pale than she already was. He knew something had happened, something so dreadful that it took the hopefulness away from her voice. All he wanted was to help her, to steal all the tears away and reinstate her laughter. Even if he *had* decided that she would no longer be the source of *his* despair.

After making peace with the decision to stay away from Xiaofan and follow the path that his parents had paved for him, Han couldn't fall asleep. How could he possibly forget the one girl who made him feel alive? But no matter how much he tried to forget about her and never see her again, he couldn't. It just wasn't in their cards.

The silence between them was comfortable. Han was there for her without needing to say a word. He sat beside her and gazed at the lights sprinkled across town. He wanted to give her some space and respect her privacy, so he decided not to ask any questions. But Xiaofan surprised him with answers, nonetheless.

"I had a nightmare about something that happened to me," she mumbled against her knees. He looked at her for a moment before glancing back toward the lights, giving her time and space to elaborate. "I thought I had moved on from this, and that I would never have to mention it to anyone," she continued, looking down at her hands. "I thought that if I pretended that it never happened, I would start believing that it didn't."

Tears started to roll from her eyes, and Han wanted nothing more than to pull her into a tight embrace and kiss her.

"When I lived at the orphanage, some of the men in town tried to force themselves on me," she admitted, her voice getting thicker and tighter with tears. "I escaped, but the memories are still alive. I can still hear their barks of laughter and feel their hands on me like it happened just yesterday. I hate it. I hate it *so much*, and all I want to do is forget about it. I've tried to move on—to forget—but I can't. I can't—" Xiaofan broke into shivering sobs.

Han was aware of her history; Zhang had told him all about her struggles—her time at the orphanage and how Xiuying found her, but he had never mentioned the men. Han was at a loss for words. He felt rage boiling under his skin, prickling his blood. Life had taken so much from Xiaofan, and he struggled to find words that would make her feel better.

Xiaofan sniffled in the silence. "I've never told anyone, not even Xiuying. I have always been petrified of people questioning my dignity and asking me to relive it by explaining what had happened. It was easier to pretend that it didn't happen at all. But you can only pretend for so long." She wiped at her eyes and cheeks with her sleeve.

"Your secret is safe with me, Xiaofan. And... well, you shouldn't question yourself."

"What do you mean?"

"I mean... this experience of yours and your vulnerability... it has only made me respect you more," Han told her, his voice steadying and growing stronger.

She looked at him as her tears dried. His words brought her comfort, and the darkness swirling in her mind had lifted. The burden of her past had been removed with only a few comforting words from this man she so admired.

"Thank you," Xiaofan whispered.

"For what?" Han peeked at her.

For everything, she wanted to say. "For staying here with me, for listening to me."

Han smiled and shook his head. "You don't have to

thank me for that. I'll always be there for you. You have my word."

Her smile was back, and he thanked the universe at the sight of it. He never imagined that he would feel gratitude over a simple smile, but here he was. And he wished for nothing more. After another moment of silence between them, Xiaofan cleared her throat.

"And what brings you here? Why aren't you asleep?" she asked.

Han shrugged. "I just couldn't, and sometimes I like to walk around to declutter my thoughts."

"Anything you want to share? I can try to alleviate some of it." Xiaofan nudged his arm gently.

"Nah, it's nothing serious." Han shook it off with a wave.

As much as he wanted to, he just wasn't ready to admit his feelings for her and why he couldn't be with her. Especially not when *he* was still confused himself. The chemistry between them was unreal, and he wished he only knew how *she* felt about *him*.

And how could he choose between someone he'd only just met and his own family? He needed help; he needed Zhang. Xiuying was Zhang's future, and Han felt almost certain that Xiaofan was his.

CHAPTER

SEVEN

Xiaofan felt different when she woke up the next morning. After last night's terror and the paradisiacal interaction with Han, she'd convinced herself that he loved her, too—that she was *finally* going to get her own happy ending. She never thought sharing this unfortunate event would bring the person she loved closer to her. And Han's support, his soft, considerate voice, and his affectionate words were still on repeat in her mind.

But she had to focus today. She had to accompany Xiuying, Kamari, and Kyrie to the dress fitting. She jumped out of bed, got dressed, and hurried to join them for breakfast. Although she was over the moon from last night, she decided to keep the interaction to herself. It wasn't that she

256

didn't trust her sister or her friends; she trusted them with all her heart. But she wanted to keep this moment of sheer happiness a secret, and she wasn't ready to reveal to them the events that led up to that moment.

While the hustle and bustle of the wedding preparations were keeping Xiaofan occupied, Han was trying to get himself out of a dilemma that was making him lose sleep every night.

He was with Zhang at the kingdom's library, impatiently waiting for the right opportunity to bring it up. Luckily, he didn't have to wait long.

"So, what's going on with you and Xiaofan?"

Han paused, and then sat next to Zhang as they stared at the painting of a mystical black dragon on the wall opposite them.

"What do you mean?" Han replied, feigning ignorance.

"Xiuying might have mentioned something."

"Like what?" Han asked, hoping that Xiuying had told him Xiaofan's true feelings for Han.

"Xiaofan is quite fond of you, I assume. I won't go into greater detail because I promised my wife that I wouldn't, but this is a hint for you in case you haven't caught on." Zhang leaned in and lowered his voice. "She is an extraordinary girl."

Han huffed out a dry laugh. "Oh, I know."

"Is there something you're not telling me?" his friend prodded.

Han took a deep breath and admitted *everything* that he had been holding in.

"I *love* Xiaofan. I feel very strongly toward her. I admire her strength, her wisdom, her passions, and her beauty, of course. Every time I interact with her, I cherish every second, and when she's gone, I long for her presence. I have never felt what I feel toward Xiaofan for anyone else. Is that crazy?"

Zhang chuckled, his smile all too knowing. "Well, that's great, right? You love her, and she has feelings for you, too. People who feel affection toward one another belong together. It's that simple."

But Han sighed in distress and curled in on himself. He ran his fingers through his hair as he rested his head on his knees. "It's *not* that simple," he whispered.

"Why not?" Zhang asked.

"You've known me since childhood, and you have met my parents. You know how traditional and strict they are."

Zhang shook his head, that smile still lingering. "Yes, but—"

"But—nothing, Zhang. Being their only child, they have outlined my life for me, made decisions on my behalf, and I have *always* agreed with them. Last year, my father decided that he would soon step down from the throne, leaving it to me. With that, my parents have already decided that the future queen would be the princess of our neighboring kingdom. They asked for her hand in marriage on my behalf *without* even talking to me first. But I am bound to follow the choices that they have made, even if I don't like them."

Zhang's eyes widened at Han's confession, but it didn't end there.

"I trusted their judgment, and at the time, I wasn't even interested in anyone else. But now... since Xiaofan..." Han tensed, and Zhang's chest constricted for his friend. "I haven't even *met* the other girl, and I don't wish to, now that I have met Xiaofan. But it isn't my choice, and I am to be married in the next six months. I don't know what to do, Zhang. My heart belongs to Xiaofan." He paused, his eyes flickering up at the painting again. "My father wants me to marry a princess so that our kingdom grows stronger. He has given his word, and he's *not* going to take it back, no matter what happens. I cannot forget Xiaofan, and I certainly cannot choose between her and my parents."

Zhang was quiet as he contemplated Han's words. His friend had a reason to be stressed; he couldn't even imagine how he must be feeling. Han was right. His parents were *never* going to understand or backtrack from their words as they never had before. But he couldn't just let go of his own love and affection for Xiaofan... now that he had found it.

"I never thought I'd find love, and now that I have, I don't want to lose it. But... I don't want to lose my family, either," Han whispered, keeping his eyes forward.

"You can't give up, Han. You have to reason with your parents if you truly love her. You have to fight for her." Zhang gently patted his friend's back. "Your parents will be here for the wedding; talk to them. They might understand."

Han remained quiet as Zhang's words tumbled through his mind. It all made sense, and what he said seemed reasonable. He had to do it. He had to tell his parents about Xiaofan, and he could only hope that his parents would listen.

"I'll talk to them when they arrive." Han's muscles visually relaxed.

Zhang smirked and added, "Besides, Xiaofan *is* a princess of *this* kingdom *and* the one where she was born. If your parents want you to marry a princess, then Xiaofan is kind of perfect. And you know, my kingdom is your ally, always."

Han sighed in relief. "I appreciate that."

Zhang stood up and patted Han's shoulder once more. "I will always be here to offer support, you know that. I can't let my best friend go into battle unprepared while fighting for the most important person in his life."

Han chuckled, the entire room lightening with his laugh. "Thanks, truly."

"Don't mention it."

Zhang then excused himself to aid Kyrie's never-ending wedding needs, leaving Han alone. Han would indeed talk to his parents, but he wanted to refrain from confessing his feelings to Xiaofan for the time being. He wanted to examine every possibility, every positive *and* negative outcome, and he didn't want to make Xiaofan a promise that he couldn't keep.

His parents were supposed to arrive at Baoshu tomorrow, so he had to stay away from Xiaofan until then. He didn't trust himself to be near her; he didn't trust himself to resist running up to her and kissing her hard on her sweet lips. But knowing that *she* also had feelings for *him* made him feel hopeful, and he was going to do everything he could to be with the woman he loved.

XIAOFAN ADMIRED THE VIEWS BELOW HER—THE WAVES CRASHING against the shore, and the ships approaching the harbor that looked like tiny ants swimming through the ocean and struggling to reach dry land—the day before Kyrie's wedding, and she closed her eyes as the breeze slowly brushed against her face and ruffled through her hair. She felt so appreciative for this moment and everything she had right now—her new incredible family, an extraordinary and overly empathic sister, a best friend whom she could share her secrets with, and most importantly, the potential love of her life.

But she couldn't help but wonder what his *true* feelings for her were. Every time she thought they were getting along, he'd disappear for hours after. And they were always meeting by chance, not by choice. Was he avoiding her?

"Men. They're always such an enigma," she whispered to herself and turned to go back inside to get dressed for the big dinner.

"Dinner? What dinner? Why didn't you tell me this sooner?" Han exclaimed to Zhang while he marched from corner to corner in his room. "I'm supposed to be *avoiding* Xiaofan until my parents come, not having dinner with her!"

"Well, it wouldn't *just* be with her. We'll all be there. And you know you can't disappoint Kyrie. She'll never get over it," Zhang told him firmly.

"But what if I accidentally say something that I'm not supposed to? I can't just ignore her if she's sitting right in front of me!"

Zhang groaned. "It is what it is, Han. You can't stop fate's bidding."

Han was hesitant, but then his pacing slowed to a stop. He gave his friend one final look before nodding once. "You're right. Let's do this."

The dinner was held at the back courtyard of the kingdom. The ground was covered with well-trimmed green grass, shadowed by rich willow trees that were in full bloom with luminous yellow flowers dancing in the breeze. A handwoven carpet was spread in the middle of the yard, and a long, thin table was placed over it. There were glass chandeliers hanging from the trees with tiny candles lit upon them, the air was fresh with a fragrance of cherry blossoms flowing through it, and oil lamps were hung on every perch.

Xiuying and Kamari were the first ones to reach the courtyard, followed by Zhang and Han. The two men were left speechless as their eyes gazed over the dinner setup. Both of them were thoroughly impressed by how ravishing and elegant it looked.

Ming and Huiqing walked in next.

"This looks like a fairytale!" Huiqing smiled in awe.

"It sure does," Ming agreed.

When Xiaofan walked in with Kyrie—the guest of honor—Kyrie started to cry at how beautiful everything looked. Zhang gave her a hug while everyone else clapped.

Han, however, couldn't take his eyes off of Xiaofan. His heart started to beat faster with every step she took toward the table. Her hair was curled with her bangs hanging loose, she wore a shimmery lilac dress, her cheeks glowed a baby pink, and he couldn't look away.

Xiaofan sat next to him, and Han struggled with the internal battle between his heart and his mind. He wanted to reach out and touch Xiaofan, but he knew he shouldn't. He held himself back. Instead, he turned toward Zhang and started talking to him, but he could feel Xiaofan's flickering glances on him, and his fingers twitched to reach out and take hers. He clenched them tightly on his lap.

The table was full of cheers as they celebrated Kyrie's last meal at home. She was always the brightest light in the room, so full of laughter and warmth. The castle wouldn't be the same without her.

But while everyone else cheered, Xiaofan felt a knife piercing through her heart. Kyrie was her friend, her *best* friend. And even though they'd only known each other for a short time, she found her irreplaceable. What would she do without her? Her mind darkened, and she looked for support to her left. Han *did* promise to always support her, be there when she needed it. And yet, Han hadn't looked at her once since she arrived.

Maybe it was all just a misunderstanding, and I misread him, Xiaofan thought as she took a sip from her soup that had now grown cold. They bonded; they had become friends, and maybe... more? *Was it all just my imagination?* He had been so open, so caring, and now... he wouldn't even look at her. She was about to lose her best friend, and now the man she thought she loved left her feeling even more alone.

All she wanted to do was run to her room and hide under her blankets so she wouldn't have to face any of this. But she couldn't. How could she leave Kyrie's final dinner? How could she let down someone who had been like a sister to her since the day she arrived? She couldn't.

Xiuying was worried when she saw Xiaofan's face darken and her body curl inwards. Han's attention was on Zhang, and Kyrie was busy interacting with her parents. She knew Xiaofan probably felt incredibly alone. Xiuying knew the feeling all too well in her past. But this feeling of isolation... it wasn't necessary. It could be avoided.

She knew how much Xiaofan loved Han, but she also knew that Han was in a sticky situation himself. She knew that all he was trying to do was protect Xiaofan by avoiding her until he figured things out, but did she *need* protection? Xiaofan was left in the dark in regards to Han's problem, and because of that, she probably thought something was wrong with *her*. Xiuying shook her head absently. Her sister deserved to know the truth; Han owed her that much.

Zhang had told Xiuying every detail of what Han was going through, and being the caring sister that she was, she was eager to save her younger sister from a heartbreak that didn't need to happen. She needed to speak to Xiaofan after dinner. If Han wouldn't support her now, she would.

A few hours later, dinner came to an end. Kyrie was emotional and wanted to spend time with her parents. Kamari was tired from all the preparations, so she bid farewell and left for her room. Zhang and Han left early to discuss some urgent issues, or so they said. This left the sisters alone. Xiuying opened her mouth to ask Xiaofan if she wanted company, but a servant came into the courtyard and called for her attention. Once Xiuying was finished, she turned back to her sister, but Xiaofan was already gone. She sighed and made her way toward her sister's room.

Xiaofan walked alone back to her room with a shattered heart. She should've known that Han was too good to be true. She should've known that a prince like him could *never* fall for someone like her. She entered her room and closed the door behind her. She looked at her bed, but her legs failed to carry her there. Instead, she sat on the floor with her head resting on her knees, and she let herself fall apart.

"Why won't he love me?" She sobbed around her wavering voice. After years of being unloved and unsupported at Jinu, and then at the orphanage, she was *sick* of being second. She was *sick* of being ignored.

"All I want is love, but no matter what I do or how hard I try, I can never have it," she whispered into her knees.

Three knocks on her door silenced her. The only person who knocked three times—Xiuying entered to find Xiaofan huddled on the floor. Xiuying slowly walked in, closed the door behind her, lit some candles to conquer the darkness, and then sat on the floor next to her sister.

"What's wrong, Xiaofan?" Xiuying whispered quietly.

"I'm tired," she croaked out, not caring if she looked

and sounded like a mess. "I'm tired of being the one to always give up what makes me happy. Why can't Han be mine? Why does he pretend to love me one day, and then doesn't even acknowledge my presence the next? I love him..." The words felt too real, too fragile. But they were out there now. "I have never felt this way for anyone else before. And now that I want him, I can't have him."

Xiaofan sniffled, her tears falling like a river down her red face. Xiuying was done seeing Xiaofan in this state, and each one of her sister's tears felt like a needle stabbing through her own heart. A part of her wanted to share what Han was going through to give Xiaofan some relief, but the other part of her insisted that it was not her story to share. Han was going to talk to Xiaofan sooner or later. She just had to hold out a little longer.

Xiuying breathed and scooted closer, wrapping an arm around her sister's shoulders. Even if this was all the support she could offer right now, she hoped it would be enough. "Xiaofan, there's so much that I cannot say right now, but remember that sometimes people have their reasons. Sometimes they have to choose a harder path to save their loved ones from dismay. So, don't jump to conclusions just yet, okay?"

Xiaofan nodded weakly, and Xiuying's heart squeezed in her chest. She wanted to do more. She wanted to help her sister more. She took a long, steadying breath.

"You are only signing yourself up for heartbreak when you expect, Xiaofan. Expectations come naturally, I understand, but they are always followed by disappointment." Xiuying wiped her sister's tears away with gentle fingers.

Xiaofan looked up at her. "What do you mean? Should I not expect him to love me back after everything that happened between us?" Xiaofan tried to wrap her mind around everything that Xiuying had said, but something tickled her thoughts. There was more to it. "Is there something you're not telling me, Xiuying?"

"Time will tell, Xiaofan. Just be patient," Xiuying said, stroking slow fingers through the ends of Xiaofan's loose strands of hair. "Even if someone loves you, they are always going to disappoint you one way or another. It's just how human beings are. The only love that's never going to disappoint you is the one that stays with you, the one that cannot be lost even with death. So, put your trust in the right place, and everything will fall in line for you, Xiaofan."

Xiaofan's tears slowed, and her lips curled into a small smile as her sister's words soothed her. "How do you always know the right things to say?"

Xiuying chuckled. "It's just something I've learned along the way." Xiuying hugged her tight and breathed in her sister's scent as they held onto each other. "Now get some sleep. It's already late, and Kyrie's big day is tomorrow."

Xiaofan nodded and thanked her sister once more before Xiuying left the room. Xiaofan climbed into bed and closed her eyes, promising herself to not jump to any conclusions before hearing from Han. After what Xiuying had said, she suspected that there was something left unsaid. She would learn what it was in time; she just had to be patient. She would wait for Han. She *had* to.

Han left the dinner with Zhang, but he went straight to his room alone. Dinner was incredibly hard for him. He had to force himself to ignore Xiaofan and was fully aware of how that made her feel. His determination almost crumbled when he saw her curl inwards and stare at her soup in silence halfway through the meal.

He hated himself for listening to his mind, he despised

himself for not telling her how gorgeous she looked, he loathed himself for not talking to her, and most of all, he abhorred his existence for not being able to confess his true feelings to her. He was certain that he had lost her.

"Why is this happening to me?!" he screamed. "Am I going to lose the only girl I have ever loved?"

The dinner made him realize how his mind weighed over his heart, and he feared that when the time came to make a decision, he might end up choosing a choice that he'd regret for a lifetime.

His love for Xiaofan was true, but their tale was utterly tragic and filled with uncertainty. Xiaofan was carrying a heart filled with love for Han, while Han was unconsciously caught up in the war that his heart and mind waged against one another.

Xɪᴀᴏꜰᴀɴ ᴡᴏᴋᴇ ᴜᴘ ᴛʜᴇ ɴᴇxᴛ ᴍᴏʀɴɪɴɢ ᴡɪᴛʜ ᴀ ʟɪᴛᴛʟᴇ ʙɪᴛ ᴏꜰ ʜᴏᴘᴇ, ignorant to what was ahead, while Han woke up tired and filled with dread. His parents arrived at the kingdom right after sunrise, but they brought a guest that no one was expecting.

It was Han's future wife! His parents thought the wedding would be a great chance for them to get to know each other, to be introduced together in a formal setting, and to mingle with the royals and allies of this kingdom. They introduced her as his fiancé without any promises being made. And before Han had even gotten a chance to talk to his parents, the entire kingdom seemed to know about his *fiancé*.

Kamari, Kyrie, and Xiuying were startled upon meeting his parents and the princess. *Nobody* expected this to happen, and they feared what Xiaofan would feel. Han's fiancé was a sweetheart at first—beautiful and proper—but after a while, her true nature started to show.

She started throwing tantrums. She didn't get along with Kamari or Kyrie. Sure, she was a princess, and she behaved like one in the worst way possible—she treated people like they were beneath her, and she insulted everyone as if they were peasants.

Her name was Rai, and *pretense* could be defined by her existence. She was a saint in front of Han and Zhang's parents, but behind their backs, she was a living nightmare for everyone around her. She sat next to Han after the parents of both families left and kept a firm grip on his hand. Han felt humiliated and irritated, both feelings visible through his face and body language.

"Oh, Han! I can't believe I'm going to be your wife soon! Girls, guess who the luckiest girl here is—it's Rai!" She laughed. The sound was whiny and grating on Han's ears.

"Who talks about themselves in the third person?" Kyrie whispered to Xiaofan.

"I don't like her," Kamari mumbled to the others while smiling at Rai and sipping her tea.

Xiaofan's face was pale, and she didn't say a word from the moment she joined them for brunch. After all the support that Xiuying had offered her the night before and the hope that she had awoken with that morning, she was fighting back tears, vowing not to cry in front of everyone.

But how unlucky was Han?! He sat across the table from Xiaofan, but he couldn't do *anything* to ease her noticeable distress without turning Rai into a monster. But it wasn't Rai or his parents or the situation that bothered him the most. What he hated most was that *he* was the reason behind Xiaofan's sorrow.

Rai continued bragging about all her riches, even if no one was paying her any attention. The other girls all rolled their eyes and constantly sipped from their cups to avoid talking to her.

"What an egotistical, self-centered b—witch!" Kamari whispered while Rai went on and on about her wealth.

"Agree," Kyrie mumbled. "Han deserves better." Kyrie reached over and squeezed Xiaofan's hand under the table, giving her friend an encouraging look. But Xiaofan's smile wobbled with effort.

"I have to go." Xiaofan pushed herself up from her seat.

"What? Where?" Kyrie's smile plummeted.

"I have a few lectures to go through before the wedding. Just some work from the university. But I'll be back before the ceremony!" Xiaofan lied and abruptly turned to leave.

Xiuying tried to go after her, but Zhang held onto her hand. "Let her be. She needs to do this alone," he said in a low voice.

"There goes the bookworm," Rai mocked, rolling her eyes in annoyance. "There's no point in reading books; it's all just fantasy. What a waste of time and money! I'd rather be doing better things—like shopping." Rai snorted, looking to Han for approval.

But Han had enough. He yanked his hand out of Rai's grasp and moved to follow Xiaofan.

"Han! Where are you going?" Rai called.

Han ignored her as he left them all behind.

He couldn't wrap his mind around what had happened. Things had blown *way* out of proportion, and now it was going to be even harder to talk to his parents. But he was determined. He would *never* marry Rai, not after seeing her true nature. He was going to fight for Xiaofan, and he would accept no one else.

He rushed toward his parents' room to have the conversation that he had been avoiding. It was now or never.

"There's our son! Oh, I have been *dying* to see your face. We saw each other for such a short time at brunch," his mother greeted him with a long hug.

"Our boy! Becoming a man *and* a king," his father added, patting him on the back.

"I was waiting for you both as well," Han said, his body tense. "But as happy as I am to see you both, I don't appreciate Rai being here."

His father's joy melted away almost instantly as he looked at his son with stale eyes. This was the first time in his life that Han had objected to a decision they made.

"What do you mean? We thought you would be happy to see her. You would get a chance to know her and show her off to our allies," his mother said, her smile dipping, too.

But Han couldn't hide his true feelings any longer. "I have seen enough of her, and I do *not* want to marry her. Please send her back," Han said firmly. "I've made no commitments to her, and I do not intend to move forward with engaging her."

His father's eyes widened, and the lines on his forehead deepened. "You are crossing a line, Han. We gave our word to her parents. They have entrusted her to us and sent her here so that she could meet you. I will *not* tolerate *anyone* going against my decision."

"If they trusted you so much, then why is there an army of soldiers here with her, Father? But like I said, I am *not* going to marry her, and that's final," Han stated.

His mother stared at him in a state of shock. She had

never seen Han so determined to stand up against something that they had decided for him. He was usually so eager to please them.

"Why are you suddenly so against this union? Is there someone else whom you would like to consider?" his mother asked.

Han hung his head; his eyes wandered along the floor, and his feet tapped an anxious rhythm. "There is."

His parents both looked at each other, and then they looked at him. He had never mentioned a girl before.

"Who is it?" his mother murmured.

"It's Xiaofan," Han said firmly. Every trace of hesitation and doubt dissipated as he confessed what was in his heart all along. "I love her. I cannot see my life with anyone else but her."

It felt like a weight had been lifted from Han's chest. Everything was brighter, the air was easier to breathe, and a warmth in his chest fluttered. Han's mother could see the affection that he had for Xiaofan when he spoke about her, and she smiled. But before she could say anything else, his father put his foot down.

"I will *not* tolerate such nonsense. Rai is the *perfect* match for you, and her presence will benefit you and our kingdom. If you refuse to marry her, you will have to walk away from us as well."

Han stared at his father in disbelief. After years of obeying every single one of his decisions, *this* was how his father reacted when Han asked to make his own for once—a decision that impacted both his future *and* his happiness. He gritted his teeth and straightened as he met his father's gaze.

"I am *not* going to marry Rai, and I am *not* going to walk away from my own parents," he said firmly. "There's more to life than power and wealth, Father. I pray that you understand that before you lose those who are important to you."

His father stared at him with a crimson face, full of rage and ready to explode. But Han didn't wait for his response. He turned and left the room with his spine still straight and his pride intact. He felt powerful. He felt free. He felt like he had been taken out of captivity, and finally, he would be able to confess his true feelings to Xiaofan... despite what his parents wished for him. His heart won over his mind this time, and the internal battle quieted. He knew there would be more to discuss later with his parents, but for now, he wanted to let his heart lead him.

Xiaofan had walked to brunch that morning in hopes that Han would talk to her, explain what had been going through his mind, and even if Han didn't reach out, she was going to talk to him anyway. But what happened was beyond anything that she had ever expected.

Han was engaged, and now everything made sense— why he'd been ignoring her. Maybe she was right after all, this was all just a fairytale.

She was so naïve! How could she even *think* that a *prince* could ever love her? All her feelings had been one-sided, and she was lying to herself to think that Han wanted to be with her also.

After walking out of brunch, Xiaofan went straight to her room and cried until her eyes were swollen.

"Horrible, isn't it?" she asked herself. "Being in love makes you vulnerable. It opens your heart to someone, and then when you're hopeful and happy, it slashes it in two." She chuckled to herself sinisterly.

Her relationship with Han would *just* be as *friends*. But it wasn't Han's fault; it was all on her. And she could cry and sulk later when she had time to pity herself, but she knew she had to gather her emotions and be her best self for Kyrie's wedding. But that alone felt impossible in this moment.

She needed to relieve her mind and vanish her thoughts, so she decided to write them down. She remembered Xiuying telling her once that writing about her feelings helped her get them out of her head and onto paper. Xiaofan couldn't talk to Han about her feelings. Maybe *this* was the only way to expose everything to him.

Han,

It's time I move on. It's time I get out of the perfect world that I have created in my head for us. You have been such a good friend to me, but I mistook that for something more.

I thought we had something, felt something for each other. I certainly did for you. But I was a fool to think that you'd ever want a nobody like me. You're engaged to a princess, even if I do think you deserve better, but now I realize that better doesn't mean me.

I love you, Han, but you are not mine.

I'll never forget you, but I have to move on.

Xiaofan

She knew she had fallen for him, but the intensity increased as she wrote it down. She went to fold the letter, but Kyrie suddenly came bursting into her room.

"I know you're not in the right headspace right now, Xiaofan, but I *really* need you."

"It's your big day, Kyrie. Anything for you." She placed

the letter on her desk and followed Kyrie out of the room and down the hall.

Han was eager to see Xiaofan. He wanted to tell her everything—the reason why he had to ignore her and stay away from her—and now he couldn't hold himself back from her anymore. He made his way to her room in hopes that he could clear everything up.

He rounded the corner of the hall and slowed as he approached her room. The door was cracked open. He knocked twice but heard no answer, so he peeked his head through the crack. No one was inside. He stepped into the empty room and looked for clues as to where Xiaofan could have gone. As he turned around, his eyes caught his name on a piece of paper that sat on her desk.

"She *did* love me," he whispered as he read her letter. "All this time, she just wanted to be with me, and I've done nothing but make it all worse. X-Xiaofan, I love you, too."

Xiaofan was moving on. After everything that had happened between them and the mishap with Rai, she was going to force herself forward *without* him. He picked up the ink quill and a blank piece of paper, and he sat down to write.

Xiaofan,

I know you don't think I like you as more than just a friend, but I do. I love you, and I can only imagine my future with you, not Rai, not anyone else. I'm so sorry for making you think otherwise as I have loved you since the day we first met.

I hope you don't move on. I hope that one day, we can finally be together because we deserve to be together. You will always have my heart, and if I were to ever get married, it would be with you.

Han paused—he only had one more chance to make this right. He had to try one more time.

I'll wait for you at midnight by the staircase outside your room, and if you decide not to come, then I promise to leave you alone forever.

With love,

Han

He folded the note and scrawled her name across the top before placing it on her desk. Then he walked away.

Xiaofan, on the other hand, was busy helping Kyrie with her wedding gown. Kyrie wore a traditional qipao with a complimenting hairstyle. She looked divine, as usual.

"You're the prettiest bride I have ever seen," Xiaofan praised her as she handed over a bouquet of white and red roses.

"You don't look too bad yourself." Kyrie grinned before softening her smile. "Han will lose his mind seeing you like this."

Xiaofan chuckled dryly. "I am probably the *last* person he's going to pay attention to."

Kyrie huffed, not even trying to hide her distaste. "I hope Rotten Rai falls off a cliff. I swear, I *cannot* tolerate her! She keeps blabbering about herself. Ugh!"

Xiaofan chuckled at her friend's forwardness, and Kamari walked into the dressing room just in time to catch the end of Kyrie's curse.

"That's what we're calling her? Rotten Rai?" She laughed, but her eyes glowed once she caught sight of Kyrie. "I can't believe you're getting married! You can still change your mind; there's still time," she added, receiving a playful push from her sister.

"Please, I would do this a thousand times over for my husband!" Kyrie giggled.

"Husband-to-be," Kamari corrected.

"Soon enough!" Kyrie grinned, posing in front of the mirror.

Kamari and Xiaofan laughed as they finished helping Kyrie get ready. The wedding ceremony would start soon enough, and there was no time to think about anything else.

CHAPTER
NINE

"The groom's here. We have to leave," Xiuying announced as she walked into the room, and Kyrie started jumping in excitement.

"Finally!" she screamed.

Zhang and Ming walked Kyrie down the aisle when the ceremony began, surrounded by friends and family. It was a scenic view. The venue was filled with lavender flowers, chandeliers with candles lit atop them, and oil lamps in every other corner. The color combination of off-white and different shades of purple was a pleasing sight for all eyes.

Xiaofan matched the aesthetic with a dark purple robe that had bell sleeves and lavender flowers embroidered onto it. She wore her hair down with blossoms pinned in the back and finished off the look with a maroon lip balm.

Han was standing in front of Xiaofan, and he kept glancing at her every now and then. Xiaofan would look away and try to refrain from any eye contact or exchanging smiles. He looked so incredibly handsome in his elegant black robe.

The wedding ceremony ended sooner than Xiaofan was prepared for. Once everyone started clapping and cheering, Xiaofan realized with dread that it was time. Her best friend was going to leave her. Saying goodbye had never been this hard for Xiaofan, but Kyrie had given her many firsts in her life. She would never forget her, *never*. As she watched Kyrie ride away with her new husband, a hole was left in her heart. She felt like she had now lost the two most important people in her life. Ming and Zhang were right. Kyrie *was* the heart of the kingdom, and a certain kind of silence took over the moment she left.

"Are you okay?" Xiuying stepped beside her and asked.

Xiaofan shook her head and started to walk toward her room.

"I understand that this has been a hard day for you," Xiuying started slowly as she walked beside her sister.

Xiaofan paused before replying, "Life seems to get harder every day."

Xiuying worried about her sister's numbness, her distance. She wanted to console her, but she had no words to say. She knew all too well how she felt. "It's not all bad," she tried. "I'm always here if you ever need to talk about anything."

Xiaofan barely nodded as she entered her room. Xiuying didn't want to leave her alone, but there was nothing else that she could do right now. Her sister needed space and time alone to decompress.

Inside her room alone, Xiaofan removed the flowers from her hair and changed into her nightgown. She sat down in front of the mirror, thinking that the day had passed by in less than a blink. She glanced over her reflection, and before she knew it, she started to cry again. Her nose turned red, her eyes were already swollen, and tears were rapidly rolling down her cheeks. She choked on a shallow, thick breaths raking her body with trembling shakes.

Xiaofan felt alone despite having people around who cared about her. She noticed how close Xiuying was to Zhang, how close Kyrie was to her husband, and how close Ming and Huiqing were to each other. Just like at the orphanage, everyone had found their missing half except for her.

She wanted her happy ending, too. She wanted to find *her* missing half.

She looked up and stared at her own reflection through blurry eyes. She couldn't recognize herself, but at the same time, she felt seen. Maybe *that* was the reason why she often cried in front of the mirror... because she wanted to be seen, heard, and understood.

Maybe.

The weather soon changed. The night sky was covered with dark rumbling clouds, and the winds were roaring, causing the windows to slam open and shut. Xiaofan stood up to close the windows when she saw the sky burst with light as a lightning bolt ripped through the darkness, with a loud thunder echoing it moments later. She closed the window and turned around to light the oil lamp sitting on her desk.

The room was now a bit brighter than before. The flame

of the lamp flickered as light breezes of wind crossed the room. That's when she noticed the letter. She moved to grab it and found her initials scrawled across the top of it. She quickly unfolded it, and her eyes started to read the curly handwriting. Word after word, she read and realized how wrong she had been. He was waiting for her; he *promised* he would wait for her. She looked outside the window and peered out into the dark. It had to be past midnight. Was it too late?

Overwhelmed by emotions, she started to feel her hands grow hot, and after a few seconds, the paper that she held in her hands began to slowly burn. Her emotions were aligning with her magical power… just as they had on the streets outside her orphanage.

"I can't let him go. I can't let him go!" she repeated to herself and scurried toward the door.

She ran as fast as she could, her breaths heavy and aching in her lungs as she pushed onward. The thunder was growing louder as the night went on, and the sky was pouring like it hadn't rained in months.

What if he left?

She grabbed a lantern and found her way through the darkness. She rushed toward the staircase, and the ground was soaked with fiery puddles as she held her light over them. She heaved a deep breath through her mouth as she stopped at the top step. She looked around but saw no one.

Am I too late?

Is he gone forever?

Her thoughts were caving into her, when suddenly, she heard a familiar voice.

"I didn't think you'd come," Han whispered with relief in his voice as he stepped around the corner and stopped just shy of the steps.

Xiaofan looked at him, warmth radiating through her even in the wet cold that was surrounding her. "I thought I was too late."

Han took a few steps toward her. "I'll *always* wait for you." He wrapped his arms around her waist and pulled her closer to him before leaning his head toward her and kissing her passionately on the lips. He could feel his heart flutter as Xiaofan kissed him back, and he never wanted this moment to end. "I love you, Xiaofan. I don't know what our future holds, but I want you to know that the love I have for you is real, and I will fight for us no matter what happens."

Xiaofan was speechless, but somehow she squeaked out, "Why?"

Han didn't hesitate. "Because you deserve it. You are worth it. And I will endure any torture in the world if it means I can spend the rest of my days with you." Han paused as they walked toward a nearby shed to sit down. He scooted closer as they huddled together to stay warm. Han's breath was hot, and his warmth was welcoming, but he wasn't done.

"I want to be honest with you, Xiaofan." She braced herself for what he was about to say. "My parents are against us. They don't want us to be together; they want me to be with Rai, but my heart disagrees. And the only reason why I've been avoiding you is because I don't know how to choose—how to choose between you and my parents."

Xiaofan listened, feeling an ounce of guilt because she felt like she was tearing his family apart. Parents were something that she didn't really have growing up, and she didn't like that Han had decided to go against his—for her, nonetheless. But she stayed silent and kept her worries to herself.

Han kept her hand firmly in his own, and after a while, he realized that her grip was warm... warmer than usual.

"Are you sick?" he asked.

Xiaofan froze.

"Is everything okay?" Han asked again.

"I have something to tell you, and it might make you see me in a different way."

Han chuckled nervously and rubbed the back of his neck. "I can assure you that'll never happen. Even if you killed someone, I can't promise you that I won't still love you."

Xiaofan took a deep breath as she focused her eyes on the ground before her. The raindrops landing in front of her soothed her nerves.

"My blood family is... different. We all have magical powers, given to us when we were born. Xiuying can control plants, mostly. And I can control fire and wind. My emotions channel them. I'm still learning how to use my magic, but my hands tend to grow warm whenever I feel... love." She looked down at their intertwined fingers.

"You love me?" Han blushed.

"I do, and I don't think I'll ever stop," Xiaofan whispered.

"Well, you were right about one thing."

"What is it?"

"I *do* see you in a different way."

Xiaofan felt her face turn red with shame, and she started to get up and leave when Han pulled her back down and into his arms.

"Your power makes you even more special. How can I ever let someone as amazing as you go?" He smirked and pressed his lips against hers.

She could feel her heart beating faster and faster

against her chest, her body turning warmer and warmer, and she was pressing so hard against him that she felt like her body was going to absorb right into his.

Han slid one of his hands slowly under her nightgown, and the skin-to-skin contact made Xiaofan's body shiver with a sensation that she'd never felt before. She kissed him even harder as he gently made his way up her body... before suddenly stopping and whispering into her ear.

"I want you, Xiaofan. I really do. But not yet, not until I figure out this mess."

"Oh..."

"Please don't think I'm pushing you away. I've only been dreaming about this moment ever since I first laid eyes on you, but it's not right to do it like this. I have to do it the right way." He paused. "Wait for me. Please? I promise you that this will all work out. I love you with all my heart, and you have my word that we *will* be together."

"I will wait for you." She smiled, and they kissed once more before he walked her back to her room and tucked her into bed.

XIAOFAN WOKE UP JUST MERE HOURS LATER TO A SUN RAY touching her face. She felt different today, better—happier. Finally, she had someone she could call hers, and that someone was Han. He was her happy ending, and she couldn't even begin to think of someone better.

Han's parents were going to stay at Baoshu over the next three days, and Xiaofan knew that those three days would decide her fate with Han. However, she tried not to let it bother her too much. He had promised her that he'd be with her no matter what, and she knew she had to trust him.

Xiaofan threw on her robe and wrapped a purple lavender ribbon around her hair, ready to head to the university. On her way out, she stopped by her sister's room.

"Finally drag yourself out of bed?" Xiuying asked in a teasing tone. "I stopped by earlier, and you were fast asleep. Did you stay up late?"

Xiaofan blushed. "Sort of. Can we meet up for tea later? I want to tell you something."

"Of course! Anything for my baby sister. We can even talk now if you want."

"No, no, you have a lot to do. I don't want to be a burden, and besides, I'm headed to the university."

"Okay... if you're sure. I'll see you tonight, then." Xiuying hugged her, and Xiaofan left.

Xiaofan went straight to the library when she arrived, eager to find the book that all her classmates had been talking about—*Dream of the Red Chamber*. This particular Chinese literature comprised of realism and romance, psychological motivation and supernatural occurrences, all things that she could relate to. And she quickly found herself invested in the pages.

After a few hours, she heard someone take a seat in front of her. She noticed the movement, but kept her head buried in the book until she finished the last paragraph of her current chapter.

She looked up to see Han sitting in front of her, holding a book of poetry in his hands.

"*This* is what I love about you. You are so passionate about the things you choose to read and study." Han grinned.

"Good to see you, too." Xiaofan chuckled.

"Why do you always sit in the corner? It took me almost ten minutes to find you. There's no one else here... if you haven't noticed," Han said as he waved his hands around at the empty tables.

"That is *exactly* why I sit here."

"Wait—you *don't* want me to find you?" Han teased.

"No, I just don't want *others* to find me."

"Understandable." He shrugged. "But I don't like it."

Xiaofan shook her head at him before glancing at his own book. "What are you reading?"

"You mean, what am I going to read to *you*? Poetry. *Romance*."

Xiaofan laughed, but Han was having none of it. He gently nudged her book aside.

"Take a break from that. I'll read to you," he said with a smirk.

"Okay, fine." Xiaofan submitted but felt the need to add, "But you can't read out loud. It's a library."

"Yeah, but you're the only human here, Xiaofan." Han laughed.

The poem was about a requited love that was still incomplete, and that made Han wonder if his own story was going to be fully complete one day. He had *his* requited love, and she wanted to stay by his side, too, but their future was undetermined.

Xiaofan was moved by the words that came out of Han. The pauses and the way that he spoke made her saw him as a true poet, portraying the strong emotions that only a lover could show.

The two of them settled together in silence, reading from their books and peeking small glimpses and smiles at each other when their love bubbled over. As the hours ticked by, and the light outside the windows dimmed, Xiaofan set down her book with a sigh.

"I should leave. I have to meet Xiuying for tea, and it's almost sunset," she said.

"Of course," Han replied and escorted her toward her carriage. But as they walked, his mind and his gaze lingered on her.

Every time he saw Xiaofan, every second he spent with her, made him realize how much he wanted her to be his queen, how much he wanted to spend every second of his life with her. But at the same time, he wanted acceptance from his parents, and he couldn't have one without the other. He had to try to talk some sense into his parents again today, with hopes that they would welcome Xiaofan with open arms, and for once, listen to what Han wanted.

Xiaofan reached the castle to find Xiuying waiting for her on the grand terrace, admiring the heavenly view. She hurried her way upstairs and rushed to meet her sister.

"I'm here!" Xiaofan sang cheerfully as she stepped onto the terrace.

"Welcome back." Xiuying grinned, giving her a hug. "Someone's in a good mood."

Xiaofan couldn't stop her smile.

"Oh, Kamari will be joining us, too. I hope that's not a problem," Xiuying added.

"Not a problem at all," Xiaofan replied and grabbed one of the moon cakes that were on the table between them. "And thanks for remembering the moon cakes."

"Always," Xiuying replied, and then she asked, "So?"

Xiaofan looked at her in bewilderment before repeating with a giggle, "So?"

"What did you want to discuss? And what changed

since last night? You were so devastated after our last conversation."

Xiaofan paused, floundering to find a way to explain what exactly had ensued. Because even after Han had confessed his feelings for her, their future was still highly uncertain, and she didn't know what would become of their story. After staying silent and taking into consideration the choice of words, Xiaofan spoke.

"I met up with Han last night. He left a note on my desk, confessing his feelings and assuring me that he wasn't actually engaged. We saw each other, and he explained his side of the story—what his parents had planned for him, and how he only wants to be with me. He loves me, Sister, and I love him back. I want to give our story a chance to come true."

Xiuying wanted to be happy for her sister, but instead, she was worried. She had been around Han's parents for long enough to know that his parents would *never* accept Xiaofan, despite how much love Han had for her. And they would forever despise Xiaofan for turning their son against them. But then again, Xiaofan was so happy. How could she take that away from her?

"I'm glad he feels the same way about you, Xiaofan. Nothing will make me happier than seeing you find love. But his parents are difficult; they are not going to just give up on their decision that easily."

"I know. But Han and I can win them over; I know we can!" Xiaofan cheered.

"I hope you do." Xiuying faked a smile, but deep down, she feared that Xiaofan was only setting herself up for disappointment.

Kamari came rushing in just seconds later, huffing and

puffing from all the stress of carrying the kingdom ever since Kyrie left.

"You need a break, Kamari. I think you're overworking yourself," Xiaofan said.

"I will... *after* the charity gala," Kamari replied.

"It's just two days away," Xiuying added. "I almost forgot!"

"What's it about?" Xiaofan asked.

Kamari took a deep breath before passionately replying, "Discount Day—a day where shops can offer to sell their products at low, low prices to help out those who can't afford them. We do this every quarter. Everyone from the community volunteers and donates—they all look forward to helping out. That's why I work so hard to make it a success every year."

"Can I volunteer to help out?" Normally, Xiaofan wouldn't be into charity, but she was so in love that she wanted to help everyone else feel the same happiness that she did.

"Of course, you can," Kamari replied, reaching forward to grab her cup. "This has gotten so cold."

"Don't worry." Xiaofan smiled, holding out her hand. "Give it to me."

Kamari was confused, and so was Xiuying. "No, I'll get it reheated by the maid. You don't have to do it for me, Xiaofan."

"Trust me," Xiaofan insisted.

Kamari raised a brow before slowly setting down the cup in her hand. Xiaofan placed both of her palms around the cup and closed her eyes. Her hands started to grow warmer and warmer by the second, and within a minute, vapor started to flow from its surface. Xiuying and Kamari looked at each other in shock.

"Here." Xiaofan passed the cup back to Kamari. When Kamari touched it, it was burning hot. She set it back down with a hiss.

"How did you do this?" Xiuying asked.

"My power. I can control fire and wind with my emotions."

"That's amazing!" Kamari exclaimed.

Xiuying felt tears of happiness glittering at the corners of her eyes. She remembered when she first discovered her own power. That moment meant a lot to her, and she was proud of Xiaofan for showing it to her and Kamari.

"I'm so proud of you," Xiuying whispered with teary eyes, and she leaned in to give Xiaofan a hug.

"Now I miss Kyrie even more!" Kamari whined, and then joined their happy embrace.

While Xiaofan's heart was filled with optimism, Han's essence was getting obscured by shadows of doubt. As time passed, he was coming to the realization that he had taken his parents a little too lightly. He knew it wasn't going to be easy, and with all the uncertainty, he was only certain about one thing. In the end, he would have to make a choice —give up on one and choose the other.

After escorting Xiaofan, he, too, went back to the castle, and on his way, he prepared himself for a conversation that he was *not* looking forward to. On his way inside, he caught a glimpse of Xiaofan laughing alongside Xiuying and Kamari on the grand terrace. The sight of her gave him the strength to fight harder. He walked toward the royal guest room—where his parents were staying—and knocked on the door. The door opened, and his mother welcomed him.

"It feels like I haven't seen you in an eternity, my son," she cooed. "Come in, come in!" She urged Han inside as she closed the door behind him.

His father was at the study desk, reading a manuscript.

"How are you, Father?" Han asked.

"My answer depends on your decision, my son. Has your mind come to its senses?" He pushed himself up, walked toward the center of the room, and sat down on a wooden chair while offering Han a seat next to him.

"I have not changed my decision. I want to marry Xiao-fan," Han replied, looking down at the ground.

"I'm afraid that is not possible. We will *not* let an orphan become a part of our legacy, our kingdom. My ancestors deserve better," his father declared.

"And what about your son? What about what I want?" Han pushed.

"You know it as well as I do. Royals have to make compromises for their legacy. We have to choose carefully, and I will *not* let you make this mistake. I will *not* let you ruin what we have built. Your immature love affair will *die* in a few days."

"It's *not* an immature love affair," Han whispered, shaking his head in disagreement.

"What was that?" his father questioned.

"I said, it's *not* an immature love affair," Han repeated while looking directly into his father's eyes. "I want her to be by my side... as my wife."

His father paused, glaring at his son before speaking, "I will *not* tolerate this. I will *not* let our only son marry a girl without an identity. This is where this conversation ends, and you make a choice. Either you listen to us and stay connected to our family, become the future of our kingdom, and inherit everything, or you choose that... orphan and forget that you ever belonged to royalty."

His father was stiff. His eyes were red with anger as he stared at his only son. Han was quiet—thoughtful. He let out a slow sigh and pushed himself out of the chair.

"Okay," he said.

"Okay, you'll forget that girl?"

Han looked at his father with a level gaze. "There is no place for me in a kingdom that does not understand me."

Han's mother had been listening to the argument silently, but when Han uttered the words that she was dreading, she could not believe her ears. "Are you—are you *leaving* your parents for a... g-girl?" she stammered with her eyes leaking thick tears.

Han looked at her, but had no words to answer her question. He wanted to console her, but what could he do? Before he could respond, his mother fainted and fell to the ground. Han and his father rushed forward.

"Look what you did! You still have time—change your decision!" his father shouted while holding his mother in his arms.

Han didn't know what to say, not when his mother was pale and fragile on the ground. It seemed that now, he didn't have much of a choice.

CHAPTER
TEN

HAN SPENT THE REST OF THE NIGHT WITH HIS MOTHER, ASSURING her that he was going to stay by her side, that he was not going to leave her.

Xiuying visited often as it was her responsibility to keep the guests at ease, and she saw everything. She saw the story unfold, how Han's mother was keeping him close, and she realized that Xiaofan had lost what had just begun. She could see the sadness in Han's eyes, the sorrow of the choice he had to make. She wondered why Han and Xiaofan were being put through a trial by faith.

While the entire kingdom was busy taking care of the royal guests, Xiaofan was in her room studying, oblivious to what had happened and how her life had just changed within a few hours. Xiuying told everyone not to tell Xiaofan about the incident. She asked Han to do it himself instead, whenever his mother fell asleep.

On the other hand, Han's father felt like he had won a war. He believed that this was his triumph. His son would now marry the girl of his choice. He knew that deep down, Han was glad that this happened, so he could keep the legacy of his kingdom alive!

He made his way over to Xiaofan's room, eager to break the news to her. He wanted to see the look in her eyes when he told her that Han would *never* marry her. And it was going to be *delicious*.

"I'm not here to greet you," he started when she opened the door, a stern look on his face. "I am here to inform you that you have brought great distress to our family. Because of you, my wife's health is suffering. We are *never* going to accept you, never. And we will *never* allow Han to marry you. If he does, he'll always blame you for causing him to go against his own family. Think wisely, my child. You are not living in a fairytale."

Xiaofan shook her head, looking down at the floor in despair. Han's father left the room and closed the door behind him without another word. Xiaofan sat on her bed and wrapped a blanket around her. Her mind was too numb to think about what had just happened. She cried and cried until her sheets were covered with tears. A strong headache took over her mind as she fell asleep.

SHE WOKE UP THE NEXT DAY WITH A HEAVY HEART AND SWOLLEN eyes. The words of Han's father were clear in her mind, but she couldn't understand if the whole thing was a figment of her imagination or not. She got out of bed and splashed cold water onto her face to bring herself back to life, but she couldn't feel anything at all. She was numb, her thoughts quiet. All she knew was that she had to leave the castle and go to the library, a place where she could escape the harsh realities of her life.

She threw on her robe and tied her hair into a braid. Her eyes were still swollen and a little red, but she ignored them. On her way, she realized how lonely she was, surrounded by so many people but still had no one. She knew she had to deal with her emotions; there was no point in running anymore. It was going to catch up to her one way or another.

When she walked in, she saw Han. His eyes looked tired and red. He kept rubbing his hands together as his eyes found everything but Xiaofan. She took a shuddering breath.

"It's alright, I understand," she whispered as tears started to roll down her cheeks.

"You know?" Han looked up at her.

"Yes, your father," she replied, but then stopped short.

"My father?" he repeated. "What did he say?"

She knew it wouldn't change anything, but she told him anyway. "He came to my room yesterday and told me what happened. And I agree with him—I will stay away from you. I love you, Han, but I can't be the reason for separating you from your family."

Han looked at her in disbelief. How could his father do that to him? Especially after he agreed to let Xiaofan go. "After I told them that I choose you, my mother fainted. My father basically forced me to reconsider or risk losing my mother forever. I had no other choice, Xiaofan. I can never forgive myself if my mother dies because of me. But believe me, I wanted to choose you; I really did." He shook his head. "Maybe we're just not meant to be together."

"That's not true, Han."

"I don't know what's true anymore, Xiaofan. I thought I would fight for us, and everything would turn out fine," Han said, seemingly disappointed in himself. "I'm sorry."

"I guess this is goodbye," Xiaofan said in a low, shattered voice and walked away without hearing what Han had to say. She couldn't give herself any more reason to believe in their false future.

"I will never forget us. I will miss you, Xiaofan, for the rest of my life," Han whispered to himself as he watched her walk away.

Xiaofan reached the castle and went straight to her room. Her eyes were filled with tears again, and as soon as she got there, she found Xiuying waiting for her. Seeing her sister sitting on her bed with her eyes locked on the door, Xiaofan started to cry even more. She ran toward Xiuying, sat down beside her on the bed, and sobbed like she never had before.

Xiuying tried to console her, but she was out of words that could make Xiaofan feel better. The kind of heartbreak that Xiaofan was feeling was unknown to Xiuying. It was distinct and extreme. Life had taken away so much from her sister that there were no hopes left in her for her future.

"I had to let him go. I had to love him enough to let him go," Xiaofan whispered. "And now I don't know how I will survive, how I will live without him being around me." Xiaofan sniffled before adding, "I don't think I will ever love anyone the same way ever again."

Xiuying's heart sank while listening to her sister explain her feelings. She had to say something, so she gathered all the strength inside her.

"You're right, Xiaofan. You'll never feel the same love toward another person that you did toward Han, but that doesn't mean you'll never find love again, just a different kind of love. And when you do, you won't even remember why you were so heartbroken. You *will* love again, Sister. I promise." Xiuying paused as she gathered her thoughts. "I know Han had a big impact on you. He loved you for who you are, and now that he's gone, you feel incomplete. But know that he's not the only one who loves you for you; we all do."

Xiaofan understood every word, and it all made sense to her, but saying goodbye to Han was harder and harder to forget. She knew that what they had was over even *before* saying goodbye. All the dreams that she shared with him were shattered and broken into invisible pieces.

"I never want to forget him," Xiaofan muttered.

"You won't forget him. He will always be in your heart," Xiuying assured her. She wiped the tears from Xiaofan's face and helped her stand on her own feet. "You are going to get through this."

Xiaofan nodded.

"Now, try to get some sleep." She helped Xiaofan tuck herself into bed and stayed by her side as she tried to fall asleep.

"Thank you," Xiaofan said. "For always being there for me."

"Always, Xiaofan. I have waited my entire life to be there for you, and I will never miss a chance to help you. I will never let you feel like you are alone."

"You are my home," Xiaofan whispered.

"And you are mine."

Xiaofan woke up to birds chirping by her room's window. The weather was gloomy, the clouds had covered the sky, and the oil lamps were still lit. Xiuying brought in breakfast for her.

"Han and his family are leaving today. I will have to bid them farewell as per kingdom tradition, but you don't have to be there if you don't want to," Xiuying said.

"I'll stay here," Xiaofan muttered.

"Are you sure?" Xiuying asked.

"Yes, we already said our goodbyes," Xiaofan whispered.

"Okay. I will be back after they leave." Xiuying turned around and left the room.

As soon as she was gone, Xiaofan's eyes teared up. She wanted to see him one last time, hear his voice one last time, but she knew that if she went, she would fall apart once again, and she could *not* put herself through the same heartbreak twice. It was best if she started focusing on those she had taken for granted over the past few weeks— her sister, Kyrie, Kamari. They were always there for her, and she had to pull herself out of her own head and return the favor.

AFTER XIAOFAN WALKED OUT, HAN COULD HARDLY GATHER THE courage to stand up and leave. If he left, it would mean that everything they had was gone, but what's the point of staying behind? Xiaofan herself had told him to leave, and that they had no future. What was he still trying to prove?

"There's no hope left," Han muttered. "I will have to live without her. She said her farewell. It's over now." Han sighed.

"It will get better with time. You did what had to be done; you saved your mother, Han. Don't be so hard on yourself." Zhang patted his shoulder, and then they stayed silent. Zhang didn't say much to Han, but he had to try one last time to make this all right. He was going to talk to Han's father.

The next day, Han saw the dusk turn into dawn, the colors of the sky change. Han had stayed up all night by the staircase. He sat alone, reliving the memories that he had with Xiaofan. He was never going to see her again, but he hoped he would get a glimpse of her before he left this castle forever.

Zhang took Han's father for a walk and explained what he had coming ahead. "The things I am going to say might offend you, might hurt you, but trust me, I am only looking out for you when I say this. You are not prepared for what is ahead. You might think that you are taking Han with you, and that he is leaving his choice behind, but you are wrong. He is always going to resent you for this. And when he is crowned king in the next few months, I fear what he will do as revenge. People change when they have power; you know that better than me. If I were you, I'd be careful."

The bell sounded, and it was time for Han's family to leave. The ships were ready to set sail, and everyone from the royal family gathered at the main entrance to bid them farewell. Han's parents arrived, and they thanked everyone for the hospitality before boarding their carriage. Zhang was hopeful that something might change after the conversation he had with Han's father, but he saw no progress.

"See you soon," Zhang told Han and reached out his hand.

"Soon," Han replied, shaking it. He looked around, hoping he would see Xiaofan.

"She's not coming," Xiuying said, noticing Han's eyes. "Take care of yourself."

Han shook his head. "Take care of her for me."

Xiuying nodded, and Han left. Their carriage left for the harbor, and so did Zhang's hope that Han's father would change his mind.

Han had grown mute when he reached the harbor. He replied with simple, one-word answers and nothing more. His behavior reminded his father of what Zhang had said. Han's mother noticed, and she blamed her husband's stubbornness.

"You are making a mistake. This will only push him away," she whispered to her husband.

"Is everything loaded?" Han's father asked his son.

"Yes, we leave in ten minutes," Han answered.

His father glanced at Han once more. He saw the despair, the grief, and the spite growing inside of him. He groaned. Zhang was right, and there was *nothing* he could do about it. "Then you should get off," he said before he could stop himself.

Han's eyes flared at him. "What do you mean?"

"I made a mistake, and I don't want you to resent me. I don't want to be the reason for your unhappiness. Xiaofan loves you. I realized that when she agreed to let you go because she wanted our family to stay together. She wanted you to be with your parents. I should have understood this then, but it is not too late. Find her, and ask for her hand in marriage."

Han could not believe his ears, but he quickly stepped off the ship. "Thank you, Father." He beamed and turned to his mother. "Are you okay with Xiaofan joining our family?"

She nodded with a gentle smile of her own. "Yes, I've always liked her. She deserves you, and you deserve her. Now go to her."

Han gave his parents a long hug before running toward the castle to reclaim his missing piece.

This was his life—his future—and he *refused* to spend one more moment of it without Xiaofan by his side.

To be continued...

THE RIGHTEOUS SON

THE LOST DAUGHTERS TRILOGY
BOOK THREE

The Righteous Son

THE LOST DAUGHTERS TRILOGY BOOK THREE

VIOLA TEMPEST

CHAPTER
ONE

For decades, the seed of hatred, oppression, and discrimination had been germinating in the soil of Jinu Kingdom. The sorrows and cries for help wafted in the eerie winds, and the kingdom that once flourished with wealth and power was now struggling.

Over the years, the kingdom had lost allies and made enemies because of Qianfan's temper and pessimism. The people of Jinu had migrated to other kingdoms after living in the deteriorating state of their own. The land had gone barren, the soil became unfertile, the water surrounding them had depleted, and with every passing second, the people were losing hope.

The king and queen had turned a blind eye to the depre-cating situation of their kingdom. For them, everything seemed normal and perfect... as long as the circumstances did not affect their extravagant lifestyle.

Daiyu, who was once the empathetic soul of the people, was now an overly desirous, self-centered bitch who only cared about herself. And while Qianfan's personality had only gotten more menacing with time, he also managed to become a narcissistic dictator.

The king and queen failed their people, and their feel-ings for each other had waned, too. The love that Qianfan and Daiyu once had for one another had now turned into pure resentment.

After the birth of their fourth child—a daughter— Qianfan blamed Daiyu for giving him a child that was of no use to him. And the love that Qianfan once had for his third child—his only son—had averted after the first five years.

Daiyu, on the other hand, reprimanded Qianfan for being a monster. He continued to abandon his children, one after another, and forced Daiyu to also turn against them. His actions and words made Daiyu suffer. She blamed him for making her numb, for killing the motherly nature that she once had inside of her. She hated herself for not standing up for her children, for not stopping Qianfan when she could've, and she couldn't live with the guilt.

She couldn't even find it in herself to love the children she still had with her. How could she stand here and love two of her children when the other two were possibly dead?

Daiyu spent most of her days locked inside her room. Whenever her children crossed her mind, she distracted herself by buying expensive clothes and jewels, spending all her time only on herself. She created a world for herself where she pretended as if her children never existed—that was the only way to keep her mind from bleeding guilt.

At the other end of the castle, Qianfan spent his time away from Daiyu, focusing his own time on whatever numbing drink he could find and building an army of mass destruction. He wanted the other kingdoms to fear him, to see Jinu as the one untouchable kingdom in all of China, and in his mind, he knew that if war were to ever erupt, he'd be ready.

As a couple, Qianfan and Daiyu had failed. They hardly saw each other anymore, and whenever they did, it was *always* an unpleasant encounter.

As parents, they were nothing more than a disappointment.

And as the kingdom's leaders, they had proven to be unsuitable.

Jinhai, the prince of Jinu, was meant to make things right. Qianfan wanted him to be a mirror image of himself. From a very young age, Jinhai was trained to be a fighter—a killer. From fencing to martial arts, he was taught *everything* that was related to violence. For Jinhai, it wasn't that bad; he liked learning new things, and he aced everything that he tried. But when he failed, his father would strike.

Every time Jinhai fell or got injured, he'd cry, and Qianfan *refused* to accept that.

"Boys do not cry," Qianfan would say every time Jinhai shed a tear. "You are weak; you *cannot* be weak."

For the first five years of Jinhai's childhood, he saw the virtuous version of his father—the one who gave him everything and treated him like an actual human being.

But little did he know, happiness never lasted long when it came to Qianfan, lasting only temporarily until he found himself longing for his next fix.

It was Jinhai's sixth birthday when things completely changed. The kingdom was decorated with red dragons and lanterns, as usual—Jinhai's birthdays were always celebrated like festivals. Qianfan distributed gold coins amongst the peasants, and he invited kings and queens from neighboring kingdoms. Daiyu was expecting another child—whom Qianfan expected to be a boy—and the day was meant to bring nothing but peace and joy.

The party began with Jinhai greeting all the kings and their sons. They had dinner together while talking over future plans that all the kings had for their sons and future leaders. But Jinhai never got along with the other princes his age. He found them too shallow and egotistical, and he'd much rather be friends with the children of the towns-people, something that Qianfan always disapproved of as the peasant boys only ever deterred Jinhai from his royal upbringing.

And he was right.

When the party came to an end, Jinhai and the rascals came sprinting down the main hall, where he tripped over the velvet rug and fell. He slammed his head onto the ground, and when he tried to stand up, his vision blurred. All he could make out was the red blood in front of him... *his* red blood. His breathing came to a stop, his lungs seized, and he began to cry.

Daiyu, who was due to give birth in a week, came running to her son's aid. But Qianfan stopped her by grab-bing onto her wrist.

"Leave him be. He needs to be strong. Let him deal with this on his own. The maids will help him clean up," he whispered.

"What's wrong with you?!" Daiyu shouted. Everyone in the room shifted their attention toward them.

"Boys are not supposed to cry," Qianfan declared, and the other kings nodded in agreement.

"In dreams of a lion, you have birthed a lamb," one king remarked, and all the guests laughed.

Qianfan hated the insult, but even *he* had to admit—they were right. His weakling of a son had turned Qianfan into a joke. He wanted nothing more than to pretend that Jinhai was never born and start over with a new son, but he couldn't just get rid of him like he had done with Xiuying and Xiaofan. This moron was the future king of Jinu, and someone would definitely notice if he were missing.

"You are a disappointment," Qianfan muttered to his son and walked out, refusing to even look at Jinhai, who was still bleeding on the ground.

The guests soon left, and the evening ended with gossip that was going to entertain their guests for months to come. Qianfan forbade Daiyu to visit Jinhai. She was furious, but her condition didn't exactly allow her to fight against it, so she went to bed with a heavy heart.

Jinhai sat alone in his room that night, surrounded by everything a boy could ever want... except for the support of his parents.

"Where did it all go wrong?" he asked himself as he stared up at the ceiling to admire the wooden carvings. "All my life, I've tried to please my father, and yet, he still hates me. If I'm not supposed to cry whenever I get hurt, what am I supposed to do? Why won't he just tell me what to do?"

The next day, Jinhai woke up with a heavy head. All he wanted was for his mother to be by his side, though she wasn't. He wasn't allowed to leave his room, as per the doctor's order, but he *was* his father's son, after all. He wanted to see his mother, and so he climbed out of bed and marched toward his parents' room. And that was when he started to hear echoes of screams. He slowly moved closer to their room, and the voices became louder —his father was shouting in rage over his mother's wavering voice.

"I cannot tolerate you or your children anymore. You have given me nothing but disappointments!" Qianfan yelled.

"You are acting as if you have compromised your entire life for me. You have done *nothing* for me!" Daiyu yelled back. "You are never happy! You wanted a son so badly that in order to get that, you abandoned *two* of our daughters. Now you have a son, but he's not like how you imagined, so now you're thinking about abandoning him, too! What kind of father are you? Do you even have a heart?"

Daiyu's voice overlapped with the shattering sound of glass. Jinhai flinched. What just happened? His heart started to race, hoping that his mother was okay. He peeked through the door's keyhole and saw pieces of a broken glass vase.

"You will *not* say a word about this," Qianfan ordered. "Next time, I won't miss."

"What else is new?" Daiyu whispered in resentment as she marched toward the door and opened it to find Jinhai standing there. At first, she was startled, and guilt stabbed at her, but the anger and hurt blanketed it.

"What do you want?!" she screamed at him. "You and your siblings have brought nothing but hurt into my life. I wish I'd never given birth to any of you!"

Jinhai's heart sank, heartbroken by his mother's words. She had always been so kind to him, treating him as if he were a porcelain doll. Never in his life had he seen her behave like this, but seeing the anger on her face, he was at a loss for words. He turned around slowly and walked back to his room, where he curled up in bed and wrapped his own arms around himself for comfort.

"How can someone be surrounded by people yet still feel so alone?" he whispered to himself.

Minutes later, his door opened. Jinhai eagerly spun around, hoping to see his mother and run into her welcoming arms. Instead, he found Haitao standing by the door, accompanied by his father, Lixin.

Haitao was one of Jinhai's closest friends. They met two years back in a fencing class and had been inseparable ever since. Haitao lived amongst the peasants inside the kingdom, and his father was nothing more than a mere cobbler. He didn't have any siblings, and his mother had died from an incurable disease several years ago.

They both entered the room, and Haitao joked, "How's your head? Do you still remember me?"

Jinhai laughed and nodded.

"Are you sure you don't have brain damage? Maybe memory loss?" Haitao asked, glancing his friend up and down.

"Yes," Jinhai replied.

"Glad to hear it, my son. Get better soon," Lixin said while patting Jinhai's shoulder. "You are a brave one. You can handle this."

Jinhai smiled and offered Lixin and Haitao a place to sit near his bed.

"Here," Lixin handed Jinhai a covered glass bowl, "I made you your favorite tofu, just how you like it."

"Thank you. It's just what I needed," Jinhai mumbled.

"You don't look so good. Is everything okay?" Lixin asked, his brows furrowed.

"Yes, I'm just lightheaded," Jinhai answered, only revealing half the truth.

"Okay, you should get some rest, then," Lixin suggested.

"No, no, it's fine." Jinhai nearly jumped out of bed with the need to keep them there. "I could use the company."

They all settled in and talked, but after a while, Lixin had to leave for work. Jinhai thanked him again for the tofu, and Lixin left with a bow. Once Jinhai and Haitao were alone, he told his friend everything that had happened. The problems were too big for their tiny minds, and they tried to make sense of the situation, but they failed to do so. All Jinhai knew was that he was hurt because of his parents, and in order to protect himself, he had to stay away from them.

A week had gone by, and no one from Jinhai's family came to see him. But he was fine; he knew how to keep his expectations low so that he wouldn't be disappointed.

Within the week, the news had spread all over the castle that the queen had given birth to a daughter, and the only person who saw this as good news was Jinhai. Daiyu had given the baby girl to a nanny the moment she was born and marked with the stone, and told the nurses that she wanted nothing to do with the child. Under the law, Jinhai was her only child. The child's room was next to Jinhai's, which once belonged to Xiaofan, and her name was Xiaosheng, named by Jinhai himself. After seeing how his mother had abandoned both him and his baby sister, he promised himself that he'd be there for Xiaosheng no matter what.

Jiayi was the name of the nanny who would now look after Xiaosheng. She had been barren her entire life, so when she learned that she'd be taking care of a child—a princess—she was more than thrilled, the best gift that she could ever ask for. She had been married and divorced several times now because of her infertility, but her wish had finally come true.

Jinhai spent his days and nights with his younger sister. He felt protective of her, and he made sure that she was properly looked after and loved. The happiness that Xiaosheng brought into his life made him forget the sorrow that his parents had given him. It made him forget how he had also been injured by them. He looked to Jiayi as his own mother, and he tried his best to forget the evil eyes that he had seen in the queen—the evil eyes of his royal parents whom he would enact revenge upon one day.

The seasons changed, and the trees saw many colors, moons, and exquisite sunsets. Fifteen years had passed, yet the memories of his parents still lived inside Jinhai's mind as if they had happened just mere days before. Jinhai was now twenty-one, a tall, broad-shouldered, and handsome-looking man with long black hair, light brown eyes, a heart-warming smile, and a glowing complexion.

Apart from his appearance, his soul was pure. He had grown up to be considerate, empathetic, charitable, and quite the opposite of Qianfan. He had spent years and years gathering the knowledge that would help him make his kingdom a better place. He had not only excelled academically, but had also trained himself in weapons development, mastered martial arts, and often disguised himself as a peasant so he could go into the kingdom and interact with his people to learn more about them.

Over the years, his relationship with his sister had

grown strong, and they had become each other's best friend. Xiaosheng was now fifteen, with similar features and complexion as her brother, but much shorter.

Jiayi looked after both of them like they were her own, and they treated her like their mother. They shared their ups and downs with her, and they came to her whenever they failed or succeeded. Daiyu and Qianfan never tried to reach out to them. They would only appear as a family when they were in the public eye. They would laugh and smile in front of the peasants, appearing as a perfect royal family, but behind closed doors, they resented each other.

Haitao and his father, Lixin, had been there for Jinhai during every step of his life. Lixin was like a father to Jinhai. He helped him become a better version of himself, and Jinhai only believed in himself because of the support that Lixin and Jiayi had given him.

Jinhai wasn't the king yet, but he knew that time was near. He was doubtful that his father would give him the crown, but he was certain of one thing—that his people loved him. They saw him strive to improve the kingdom, and when the time comes, they would all stand behind him.

"What took you so long?" Xiaosheng asked as he entered his room after a long day of fishing at the sea.

"Fishing?" Jinhai laughed.

"I was waiting for you. I haven't had dinner yet," Xiaosheng murmured.

"I've told you many times to not wait for me," Jinhai answered in a polite tone as he sat down next to her, and they both started to dig into their plates.

Xiaosheng took a bite before looking up at him. "Got your favorite tofu made."

Jinhai smiled. "Yes, I can see that. Though, the one that Haitao's father makes just hits different." He chuckled.

Xiaosheng nodded with a slight shrug. "Nothing can beat his."

"So, why the long face? Is everything okay?" Jinhai asked, noticing how Xiaosheng was quieter than usual, and her cheerful smile was missing.

"I don't know. Lately, I've been feeling out of place, useless, like I have no purpose. I keep roaming around the castle like a ghost."

"Well, that's not necessarily a problem. Tell me, Sister, what are your dreams?"

"What do you mean? Are you making fun of me?" Xiaosheng sneered.

"I certainly am not. Everyone has dreams. They are everything a person needs to stay inspired and hopeful. Having a dream makes you want to get up every morning and work for it. It gives your life a purpose. If you have none, you'll feel like you are lost. You'll feel like you're less motivated. A mind that is knitting dreams is less likely to fall to negative thoughts," Jinhai replied earnestly.

"I haven't thought about it that way." Xiaosheng grinned.

"Think about it, then. Find a dream, follow it, and I will be right here to support you every step of the way." Jinhai smiled

"What if I can't do it? I'm not strong like you."

This reminded Jinhai of the time when he felt the same, and Haitao's father made him understand something important. "Xiaosheng, it took me a great deal of time to understand this, and I want you to know that nobody is perfect. Everyone has weaknesses, insecurities, and self-doubts. The best thing you can do is be aware of them. It will help you be less judgmental, more mindful of your actions, and it will help you stay grounded and have self-control. You are saying that you are weak, and that's exactly how you start. You point out your weaknesses, and you work on them, push yourself to overcome them, and become an improved version of yourself. I have weaknesses, too, and sometimes the things that you think are weaknesses turn out to be your biggest strengths."

Xiaosheng smiled. "How do you always have all the answers?"

"It's because of all the experience that I have. I was born six years before you. Have you forgotten that already?" Jinhai quipped.

"Oh, I must've forgotten—the six years when you were just a *child*," Xiaosheng teased.

"Hey, don't underestimate your brother. I had the wisdom of a monk at that age!" Jinhai laughed.

"Maybe," Xiaosheng chuckled, "but I'm going to bed, Sir Wise One."

After Xiaosheng left, Jinhai was left in his room all alone. He felt at peace because he was happy. He could be there for Xiaosheng, and he was relieved that she had a family she could turn to. He was still keeping the promise that he'd made to his younger self.

He woke up early the next morning and began to prepare for his day. The food drive for the local community was scheduled for this evening. This was something he did every month to connect with the people who needed support, to interact with those who thought the prince was not within reach, and most importantly, he did it for himself. He'd saved all the coins that he'd gotten from his father and the other royal kings when he was born, just for this occasion. He felt like he didn't need or deserve any of it.

The kingdom's treasure was more than enough, while the basic needs of the people were hardly being met. It was unfair to them, and if he used the coins for himself, he would never be able to forgive himself.

The door to his room resounded with a knock, and when he didn't reply, it opened. To his surprise, in walked his father, Qianfan.

"My son!" Qianfan exclaimed with excitement.

Jinhai raised his brows at him. "Now you remember you have one? After fifteen years? How about a daughter?"

"Yes, at least I remember, unlike you," Qianfan shot back.

"Why? Are you the only one who's allowed to forget about or abandon people?" Jinhai questioned.

"You are forgetting that you are talking to your father," Qianfan stated flatly, all the pretense of excitement gone.

"A father who forgot that I existed for almost six years of my life," Jinhai corrected. "You cannot choose to become a father whenever it is convenient for you."

"Keep it up, and I promise you will lose the crown that isn't even yours yet," Qianfan warned.

"I'm not worried about that one bit." Jinhai laughed sarcastically as he walked toward the windows to close them.

"The reason why I stopped by was to ask you to *not* do the food drive today," Qianfan confessed, ignoring his son's jab. "It creates chaos and disrupts the roads near the harbor."

"It only becomes chaotic because the people of your kingdom are struggling to afford a decent meal. This is something you have to think about—something you have ignored. And I will *not* hold myself back from helping them now. Sorry to disappoint you, like always." Jinhai sneered.

"Kings are not supposed to sit with the peasants on the streets!" Qianfan bellowed.

"You have simply forgotten what being a king means," Jinhai replied. "Maybe you should think about the sins that are holding you back, the sins that are affecting your good nature."

Qianfan boiled in rage. "How *dare* you speak to your father like that?"

Jinhai grinned, and then calmly uttered, "Pardon me, I have to go. I'm running late for the *food drive*."

He left the room, leaving Qianfan standing there alone with an army of guards that were gathered outside Jinhai's door. Jinhai knew that his father was powerless to stop him, and he *never* let him get on his nerves. Their encounters were entertaining for Jinhai, just as they were humiliating for Qianfan. Their exchanges were only words for now, but Jinhai knew that when he takes the throne, Qianfan would only make things difficult for him.

Jinhai quickly wolfed down his breakfast, then left with Xiaosheng for the main market down by the harbor—the hub for all the trading shops and where many of the homeless resided. When they arrived, there were already many residents carrying boxes full of clothes and food to donate, all willing to help out wherever they could. Jinhai wanted Xiaosheng to see how helping others had a ripple effect— how one person's small offering could give others a chance to pay it forward. Haitao and his father were there, too, but they were standing next to someone that Jinhai had never met—a beautiful woman.

"Jinhai!" Haitao shouted from a distance.

"Haitao, my friend!" Jinhai shouted back, and then they shook each other's hand. "Good to see you!"

"Always a pleasure to see you doing great things, my son," Lixin commented.

"It's all because of you," Jinhai assured him with a grin.

"Oh, I almost forgot—meet Fia. She just moved in next door. She's new to town, so we thought we'd bring her along and introduce her to the community." Haitao winked at Jinhai.

"Hi!" Fia cheerfully greeted.

She had a thin face with rosy cheeks, a fair complexion, and her smile was accompanied by dimples on both her cheeks.

"Hi," Jinhai greeted back with a grin. But then he abruptly excused himself when someone called for him.

Jinhai was never into romance or attracting attention to himself. He knew he easily caught the eyes of many women around him, but he never gave them a second thought. He stayed away from anything heartfelt, and from afar, he seemed extremely unapproachable. His parents' relationship had affected him a great deal. They made him think that love between two people would always be temporary—a waste of time—so there's really no point in chasing it.

He had his boundaries set, and he never crossed them... until now. Fia. He couldn't stop thinking about her. Her beautiful smile, her bubbly personality. She brought him a certain sense of... comfort. She felt like pure light to him.

People all around him were preparing for the food drive. Wooden tables were set up on a red carpet that was spread along the pathway, containers full of food were brought in, and everyone was invited to take their places while the volunteers started to serve them.

Fia was one of those volunteers, and the way she committed to the cause caught Jinhai's attention. She approached people with a smile and asked them how they were doing in a welcoming tone. They complimented her, and she laughed before moving onto the next person, making them all feel at home. Jinhai caught himself looking for her many times when she disappeared from his sight, and then he'd tell himself to snap out of it.

"Don't do this to yourself. You will become *nothing* but a hopeless romantic."

Haitao and Jinhai worked together at the drive. They refilled the food containers as soon as they were empty. There were more than two hundred people who had shown up, and after they were all fed, the leftovers would be packed and sent home with them.

"You seem distracted today," Haitao teased.

"Why would I be distracted?" Jinhai asked.

"You tell me!" Haitao laughed.

"What do you mean?"

"I've noticed that your attention is on... a certain someone."

"Well, maybe you should be noticing how you're spilling beans all over the floor," Jinhai replied with a sneer.

Haitao looked down at the beans that covered his shoes before laughing. "The beans have fallen, just like you."

Jinhai shook his head, speechless.

After serving the food, all the volunteers gathered around the food containers to pack the leftovers. They all sat down in a circle and quickly filled up the bags around them. Jinhai couldn't help but notice how Fia and Xiaosheng had gotten very close, almost like they were sisters.

A middle-aged woman from the circle spoke up as she filled a bag, "All these people are suffering because the kingdom is failing. How is this ever going to get better?"

The townspeople of Jinu felt comfortable voicing their

concerns to Jinhai, despite him being a prince. Unlike his father, he listened, and he never judged them. But before he could answer, Fia chimed in.

"You know how when stars fall, we make a wish? But we don't see those stars as falling; we see them as a chance to pray for a miracle. Think about our situation in the same way. Sure, things aren't that great now, but I believe that if we want it enough, a miracle will soon happen."

"I never thought of it like that," the woman replied.

"What a wonderful comparison, Fia!" Lixin exclaimed.

"I agree!" Xiaosheng added and looked over at Jinhai, who remained silent.

The sun soon started to set, just as the volunteers were finishing up. The sky had turned dark blue, and as the light slowly dimmed, the wind grew stronger, and the waves of the ocean aggressively crashed into the shore.

LIXIN INVITED THE GROUP BACK TO HIS HOME FOR SOME TEA, AND Jinhai and Xiaosheng eagerly accepted. After all, they called that place their *home*, the one place they felt safe in ever since they were just children. And the only reason they stayed at the castle was because of Jiayi. As a servant to the royal couple, she was never allowed to leave.

When they walked inside, Haitao, Fia, and Xiaosheng went to sit by the fireplace. Jinhai lit the logs before heading into the kitchen to help Lixin with the tea. Ever since Jinhai was young, they'd always bonded that way.

"My father visited me today, wanted me to stop the food drive," Jinhai said.

"And you made the right decision," Lixin assured him.

"He's always trying to make me a version of him, always trying to kill my compassionate side," Jinhai let out in frustration. "I like that I can feel other emotions and understand what others are going through. It helps me understand them better, and I come up with better solutions when I can relate to people."

Lixin smiled with a sense of relief. "That is your strength, Jinhai. You will never be able to experience any other emotion fully if you don't also let yourself feel the negative ones. You are in touch with your emotional side, and it is a blessing. You don't have to be strong and follow what your father tells you. I am proud of who you have become." Lixin paused, picking up the tea that he had just poured into the wooden cups, and then continued, "You are going to make a fine leader one day."

Jinhai nodded, grabbed the plate with baked bread and sliced cakes off the counter, and followed Lixin back into the living room.

"My favorite!" Xiaosheng jumped up excitedly and grabbed a slice of cake.

"This is literally the best bread that I have ever had," Fia added. "I will certainly take some home."

"Me, too!" Xiaosheng approved.

"So, who's this prince that everyone keeps talking about today? The entire kingdom seems to like him, and they say he's their last hope," Fia then asked.

Xiaosheng looked at Jinhai, and they all soon realized that Fia had no idea that Xiaosheng and Jinhai were royalty —that *they* were the future of this kingdom.

"I'm curious myself," Haitao joked.

"What do you mean?" Fia chuckled. "You've never seen him?"

"Fia," Lixin grinned, "I believe you have not been properly introduced." He paused, and then pointed at Jinhai. "Meet Jinhai, the *prince* of Jinu."

Jinhai looked into her eyes and smiled.

"Oh...," Fia murmured, embarrassed.

"And meet Xiaosheng, the *princess* of Jinu," Lixin revealed.

"Hi!" Xiaosheng laughed.

"Why do you seem so disappointed?" Haitao asked.

"I'm not disappointed, just... surprised," Fia replied, and then continued in an apologetic tone, "I hope I didn't offend anyone. I didn't know."

Haitao laughed again, and then jokingly said, "You have, and now you're going to prison for life!"

"Haitao's just messing around. You didn't offend us. I prefer *not* to be treated like royalty anyway," Jinhai finally spoke.

Fia was still shocked that the cute boy she'd been hanging around all day, one who looked just like everyone else in town, was actually the prince of this kingdom, the one destined to save it from poverty and destruction. He's so... so... different, so kind. Suddenly, she found herself being drawn to him, but had to take a step back. "I should get going. It's getting late."

"Alright, don't forget the bread!" Haitao reminded her.

"Oh, yes." Fia beamed, and Lixin handed her a box filled with some. "Thank you."

"It was nice meeting you. See you soon!" Xiaosheng waved.

"See you soon," Fia replied.

She didn't say anything to Jinhai, but their eyes met before she walked out of the door.

"I really like her," Xiaosheng sang.

"Seems like you're not the only one," Haitao added.

"Who are we talking about?" Jinhai asked.

"Oh, don't act naïve," Haitao teased.

"Wait… Jinhai?" Xiaosheng chuckled.

"Xiaosheng, have you ever seen your brother this quiet?" Haitao asked.

Xiaosheng paused, and then shook her head. "No, I haven't." She shot her gaze over at her brother. "You like her!"

Jinhai muttered, "I just met her." He shook his head. "I don't even know her."

"You're not denying it, though," Haitao teased again.

"I am not agreeing, either," Jinhai insisted.

"Alright, alright!" Xiaosheng laughed.

"She's a strong one. Fia's parents died when she was very young. She spent the majority of her childhood at an orphanage that wasn't safe for anyone. She only recently moved here because she wanted to start fresh, to find a new home. Even now, she's living alone, and she works at the flower shop to support herself. She mentioned that when she's financially stable enough, she'll dedicate her life to helping orphans who can't help themselves, so they don't have to go through what she went through," Haitao explained.

"What an inspiration!" Xiaosheng exclaimed.

"Yeah," Jinhai murmured.

Later that night, Jinhai and Xiaosheng walked back to the castle, where they found Jiayi cooking up something delicious. Xiaosheng rushed over to hug her.

"How was your day?" Jiayi asked as they sat down for dinner.

Xiaosheng told her everything, including how they'd

met a woman who was *perfect* for Jinhai. "She's pretty. She's kind. She's perfect!"

"You're blushing, Jinhai, something I've never seen you do," Jiayi pointed out. "There seems to be a bit of truth in what Xiaosheng is saying."

"There's nothing going on. We *did* just meet," Jinhai assured them.

"Only time will tell." Jiayi nodded.

Jinhai went into his room after dinner and closed the door behind him. His room was huge, with different types of swords hanging on the walls and painted portraits of martyrs whom he admired. The sheets on his bed were made of blue silk, and the walls were white but covered with velvet curtains.

It had been a long day, and while he was tired, he couldn't fall asleep. He just couldn't get Fia out of his mind.

"How could someone have gone through so much but still have such a positive outlook on life? I don't understand."

Jinhai woke up the next morning to the sound of roaring thunder. He rolled out of bed and looked out the window. The wind was strong and getting stronger by the second, the streets were emptier than usual, and the sky was covered in dark gray clouds that looked menacing and threatening.

He could see the harbor from his window. The waves in the ocean were unsettling, hitting the rocks by the shore with force, and ships were swinging from side to side. Jinhai had never seen the weather this bad before, and he was worried about his people, especially the ones without shelter.

However, it wasn't raining yet. He still had time to get everyone safely inside somewhere before it began to pour. He rushed over to his closet to get dressed, choosing a traditional attire over the old rags that he usually wore. He needed to feel powerful in order to complete this morning's mission.

As he secured his kingdom's broach onto his lapel, he looked in the mirror and grinned at his reflection.

"There's no mistaking that I'm a prince now."

Suddenly, he heard a knock on his door, and it swung open to Qianfan walking in.

"Spying on me, Father?" Jinhai asked, staring at his father's reflection in the glass.

"Trust me, I wouldn't be here if I didn't have to be," Qianfan said in a stern voice before asking, "Have you discovered your power yet?"

Jinhai knew about the power that had been bestowed upon him and the stories of the magical stone, but he had never experienced anything magical in his life. He didn't even know where to begin.

"I have not," Jinhai replied.

"Always a disappointment," Qianfan huffed. "I knew you were weak the day you were born. Your chances of becoming king are dwindling by the minute."

Jinhai remained silent and let patience take over his mind with a deep breath. He was using everything he had to not explode at his father.

"What a wimp," Qianfan taunted and dramatically left the room, slamming the door shut behind him.

Jinhai was worried—not because of what Qianfan had said, but because he felt incomplete without his power. If he was blessed with one, then why was it taking so long to come to fruition?

He quickly pushed the thought out of his head and joined Jiayi and Xiaosheng for breakfast.

"The weather outside is so scary! Have you seen it? It feels like the night has eaten the sun." Xiaosheng gestured toward the window while sipping her tea.

"Yes, stay indoors today, Xiaosheng. You, too, Jiayi. Please stay with Xiaosheng," Jinhai muttered as he walked in.

"What about you? Where are *you* headed?" Jiayi asked a bit sarcastically.

"The weather is bad... and only getting worse by the minute. Our less fortunate brothers and sisters are sleeping by the harbor; they are going to need shelter. I have to make sure that they are taken care of. I'll be fine. Do not worry," Jinhai assured.

"Can someone else not do it? It's not safe out there. The wind is angry, and I can sense a vicious storm brewing."

"No. This is our kingdom, our people. We *have* to take care of them; we *have* to be there for them." He gently touched Jiayi on the hand and whispered, "I promise to come right back once my duties are done." He stood up hugged them both before grabbing his belongings and walking out to his carriage.

When he reached the harbor, there were crowds of people running around in a panic. One of the ships had crashed onto the land, damaging several homes and injuring many with no help in sight. The waves of the ocean were growing higher and higher with every push, and the ships that were still standing were starting to lose control against the strong currents. A crowd had gathered around the site of the crash—men, women, and children all desperate to save those trapped beneath it.

"We need to get everyone back into their homes or into one of our military-grade shelters! Now!" Jinhai shouted over to his guards.

As he uttered his last words, one of the waves began to levitate the largest ship over the ocean. Jinhai saw the scene unfold before him in horror and looked over at the crowd that stood in front of it.

If this falls, it will be a bloodbath, a great tragedy. I cannot have this on my conscience.

He felt shivers rush through his body, but he knew he needed to do what he came out here to do—protect the people. He rushed over to the crowd and began pushing them aside, flailing his arms in every direction in an attempt to clear the path.

"Move out of the way!" he screamed as he glanced over at the ocean and saw the wave push the ship toward the harbor with a mighty force. "No!" he shouted as he moved both of his hands toward the ocean and squeezed his eyes shut.

His heart was pounding in his chest, and he felt a sinking feeling in his stomach. He clenched his fists in anticipation for the loud crash and screaming cries that would soon lead to death. He waited for all of it.

But it never came.

Silence.

No screams.

What happened? A miracle?

Jinhai slowly crept his eyes open, still expecting to see a massacre before him, but what he saw was much... stranger.

His hands were still lifted in the air, toward the ocean,

and the deadly wave appeared as if it were frozen. The people all looked at Jinhai in shock, then they started cheering for him. Not knowing what to do next, Jinhai slowly brought his hands back down, and to his surprise, the water followed, and the mighty waves merged back into the water.

He fell onto his knees with his hands over his head. He could only feel gratitude—the scene had been witnessed by the people of his kingdom who would now think of him as a hero. Fia, Haitao, and Lixin, who were all there to help the homeless move into shelters, had also witnessed his heroic act.

Suddenly, a bright light flashed from the clouds as a streak of lightning struck the ocean nearby, and a loud clap of thunder boomed as the wind grew stronger again.

"Everyone needs to leave!" Jinhai yelled as it began to rain heavily, and the crowd started to disperse.

"You, too. I'll stay behind to make sure everyone's gone." Jinhai turned toward Haitao and Fia.

"No, we're not leaving you," Fia fought back.

"Agree. We will stay and help."

"Where's Lixin?" Jinhai asked.

"At the shelter. He took a bunch of people with him."

After hours of thoroughly searching the harbor, making sure no child was stuck under a rock and no father was lost trying to find his way, they all walked toward the shelter. The rain was getting heavier and heavier as time passed, and they were soaking wet by the time they arrived.

Jinhai was greeted with applauses of encouragement and chants of appreciation as he walked inside. Family after family came up to him, thanking him for everything that he did. The prince bowed his head in respect every time someone shook his hand, and Fia admired him from afar.

The affection. The determination. The respect. Something that she had never seen before.

And the shelter itself, a former military unit for the storage of firearms and armor, was massive and stocked with everything they'd need for the night. There were enough warm meals to go around, hot tea to cool down those coming down with an illness, and the injured were quickly treated. The people of Jinu residing there all gathered around the fireplace, reminiscing their experiences of the prince's magnificent miracle.

"A miracle. It truly *is* a miracle," Jinhai repeated over and over to himself as he changed into garments that were less damp. "Almost too good to be a miracle—"

"You finally figured it out," Lixin interrupted from around the corner, causing Jinhai to slightly hop.

"The Universe figured it out for me."

"*You* did this, all on your own, Jinhai. Have some faith in yourself." Lixin smiled. "Look around you. All these people are safe for another day because of *you*, because *you* woke up this morning and decided to risk your own life for them. You could've stayed home, much like your father did, but you didn't. That's the difference between a great leader and a coward."

Jinhai gave him a shy grin.

"And all it took was a little bit of emotion," Lixin continued.

"What do you mean?" Jinhai asked.

"Legend has it, the powers that your family has only reveal themselves through pure emotions. You must've been holding back all these years, and when you allowed yourself to be scared and concerned over the safety of the people back at the harbor, that's when your power came to life."

Jinhai's shy grin turned into a full smile. He turned around and looked for Fia in the crowd, where he saw her wrap a tiny four-year-old child in a blanket.

"You will catch a cold." He heard her faint voice from a distance.

How can you fall for someone you barely know? he asked himself.

"It's all because of her," he caught himself saying out loud.

"Because of who?" Lixin asked, and then noticed Jinhai blush. "Are you hiding something from me? You are, aren't you?"

Jinhai chuckled. "I think I have feelings for Fia. I can't stop thinking about her. I can't stop dreaming about her beautiful face. I believe that it's because of her that I am able to become emotionally vulnerable. I feel like she is my soulmate."

"You know, when my wife died, I couldn't believe it. For months, I was a wreck because I felt incomplete without her, like someone had taken away a piece of my heart. Losing her made me realize how much I took her for granted, her smile, her laughter, even her words. Even my own name sounded different after she was gone. But at the same time, it made me want to cherish the one thing that I had left of her even more, my son. So, I pieced myself together, put on a brave face, and promised her that no matter what, I will take care of our child. I will live for the both of us." Lixin sighed before continuing. "Treasure the way that you're feeling now... because you never know when you'll feel the same way again. Tell her how you really feel. Don't take her for granted like I did."

CHAPTER
THREE

The shelter soon calmed, and silence took over as the night went on. The children had stopped running around, and everyone was growing sleepy after their large dinner of boiled white rice and garlic-seasoned chicken.

"Prince Jinhai, we have informed Xiaosheng and Jiayi about your safety, and that you will be staying here for the night," one of the guards told Jinhai.

"Thank you," Jinhai replied.

After the guards left, the prince took a deep breath. "I hope they weren't too worried. Jiayi *did* have a hunch that something bad was going to happen. She must be under great levels of stress. I am ashamed of myself for having caused that."

Haitao had fallen asleep, and Lixin was silently sipping his fourth cup of tea.

"It's not your fault," Fia comforted him. "You were exactly where you were meant to be. Right place at the right time. You have saved so many lives today. Jiayi is only going to be proud of you." She smiled. "Imagine how many families you have saved from being broken, how many children you have protected, Prince Jinhai."

"You don't have to call me that. You can just call me by my name. You are just like Haitao to me, a friend. Thank you for sticking around and helping out."

Before Fia could say another word, Lixin chimed in.

"Goodnight, both of you. I'm off to sleep. I'll see you all in the morning."

"Goodnight," Jinhai whispered.

"Sleep well," Fia wished to Lixin as he walked off.

For the first time since they met, Jinhai and Fia were finally alone, sitting in front of each other by the fireplace. Fia's face was glowing as the orange light of the fire met her face, and it made her smile even warmer, which softened Jinhai's heart.

"Aren't you tired? It's been a long day," Jinhai asked.

"No." Fia shook her head with her eyes glued to the flames of the fire. "This is nothing compared to what I'm used to."

"I can believe that. Haitao mentioned your past struggles. Your resilience is admirable."

Fia blushed. "Thank you."

"Can I ask you a question?"

"Of course," Fia responded.

"You've been through so much and have faced so many

injustices. I'm sure living without parents and at an orphanage is *not* easy. But you still have this calmness in your soul, this willingness to still help others even when no one helped you. How?"

As Fia listened, she realized that Jinhai *had* been thinking about her, and her heart tingled slightly. "There are so many things in our lives that we cannot control... except for our reactions to those things. I just don't see a point in letting the bad destroy me when there's nothing that I can do to stop it from happening." Fia paused, then continued, "There's always a silver lining if I look hard enough."

"Every time I interact with you, you leave me speechless. Your point of view is so different from that of others. It's extremely uplifting, even in the darkest of days," Jinhai muttered in a low voice.

"I leave you speechless?" Fia asked as she laughed.

"Yes, you do. I'm not usually someone who gets quiet around people, but around you, I... you make me nervous."

"Nervous? Around me? I'm the one who should be nervous around you! You're a prince! And you're magical!"

"B...," Jinhai stuttered, "because I... because I like you."

"What are saying, Jinhai?" Fia asked.

"I'm saying that I am drawn to you, that you complete me. You are the reason I was able to save lives today. Before today, I had no control over my power. I was even growing distraught because I thought I didn't have any. It wasn't until I met you and started becoming emotionally vulnerable did it finally unleash. You were the key that I needed." He looked down at his feet and shuffled. "I understand if you do not feel the same way. Lixin made me realize today that life is too short to hold in my feelings any longer. I just needed you to know. I want you by my side day after day."

"Truth is, Jinhai, I sort of felt the same way, but you're a prince! How could an orphan girl like me even have a chance? You could have anyone you want in this entire kingdom... plus more! I'm outnumbered!" Her eyes started to fill with tears as she spoke.

"Hey, why are you crying? This is great news!" Jinhai tried to console her, wiping away her tears.

"But it's never going to work. One day, you will become King. And you are destined to marry a princess. I don't even have a family!"

"So? Those things don't matter to me. The throne doesn't matter to me. I only care about the people around me. Xiaosheng loves you, Haitao and Lixin praise you, and Jiayi will be over the moon to meet you, I promise. *You* matter to me, not some stupid crown or the label of royalty." Jinhai held onto her hands as Fia shifted herself closer to him and rested her head on his arm.

"I should go to sleep. It's getting late," Fia whispered.

"See you tomorrow?" Jinhai asked.

"Of course." Fia smiled. "Goodnight."

Jinhai was shocked by what he had just done. That was the most spontaneous he'd ever been his entire life! And he didn't fall flat on his face. He was grinning from ear to ear. No more fighting with himself and wishing for some girl in the corner of his room. She liked him back! He vowed to himself that he'd protect her and keep her close from now on.

Fia, on the other hand, was overwhelmed, but she wasn't complaining. A prince had just told her that he wanted her! Her whole life, all she ever wanted was to be wanted, and what she got was way better than she'd expected. Jinhai brought out the best version of her. She felt like herself around him—she smiled a little brighter, laughed a little louder. He completed her, just like she completed him. She just hoped that things would work out between them, and that the Universe wouldn't test her like it always did.

IT WAS A NEW DAY, BOTH LITERALLY AND METAPHORICALLY. THE sun shone in the blue sky with hints of white clouds, and the birds were singing with joy. The storm had passed, but a lot changed for both the kingdom and for Jinhai.

He woke up to the smell of tofu and realized that Lixin was making breakfast. He quickly got up and looked around —everyone had gone back to their homes. Only Haitao, Lixin, and Fia were left inside the shelter, waiting for Jinhai to wake up so they could all eat.

"Prince Sleepyhead is finally awake," Haitao teased.

"Why didn't anyone wake me?" Jinhai asked in a tired voice.

"You seemed like you were enjoying your rest. We didn't want to disturb you," Fia replied and gave him a flirtatious wink. Jinhai blushed.

"Breakfast is served," Lixin interrupted the three and placed an enormous pot of steaming hot tofu in front of them.

After a heavy breakfast, Lixin and Fia walked back to their village while Haitao stayed behind with Jinhai for a little longer.

"So?" Haitao asked as they walked out of the shelter and into the blazing sun.

"So?" Jinhai repeated.

"You have fallen for her pretty face, haven't you?" Haitao teased.

"The human face does not reflect the beauty that the soul within holds," Jinhai responded. This was his way of teasing Haitao back; he knew how much he hated poetic replies.

"Oh, stop with this nonsense," Haitao said with a sneer.

"Fine, fine. Yes, I have fallen for her pretty face!" Jinhai laughed. "Xiaosheng is definitely going to be happy when she hears this."

"I never thought this day would come. Jinhai, the boy who once swore to never become emotionally attached to anyone, has fallen in love."

"Yeah, well, people can change… I should probably get going. Jiayi must be worried sick." Jinhai waved farewell to his friend and walked off in the opposite direction.

Jinhai found Jiayi and his sister both waiting for him in his room when he reached the castle.

"Morning," Jinhai mumbled in a tired tone.

"Thank goodness! You're okay!" Xiaosheng screamed in relief and ran over to hug him tight.

"I am *so* proud of you. I've heard many stories about your bravery at the harbor," Jiayi praised with a smile and prideful eyes. Her words made him realize how Fia was right—Jiayi *was* the first to praise him.

"Thank you." Jinhai bowed his head.

"And I've heard about your newfound power. It's so cool that you can control water!" Xiaosheng exclaimed in excitement and hugged him again.

"Now you'll have to think twice before playing anymore pranks on me… unless you want to drown," her brother taunted while Xiaosheng gave him a playful push. Then his tone grew more serious. "And… I told Fia how I am attracted to her, and how I want to be with her."

"What did she say? Did she reject you?" Xiaosheng asked. She was not surprised at all by his confession.

"She said…" Jinhai stopped.

"Well, tell us!" Jiayi urged.

"She said she likes me, too." Jinhai grinned.

"I can't believe this!" Xiaosheng screamed and jumped up and down.

"I was hoping I could bring her over for dinner tonight… if that's okay with you, Jiayi," Jinhai requested.

"I don't see why not!" Jiayi agreed.

"But keep it low-key. I don't want anyone knowing about this just yet. You know how word travels fast around here."

"My lips are sealed," Jiayi assured the prince.

About an hour later, Jinhai took a quick bath and got ready. He was going to go down to the harbor and invite Fia over for dinner. He threw on a royal blue qipao and pinned on a brooch that had a bird engraved onto it, symbolizing peace and harmony. He then summoned his carriage, gathered his guards, and left for the harbor.

The conditions at the harbor were bad, really bad. What used to be the pride and joy of Jinu was now heavily damaged and falling apart. He walked around and inspected every inch of his surroundings, giving orders to his guards on suggestions that he had to fix up the place and quickly.

Suddenly, someone tapped him on the shoulder. Jinhai quickly spun around, expecting to see Fia, but instead, he saw an elderly woman standing behind him. She was quite petite and had silver hair. Her face was covered with wrinkles, and she limped while leaning on her wooden stick for balance.

"Yes?" Jinhai politely answered the tap.

"Thank you," the old woman whispered. "You saved my son yesterday. If you hadn't been there, I would be mourning his loss today." She bowed respectfully. "I wish for you to overtake your father and rule the land. You deserve to seize the throne."

Jinhai never really knew what to say whenever someone complimented him. Instead, he simply bowed back and accepted her gratitude.

"If you had been born sooner, your sisters may not have suffered the fate that they had," the woman continued.

Jinhai's heart briefly stopped, and his stomach dropped.

"What do you mean?" he asked.

"You do not know? Your older sisters, Xiuying and Xiaofan. They were both abandoned because your father so desperately wanted a son. Xiuying's nanny was my sister, Mei, and your father sentenced her to life in prison."

Jinhai could not believe his ears. How was this the first time he was hearing about all this?

"Are they... are they... alive? Do you know what happened to them?" Jinhai asked frantically. His entire life, he thought he only had one sister, Xiaosheng.

"I know as much as you do. My child, it is almost as if they had been forgotten. Not many people in the kingdom know about them. I only know bits and pieces of what had happened because my sister witnessed everything with her own two eyes." The woman then added, "Everyone who knew about your sisters were either imprisoned or killed by your father."

Jinhai stood silent, trying to process everything that he had just heard within the span of five minutes. "There must be *someone* still around who knows what *actually* happened to them! Think, who else knows?"

The old woman hesitated for a moment, but then she

revealed, "You have to meet Huiqing. He was Chief of the Military at the time and imprisoned with Mei as an accomplice. He might know something that nobody else does."

"Where? Where can I find him?"

"Locked inside a prison cell deep within the castle. You could try, but he might already be dead," she replied.

Jinhai nodded his head. "Thank you for telling me this."

"Do not let this information go to waste, my child. You are the only one who can save your sisters."

As the woman strolled away, Jinhai stared out into the ocean, where the waves were crashing against the shore. "My father is an evil man. There is no denying that he is capable of something like this. I have to get to the bottom of this."

The guards were all given orders to tend to the harbor while Jinhai had more important things to worry about. Fia. With the words of the woman and his father's atrocious actions still in his mind, he hopped inside his carriage and rode away.

CHAPTER
FOUR

After a short ride, Jinhai reached his destination and walked down the street toward Fia's shop. He stood there for a minute and watched her put together a bouquet of flowers, placing each stem carefully in its place. Her hair was tied with a ribbon that matched the robe she wore, and he admired how she always made sure her colors matched. There was just something about her that gave him peace amidst all the chaos around him.

After a few more minutes, he walked in. He had spent much too long staring at her through the window that it was starting to get weird.

Fia greeted the prince with a cheerful tone when she saw him. "Hi! What are you doing here?"

"I had some things to take care of in town and thought I'd pop in to see you."

"Really?"

"No," Jinhai admitted.

"Then?" Fia chuckled as she asked.

"I came here to invite you over for dinner tonight. I want you to meet Jiayi. She's been a mother to me my entire life when my birth mother didn't want me."

"Well, if you put it like that, how can I possibly refuse?" Fia smirked sarcastically.

"I can have a carriage come by later to pick you up," Jinhai offered.

"No, no. It's fine. I'm a grown woman. I'm sure I can find my way there. Besides, it's not like I can see it from here or anything." Fia pointed over to her left. And when Jinhai looked over, he saw one of the large castle towers looming over the village.

"Fair point," he acknowledged, "but let me send one anyway. It'll be my way of showing my appreciation for all that you do."

"If you insist." She grinned, though there was still hesitation in her voice.

When Jinhai left to head back to the harbor, Fia still felt a pang of guilt. The differences between her and Jinhai were infinite. They weren't even part of the same social circle! He came from wealth and gold while she came from poverty and destitute. How was she ever going to stand a chance with him without everyone around her mocking her and judging her? She would forever be labeled a *gold digger*, or even worse, a *prostitute*.

On the other hand, she knew that Jinhai didn't see her

in that way at all, and she knew she couldn't let the sneers of others cut in between them. Their relationship was between the two of them, not the world around them.

After making sure that everything was in order at the harbor, Jinhai went back to the castle with just one intention—to visit Huiqing and find out the truth. Part of him prayed that the old woman was just delusional and spewing nonsense, but the other part of him didn't expect anything less from his parents.

It was already late in the afternoon when he got back. He slowly made his way down the halls, ones that he wasn't very familiar with as he was usually confined to his room, and headed down the dark staircase into the abandoned hall of the basement. There were two guards protecting the only door, surrounded by lit oil lamps and the freezing cold air.

"No one is allowed inside," one of the guards stated firmly.

"I believe you are forgetting who I am. I may just be a prince right now, but soon, this will be *my* kingdom. Your actions now will surely determine your fate in Jinu," Jinhai warned them with a strong yet soothing tone.

"Yes, your highness," the guard replied and opened the door of iron rods, sealed with chains and locks.

Jinhai knew that the door wasn't to be opened without the king's permission, and so he assured the guards that this would stay between them as he stepped inside. He walked into a small alley that had tiny rooms on both sides with no windows. They were also covered with iron rods, chained and locked in the same manner as the front door.

He shivered as he walked past three empty cells, and then three more that housed people who were on the verge of dying. He could see that the lack of food, water, sunlight, and hygienic facilities had made it challenging for them all to survive.

"This is torture," he heard himself mutter.

It was so dark that it felt like it was past midnight. There were rats crawling all over the floor and water coming out of the broken pipes.

"How? How is this justice? I get to sit upstairs on my golden throne while these people down here are forced to eat their own excrements."

Jinhai walked to the end of the alley, finding two more cells that faced each other. One of them was empty with nothing but a tiny window inside, while the other housed a very ancient man with a long beard and a pale face. He was sitting up, staring out the tiny window, so focused on the light coming in that he didn't realize that someone had approached him.

"Huiqing?" Jinhai spoke softly.

The man slowly glanced up at him, frightened.

No one had come to see him in years, left alone to relive his terrifying memories.

"I have not heard my name in ages," the man whispered in a strong voice.

Jinhai was shocked when he heard the man's voice. For someone who seemed so weak, his voice didn't match his appearance at all.

"Who is here to see me?" Huiqing asked.

"Jinhai," Jinhai replied.

Huiqing paused. "The awaited Prince of Jinu? I have heard good things about you. I have heard that you are quite the opposite of your father. What is someone so high and mighty like yourself doing down here in the cells?"

The question haunted Jinhai. Huiqing was here, imprisoned, and the possibility of the tale being true was elevated. Did he even have the courage to learn the truth?

"Seems like you're a little lost, Little One," Huiqing continued.

Jinhai took a deep breath and sat down beside the iron rods that separated him from Huiqing. "The search for peace—for truth—brings me here to you, Huiqing. I have been told a tale by someone who claimed to be Mei's sister," Jinhai said, looking down at his hands.

"You seem anxious, Little One, and rightfully so. It is not just a tale that you have been told, but it's the truth that, I assume, has been hidden from you for decades. It is what has happened before you. It is what people have experienced for only showing kindness, for only wanting love. It is the injustice that took our lives away," Huiqing explained almost poetically. His voice was firm but painful that it sent shivers down Jinhai's spine.

"Xiuying was born first, the eldest. Your mother adored her, but your father so desperately wanted a son instead. So, they gave her to Mei. Your parents abandoned her, and they announced to the kingdom that Xiuying had died at birth. But shortly after, the queen—your mother—started to feel resentment toward Mei for being Xiuying's first priority. Because of all the trauma, Xiuying attempted to take her own life one night. Luckily, she survived. Mei, with her motherly instincts, went against the queen and king, fought for Xiuying's rights and the love that she needed, but in return, she was forced to spend the rest of her life here." He pointed toward the empty cell in front of his, the one with the tiny window.

"I was ordered to drop Xiuying off on a deserted island to die so that your parents could be free of their mistake, but I couldn't do that to her. Instead, I left her in the care of some amazing village people whom I knew would care for her well. She was wronged by everyone here, and life was extremely difficult for her, being sent away by her own blood mother, after all. However, when I came back, your father soon found out what I had done and sentenced me to spend the rest of my life down here."

Jinhai stayed silent. He didn't know what to say. He hated the way that his father had treated him, but to force someone who had once been loyal to him to die of starvation was much worse than he could've imagined. Qianfan. He just wasn't human!

"I'm so sorry," Jinhai apologized on his father's behalf. "I didn't know about any of this."

"I loved her. Mei. We spent years and years together down here. She continued to praise Xiuying until the day she died and told herself that it was all worth it. Unfortunately, the torture that she underwent would be fatal for anyone. They forced her to stand on swords for hours, starved her for days at a time, and mercilessly whipped her until she admitted that she never loved your sister—which she'd never do. She was beaten to death simply because your mother resented her. Your mother constantly blamed Mei for Xiuying's hatred for the queen. Always blaming everyone but herself and her own damn husband."

Huiqing broke into tears and started to cry. Jinhai's eyes turned red with rage, remorse, and regret, tears rolling down from them. His heart had become too heavy. He could feel himself drowning in the pit of despair. He was so oblivious, so unaware... that his parents were the human version of the Devil. With no words to describe the sorrow, no will to speak for the injustices that his father had done, the lives he had destroyed, Jinhai thought it couldn't get any worse... but then Huiqing continued.

"Xiaofan was born next. Your father played his cards with this one. At first, Xiaofan was accepted, welcomed, and celebrated. Your mother was at ease with the fact that Qianfan had accepted a girl, but to him, Xiaofan was only a pawn, a gateway to finally bearing a son. And when you were born, everything changed. Now that the king finally got what he wanted, he no longer saw a need to keep Xiaofan around. So, he sent her away to an abandoned orphanage in the middle of a destitute town known for its darkness and horrendous crimes. And of course, the queen stayed silent throughout all this, as usual. She'd never go against her husband." Huiqing paused for a moment to swallow his tears. "Oh, and don't even get me started on your evil grandmother. She was the worst of them all when it came to Xiuying."

Qiang had always been nothing but a saint to Jinhai, the sweet grandmother who took care of him and fed him. He couldn't imagine someone like her ever being capable of anything else.

"Do you know where they are? Are my sisters still alive?" Jinhai nervously asked.

"Qiang was supposed to meet them. They are alive, and they live together, but that is all I know. Your grandmother mentioned this when she last visited me, and right after, she hopped on a boat to go see them," Huiqing replied.

Jinhai remembered the voyage that his grandmother took just before she died. It took her over two weeks to come back, and Jinhai remembered the argument that Qiang had with his father the night she died. Jinhai was shaken to know how much clearer everything was. It all made sense now.

"I am sorry about your grandmother's passing. My

condolences… but something inside me tells me that it was not a coincidence," Huiqing spoke.

"What do you mean?"

Ignoring Jinhai's question, Huiqing continued, "I don't know what happened after or what happened at the voyage, but there is a way for you to find out. Your grandmother always carried a journal. Every time she came down here, she would write down all our conversations. For sentimental reasons? Maybe. But I think it's to catch anything I say that could lead to my impending death. If you find it, I'm sure you might be able to find some answers."

"Yes, yes!" Jinhai jumped up as he remembered. "She *did* take her journal with her, and she *did* bring it back. It must be in her room somewhere. Thank you, Huiqing, for everything." Jinhai paused. His voice was shaky as he stood up, holding onto the iron rods with his sweaty palms. "You took care of my sister when my parents did not. You protected her when my parents had left her to die, and I will never forget that. I am in your debt with all that you have done, and I promise that I will find a way to get you and everyone who have faced injustices at the hands of my father out of here. Until then, I will make sure that you have everything you need to live comfortably."

"I wish to see the sun one day and the crown on your head. But now, you must leave. It's getting late, and if your father catches you, he'll lock you down here, too," Huiqing replied. "And remember, don't let your father know that you are aware of his wrongdoings. Use this as your weapon. Don't let it become your weakness."

CHAPTER
FIVE

THE SUN HAD GONE DOWN, AND DARKNESS HAD TAKEN OVER WITH stars shimmering within the abyss. Jinhai had completely forgotten about dinner, and the fact that he had invited Fia over to meet Jiayi.

He sprinted out of the prison chambers and straight into Qiang's room... which he found bolted with thick metal chains. But he was tenacious, and he was *not* going to just give up. He needed to learn the rest of the story, and the anger that he held for his father was increasing with every second of anticipation. All he could think about was getting revenge—he was *not* going to let his dictator of a father get away with all that he had done. Jinhai was determined to

352

take the throne and crown away from him, everything that had turned him into the egotistical and prideful snake that he was.

Over on the other side of town, Fia had spent her entire evening debating over what she was going to wear, how was she going to style her hair, and what she was going to say to one of the most important people in the prince's life. She was nervous, timid, but she was also super excited that something as amazing as dinner at the castle was actually happening to her.

But a big part of her missed her friends. If they were here now, they would've helped her with choosing the perfect outfit, and also tell her that she was being silly for doubting herself. Especially Xiaofan. She always liked to tease her. If only they could've all stayed together... But Xiaofan was with her sister now at a much better place than the orphanage, and she was sure the other girls also found a safe place to stay. *Anything* was better than that wretched town.

The overwhelming thoughts were eating her alive, and the sun had already set. She made herself a cup of oolong tea to calm her nerves, and then threw on the outfit that she had chosen. She finally decided on a traditional red qipao that covered her feet, and to finish the look, she clipped on her favorite necklace that had a tiny bird at the very center. She then walked over to her mirror and brushed a hint of pink across her cheeks and lined her lips with the darkest red gloss that she had.

When she finally stepped back, she looked different. She *felt* different. But she felt beautiful, and hopefully, that was enough to impress the prince. As she glanced outside the window, the color of the sky had shifted from a dark blue to a midnight black, but the stars deep within it continued to twinkle. She looked at them, and a smile grew on her face.

"This is really happening," she whispered to herself and took a deep breath. "For the first time since forever, I am finally getting what I've wished for."

She took in another breath and walked away from her window, eagerly waiting for the carriage to arrive as she sipped on her tea again. Within the next few minutes, she heard the sound of a bell outside. Her carriage had arrived.

"You look absolutely divine!" Xiaosheng blushed and complimented Fia as soon as she stepped inside the carriage.

"So do you!" Fia complimented back, and then they started catching up on each other's lives since they had last seen each other.

Jinhai was trying everything he could think of to break the lock on Qiang's door, but the more he tried, the more he was failing. He needed to get in, and he wondered why the room was even locked in the first place. What the hell was his father trying to hide?

There was an old willow tree just outside of Qiang's room, with thick branches that extended to her window. As a child, Jinhai used to climb across them and scare his grandmother, but he stopped after the day that Qianfan caught him and scolded him for disgracing the family name. That very memory flashed in his mind as he rushed toward it out in the garden.

It wasn't very dark outside, but it was just dark enough where no one would notice a grown man climbing up a tree. At the very least, he had to try. It was his only chance of getting inside the room. He tipped himself over onto his toes and hoisted himself up the trunk, frantically grabbing every part of it to keep himself from tumbling back down.

This was so much easier when I was a child.

When he finally made his way up, he carefully shifted his weight across one of the branches and toward Qiang's window. Luckily for him, it was unlocked! He grasped onto the ledge and jumped inside. Everything in her room was scattered haphazardly... as if someone had recently been in here, as if someone had been searching for something but failed to find whatever it was.

Jinhai lit a small candle and started to look around. He searched all the wooden boxes, her rustic shelf of books, and even her closet, but he couldn't find her journal anywhere.

"Come on, please, I really need this," he whispered to himself in distress and sat down beside her bed. He tilted his head down with his hands wrapped around his knees.

"What am I going to do?" he asked himself as his eyes wandered across the floor, when suddenly, he saw a crack in between two floorboards.

"The secret box?" he whispered. "The secret box!"

The secret box was the hidden compartment beneath the floorboards of Qiang's room, where he used to hide his valuables from Xiaosheng. Oh, she was such a messy child, drawing all over everything she came across and smashing whatever would break against the ground. Jinhai thought it was a miracle the day he found this crack, a true refuge for all his special belongings.

"It's the secret box!" he repeated and rushed to open the crack.

THE CARRIAGE ARRIVED AT THE CASTLE, AND XIAOSHENG HELD onto Fia's hand as they both stepped out. This was Fia's first time ever seeing the luxurious sight around her, and she was even being treated as a royal as the guards that lined the staircase all bowed to her as she walked up the steps. The staircase was huge, and the wall was covered with wooden carvings and paintings. That, plus the marble floor and intricate statues, all made her feel very small, but she was excited to see what else was in store.

"This is my room, and right next door is Jinhai's room." Xiaosheng pointed from room to room before ending her finger toward the largest one in the hallway. "And this right here is where we're having dinner tonight. Come on!"

The dining room was simple yet still elegant. A long but short wooden table sat in the center of the room, and the floor was covered with a handwoven carpet that made Fia feel like she was walking on a cloud. The walls were decorated with oil paintings of what seemed to be childhood portraits of Jinhai and Xiaosheng. And a delicious aroma of chicken broth and fresh herbs filled the entire room. It was enough to make Fia's stomach rumble.

"I hope you're hungry!" Xiaosheng smiled beside her. "Jiayi makes the BEST noodle soup!"

"You must be Fia!" Jiayi sang as she walked in to greet them. "It's so nice to finally meet you! Jinhai has been singing your praises nonstop."

"I've heard a lot about you, too," Fia replied and bowed,

to which Jiayi waved a hand to tell her that it was unnecessary.

"Where is Jinhai?" Jiayi asked Xiaosheng.

"I haven't seen him all day." Xiaosheng shrugged, reaching across the table to help herself to a warm custard bun. "And he's not usually late for dinner, either."

"Hm, you're right. That's not like him at all," Jiayi wondered out loud. "I wonder where he could be."

CHAPTER

SIX

Jinhai leaned over to open up the crack, hoping to find a childhood memorabilia inside. Instead, he found something much, much better. His grandmother's journal! She must've wanted whatever she wrote inside to stay a secret. And this intrigued Jinhai.

When he opened up to the first page, he saw his name.

Dearest Jinhai,

The blessed son who came into this family during the darkest of times. Your heart is pure like the water that the sea holds, and your soul radiates sunshine that represents the golden light within you. I have sinned my whole life, and I shall always regret

358

it. Do not become like your father. It is too late for him. Rise, and be the king that Jinu needs.

Read my journal with your heart. With every written word inside, you'll learn about a terrible past that's awaiting your rectitude.

I will always love you.

Grandma

Jinhai's eyes watered, and he turned the page. Inside, were all her conversations with Huiqing, tons of details about his torture tales that he didn't disclose down in the dungeon. But it's never easy talking about something traumatic.

Apparently, Huiqing was branded a spy in the kingdom —a traitor—and was blamed for things that he never did. Rumors had spread that he'd been disloyal to his land, his kingdom, and his people, and everyone in Jinu turned against him, even his own siblings. Huiqing was forced to confess to the public because if he didn't, Qianfan threatened to burn his siblings alive.

Jinhai turned the pages, reading each and every word, and eventually reached the page where Qiang wrote about her voyage—the voyage that changed her life.

I have reached the kingdom where Xiuying resides. I had informed her beforehand of my visit, and to my surprise, Xiuying came with royal favors to meet me at the harbor, despite how terrible I've treated her in the past. She is married to Prince Zhang Wei of the Baoshu Kingdom, and he loves her like I've never seen my own son love his wife. She reminds me of her mother, but Xiuying is much more human than her. For Heaven's sake, she refused to even let me apologize! Instead, she welcomed me with open arms and gave me a place to stay at her castle.

Xiaofan is also living with her. Xiuying searched everywhere for her after discovering that her parents had also abandoned her, eventually finding her at a run-down orphanage and bringing her here. I knew all this, and I should've done something—anything—other than promote it and encourage my son, but I didn't. All I did was sit back and did nothing. I'm no less of a monster than my own son.

But I'm glad they're doing better... even after their parents took everything from them. They seem happy, successful, a queen and a princess... no thanks to me. To this day, I regret what I've done. Both of them suffered greatly to get to where they are today.

Xiuying's final days in Jinu are still nothing but emotional baggage. She'd still hear the angry roars of my son and the hateful cries of her own mother. Such a tragic experience for a young child. She'd freeze and lose control of her body whenever memories of the past crept in, and despite being surrounded by loved ones now, part of her would always feel like she isn't good enough, that she'd be abandoned again one day.

Xiaofan's memories aren't much better, even more unsettling, I'd say. If her memories of the raggedy orphanage and the evil headmistress weren't enough to send her for the hills, then the assault that she'd experienced on the streets by a bunch of thugs certainly was. And though she eventually managed to escape it all, she'd still wake up frightened by her nightmares of the past. But she tries to remain strong! Oh, she always tries to remain strong. But when she doesn't and begins to cry... my heart goes out to her.

I have failed to protect my granddaughters.

I have failed as a human being.

Don't get me wrong, Jinhai. Your sisters did come to the castle when they found out about you and your sister, Xiaosheng. I guess they were scared of what your father would do to you both if they didn't save you. And I don't blame them. But your father kicked them both out and threatened them with death if they were to try and come back.

Zhang and Han were both ready to attack, but your sisters stopped them. They believe in you, Jinhai. They believe that you have the power to overturn your father without any bloodshed. Prove them right.

Over the years, your father has only thought about himself, his power, and his status. He has murdered people for the sake of murdering them and nothing else—brothers, fathers, sons. And your mother is aware of all this, aware of all the evil doings, but she chooses to stay silent and support her husband, like an honorable wife should. But this is wrong. This is all wrong.

The hunger that Qianfan has for blood and tears is going to destroy this kingdom one day unless you stop him. And by the looks of it, the kingdom is already falling apart.

When I arrived back at the kingdom, I wanted to tell you about your sisters, Jinhai. I wanted to tell you that they're still alive and want to see you defeat your father. But when my son found out what I was up to, he smashed a glass vase and threatened to cut me with the sharpest piece. He has never spoken to me in that tone before. I must've done something wrong as a mother.

But I'm not scared. I know he will fall on his face one day. And when he does, I'll be laughing. From where? I do not know, for Qianfan has put a death card on my life, and I don't know when I'll ever see the light of day again.

Hopefully, you'll find this journal before he does and make sure that everyone knows the truth. If you don't, my son will set it on fire alongside my body.

If my instincts are right, and if this is goodbye, always remember that your grandmother loves you and Xiaosheng. And if you ever get a chance to meet your sisters, tell them that I am truly sorry and that I've tried to make things right. But some-

times, it's not possible when it comes to Qianfan. Tell Xiaosheng about your sisters. How Xiuying loves to paint, just like she does. And how Xiaofan's best friend, Fia, is planning on joining the Jinu Kingdom very soon. Those two were inseparable at the orphanage.

Lastly, Jinhai, don't forget to believe in yourself. You have the ability to feel what others feel, and that is a rare gift. Connect with your people, and let them guide you to victory.

Jinhai turned the page to find it blank. The pages were all covered with his tears, and his eyes were swollen. He was in a state of shock. Could his father have really murdered his grandmother? His own mother?

Qiang died three days after she came back from the voyage, and she was perfectly healthy when she did. She definitely didn't die from health complications like his father had told everyone she did. There was also zero sadness on the king's face, completely apathetic, like he didn't even care about the death of his own mother!

Jinhai felt dizzy. Nauseous and sick from what he'd just found out. He got up and sat down on his grandmother's bed, placing his head in his hands. He closed his eyes and took a deep breath. The first face that popped in front of his eyes was Fia's, and he smiled over the fact that the reason why he'd felt so connected to Fia was because the Universe sent her into his sister's life before he even knew about her. It *wasn't* just a coincidence that he found himself attracted to her.

"Fia! Dinner!" He glanced over at the clock. "I'm late!"

Jinhai had been so focused on finding out the truth that he'd completely forgotten! He quickly placed the journal back in between the floorboards, carefully sealing it so no one else would suspect that something was underneath.

When he stood back up, his eyes caught sight of a small

teacup that sat on Qiang's desk. There was a green liquid inside, almost clear. Green tea, maybe? And a delicate flower sat at the bottom center. On closer inspection, Jinhai's stomach dropped.

That was no ordinary flower. Nerium oleander. A poisonous flower!

And beside the cup was a note.

Making temporary amends, Mother. Night, night.

Qianfan

CHAPTER
SEVEN

ANOTHER TWO HOURS HAD GONE BY, AND IT WAS ALMOST midnight. Jiayi and Fia wanted to continue waiting for Jinhai, but Xiaosheng insisted that they start without him. She was starving, after all, and Fia's stomach was also growling.

"He probably fell asleep or something. Everything's getting cold, and if I don't eat something soon, I will pass out!" Xiaosheng exclaimed.

"Can you be a little more dramatic?" Jiayi asked.

Suddenly, they heard footsteps approaching the front door of the dining room.

"That must be Jinhai!" Xiaosheng screamed in excitement, more so for her stomach than for her brother's appearance. "What took you so long?"

But the face that walked in didn't belong to Jinhai. It belonged to someone she'd never expect to see again, to someone she didn't want to see again.

"Nothing, I simply was not invited, my dear daughter," the queen answered in a taunting tone.

"I am *not* your daughter, and you are *not* my mother. No, you were not invited, and you are certainly not welcome here!" Xiaosheng shouted at Daiyu, crossing her arms over her chest.

"Have you forgotten your manners, Jiayi? No offering for the queen's arrival?" Daiyu turned to face Jiayi and asked.

Jiayi stood up with her heart beating fast against her chest, but before she could say anything, Daiyu started to walk toward Fia.

"You know, word travels fast in this castle. I don't know why, but you all seem to forget that this is *my* castle, *my* kingdom, and I know *everything* that happens within these walls," Daiyu firmly claimed while looking from Fia to Jiayi and back. "And you think you have gotten yourself a prince? Ha! What a joke! My son is *never* going to marry some low-class trash like you." Daiyu glared into Fia's eyes and smirked.

"That's where you're wrong, Mother," Jinhai jumped in when he entered the room.

His sleeves were rolled up, his eyes were a little red and swollen, but his voice remained firm, strong. But his appearance at that moment startled everyone in the room.

"You may be the queen of this kingdom, Mother, but that is all you are," Jinhai spoke and walked toward Fia. "You don't know the prince, and you certainly don't know your own son. The woman standing before you is going to take your place very soon. So, I suggest that you show some respect if you don't want your future to be in jeopardy."

Daiyu was surprised. Jinhai had *never* spoken to her like that before, never disrespected her like that before. "How *dare* you speak to your own mother so dishonorably?" Daiyu shouted.

"Mother? Are you serious? You have abandoned us. You can't just walk back in whenever it's convenient for you and expect us to respect you. You mean nothing to us anymore. You and your demented husband can both die, for all I care." Then he pointed toward the door. "Now, please leave, and never come back."

Xiaosheng drew an evil grin on her face. She loved seeing her awful mother get what she deserved. Daiyu stood there speechless for a minute, and then stormed out of the room, along with the guards and maids who had accompanied her.

The room fell silent after she left. Jinhai wrapped his arms around Fia and assured her that she had nothing to worry about. "I'm sorry I was late."

Turning to Jiayi, he asked her to bring in some tea as he had important matters to discuss with them all.

"What is it, Jinhai? You're making me anxious!" Xiaosheng was the first to say. "Is everything okay?"

"It is now," Jinhai answered mysteriously, still holding Fia's hand.

"If this is important, maybe I should leave you three alone. Besides, it's already pretty late," Fia whispered quietly, still shaken by what the queen had said to her.

"No, you need to hear this, too. I want you to be here, Fia. Please."

"You seem so tired," Fia pointed out.

"I am, but it's okay," Jinhai replied while looking down.

Jiayi came in with some hot oolong tea for everyone and sat down beside Xiaosheng.

"Now, can you please elaborate on what has been happening? Jinhai, you have made me so worried!" Jiayi urged.

Jinhai took a deep breath, then after taking a sip of his tea, he started to unfold the events that had occurred earlier today. He explained every detail, from his meeting with Huiqing to discovering Qiang's journal, and finally, to exposing the truth behind the death of his grandmother.

"I know this is a lot to understand, to accept, but look on the bright side, we know the truth. And we can bring justice to others and fight for what's right. Xiaosheng, you've always complained about wanting an older sister. Well, now you have two, two who love you dearly from afar. We must take the kingdom away from my conniving father. We shall *not* let our grandmother's sacrifice go to waste!"

Xiaosheng wiped her tears and agreed, muttering, "Yes."

"Xiaofan was my best friend at the orphanage, and we used to share everything. When she first came in, she was very quiet and had a hard time adjusting to how things functioned there. She was very strong and brave, but something in her broke after she was attacked, and after she left, something similar happened to me. Two men came into the courtyard when I was alone and grabbed me. I tried to fight them off, but I wasn't strong enough. They were huge! But luckily, Xiaofan sent over an army of guards that came to my rescue, and shortly after that, the orphanage dismantled, and all the girls were sent to different kingdoms. That's how I came here. Xiaofan specifically told me that Jinu would be the safest place for me. I didn't know why at the time, but now it's pretty obvious... because of you two." She nodded her head toward Jinhai and Xiaosheng.

"The more I think about it, the more I am unable to understand the mysterious ways that the Universe works, but the one thing I can say for sure is that those who go out of their way to help others always get rewarded in the end," Jiayi said with a grin, and then added. "The Universe will always have your back, Fia. I just know it."

After Fia headed back home, Jiayi and Xiaosheng proceeded to their own rooms to get some rest, promising each other that they wouldn't tell a soul about what they had just learned from Jinhai.

Jinhai stood alone in his room with a solemn heart. He always knew that one day, he had to become a king, but now, that reality was absolutely necessary. He just had to figure out how to do it. He knew his father was much more powerful than him, but Qianfan was also a fool. Jinhai would outsmart him somehow. Maybe Lixin and Haitao would have some words of encouragement. He'd go and talk to them in the morning. For now, he wanted to let himself bask in the sorrow of losing those who've loved him. If anything, the overthrow of Qianfan would be the way to avenge them.

THE NEXT MORNING, JINHAI WOKE UP EARLY TO THE BRIGHT RAYS of sunlight burning his face. He opened his eyes and realized how different things were going to be from now on, how today was going to be the first chapter in his new life. For once, he was not oblivious to his family's wretched past. He strictly forbade everyone around him to talk about the news that he had unveiled. While many of the castle residents despised the king and queen, many were still loyal to them.

Jinhai jumped out of bed and quickly got dressed. He then left to go see Lixin and Haitao. It was still early in the morning when he arrived at their home, and he walked in on them eating breakfast.

"Jinhai, what a surprise, my son! Come, grab yourself a plate!" Lixin welcomed him in.

"Why the long face?" Haitao asked.

"Is everything okay?" Lixin followed up, and within a matter of minutes, Jinhai told them everything.

"Lixin, you never knew anything about my sisters?" Jinhai asked.

Lixin sighed, and then replied, "I had heard some rumors around town, but I was never certain, so I figured it was best to not even mention them to you. It would only hurt that much more if they were false."

"We're always here for you. You know that, right? Let us know whatever you need, whenever you need, and we got you. You don't have to go through this alone," Haitao firmly said and gave Jinhai a pat on the back.

"I know. That's why I'm here. I won't be able to do this alone. And Haitao, no need to stop cracking jokes. Sometimes a little bit of distraction is good during rough times."

"Always." Haitao beamed.

"With time, everything is going to unfold in a way that works out in your favor, Jinhai. But for now, you need to take it one day at a time. You're stressed. I can tell. And that usually causes you to make hasty decisions. Once you take the time to clear your mind, I'm sure the solution will be much clearer to you," Lixin explained.

"And how do I do that?" Jinhai muttered.

"Well, if you ask me," Haitao jumped in, "I've seen the

way you handle stress, and it is *not* good, my friend. Father is right. You need to relax a bit. Why not spend some time with the girl next door? You know, her name starts with an F and rhymes with Pia." He started jabbing Jinhai on the side while chuckling, and Jinhai flailed his own arms at him.

Jinhai had never been much of a romanticist, so when it came to spending time with someone of the opposite gender or surprising her with some big romantic gesture, he was utterly confused. But he wanted to do *something*. He didn't want to become like his father, whose greatest gesture was having a child with the woman he loved and then throwing it away. No, he needed to be better than that!

Then he remembered something. The small wooden terrace near the lake that he and Xiaosheng had built when they were kids so they could sit and watch the birds. And even better? The terrace was far away from the castle, kept hidden from even the guards and maids! This was where he used to go with his sister to escape the problems of the castle, a place where they could just sit for hours and hours without a worry in the world.

And it had been years since he'd visited, and since the place held such sentiment in his heart, he decided that it would be the perfect place to take Fia. After all, there was nothing more romantic than showing her a little part of his world that mattered a lot to him.

EIGHT

It was half past noon on a sunny winter day when Jinhai arrived at Fia's home. The sun was shining through fluffy clouds in the blue sky, and birds were chirping songs of praise overhead. Jinhai knocked on the door, crossing his fingers in hopes that Fia would answer. He'd never been more nervous in his life.

"Oh, hi!" Fia greeted, surprised to see Jinhai.

"H—what's on your face?" Jinhai stopped talking. *What's wrong with you? You don't say that to a woman! Idiot!* "S-sorry, I didn't mean it like that."

But Fia just giggled. "You must be talking about the

chocolate smeared all over my face." Jinhai nodded. "Let's just say, chocolate-covered dumplings sounded like a good idea, but it's definitely pretty disgusting." She giggled again. "So, what brings you here?"

"Nothing much," Jinhai smirked. "I just came by to see if you were busy. I thought I'd show you a place that means a lot to me. A special place."

"Nope, not busy at all! I just, you know, need to clean up a bit before I go out in public." Then she thought about what Jinhai had just said. "What special place?"

"It's a surprise." Jinhai winked. "I guess you'll just have to come with me to find out."

"You're such a tease. Let me go get changed, and I'll meet you outside."

Jinhai nodded and walked back to his carriage to wait for her. A few minutes later, Fia walked out looking like a completely different person! Her face was as clean as clean can be, her hair was tied up in intricate braids, and she carried a small woven basket on her petite wrist. Jinhai could feel his heart beating faster and faster as she approached him.

"You clean up good," he complimented.

"Anything for you, my prince." And Fia bowed.

After a long and bumpy ride on an old dirt road, they finally reached the lake. They stepped out, and Fia's eyes widened with amazement. She was surrounded by beautiful cherry blossom trees that wrapped around the lake, white doves that circled above her head, and the grass was much greener and softer than what she'd been used to. And over to her left, there was an old oak tree that had a wooden platform built into it with stairs leading upwards.

"This is incredible," she whispered as she continued to

look around, basking in the petals that fell over her as she did.

"It really is. Xiaosheng and I used to come here all the time to get away from our parents. Besides you, no one else knows about it."

"I'm very flattered." Fia bowed again.

Jinhai grabbed Fia by the hand and led her up the staircase. As they climbed, she smiled at the incredible view of the lake and the different colors of the sunset. The sky had turned into shades of pink, yellow, and orange, and Fia felt like she was living inside a fairytale.

"A year ago, I would've never imagined my life turning out the way that it did. I was just a young man trying to get through life and make sure my father doesn't ruin my life. Now I'm preparing to take down my father and find my long-lost sisters. It's crazy how much things can change with time. Sometimes for the better, sometimes for the worse."

"Well?" Fia asked.

"Well, what?"

"Has your life changed for the better or for the worse?"

"Hard to say, really." Then Jinhai wrapped his arm around her waist and pulled her in close. "But with you by my side, I'd have to say for the better, much better." He slowly leaned his face down toward hers and planted a kiss on her lips. He had never kissed anyone before, and he didn't know what he was doing, but Fia's lips just felt so... so familiar that he didn't want to pull away.

"I could say the same about my life. It's not every day that a poor orphan girl gets to be with a royal prince," Fia whispered when they slightly parted.

"I hope I'm able to make life better for you." Fia nodded,

and Jinhai leaned in to kiss her once more. When they finally parted again, Jinhai continued. "I want to apologize for yesterday, for being late. I know there's no excuse on my part, inviting you over and then disappearing for hours. If it wasn't for me, Daiyu may have never made an appearance. I'm sorry I wasn't there to protect you from her. I should've been there." He pulled her in for a hug. "Just know that no matter what she says or what anyone says, my heart belongs to you, and I'd choose you over a princess any day."

"Jinhai, it's okay. You have nothing to apologize for. You stuck up for me, and that's what matters."

Jinhai let out a sigh of relief and muttered, "Thank you for understanding."

"Always."

Jinhai then climbed down and started a fire to make some tea.

"You know how to do this?" Fia asked in shock.

"Yes, plus a lot of other things. When it comes to making tea, I am considered an expert." Jinhai laughed.

"Well, then I have the perfect thing to go with it!" Fia made her way down also and laid down a red sheet for them on top of the grass. "Good thing I brought some dumplings with me."

"I was wondering what you had inside that basket. Thought it might've been a human head or something," Jinhai joked.

The sun soon started to set, and the lighting dimmed as time passed.

"Sometimes I wish I could just get a break from all the constants problems in my life," Jinhai pondered while pouring the tea into tiny cups. "As I grow older and older, I realize how much different life is from when I was just a child. The scary tales that I used to read in books are now all coming to life."

"I get how you feel, but letting uncontrollable situations run our lives is definitely not the right way to go. Instead, it's better to use those dark moments as fuel to make a change."

"I guess you're right. You always know the right things to say, Fia." Jinhai took a sip of his tea and sighed. "I really needed this."

"Me, too." Fia smiled. "And this tea is magnificent. You really are an expert!"

"Told you so." Jinhai laughed.

An hour later, the sun had completely set, and it was time to head home. On the way back, Jinhai saw the fireflies around them glimmer against the night sky, like tiny stars were floating around them. And in that moment, he knew that they belonged together. That the Universe had put Fia in his life for a reason.

When they arrived at Fia's home, she turned to him and said, "You know, whenever I think about Xiaofan, it makes me think about how ironic it is that every moment in our lives is connected somehow to what's ahead of us. How every person who crosses our lives brings some sort of significance. It's crazy if you really stop to think about it."

"Yeah, but I'm not complaining." He gave her one last kiss on the cheek and hopped back inside the carriage to head back to the castle. He was slowly falling in love with her, and in the past, this would've been his sign to run in the opposite direction. But he had a good feeling about Fia, and he couldn't even begin to imagine his life without her.

When he finally arrived back, he walked straight toward his room. He didn't want to risk the possibility of running into his parents or any of their loyal minions. He just wanted to find Jiayi and Xiaosheng. Hopefully, they're still awake. But when he went into their rooms, he found them both empty. Heart pounding, he started to get worried.

What if Qianfan got to them already? What if he knows that I know? They could be dead by now!

Then he heard footsteps behind him, and when he spun around, expecting to see his father's cynical smile, he saw his sister instead.

"Where were you? I was looking for you! And Jiayi!" Jinhai exclaimed as soon as he saw her. "I thought our father had gotten to you or something and sent you away."

"Oh, stop being paranoid. I just went for a walk out in the garden with Jiayi," Xiaosheng told him. "Besides, I can take care of myself."

"Why do you have a weird smile on your face? What are you up to?"

"I have to tell you something."

"Okay... What is it?"

"No, wait. No! It's not something I can tell you," Xiaosheng corrected herself.

"What? What's wrong with you?"

"It's something I have to show you!"

"Okay...?"

Xiaosheng then closed her eyes, and it even confused Jinhai even more.

"Are you okay?" he asked but was ignored. Then after about two seconds, the book that was sitting on the table beside them started to levitate over his head. "What? Xiaosheng, what's this?"

"I got my power! I got my power!" She jumped up and down with excitement, her focus dwindling from the book, and eventually, it fell onto Jinhai's head.

It stung, but he didn't care. His baby sister finally got her power, and he couldn't be prouder.

Suddenly, he heard a bang, a thud, followed by a faint scream.

"What was that?" Jinhai asked.

But Xiaosheng just shrugged. "I didn't hear anything."

"Hm, must've been an animal or something. Anyway, Xiaosheng, that's fantastic! I'm so happy for you!" Jinhai gave his sister a bear hug. "You are finally growing up, but it still seems like you were born just yesterday," he whispered.

"Oh, don't get all emotional on me now!" Xiaosheng teased. "Just expect things to be thrown at you whenever you annoy me."

"You do that, and I'll drown you in a sea of water," Jinhai teased back.

"Really?"

"Maybe." Then he winked.

Xiaosheng getting her power could not have come at a better time. Jinhai needed all the strength and support that he could get during this time, but it also made him realize how much of an emotional toll his sister must've gone through with everything happening around them. A part of him felt guilty for putting his sister through so much. He was supposed to protect her, not expose her to the tragedies of reality. But at the same time, she was now officially a member of the magical Jinu Kingdom, and he promised himself that he would teach her, and himself, how to use her power well.

THE NEXT MORNING, JINHAI DIDN'T WASTE ANY TIME. HE FELT LIKE he was in the right space mentally, and he knew it was time to come back to reality and plot out his revenge against his father's reign of terror.

But first, a visit to see Huiqing. It had been a few days since he'd requested the guards to send him a few more supplies, and he wanted to make sure the man was still alive. He walked to the front door of the prison and found the same guards standing there.

"All the changes done?" Jinhai asked discretely.

"Yes, sir," they both answered simultaneously and unlocked the iron gate for Jinhai to enter.

And as soon as he walked in, he noticed all the visible changes. Warm blankets were distributed to all the prisoners, the leaking pipes were sealed, and the odor that previously lingered in the air now smelled like fresh mint.

Jinhai walked toward Huiqing's cell and sat down in front of him.

"Something in you has changed, my child," Huiqing whispered.

"A lot has changed, actually," Jinhai replied and told him all about Qiang's journal and what she had written inside.

"I am happy for your sisters. They deserved every bit of it." Huiqing smiled weakly.

"And you were right," Jinhai continued. "Grandmother's death was not just a coincidence or a health complication. She was poisoned, and I have proof. My father was a fool to not clean up after his own mess. And now, he is going to pay for trying to play God."

"The best punishment for someone like Qianfan would be to take away his power, the one thing that makes him invincible," Huiqing told him.

"It is time we dethrone him. The people of Jinu are already against him, and once the truth comes out, they will join me and stand up against him. I will reveal the truth about their precious king, and I will clear your name, Huiqing. I will make sure that you get out of here alive, one way or another."

"I hope you do. You are a man of your word, but remember to always have a backup plan. You don't know Qianfan and how evil he can truly be. Perhaps you can join forces with your sisters. You are not the only one whom Qianfan has wronged. Together, you can all unite and take down your father."

Jinhai nodded and bowed, thanking Huiqing for all that he had done. "Stay strong, Huiqing. This will all be over soon." He stood up and headed toward the exit, hearing shouts of praise from the others as he passed them.

When he got back to his room, he immediately started drawing up his plans. He knew the people trusted him, and he definitely had the support of Haitao and Lixin, but Huiqing was right. He needed the powers of his magical sisters. It's the only thing that's powerful enough against Qianfan. Plus, his sisters deserved to know what's happening in their own kingdom, so he pulled out a quill and started to write.

Dearest Sisters,

My entire life, I have believed that I was the eldest... until recently. Our father is a cunning man, how he was able to cover up his wrongdoings all these years, the torture that he had inflicted on the both of you. I feel utterly ashamed for not having discovered this earlier, for not being there for the both of you. But now I know the truth, thanks to Mei's sister and Huiqing. I'm sure you both know them well.

I think it's time we all take a stand against Father. End this misery for our family and the people struggling on the streets of the kingdom. It is time his reign ends. It is time that the people of Jinu live under a ruler who has their best interest at heart.

I must dethrone the king, but to do that, I will need your help. Xiaosheng will need your help. There is a reason that I found out about you and a reason we all have powers... because it's in the Universe's plan to reunite us and make a difference in this world. I know you're probably both very happy where you are, and I want nothing less than for your lives to stay that way, but I'm sure, that like me, you are both also hungry for revenge. Plus, your little sister will be thrilled to finally meet you.

Xiaofan, I have met Fia, your best friend. And it just so happens that I have fallen in love with her. Life is too short to live in fear under our father.

I hope you both consider joining me in this fight.

Your brother,

Jinhai

He then sealed the letter with wax, rolled it into a scroll, and walked down to the harbor to deliver it himself. He refused to take any chances when it came to this. It was too important to put into the trust of someone else.

"I have a plan," Jinhai announced when he walked into Lixin's shop afterwards and told him all the details.

"Are you sure the military will support you in this? What if they retaliate? The chief *is* your father's ally, after all. He is *never* going to betray him," Lixin questioned with concern.

"I've done my research, and besides the chief, every other soldier is on my side. They all despise my father, and they've all been waiting for the day when they can finally be free from his grasp," Jinhai explained.

"Sounds promising."

"I also wrote to my sisters. I need their powers in this fight. I am hopeful that they show up," Jinhai said.

"So, what do we do now?" Lixin asked.

"We wait for a response, and then we take action."

Lixin had doubts that he didn't voice. He knew that Jinhai was doing the right thing. This was what the kingdom needed, what the people needed, but Qianfan was *not* someone who would easily back down in defeat. Jinhai's approach to wait might give Qianfan a slight advantage and attack, but Jinhai needed support, and that was what Lixin needed to give him. This was the ultimate test of his patience, and he tried not to let his worries get the best of him.

"Jinhai, I have known you ever since you were just a little boy. You are much stronger than you give yourself credit for, and the only way your plan will succeed is if you believe in it. Don't doubt yourself," Lixin said when he noticed Jinhai rubbing his hands together. He usually did that whenever his thoughts conflicted with each other.

"Thank you, Lixin. I will do my best."

THREE DAYS HAD GONE BY, AND JINHAI STILL HADN'T HEARD FROM his sisters. He was on the verge of losing hope, when suddenly, he heard a knock on the door.

"Letter for you, Prince Jinhai," a guard spoke from outside the door.

Jinhai rushed over to open it, quickly yanked the scroll out of the guard's hands, and slammed the door shut. He then ripped it open as fast as he could and read.

Beloved Jinhai,

We hope this letter reaches you before we do, and we are both so proud of you for taking a stand against our awful father. And to be honest, nothing would make us happier than to watch him burn. You have our full support, and however this fight ends, at least we are all together.

We hope to arrive at Jinu soon, and we can't wait to finally meet you and Xiaosheng.

Your sisters,
Xiuying and Xiaofan

CHAPTER
NINE

Hope, a simple four-lettered word that makes people trust in the unknown and hope for the best against any evil.

That is exactly what Jinhai had done. He had hoped for his sisters to show up for him, and now he was hoping that everything would go as planned, that justice would be served without any bloodshed.

He kept the scroll hidden inside his room and decided to keep the news of his sisters' arrival to himself. He wanted to meet with them alone first without generating a crowd, and he wanted to give Xiaosheng the same experience.

He didn't know what he was going to do when he faces

his father. He had originally envisioned himself speaking to his father in a calm and civil manner, but that idea was quickly brushed out the door when he realized that the king would never be reasonable. With Qianfan, there was never a dull moment; tantrums and threats of death always did the talking for him. But still, Jinhai was nervous. His father always managed to demean him as a child. What would make it any different now?

While Jinhai was occupied with his thoughts, Xiaosheng and Fia were getting ready for brunch over at Fia's home. Xiaosheng was super excited to spend some time alone with her. Whenever Jinhai was around, he took all of Fia's attention, but now, Xiaosheng had her all for herself, and she liked feeling like she had a sister. She wondered what it would feel like if her blood sisters ever came to visit. Would it be like meeting a stranger? Or would she feel right at home with them?

On her way out the door, she turned back around to say goodbye to Jiayi. She hadn't seen her since last night, which was odd since Jiayi was *always* around. But Xiaosheng was in a hurry and didn't give it another thought. Besides, Jiayi had a lot of responsibilities in the kingdom. She was probably just busy.

Xiaosheng checked Jiayi's room one last time, and when she didn't see her, she left to go meet Fia. After riding through the busy streets and rocky pathways, Xiaosheng finally reached her destination and was greeted with open arms.

Fia's home was small, more of a cottage than a house, with wooden floors, mustard-colored walls, herbs planted in every corner, and the windows were all open to let in the cool breeze. It reminded her of one of her doll homes that Xiaosheng had growing up, and she remembered how she often wished that she was tiny enough to walk through one of them. She giggled as the thought crossed her mind.

"What's so funny?" Fia asked, placing a basket of baked buns in front of Xiaosheng along with a pot of warm tea.

"Oh, it's nothing. Your house just reminds me of one of the dollhouses I had when I was younger. It feels like I'm inside one of them."

Fia chuckled. "I never thought about it that way before. It does look like one."

"So, how did you know that Jinhai was the one for you?" Xiaosheng asked. "How do you know when you've found that special person?"

Fia looked outside the window, noticing the birds flying in pairs across the bright blue sky. "I don't know how to put it in words, exactly, but you just feel it in your heart when you meet someone who's right for you. You feel like you can talk to them about anything, and you feel like the best version of yourself around them. Does that make sense?"

"I guess. I hope I can find my own true love one day." Xiaosheng sighed.

"Don't feel like you have to rush into it. You will meet countless people in your lifetime, some good, some bad. Some deserving of your love, others not so much. Most are going to take you for granted and then just leave. But the ones who stick by your side during all the low points in your life are the ones worth keeping." Fia held Xiaosheng's hand tightly. "Don't sacrifice your own life for someone else. Just keep that in mind."

"You're right, Fia. Sometimes I just get so caught up in growing up and wanting what others around me have that I forget I still have many years to live. Thank you. You've been like a big sister to me."

The ride back to the castle made Xiaosheng feel

anxious. Her heart was racing, and she didn't really know why. But whenever it did, something bad usually happened right after. Hopefully, her intuition was wrong this time. When she walked in through the front door, she looked for Jiayi. Most nights, she'd just be in the kitchen, cooking up something delicious, but when she found the kitchen empty, she felt a wave of sadness.

"Have you seen Jiayi?" Xiaosheng asked one of the maids instead.

"I haven't seen her all day," the maid replied.

"What do you mean?" Xiaosheng asked.

"I mean, I don't know. Look for her somewhere else," the maid hissed angrily and walked away.

Xiaosheng didn't respond, but she overheard the maid whisper something to another as she left. She continued to look for Jiayi throughout the castle, but Jiayi was nowhere to be found. This was very unlike her, disappearing without saying a word, and Xiaosheng immediately started jumping to the worst possible conclusions.

When she arrived back at Jiayi's room, she noticed that the door was already open. And when she walked in, the room was a mess! It so was unlike Jiayi, who was usually the most organized person she'd ever met. It looked like a fight or a fit of rage had taken place here, like someone had purposefully smashed everything inside. All of her things were thrown from one side to the other, the sheets were torn and scattered all over the floor, and the vases that used to carry the most beautiful of flowers were all smashed against the ground, glass shards sprinkled throughout the room.

Something bad had happened here. Something really bad. Xiaosheng quickly rushed to Jinhai's room and started banging violently against the door.

"Open up, Jinhai!" Xiaosheng's voice was in such a panic.

Jinhai rushed toward the door to open it, and Xiaosheng quickly rushed in and slammed the door behind her shut as she paced around the room from one end to the other.

"Jiayi is gone! Jiayi is gone!" Xiaosheng repeated frantically.

"Xiaosheng, I don't understand. Can you calm down for a second?" Jinhai asked, but Xiaosheng continued pacing back and forth. Jinhai then held her by the shoulders and forced her to stand still. "What's going on?"

"I haven't seen Jiayi since yesterday, and I tried to look for her this morning, but I couldn't find her anywhere. When I came back from Fia's, I tried looking for her in the kitchen, but she still wasn't there. And the other maids were whispering, whispering something that they clearly didn't want me to know about. Then I went into her room..." Xiaosheng stuttered and broke into tears.

"You went into her room and then?" Jinhai urged his sister to continue.

"She wasn't in there either, and her room was an absolute mess! You know Jiayi would *never* leave it like that. Something happened in there, a fight, a struggle. I think someone took Jiayi!"

There was no doubt in Jinhai's mind that this was the work of his parents. Someone must've overheard them talking and took Jiayi as collateral. A bird couldn't even move around the castle without them finding out.

"I will find her, Xiaosheng," Jinhai told his baby sister as he wiped down her tears and hugged her tight. "She's going to be here with you soon, I promise. But I need you to stay right here until I come back. Do *not* go anywhere else! Lock the door and the windows, and I will be back as soon as I can."

Jinhai pulled away and headed toward the door when he heard a knock. He opened it and found a maid standing there with her head down.

"Jiayi was taken by the queen," she whispered. "She is going to be executed tomorrow. Please don't tell anyone that you heard this from me." Luckily, Xiaosheng didn't hear anything, and Jinhai intended to keep it that way.

Executed? Jinhai thought to himself as he closed the door behind him and marched toward his parents' room.

AFTER JINHAI EMBARRASSED DAIYU WITHOUT ANY HESITATION that night, she had fallen into a pit of self-doubt that she thought she would never experience again in her life. That incident took her back to the night when Xiuying tried to take her own life. It reminded her of how Mei had spoken to her and how much she'd despised that, and now, years later, her own son—her own blood—was doing the exact same thing, like he had absolutely no respect for her. She blamed Jiayi and the way she'd raised him. To Daiyu, Jiayi and Mei were cut from the same cloth.

Daiyu felt like her children loved Jiayi more than her, and it made her feel insignificant. How dare Jinhai talk back to her like that? She was his mother! Someone had to pay for his disrespect, and Jiayi—their pathetic nanny—was the perfect *prey*.

"You know what I hate most about my life?" Daiyu asked cynically when Jiayi walked back into her room the night that Xiaosheng discovered her power to discover the queen sitting on her bed. "It's women who try to take my children away from me. First, it was Mei, the maid who tried to make Xiuying her own, and now, it's you, the *bitch* trying to take Xiaosheng and Jinhai. It's always *someone*, isn't it?" Daiyu hissed with a sinister laugh. "But women like you forget that you can *never* be a mother to them; you can *never* take my place!" Daiyu shouted and smashed a vase against the floor, glass shards flying off in all directions. "Women who turn children against their mothers deserve to rot, and that is *exactly* what will happen to you."

"I never turned them against you. I have only given them the love and affection that you failed to!" Jiayi pleaded.

"Liar! I will personally make sure that you will *never* see the light of day again! Guards, take her to the dungeon!" Daiyu ordered and left the room with her maids.

"No!" Jiayi shouted, stepping back as the guards approached her. Her feet were bloody as the shards cut through her skin. "Please, don't!" She screamed for mercy and tried to fight off the guards, but they held onto her arms tightly and dragged her to the basement.

Jiayi was kept inside the dark cell in front of Huiqing. Huiqing could hear her cries and tried to comfort her, but nothing helped. Jiayi was different than Mei. She was easily frightened, sensitive, and this was taking a toll on her. She hoped that Xiaosheng and Jinhai would soon find her, but that hope was dwindling as the days passed. This was her fate now. She always hated working for the queen.

"Where could she be?" Jinhai asked himself as he stormed toward the king and queen's quarters of the castle. When he reached there, to his surprise, they were both sitting together and dining on the grand terrace, which only made Jinhai fume even more. But when Daiyu saw him, she simply smiled.

"My son, to what do I owe the pleasure of this visit?" Daiyu asked, her sickly tone exuding fakeness.

"Why did you take Jiayi? And to execute her? What's the matter with you?" Jinhai screamed in resentment toward the woman who birthed him.

"I can do anything as the Queen of Jinu, stupid child!" Daiyu cackled while clapping her hands.

"Forget Jiayi, my son! We are celebrating this kingdom's first execution. Come, join us. This event will go down in history!" Qianfan chimed in jovially.

"How many more lives need to perish for your own amusement? This is injustice!" Jinhai exclaimed.

"There *is* no injustice, you fool! Jiayi is nothing more than a filthy servant who wants our gold and our throne by *brainwashing* our children. Trust me, Jinhai, she doesn't love you or your annoying sister. She is only doing this for herself," Daiyu declared.

"No! She has been more of a mother to us than you have ever been, than you ever will be! And you're right. Tomorrow *will* go down in history, but not for the reason you think. I will do *everything* in my power to prevent that from happening!" Jinhai hissed as he violently pushed away the cup of tea that was being offered to him, causing the glass to smash against the floor.

"You are all words and no action, my son. You are as soft as a feather. A wimp. A coward. Ever since you were just a baby. You are no match for me." Qianfan sneered while Daiyu stared at Jinhai with hatred in her eyes as he stormed out of the room.

"Where could she be? Where could she be?" he kept whispering to himself. Then he paused. "The prison! Of course!"

He rushed down to the basement, and when he reached the entrance, he found six military guards standing there with sharp swords in their hands, guarding the iron gate.

"Let me in," Jinhai ordered.

"No one is allowed to enter this part of the castle. We have strict orders from the king," one of the guards answered.

"I am the prince of this kingdom. I command you to open this gate at once!"

"I'm afraid we cannot do that. If we let you inside, the king will have our heads," another guard muttered.

"Ugh! I hate my father and his tyrannical ways!" Jinhai screamed at the top of his lungs and stormed back toward his room.

It was almost dawn when he passed by Jiayi's room and saw tiny droplets of blood on the carpet. His parents had gone too far this time, and he swore to himself that he will make them pay for all of it, no matter what it took.

His mind muddy and his blood still boiling, he went to his own room and found it closed but unlocked. Jinhai quickly rushed to check on the scroll. Luckily, it was still where he'd left it, untouched, untampered with. Feeling a rush of relief, he then sat by the window and watched the color change in the sky before dozing off.

A few hours later, he woke up to Xiaosheng's voice as she walked into the room with breakfast and closed the door.

"What time is it?" Jinhai asked, startled.

"Almost noon," Xiaosheng answered before she hesitantly asked, "Find anything?"

Jinhai nodded and spoke before he could stop himself. "Jiayi is still alive, but she has been imprisoned by Daiyu. She's fine for now, but they plan to execute her, and I must stop it before it's too late."

"She can't do that! If she does, I will *never* forgive her. Never!" Xiaosheng began dripping tears from her eyes.

"And...," Jinhai started, quickly changing the subject, but paused.

"And?" Xiaosheng repeated while she sniffed her nose.

"Xiuying and Xiaofan are also arriving today. I haven't told anyone yet because I want us to meet them first." Jinhai smiled.

"What a pity! This should be the happiest day of our lives, but instead, we're worried about Jiayi's life," Xiaosheng huffed. "Those two morons sitting on their thrones have ruined our lives since day one. When's the execution supposed to happen?"

"Today. At sunset." *Might as well let it all out.*

"And... and when are Xiuying and Xiaofan supposed to arrive?" Xiaosheng probed.

"Probably in the next three to four hours, but I can't say for sure. You know how tough voyages are."

"I really hope they make it. It just feels like the Universe is against us right now."

"Don't say that, Sister. It will only get better from here." Jinhai tried to comfort her.

"How can you be so calm during a time like this?!" Xiaosheng shouted.

"As you grow older, you come to realize that even when all the odds are against you, they cannot defeat you unless you allow them to. I learned that from Fia," her brother whispered. "Speaking of Fia, would you like to go visit her? I need to head over to Lixin's." Xiaosheng nodded and extended her hand out for him to take. "Come on. I think we *both* need a good distraction."

CHAPTER
TEN

MEANWHILE, THE OTHER SIDE OF THE CASTLE WAS DRAPED IN darkness. After years of separation, Qianfan and Daiyu were finally back together again. With time, their hearts had turned cold, and they had found solace in torturing others.

"You know what we should do?" Daiyu whistled as she raised her glass of red wine up to her lips. "We should make an example out of this."

"How so?" Qianfan asked, intrigued.

"We should execute the bitch in front of the entire kingdom so that nobody ever tries to conspire against us ever again!" Daiyu cackled. "This will make all the peasants fear us even more."

"I love it! Punish anyone who even dares to utter a word of disrespect to us, slaughter those who dare to stand in our way." Qianfan laughed as he walked back and forth with his fingers wrapped behind his back. Then he whispered to himself, "Fear is the only thing that'll help me keep this crown." He turned to face the door and shouted, "Guard!" One of his loyal guards came rushing in within a second of his bellow, carrying a scroll and quill in his hands. "Start writing," Qianfan ordered him.

"Make it good, my husband. I need everyone to know who's in charge here," Daiyu called out.

The king cleared his throat and began speaking, "Peasants of the Jinu Kingdom, I hereby invite you all to witness our first-ever execution, and I expect you all to be there with bells on. Witness what happens to those to dare defy me, for if you do, it shall forever deter you from going against my orders. Come to the castle at sunset to see justice served! Yours truly, the King of Jinu." The king then waved the guard away. "Oh, wait, one more thing. Those who do not show up will all witness their own executions." He then waved off the guard once more. "Now go! Take the scroll to the harbor and make the official announcement!"

The guard hesitated, but before Qianfan could wave a second time—the fatal wave—he quickly bolted out of the room and ran as fast as he could down the hall and out of the building.

Oblivious to the king's demand, Jinhai and Xiaosheng arrived at Lixin's on the other side of town. Fia was already there, helping Haitao plant new flowers to celebrate the new upcoming year.

"Jinhai! Xiaosheng! What a pleasant surprise! What brings you two here?" Lixin asked with delight.

"Our lives," Xiaosheng murmured with a stale face.

"What happened?"

Haitao and Fia also stopped what they were doing and looked up.

"My father has gone too far. He has imprisoned Jiayi," Jinhai revealed and politely asked everyone to head back inside.

They all settled in the living room with the window open, highlighting a beautiful blue sky and the vast ocean. It was a busy day at the harbor, and they could see local ships departing on their voyages.

"How exactly are you going to confront the king? You can't just walk in and seize the throne. He'll kill you!" Haitao asked after Jinhai finished explaining everything that had been going on.

"Only time can guide us now. But first, I need to focus on meeting my sisters and saving Jiayi," Jinhai firmly stated.

"Your powers can help with saving Jiayi, right?" Fia chimed in and asked.

"Yes, most definitely. Xiaosheng and Jinhai can both use their powers to help Jiayi escape. Xiuying and Xiaofan can also help them out. Together, they are bound to be invincible," Lixin replied.

"Only if they get here in time," Xiaosheng mumbled, deflated.

"There they are! Look!" Fia jumped up excitedly while pointing toward the tiny ant-sized boats arriving at the harbor. "I recognize the flag of the Baoshu Kingdom!"

"Really? No way!" Xiaosheng stood up and ran toward the window. "They're really here!"

"They are going to arrive any minute now, Jinhai," Haitao said.

"Yes, you both should go meet them. We will wait for you here." Lixin lightly touched Jinhai's shoulder and nodded.

This was really happening! Jinhai's heart was pounding in his chest, and he was feeling so many different emotions all at once. He didn't know what he was going to say to them, how he was going to react to seeing them for the first time, but he left for the harbor with Xiaosheng anyway.

The closer their carriage got to the harbor, the clearer he could see the ships and the flag of Baoshu, and it was a beautiful sight to see. The harbor was crowded with people by the time they arrived, merchants going to and from the island on the one day where the flowers seemed to magically bloom. Luckily, there were so many other ships at the dock that no one seemed to really notice the royal ships arriving, just like Jinhai had wanted.

He stood there with Xiaosheng, heart racing and squeezing her hand, when suddenly, someone around his age came running out and straight toward Xiaosheng.

"Xiaosheng! I can't believe it's you!" the woman cried. "I'm Xiaofan, your sister!"

Xiaosheng started to tear up while tightly hugging her back. Jinhai stood next to them with tears in his eyes as Xiaofan soon let go and hugged him next. "Oh, look at you! You have gotten so big. The last time I saw you, you were just a baby."

Jinhai hugged her back, too choked up to find the right words to say, when he soon saw someone who resembled Xiaofan coming up behind them.

"You must be Xiuying, the eldest," Jinhai said and bowed.

"Oh, no need for formalities, Little Brother. We're all family, and I'm so happy that we are finally all here together." Xiuying beamed and wrapped her arms around Jinhai and Xiaosheng.

"Are we even welcomed here?" Zhang teased as he stepped off the ship.

"Don't think so." Han laughed as they walked toward the four siblings.

"Always have to be the center of attention, don't you?" Xiuying teased back and pulled Zhang to her side. "Jinhai, Xiaosheng, meet Zhang, my husband and the King of Baoshu."

"And this," Xiaofan pulled Han over next to her, "is Han, my fiancé."

"So, lead us to Father." Xiuying clapped her hands together. "It's been so long since I've last seen the man who changed my life forever."

"Not just yet," Jinhai said. "We're going to Lixin's first so we can finalize out plan. Plus, I'd like you all to meet the man who practically raised me."

"Lead the way." Zhang gestured.

As they headed toward the carriages, Jinhai noticed the king's own carriages arriving at the harbor and guards beginning to round up the crowd.

"What's this?" Xiaofan asked.

"I have no idea." Jinhai glanced around, frightened for what was about to happen.

One of the guards started to read from a scroll, and every word made Jinhai's heart stop. Even the guard himself was trembling with the words that he was forced to say, but he had to keep going for the sake of his life. The faces of the crowd turned pale, and not even a whisper graced the air—only shivers of fear and silence.

He was announcing the public execution of Jiayi, not only as a punishment for her, but as a threat of death for all those who failed to obey every order from the king. This was an order to incite fear in the hearts of the people.

"What's happening, Jinhai?" Xiuying asked with trepidation in her voice.

"Jiayi? Isn't that the woman who looked after you and Xiaosheng?" Xiaofan added.

"We need to go. Now! We're running out of time! I need to do everything I can to *not* let this happen." Jinhai nodded.

They all quietly scampered toward the carriages without creating any attention from the crowd. The girls all sat in one carriage while the boys took the other. None of them had a clue as to what was going on, but Zhang was certain of one thing—Jinhai had potential in him, and he was confident that the prince knew what he was doing. To Zhang, Jinhai was born to be a king.

When they arrived, Fia was over the moon to reconnect with Xiaofan and Xiuying, and Lixin greeted them with open arms. Haitao's jaw practically dropped when he saw Xiaofan, and Jinhai knew he had a little crush on her, but he kept his distance. Besides, Han looked strong enough to beat the both of them up.

"Jiayi took care of Xiaosheng when our mother abandoned her at birth, and she also took me under her wing when Father grew ashamed of me and tried to hide me from the rest of the castle. But even still, Daiyu blamed Jiayi for her children hating her, never herself, just like she'd blamed Mei for Xiuying turning against her. So, to make herself feel better, she threw Jiayi in prison, just like she'd done to Mei and Huiqing. Just like Father had killed his own mother for questioning his sickening ways," Jinhai explained.

"I'm not even surprised. Truly, nothing has changed," Xiuying whispered.

"I don't think they'll ever be capable of change," Xiaofan added.

"This is why we need to bring change to this kingdom as soon as possible. Otherwise, more and more people will keep dying." Lixin sighed.

"Good thing Jinhai here is the right man for that!" Haitao exclaimed and threw a wink over at Xiaofan.

"But... but how exactly are we going to save Jiayi?" Xiaosheng stuttered. "I don't want to lose her!"

"We won't let anything happen to her. I will do everything in my power to make sure of it," Zhang assured her.

"You need to get the people on your side, Jinhai," Han told him. "Qianfan is going to fall into his own trap. I doubt any of the townspeople are going to support the execution, and if you can gather the crowd on your side, you might have a chance of stopping him at sunset."

Jinhai was intrigued. "I need to tell them all the truth. If they know just how evil their king is, they will join forces with me. My father isn't unstoppable."

"He's going to think that the public is there to witness the execution, and we will all take him down with the element of surprise." Zhang smirked.

"Zhang, maybe you can accompany Jinhai. For protection," Xiuying suggested.

"Might be better if Han goes. I'm pretty sure your father still remembers me from the last time I mouthed off to him."

"Agree, and we should leave now before it's too late," Han said.

Xiuying, Zhang, and Fia stayed behind at the house while everyone else headed back toward the harbor to gather the people.

"Jinhai, wait!" Fia called out after him, running up to him and wrapping her arms around him. "Promise me you'll stay safe."

"I'll do everything in my power if it means coming home to see you again." Jinhai pressed his forehead against hers and leaned down to give her a passionate kiss. He wrapped his arms around her waist and pulled her in tightly before letting go again. "The Universe is on my side." He gave her another quick kiss and rushed toward the carriages.

When they reached the harbor, some of the merchants and townspeople were still frightened by the news, whispering sounds of nervousness to everyone who passed them. On the right side of the harbor was a large and menacing bell, a bell that was only rung when tragedy struck the kingdom and the people needed to prepare for war. The group of five walked toward it and stood there for a second as Jinhai took a deep breath.

"Are you ready?" Han asked.

"Yes," Jinhai whispered as Xiaosheng held onto his hand. "I can do this."

Jinhai then stepped onto the stone pavement and pulled the rope, sounding the bell exactly three times.

Hearing the sound of a bell that was usually never rung, the people at the harbor all stopped and looked over to see the prince. Even those from afar left their homes and ran over to see what the commotion was all about. Within a matter of minutes, the space before them was filled with the people of Jinu.

Jinhai didn't even need to look first before speaking. He

knew his father wouldn't leave his precious throne even if the entire kingdom was burning down. Besides, he'd probably just assume that a guard had rung it for the execution.

He stepped forward toward the people and started to speak.

"Beloved people of Jinu, I stand here today with a heavy heart and a confession, a truth that you all deserve to know. The king, my father, has been hiding secrets, and it's about time they come out. As many of you may not even know, I am not the eldest child. I have two older sisters, the princesses of Jinu, both of whom my father sent away to die. And those who helped them? Well, let's just say things didn't turn out very well for them. And then there's me and my younger sister, Xiaosheng. We were both treated like royalty, sure, but we were never really wanted either. Qiang, our grandmother, and Jiayi, the woman about to be executed raised us, and as a result, they are now either dead or destined to die. This just goes to show that anyone who dares to stand in the way of the king and queen will be killed... one way or another, and this needs to stop! I am standing before you today, begging for you to join me in my fight against injustice, begging you to stop allowing my father to treat us like his own personal puppets. He doesn't care about us, any of us, not even his own children. At sunset, right before the execution is set to commence, we will rise and show him who's boss."

CHAPTER
ELEVEN

Jinhai glanced at the crowd, and during those first few minutes of silence, his hope began to shrivel, but then out of the blue, he heard a voice.

"We're with you, Jinhai," one man shouted.

"Time to take down the rotten dictator," another joined in.

And soon, the crowd burst into chants and started cheering for Jinhai. Eventually, everyone else chimed in and started to yell, "Burn, Qianfan, burn!"

Just like Jinhai had wanted.

The sun was almost setting, so Lixin and Haitao rallied the crowd, and they all began marching toward the castle.

There was no panic, no fear, only the determination to save a life.

When they reached the front gate, even the iron bars and army of guards weren't enough to hold them back. The crowd was too big, and people were pushing down everything in their path to get inside. This moment was indeed a revolution, and the enthusiasm of the townspeople was even more impeccable than anyone could've anticipated.

They arrived to the courtyard—where the execution was set to be held—and found Qianfan and Daiyu standing at the center, surrounded by armed guards. Jiayi was down on her knees with her hands tied behind her back and a black silk cloth covering her eyes. The sky had turned a deep orange as the sun slowly faded away, and the gust of wind sent chills down everyone's spines. Evil was certainly in the air.

"What a magnificent turnout!" Qianfan laughed. "It looks like the entire kingdom is here to witness the execution of this filthy animal."

"And look who finally found his place and decided to bring them all here!" Daiyu grinned with pride. "Our bastard of a son!" Then she leaned down. "Oh, Jiayi, how I wish you could see this. Everyone here to watch you die. Guess they really are *my* children after all."

Just as she finished her last word, the crowd started to chant, "Burn, Qianfan, burn! Burn, Daiyu, burn!" The voices grew louder and louder until Jinhai stepped forward to face his parents.

"We know everything. The people here know everything, the abandonment of your daughters and the death of those who once loved you." He raised up his hand and gestured to the crowd. "Do you see all these people around you? They are not here to watch you execute Jiayi; they are here to watch you burn, take you down. And the guards? Ha! You really think they're on your side? They fear you more than they respect you, and once they realize that there's power in numbers, *no one* is going to stop this mob."

Jinhai stared straight into his father's eyes as Qianfan darted his eyes around to the angry hoard that surrounded him. "There's nothing you can do anymore besides walk away... for your own safety. The people no longer fear you," Jinhai finished.

Qianfan felt like a dagger had just been pierced through his heart. Betrayed by his own son. *His own son!* And beside him, Daiyu was trembling for the first time in her life. They both couldn't understand how their plan had failed. It was foolproof! But they remained silent, and their faces pale, they slowly walked back into the castle.

The crowd cheered as Jinhai untied Jiayi from her restraints, and Xiaosheng rushed over to embrace her. She removed the cloth from her eyes and cried into her shoulders.

"I thought I'd never see you again," Jiayi cried.

"I would *never* let anything happen to you!" Xiaosheng exclaimed.

"It's time for us to go," Jinhai whispered and lightly touched Jiayi's shoulder.

"Where?" Jiayi asked.

"Home," Xiaosheng replied.

They all walked off the castle grounds, and the crowd dispersed after wishing Jiayi the best for her life ahead. They walked to the harbor and rode the carriages back to Lixin's house. The ride back was peaceful, the sky had turned dark with infinite stars shining bright, and the aroma of blooming flowers wafted through the air. Xiaosheng stayed with Jiayi and held onto her hand.

"Let's just give them a little scare, shall we?" Han suggested when they arrived. "Tell them our plan had failed and see how they react."

"Diabolical. Let's do it!" Jinhai laughed.

Jiayi stayed in the carriage while the rest entered the house. Xiuying and Fia had decorated it with fresh flowers and oil lamps, and delicious moon cakes were served on the table with a small pot of tea.

"There's nothing to celebrate," Han said in an ominous tone.

"Is this some kind of joke?" Jinhai added.

Fia was the first to stop. "Wait... what? Tell me it's not true."

"How could you let this happen?" Xiuying nearly shouted.

But Zhang remained silent. He could see the faint smirk on Han's face and knew he was clearly up to something... he just didn't know what.

Jinhai then looked over at Han, and they both started to laugh.

"That's not funny!" Xiuying yelled and gave Han a playful push.

"Really, Jinhai?" Fia darted her eyes over at Jinhai.

"Hey, don't blame me! It was Han's idea." Jinhai raised his hands in the air.

"Me? Everyone knows that I'm not one to play such childish games," Han teased and chuckled as Jiayi was welcomed inside with hugs and kisses.

That night, it truly felt like the entire family was back together again. Haitao and Han did their best to lighten the dark mood with all the jokes they had in their pockets. Xiaofan and Fia caught up with each other after years and years of being apart. And Xiuying went inside the kitchen to brew some more tea, accompanied by her little brother.

"Never in my life did I ever think this day would come," Xiuying pondered. "Look around; this feels like *home*."

"Home is where your heart is, right?" Jinhai mumbled.

"Right, but in your case, your heart is somewhere else. Inside a very special person, I might say."

"It's not like that." Jinhai blushed.

"She's different. Resilient. Strong. And you love her. I see it all over your face. Why not ask for her hand in marriage?" Xiuying asked.

"Just waiting for the right time, I guess."

"You will always continue waiting if you keep waiting for the right time. The right time is never going to come. You need to make it the right time. And besides, with how things are going in this kingdom, the right time is running out." She turned to face her brother. "If you feel like you are ready, just go for it."

"You're right. I *am* ready." Jinhai nodded and started to tear up.

"What happened?" Xiuying asked.

"It's just that... I've never had an older sibling to help me through life. My entire life, I've felt like I've had to be strong and stay brave for the sake of Xiaosheng. It just feels like such a relief to know that all the burden isn't just on my shoulders, and that I have someone to turn to in times of need. It's something I've been missing my whole life."

"My only wish is that I could've been here sooner. So much has been taken away from us," Xiuying mused.

"We just have to make up for lost times." Jinhai grinned, and they both walked back out with two fresh pots of tea.

Jinhai felt a comforting warmth inside his heart. He felt

protected, supported, but at the same time, he knew his father wouldn't just give up. He was planning something; he could feel it. Tomorrow, they would all go visit Qianfan. After the humiliation that he'd put his father through today, he was terrified of what would come next.

"I bet everyone in town is celebrating the major win from today. We should go join them!" Xiaofan said after taking her first hot sip.

"Totally! We should all be there, especially Jiayi," Xiaosheng added.

"Let's go! I can't wait to stuff my face with everyone's delicious baked goods." Haitao jumped up.

"You all can go ahead. I'm feeling a bit tired. I might just turn in early," Fia said as she yawned.

"I'll stay with you, keep you company," Jinhai said to Fia.

"Perfect! We shall leave you two alone," Xiuying said and gave Jinhai a quick wink.

"We also need to stop by the ship. All our belongings are still in there," Xiaofan reminded everyone.

"Your wish is my command," Han replied as they all marched out of the house and boarded the carriages.

The house became silent after they left, leaving Fia and Jinhai alone. Fia stood up and began cleaning up the porcelain dishes and cups.

"Are you still upset from what happened earlier?" Jinhai asked.

"Maybe," Fia whispered.

"It wasn't my idea," Jinhai insisted.

"Maybe."

"Do you need any help with that?" Jinhai asked as Fia started to wash the dishes inside the kitchen.

"Maybe."

He walked up to the sink and stood beside her. "I'm sorry."

"Maybe." Fia giggled.

"What does that even mean?" Jinhai asked with a chuckle.

"It just means maybe, a possibility," Fia replied.

"So... will you marry me then?" Jinhai asked, shyly looking away. "Maybe?"

"Yes," she said, her eyes locked on the floor.

"Is that for the maybe or for the question?"

"For the question!" Fia laughed, and Jinhai pulled her in for a long hug.

THE MOMENT QIANFAN ENTERED BACK INTO THE CASTLE, THE ONLY thing he could feel was humiliation. Embarrassment!

"The audacity of that stupid child!" he yelled and hurled his sword toward the mirror, shattering both the glass and his reflection.

Daiyu, on the other hand, was finding herself back in a similar situation, caught between her children and husband, but this time, she had already picked a side, and there was no turning back.

"He is going to regret *ever* crossing me!" the king shouted.

"Qianfan, you need to calm down," Daiyu whispered in a soft voice.

"No! How can you even *think* about calming down during a time like this? This is *war*, and our foolish son has declared it. Does he really think rallying a bunch of peasants can help him seize the throne? No! I have everything. I have the magic stone, a power that nobody else has! He is a fool to have crossed me. If it means bloodshed to keep the throne, then let it be. He has no idea what he has gotten himself into!" Qianfan bellowed and stormed down the hallway, smashing anything and everything that stood in his way.

To Daiyu, the situation was out of control. It was one thing when the chaos remained within the walls of the castle, but having the public turn against them was unacceptable. It was something that their ancestors had never faced, and to make it worse, it was provoked by their own children. Such shame!

Qianfan's heart had turned stone cold over the years, and the only emotions he felt were ones that drained his ability to channel his power. The negativity inside of him took away his greatness. Even the love that he used to have for his wife had now dissipated, the one emotion that made him who he was in the first place.

The only power he had now was the magic stone. The magic stone was the main source of energy for all the elements in the Universe, even the ones unknown to humankind. The one who held the stone was the most powerful because the powers could be unleashed with just the mind, regardless of emotions. For that very reason, the stone was kept inside the royal chamber, locked away from everyone who walked within the castle walls, and the only person who could ever access it was the king himself.

THE NEXT MORNING, JINHAI WOKE UP TO THE SCENIC VIEW OF THE ocean, colorful flowers in bloom, and best of all, all the people he loved. But as much as he wanted to remain in bed and bask in the moment, he suddenly remembered what day it was—the day that the king would reunite with the daughters he'd abandoned and face the wrath of the son he'd so desperately wanted then also kicked aside. Sure, he felt guilty turning against his father. As a child, all he'd ever wanted was for his father to love him, accept him. But what other choice did he have? Let Qianfan destroy the kingdom and kill the people of Jinu? He couldn't let that happen!

"You missed the fun party last night, Jinhai. The townspeople are such wonderful people! We danced, we sang, and we ate some of the best food I've ever had in my life. It was such a delight!" Zhang exclaimed.

"We missed you," Xiuying said with a smile on her face. "It would've been fun to have our little brother out with us."

"And we also visited the main market. What a place! Things have definitely changed around here over the years," Xiaofan chimed in.

"With time, things change. It happens," Han replied, holding onto Xiaofan's hand.

"I need to tell you all something very important," Jinhai announced, changing the topic. He then gestured his hand toward Fia. "Can I have you by my side?" Fia gladly took his proffered hand and stood beside him. "Last night, I proposed to Fia."

"And?" Xiaosheng asked sarcastically, already knowing the answer given the massive smile on Fia's face.

"We're getting married!" Jinhai cheered excitedly and swung Fia's hand into the air.

"I knew it!" Xiaofan screamed and ran up to hug her little brother.

"Congratulations!" Xiuying sang and joined into the hug.

"Leave some space for me!" Xiaosheng whined as she squeezed her way in.

"We are *definitely* going to have the wedding before we leave," Xiaofan said. "If that's okay with you two."

"Of course!" Fia agreed. "I wouldn't have it any other way."

Jiayi then remembered a vital piece of information that Huiqing had revealed to her in prison. He used to be Qianfan's closest confidant and knew about the magic stone. "Jinhai, there is something you should know. The magic stone. It's locked inside the royal chamber, the same stone that was used to mark you and your sisters, and the very stone that gave you all your powers. However, the stone is more powerful than all of you combined, and it contains every single one of your powers plus much, much more." Then she swallowed hard. "And Qianfan has it."

Jinhai gulped, and he felt his confidence begin to dwindle. He was so sure that with the help of his sisters, he could take down the king. But after knowing this, after knowing that Qianfan was still more powerful than all of them combined, made him start to doubt whether his plan could actually be successful. He was afraid, but he knew they had all come too far to back down.

"It's okay, Jiayi," he assured her. "There is nothing to worry about. I can handle this."

Jiayi smiled as she touched Jinhai's face with motherly affection. "I hope so."

"But just to be on the safe side, maybe you should touch some wood," Haitao said.

"I don't think that's how it works—" Jinhai began.

"Just touch it!" Xiaosheng exclaimed.

Shrugging his shoulders, Jinhai bent down and touched the wooden floor. "Whatever you say."

"You could have touched the door," Xiaofan said.

"That's for the weak," Xiaosheng mumbled with a snort.

"Alright!" Jinhai clapped his hands together. "The wood has been touched. Now we head to the castle."

TWELVE

The gates of the castle opened wide, and all the horrific memories of her childhood came rushing back into Xiuying's mind. She remembered the carriage ride that sent her away for good, the carriage ride that was meant to kill her. To this day, nightmares continued to haunt her, and even though she'd sworn that she would never return to the place that ruined her life, she continued to find herself back here over and over for the sake of her siblings.

"You are not weak. Remember what you came here for," Zhang comforted her when he noticed his wife's eyes tearing up.

By the time their carriages arrived at the main entrance,

the guards had already informed the king and queen of the unexpected visit. Qianfan had taken the stone out of the chamber and placed it at the center of his crown.

"It doesn't even smell the same anymore, but it still reminds me of my awful childhood," Xiaofan said as they entered and looked around, taking it all in. It's all a reality now. The place that was meant to be their home now felt so foreign and unwanted.

Suddenly, they heard footsteps storming toward the entrance and saw Qianfan approaching them, with Daiyu draped around his right arm.

"Here we go," Han joked in a low voice.

"Not now, Han," Xiaofan whistled.

Jinhai noticed the magic stone sitting on the king's crown, and he knew his father had a plan—or a trick—up his sleeve. He was going to fight them, fire with fire, or he'd die trying.

"The stone. It's in his crown. We need to get it away from him; otherwise, we don't stand a chance," Jinhai whispered.

"How many times will it take to get rid of you all for good?" Qianfan yelled when he saw the faces of his children.

"What is this? Sabotage?" Daiyu asked.

"There is no need to be upset or draw weapons. We can discuss this like adults," Xiuying politely said.

"We are here to give our family a chance, but only if Father steps down from the throne and hands the crown over to Jinhai. The time has come, Father. You are getting old, and the kingdom needs a new king," Xiaofan added.

"Are you serious?" Daiyu laughed. "Do you really think Qianfan is just going to hand over everything he'd worked so hard for? Everything that he deserves? You were right, my husband. Such foolish souls. I pity them." Then she spat on the ground.

"And you? You little brat!" Qianfan hissed, pointing at Xiaofan. "You think I can't handle the responsibilities of being King? And who can? Your overly emotional brother who acts more like a princess than a prince?"

"You will only ever get the crown in your dreams," Daiyu taunted.

"Now leave!" Qianfan ordered.

"We are not leaving without the crown. The throne is Jinhai's, and the people of this kingdom do not want you as their king," Xiuying said sternly and stood her ground.

"Yet Jinhai is letting all the women advocate for him. Only a *weak* man uses women as a shield. He wasn't powerful enough to take the throne himself, so he had to call on his sisters. What a joke!" Qianfan blurted with a loud laugh.

"I'd much rather have someone who relies on his family to be the king than someone who abandons them. You're no leader, Father. You are a dictator. A *monster*," Xiaofan declared.

"Monster? A monster? How dare you speak to your father—your king—in such disrespectful manner?!" Fury filled Qianfan's eyes, and within seconds, his hands turned into fire, and he threw a fireball straight at Xiaofan.

However, before it could hit her, Han pushed her out of the way, injuring himself instead.

"Han!" Xiaofan shouted, running over to treat the minor wound.

"Are you out of your mind?" Xiuying screamed at Qianfan.

"Qianfan, let me make this very clear to you. We both know that my army is much larger than yours, and as we speak, I have three ships docked at your harbor filled with armed guards and the most powerful weapons that this world has ever seen. Attack one of my own again, and I can have them all here with the snap of a finger," Zhang stated and slowly walked toward Qianfan with his sword.

"Nobody threatens me in my own kingdom!" Qianfan bellowed, ready to shower Zhang with enough fireballs to kill him. But nothing came out... nor did his hands light up. "What?" He reached his hands up to feel around his head but also came up empty. It was no longer there!

Then he saw it. From the corner of his left eye, he saw his precious crown floating in the air, finding its way on top of Jinhai's head with the help of Xiaosheng and her newfound power.

"Whoever possesses this crown is King, to me and to everyone else," Xiaosheng declared with a smirk on her face.

"You little prick! I knew there was a reason I've always hated you!" Daiyu screamed and turned to her husband. "Do something, Qianfan! Use your power. Kill them! We need to kill them all!"

But despite his wife's cries, his dear wife whom he used to do anything for, Qianfan could not hear a thing. His mind and body had both grown numb, and for the first time in decades, he felt like he was losing control. He knew he'd been defeated, that his last hope for victory was now sitting on the head of his one and only son. His vision grew blurry, his arms grew weak, and all of a sudden, he vanished into thin air, as if someone had snatched him away.

For a minute or two, no one understood what had happened, but the longer they waited, the more evident it became that he was not coming back. Their nightmare was finally over.

As for Daiyu, she no longer had the king to hide behind, and she soon faced her own nightmare of being completely alone and surrounded by all the children whom she'd tossed aside.

"Please, forgive me," Daiyu pleaded. "Have mercy, for I *am* your mother, after all."

"You were *never* our mother. You've never stood up for any of us against that evil husband of yours," Xiaofan hissed.

"You showed no mercy to Mei, so why should we show mercy to you?" Xiuying jeered.

"And don't forget about what you didn't show to Jiayi," Xiaosheng added resentfully.

"Guards, please take Daiyu to the prison, and lock her in the same room that Mei and Jiayi were kept, so that she will forever remember what she had done. And I want all the other prisoners set free, especially Huiqing. They do not deserve to be in there a second longer," Jinhai ordered.

Xiaosheng came running toward her brother once he finished his order. "We are finally free! No longer will we have to live in fear."

"Thanks to you!" Xiaofan hugged Xiaosheng.

"You saved the day, Little Sister," Xiuying agreed.

"Little one's a champ," Han said appreciatively.

"She sure is." Zhang smiled.

"You know what we need? A proper ceremony! To inaugurate Jinhai as the new King of Jinu!" Xiaofan suggested.

"Yes!" Xiaosheng shouted excitedly.

"Is that really necessary?" Jinhai asked humbly.

"We wouldn't have it any other way," Xiuying whispered beside him. "And as the eldest, it would be my honor to crown you."

A few minutes later, the guards brought Huiqing into

the room. He was old, weak, and had trouble walking on his own, but when he saw Xiuying, he couldn't contain his feelings.

"My child, you are here!" he exclaimed when he saw her. "I never thought I would ever see you again." He placed his hand on Xiuying's head. She struggled to find words through all the happiness that she was feeling... so she didn't.

"Thank you for all that you have done, Huiqing," Zhang said while shaking his hand. "If it weren't for you, Xiuying would not be alive today."

"I am so sorry that you had to spend your life in prison because of me. If I had known about this, I would've done my best to free you," Xiuying finally said, gasping for air.

"No, my child. This was all in the Universe's plan. It was all to bring you and your sister back to Jinu and save the kingdom." Huiqing smiled. "Everything worked out like it was supposed to."

"Huiqing, I want you to know that I have cleared your name to the public. That you were mistreated and wronged. And," Jinhai cleared his throat, "I would like to reinstate your position as Chief of the Military. It would be an honor to have someone like you protecting this kingdom."

"Thank you, my child." Huiqing bowed. "I knew I've always liked you."

"What happened?" Jiayi rushed in, interrupting the conversation.

"Where are your parents?" Fia asked.

"Is everything okay?" Haitao added.

"Once voice at a time, please!" Han laughed.

Xiaosheng sat them all down and started to explain everything that had happened. Once she finished, Jiayi said, "I still don't understand Qianfan's disappearance."

"Urban legend has it," Lixin started with a deep voice, "that when evil spirits realize their wrongdoings, their souls are taken by the dark shadows of Hell, trapped and tortured for eternity. For centuries, criminals and dictators have disappeared without a trace. The same thing must've happened to Qianfan."

"Wow…," Xiaofan said. "And I've always thought those legends were all just stories. Nothing more."

"Oh, whatever! We have more important things to focus on today," Xiaosheng exclaimed. "We need to prepare for the crowning ceremony!"

Xiaofan chuckled. "You're right. I'll get all the castle maids to start preparing."

As Jinhai watched his loved ones around him, he finally felt like he was home. Despite everything that had happened in this castle and all the trauma he'd dealt with as a child, things were finally looking up, and he no longer feared living inside these very walls.

EPILOGUE

Jinhai's inauguration was celebrated like any other traditional holiday. He wanted it to remain small and close-knit, only inviting those within the walls of the kingdom. Qianfan was always focused on trying to impress the other kings, but Jinhai cared more about impressing his own people. In Jinhai's kingdom, nobody slept under an open sky or with an empty stomach, and he completely abolished the one-child rule in Jinu so that little girls born no longer had to be killed or sent away in hopes of having a boy.

A week after the ceremony, Jinhai and Fia got married, and the kingdom now had a wise and empathetic queen.

Jiayi and Xiaosheng lived with them in the royal chamber, and they continued eating their meals together, just like old times. Jinhai offered Haitao and Lixin their own place at the castle, but they refused and insisted on staying inside their own house. Huiqing was given a piece of land and sacks of gold coins to start his new life, and he eventually reunited with his family once Jinhai cleared his name.

Xiuying and Zhang left after the wedding to head back to Baoshu, and a week later, Jinhai received a scroll that Xiuying was expecting her first child, a little girl. Han took Xiaofan back to Shénhuà, but only after he vowed to Jinhai that Shénhuà would become Jinu's trusted ally during times of conflict and war.

As for Daiyu, she stayed within the confined walls of prison, accompanied by silence and loneliness. She had everything that she needed physically—food, water, and warm blankets—but her mind continued eating at her with each passing day with one unanswered question.

Was it the legend that made Qianfan disappear? Or did he finally manage to generate his own black magic spell that he used on himself?

That's a question that no one would ever be able to answer, and Qianfan was a man whom everyone hoped would never return.

The End

ABOUT THE AUTHOR

Viola Tempest is a dystopian fantasy and paranormal romance author who yearns to expose the truth of those in the modern world: the good, the bad, and the ugly. Her inspiration primarily stems from life experiences, those who annoy her, ex-boyfriends, and the crazy dreams that pop into her head every once in a while.

The Lost Daughters

COMPLETE TRILOGY

VIOLA TEMPEST